PRAISE FOR *NEW YORK TIMES* BESTSELLING AUTHOR CATHERINE COULTER

"Bawdy fare, Coulter-style . . . romance, humor, and spicy sex talk." —*Kirkus Reviews*

"A hot-blooded romp." —*People*

"Coulter is excellent at portraying the romantic tension between her heroes and heroines, and she manages to write explicitly but beautifully about sex as well as love." —*Milwaukee Journal Sentinel*

"Unexpected plot twists, witty dialogue, and an engaging cast of characters." —*Publishers Weekly*

"Catherine Coulter delivers . . . straightforward, fast-paced romance." —*Minneapolis Star Tribune*

"Sexy." —*Booklist*

"Coulter's characters quickly come alive and draw the reader into the story. You root for the good guys and hiss for the bad guys. When you have to put the book down for a while, you can hardly wait to get back and see what's going on." —*The Sunday Oklahoman*

"Charm, wit, and intrigue. . . . Sure to keep readers turning the pages." —*Naples Daily News*

Titles by Catherine Coulter

The Bride Series
THE SHERBROOKE BRIDE
THE HELLION BRIDE
THE HEIRESS BRIDE
THE SCOTTISH BRIDE
PENDRAGON
MAD JACK
THE COURTSHIP

The Legacy Trilogy
THE WYNDHAM LEGACY
THE NIGHTINGALE LEGACY
THE VALENTINE LEGACY

The Baron Novels
THE WILD BARON
THE OFFER
THE DECEPTION

The Viking Novels
LORD OF HAWKFELL ISLAND
LORD OF RAVEN'S PEAK
LORD OF FALCON RIDGE
SEASON OF THE SUN

The Song Novels
WARRIOR'S SONG
FIRE SONG
EARTH SONG
SECRET SONG
ROSEHAVEN

The Magic Trilogy
MIDSUMMER MAGIC
CALYPSO MAGIC
MOONSPUN MAGIC

The Star Series
EVENING STAR
MIDNIGHT STAR
WILD STAR
JADE STAR

**Other Regency
Historical Romances**
THE COUNTESS
THE REBEL BRIDE
THE HEIR
THE DUKE
LORD HARRY

Devil's Duology
DEVIL'S EMBRACE
DEVIL'S DAUGHTER

**Contemporary
Romantic Thrillers**
FALSE PRETENSES
IMPLUSE
BEYOND EDEN

FBI Suspense Thrillers
THE COVE
THE MAZE
THE TARGET
THE EDGE
RIPTIDE
HEMLOCK BAY

The Offer

—◆—

Catherine Coulter

Previously published as
An Honorable Offer

A SIGNET BOOK

SIGNET
Published by New American Library, a division of
Penguin Putnam Inc., 375 Hudson Street,
New York, New York 10014, U.S.A.
Penguin Books Ltd, 80 Strand,
London WC2R 0RL, England
Penguin Books Australia Ltd, 250 Camberwell Road,
Camberwell, Victoria 3124, Australia
Penguin Books Canada Ltd, 10 Alcorn Avenue,
Toronto, Ontario, Canada M4V 3B2
Penguin Books (N.Z.) Ltd, Cnr Rosedale and Airborne Roads,
Albany, Auckland 1310, New Zealand

Penguin Books Ltd, Registered Offices
Harmondsworth, Middlesex, England

Published by Signet, an imprint of New American Library, a division of Penguin Putnam Inc. Previously published in a Topaz edition. Originally published in a somewhat different version in a Signet edition under the title *An
Honorable Offer.*

First Signet Printing, April 1999
10 9 8 7 6 5 4

*To my sisters of more years
than any of us would care to count.
Here's to the second time around.
Aniko, Ildi, Ursula, Leslie, and Zita.*

where she was. She remembered reading that in
Dante's inferno the deepest circle in hell was cold, not
hot. She was ready to accept it without question. She
knew now this was what hell was like—a colorless
cold, so cold, so intense, that her breath froze into
nothingness in the frigid blank air. She clutched the
palm of her gloved hand against her breast for warmth
and drew to a stumbling halt against a large gnarled
elm tree. She hugged its trunk and let the rough bark
dig into her cheek. It hurt. At least she could still feel
her face. She felt the bark through her cloak, digging
deeper, through her gown, through her chemise. She
savored for the moment the illusion of shelter it offered. The wind swirled about her, making her cloak
billow at her ankles, making the naked branches overhead whip back and forth, tangling with other branches,
rending and tearing, like fingernails pulling at flesh.

She gazed up. The snow wasn't too terribly heavy
yet. But the full fury of the storm would soon be upon
her, and she knew that unless she found her way out
of the forest, she would die. She forced herself to look
about again. Was the snow coming down harder?

She pushed herself away from the tree and forced
her feet to move forward, in what she prayed was a
southerly direction. She had been so certain of herself,
even after her mare had gone lame, sure that she
would find her way through Eppingham Forest. After
all, she'd lived here all her eighteen years and knew
the forest well. She wondered now if she would ever
find her way before the thickening snow blanketed
any landmarks she might recognize.

The thorn of a bramble tore into her beautiful crimson velvet cloak, a present from her grandfather the
previous Christmas. She bent to pull the cloak free.
The pain in her chest gripped her again, and she doubled over with the cough that had become harsh so

very quickly, and tears fell, cold and slick down her cheeks. She dashed her hand across her eyes, but when her vision cleared, it was Trevor's face she saw again, a pretty face, indeed, its finely chiseled features almost too pretty for a man. She saw his hooded pale green eyes were darker now as he stalked her. His lashes were too long and thick for a man, her sister Elizabeth had told her, but perhaps if she birthed a daughter, she would have her father's beautiful eyes and lashes.

Trevor had followed her to the portrait gallery in the east wing of Monmouth Abbey, where she painted when the weather was fine. That day she'd wanted to copy a portrait of Isolde, the sixteenth-century countess who'd once caught the eye of Henry VIII. Sabrina forgot about her work quickly enough when Trevor had shown himself.

She could clearly hear him say again, "Don't fight me, my little Sabrina. You've led me a merry chase and I'm not a particularly patient man. But you were different. You have teased me, made me want to shatter the illusion of innocence you've cloaked yourself in. But the chase is now over. No more of your clever games. I know why you came to this isolated gallery. Your plan is perfect. Come to me now, tell me how much you want me."

She was pressed hard against her great-grandfather's picture frame. She could retreat no farther. Reason, she had to try to make him see reason. "You have mistaken me, Trevor. I am your sister-in-law. You are newly married to Elizabeth. She is your wife. I have not tried to attract you. I have not wanted you to chase me. I don't want you and never have. I'm not lying or playing games. Please, leave me alone. I came here only to study a portrait that I wish to paint."

He smiled at her, saying nothing.

She wasn't blind. There was raw hunger in his eyes, but also something else. Determination. He wouldn't listen to reason, not Trevor. He heard only what he wanted to hear, saw only what he wanted to see. There were always servants about, but she'd neither seen nor heard a single one since Trevor had come. She allowed the contempt she felt for him to come out. "Listen to me, Trevor, Elizabeth is your wife. She trusts you. My grandfather trusts you. I haven't trusted you, but that doesn't matter."

He laughed, his head tilted to one side. His light green eyes were filled with more hunger than just the moment before. "You look lovely in that dark gray gown. I would have thought it would make you pale, but it doesn't. It must be that beautiful auburn hair of yours. You do have beautiful hair, you know, Sabrina. I've watched you shake your head, making that glorious hair of yours fall around your shoulders when you knew I was looking at you. As sinful as a woman's red lips, your hair."

He was not a large man, but he was still considerably larger and stronger than she was. What to do? She was very angry now and shook her fist at him. "Listen to me, Trevor, stop it! I have done nothing to attract you. The truth is I don't even like you. That's right. I wish you had never come, but there was no choice, was there? There was no direct male heir, so Grandfather was forced to recognize you, his brother's grandson.

"Leave me alone, Trevor. Go away." When she tried to walk by him because he hadn't moved an inch, he just stood there smiling at her.

"Oh yes, you're right, Sabrina," he said, his voice lower, softer, slippery as her satin sash. She shuddered. "But everything will be mine once that damned old relic has shucked off his mortal coil. It shouldn't be much longer now. Soon all this will be mine. Elizabeth will soon call me her lord, her master, as will you, Sabrina. I like those words from a soft mouth when I reach my pleasure. Ah yes, and a warm woman's breath on my flesh, it heightens the experience.

"You know I would have preferred to wed you, but it was not to be. The old earl forced me on Elizabeth. Elizabeth was older, she must wed first, it was only fair, he said. The old fool didn't want me to have you, truth be told. No, I couldn't have you as my wife, but you are still here, and we can be together."

As he leaned toward her, she pressed her palms against his chest, shoving as hard as she could. "Get away from me, Trevor, get away. I shall scream. The servants will obey me, not you."

He laughed, now so close to her face that she could smell on his breath the turtle soup he'd eaten for luncheon. "Yell yourself hoarse, Sabrina. No one is about to hear you, but you already knew that, didn't you? Ah, I feel you trembling, my pet."

"I'm not your damned pet, you bastard!" His fingertips brushed lightly over her cheek. She rammed her fist as hard as she could into his belly. As she felt the soft flesh give, she jerked away, almost free of him.

His hand grabbed her upper arm, pulling her back. Then his hands were around her neck. Her fingers clutched about his, her nails digging into him, but she could not get free.

His fingers tightened about her neck and his face blurred above her. He suddenly released her and she gulped in air. Then she felt his mouth slam against hers. His tongue probed at her lips to force them apart. She opened her mouth to yell at him and felt his tongue go deep. She gagged and bit down hard.

He jerked back and she released him. "You little bitch!" He was panting with rage and pain as he drew

2

In the next instant she realized that her insults pleased him. She knew it, could see it as the rage faded from his face, and he laughed. "I've always liked my women to have a bit of spirit, not to just lie stiff and silent beneath me like martyrs, like that damned sister of yours. When I'm ramming really hard into her, I like to watch her go pale, bite her lips and moan." He saw she didn't understand what he was saying. He laughed with pleasure. He'd wanted to be the one to break her from the first moment he'd set eyes on her.

"Yes, I like a girl with spirit, Sabrina. Fight me, do, if you like that game. A fine, aristocratic young lady you are, so proud, so sure of yourself and what you are and what is owed to you. I wonder when I take you, if your virgin's blood will flow as heavy as Elizabeth's. There was so much of it. I fear my poor little bride believed that I'd killed her. More's the pity that I hadn't."

It hit her with full force in that moment that he fully intended to rape her. He was pulling her wrists over her head. He moved in. She yelled in his face, "No, Trevor. I'll tell Grandfather what you are, don't you doubt it. When I tell him, he'll have you flogged and thrown out of Monmouth Abbey. He'll disown you."

"Ah, I wondered if you'd try that, Sabrina. If you

open your sweet mouth to him, then I assure you that I shall assist him to his final resting place. It wouldn't take much to nudge him into the grave, you know.

"Now, my dear, enough of this flightiness. I've waited with great patience for you. I'll wait no more."

His pale green eyes were narrow with purpose. He grabbed the neck of her gray wool gown and jerked it down. She knew he was staring at her breasts. She wouldn't let his hands touch her bare flesh. She lunged forward, striking at his face with her fists.

Then he managed to grab one of her arms. He twisted it, jerking it upward behind her. She screamed again, the pain clear in her cry. She saw then that he enjoyed causing her pain. He twisted her arm even higher but she kept her scream in her throat.

"Very well," he said. With his other hand, he grasped the edge of her chemise and tore it down to her waist. His eyes were blazing as he gazed at her breasts. "My God, you're a beauty. I imagined you would have nice breasts, but they're exquisite." He grabbed one breast and squeezed.

It hurt but still she held her pain inside. She wouldn't give him the satisfaction of knowing that he was hurting her beyond what she could bear. She leaned down and bit the back of his hand as hard as she could.

He backhanded her. "I will teach you obedience to your lord, to your master, to me. You bite me again and I'll make you very sorry."

His hand squeezed her breast again, then quickly he was at her stomach, his fingers digging in to find her through her gown and chemise.

"No!"

He laughed, and toppled her onto the hard wooden floor. She was struggling for breath. His body slammed down on top of her. He reared back and she felt that male part of him pushing hard against her belly. She jerked her hand free and smashed her fist into his nose.

"You bitch, you miserable little bitch!" He began to slap her, again and again, until she saw nothing except explosions of white pain. He was howling as he hit her, his eyes wild.

Suddenly he stiffened above her and she saw his eyes widen, then become glazed and vague. He slapped her again, cursing her, but this time his voice was soft, drowsy-sounding. He growled deep in his throat. "Damn you, damn you." He froze above her, stiff as a board. Then he rolled away from her to lie on his back, his legs spread.

She was on her feet in an instant, staring down at him. His breathing was harsh and low. He was looking up at her, his eyes tender, a gentle smile on his mouth. His smile widened when he lightly touched his fingers to himself. There was a wide stain on his breeches.

She took a step back from him. She was shuddering with reaction, with utter rage. Without thought, she kicked him in the ribs. "You filthy animal, filthy, filthy. God, I hate you."

He tried to grab her ankle but she jumped back in time. He rolled to his back again. He gazed up at her and touched his bloody nose, his features once again beautiful and calm. "You won't kick my ribs again, but I can't say that I blame you. You overexcited me, Sabrina, this time, and I had no chance to pleasure you, to plunge deep into your virgin's body. Ah, but next time.

"Pain and pleasure, little pet, beautifully and irrevocably intertwined. I shall have you, and no one shall stop me, least of all you. Don't even try to lock your door against me, else I shall tip the balance to pain. You know, I think next time I shall have to tie you down. You've bloodied my nose just like a schoolboy. My ribs ache, ah, and I've spilled my seed on myself. Your fault, of course. I haven't known such excitement in a very long time, certainly not with your bloodless sister, or any of those silly maids. Not an auspicious beginning for us, but a beginning nonetheless.''

Sabrina turned and ran from the portrait gallery, the low heels of her slippers clipping the wooden floor, ringing loud and hard in her ears.

She heard the cat-soft footsteps of a footman and huddled into a small embrasure until he passed her. She ran into her bedchamber and with trembling fingers quickly twisted the key in the lock. Stepping to a long mirror beside a walnut armoire, she touched her fingers to her ravaged face. She gazed dumbly at her puffy eyes, still wet with her tears, and her swollen, stained cheeks, still marked by his blows, still hot and tender to the touch. She stared at herself in silence, raging against her own impotence, her helplessness against him, a man.

She remembered when he had first arrived from Italy but a month and a half before, so winsome in his charm, almost boyishly eager to win approval, particularly from Elizabeth. She thought about the first time she'd noticed his hands, soft and white, like a woman's. Grandfather had growled under his breath that Trevor was naught but a pampered, vain fop.

Grandfather. Sabrina turned away from the mirror and sat, shoulders slumped, upon her bed. If she told him that Trevor had tried to rape her, after only two weeks of marriage to Elizabeth, he would go into a rage. She swallowed a sob. Only her grandfather stood between her and her cousin, and he was too old. Sabrina rose with sudden decision. She would go to Elizabeth. Together they would decide what was to be done. She quickly dashed cold water on her face. She still looked a fright. Well, Elizabeth would see the proof of his blows; she wouldn't have any doubts as to the sort of man she'd married. She stuffed her torn clothes into the corner of her armoire, and changed quickly into an old brown wool gown.

She found her sister in her bedchamber, seated at her small writing desk, penning letters, Sabrina thought, to the wedding guests.

"Leave us, Mary," she said to the maid.

Elizabeth raised pale blue eyes to her sister, but said nothing until Mary had finally and reluctantly closed the bedchamber door. She laid down her pen and out of habit smoothed a wisp of pale blond hair back into its knot at the nape of her neck. Both Trevor and Elizabeth had soft blond hair. Where Trevor's eyes were a pale green, Elizabeth's were blue. "There's no need for you to be rude to Mary. She's a sensitive girl. I don't wish to see you behave like that again. Now, what do you want? As you can see, I am quite busy. How am I to thank the Viscountess Ashford for that hideous cachepot? Can you imagine, blue tulips strewn all over the thing? Trevor laughed and laughed."

"The cachepot is ugly but Mary Louise meant well." Sabrina slashed her hand through the air. "That's not at all important. Listen to me, Elizabeth, I must speak with you. I know that this will come as a shock to you, but you must help me. It's Trevor, Elizabeth— he just tried to rape me."

Elizabeth arched a pale blond brow and glanced over at the clock on the mantelpiece. The brow went higher. There was a twisted smile on Elizabeth's mouth. "First you are rude to my Mary. Now you tell me that my husband of two weeks tried to rape you. Is this some kind of game, Sabrina? Are you that envious of my new status? Such a thing is scarce possible, particularly when it is only three o'clock in the afternoon."

Sabrina gazed dumbly at her sister, unwilling to believe the iciness in her voice. No, Elizabeth simply didn't understand. She rushed forward and laid an urgent hand on Elizabeth's sleeve. "Look at my face. He struck me repeatedly. It gave him pleasure to hurt me. Look, damn you!"

Elizabeth shrugged. "So, your face is flushed, nothing more that I can see. You are always in the sun so that is no surprise."

"It's winter, Elizabeth. We haven't seen the sun for days until just this afternoon." Sabrina couldn't believe this. She went on her knees beside her sister, clutching her hand between hers. The sunlight was fierce on her face. She knew that the redness and swelling were clear to see. "You must listen to me, Elizabeth. It would make no difference to Trevor if it was day or night. I went to the portrait gallery to look at the countess's portrait. I want to paint it. Trevor followed me. You know how isolated the gallery is. No one was near to help me and he knew it. That's why he followed me there. Elizabeth, look at my face. Don't tell me it's simply flushed. No, he slapped me and slapped me. He's vicious and cruel, Elizabeth. He's proved he has no honor. He even threatened to kill Grandfather if I told him what he'd tried to do. You must help me decide what we must do."

Elizabeth shook off her sister's hand, as if her touch was distasteful to her. She rose slowly from her chair. Sabrina also got to her feet. Elizabeth was some three inches taller than her younger sister. She looked down at her now, and there was intense dislike in her pale blue eyes. "I forbid you, Sabrina, *forbid you,* to speak any more such absurd nonsense. Pray remember that you are speaking of my husband and our cousin. Does it mean so little to you that he will be the Earl of Monmouth after Grandfather's death?"

Sabrina took an involuntary step backward. "Elizabeth, haven't you heard me? Did you not understand what I said? Damn you, look at my face! You can see his handprints! My skin is still hot from the force of his slaps. None of it is nonsense. I'm sorry for this, but you must believe me. Trevor is vicious. He tried to rape me. I'm not lying. He isn't worthy of you. He told me if I tried to lock my bedchamber door against him, he would hurt me even more. Please, what are we to do?"

3

Elizabeth sat back down on the delicate French chair and tapped her fingertips softly and rhythmically together. She smoothed her pale blue wool skirts. She looked at the glittering diamonds on her heirloom wedding ring, the huge faceted emerald that sat high in the middle. Finally, she looked up and smiled at her sister. The sight of her ravaged face was balm to her soul. "I gather you are still a virgin, Sabrina?"

Sabrina stared at her sister's calm, impassive face as her question rang in her ears. She sounded bored, indifferent.

"Well, are you? Are you stupid? Can't you speak?"

Sabrina didn't want to, but she turned red, remembering Trevor's howling yell, seeing again the stain spread on his breeches. God, she hated him, she hated what he'd made her learn, all in an instant of time. "Yes, I'm still a virgin, no thanks to that bastard."

Elizabeth's lashes nearly closed over her narrowed eyes. "So, my dear little sister, what happened is that you teased Trevor, and being a man and weak of flesh, as all men are, he gladly accompanied you to the gallery. You then ran away from him when you realized he had every intention of taking your teasing seriously. Were you afraid he'd make you pregnant, Sabrina?"

Sabrina grabbed her sister's arm, saw the disdain in her sister's pale eyes, and dropped her hand. "Listen to me, Elizabeth. You cannot believe what you just said. You make it sound as though I purposefully tried to seduce your husband. I tell you, he is vain and cruel, a strutting evil man who scorns us all." She wasn't about to tell her sister what her bridegroom had said about her. "Please, Elizabeth, you cannot ignore this, you cannot pretend it didn't happen. You must help me, help yourself."

Elizabeth stood abruptly again, standing on her tip-toes so she could tower over her sister, and flattened the palms of her hands on the desktop. "Now you will listen to me, you pampered little wretch. For years, even before our parents died, I have watched you twist Grandfather around your little finger, wheedle your way so firmly into his affections so that he had no love left for me. Oh yes, Grandfather allowed me a season in London with Aunt Barresford, hoping that I would find a husband so he would be rid of me. But I always knew that my place was here, even though at every turn you have tried to usurp my position and my authority as the eldest.

"No more, Sabrina. I am Trevor's wife." She squared her shoulders, standing even taller, the sun-light lacing through her blond hair, forming a pale golden halo round her head. She looked like a princess, tall and proud. Then she said, her voice colder than the wind that was tangling through the oak branches outside the window, "When that miserable old man dies, I shall be the Countess of Monmouth. On that day, my dear sister, I shall be the undisputed mistress here and you will be nothing more than I wish you to be. I wonder if I will even allow you to live here. Perhaps the dower house is the place for you. I doubt I'll waste my money on a London season for you."

Sabrina drew back at the naked hatred she saw on

her sister's face. Dimly she realized that the cold aloofness Elizabeth had always shown the world, had always shown to her sister, masked a bitterness that went very deep. Had she somehow been responsible for that? She was appalled. No, she hadn't done a thing. She was eighteen years old. She'd laughed and played, wept bitterly when her father had been killed on the Peninsula and her mother had died but a year later so needlessly, in the boating accident in the fall of 1811, but her grandfather had been there for her, and she'd accepted his love, his warmth, never realizing that Elizabeth saw herself standing on the outside. Grandfather loved both of them equally, surely he did.

She struggled to understand her sister, understand her hatred, her defense of a man who didn't deserve to be her husband. But she'd wanted him because she wanted to rule, to order. She said slowly, "Elizabeth, surely you cannot mean that you married Trevor only so that you would be the Countess of Monmouth. No, you would not have done that."

The bleak five years since her eighteenth birthday and her one season in London stretched out endlessly in Elizabeth's mind. Five years watching this precocious child grow into womanhood. She said with deadly calm, "I have done exactly what I intended to do, and you, Sabrina, never had, and never will have, anything to say in the matter. My feelings for Trevor are none of your affair. He is my husband and he shall remain my husband, his reputation unsullied by you, you filthy little liar."

Sabrina felt a knot of fear clog her throat. "Elizabeth, I'm not lying! Trevor threatened to come to me again, even to my own room. He said he would hurt me if I locked my door against him. He hurt me this time, Elizabeth. He's not natural. Surely most men aren't like he is."

"Shut up!"

Sabrina stared at her sister's set face. She'd never felt so helpless in her life. "I had never thought that you so disliked me, Elizabeth," she said finally, striving to sort through all the ugly words her sister had hurled at her. "I have never done anything to harm you. I can't believe that my loving grandfather made him care for you less. Don't turn away from me, Elizabeth. You are my sister and I seek only to protect you and me from that terrible man."

"Get out, Sabrina. I will hear no more of your pathetic lies."

Sabrina drew herself up to her full height. "If you will not believe me, then I must go to Grandfather. I can't simply ignore what Trevor has threatened to do to me. He said he would come to my bedchamber. I won't wait like a whimpering helpless female for him to come and abuse me." She turned on her heel and walked quickly to the door.

Elizabeth yelled, "If you have the audacity to carry your filth to Grandfather, I shall tell him that in your jealousy, you threw yourself at Trevor and that he repulsed you. Think, you little wretch, just think of what would happen. Everyone would revile you. You would disgrace your family. You would disgrace Grandfather. Know that you will get no quarter from me. Just what do you think Grandfather would think then, Sabrina?"

Sabrina felt suddenly like a hated stranger in her own home. She stood uncertainly at the door, staring bleakly back at her sister.

Elizabeth pursed her thin lips and said more calmly, her words all the more deadly because of their emotionless calm, "No, Grandfather wouldn't believe you. You know, of course, what Trevor would say. Go ahead, Sabrina, go to him. See how quickly he loses his doting affection for you. Trevor is his heir, you fool. He would take the side of his heir because through Trevor he gains his own immortality and the immortality of his precious line. Mayhap such a filthy story would topple him into his grave. Would you like Grandfather's death on your hands? Well, would you?"

Sabrina remembered Trevor's threat. No, surely he wouldn't try to kill Grandfather. But what would happen? She shook her head back and forth, unable to find words. Her face ached where Trevor had struck her. She saw the stain on his breeches and felt such hatred she was certain she'd choke on it.

"You know, Sabrina," Elizabeth continued, carefully watching her sister, "there is really nothing left for you here. If indeed you are so concerned about my husband's attentions toward you, perhaps it would be better if you left." She saw wrenching fear in her sister's vivid eyes, an incredible violet that everyone so admired, and turned abruptly away from her. She'd said enough. She wanted to smile, but she didn't. She'd nearly won. "Leave me," she said, her voice as cold as the winter wind that was beginning to howl against the windows. A storm was coming. A very bad storm. "Leave me. I do not wish to look on your face again."

Sabrina licked away a tear that had fallen down her cheek onto her upper lip. She tried to talk some purpose into herself, to force herself to bury for the moment at least the terrible memories of the previous afternoon. She'd spent the night in a large cupboard in the old nursery, waking at dawn, dressing, and sneaking to the stables. Had it just been the day before that Trevor had attacked her? It seemed like a week had passed, a week alone in the dizzying cold, watching the sky darken and fill with snow. She

pressed her hand against her chest and felt hope at
the thought of the three pounds tucked safely inside
her chemise. It would be enough to buy a stage ticket
to London, to her aunt Barresford. It would be dark
soon. She didn't have much time. She couldn't press
against this tree forever.

She pushed back a heavy lock of hair that had come
loose over her forehead, and looked about her. Surely
she had walked in the right direction. It could not be
too much farther to Borhamwood and the warmth and
safety of the Raven Inn.

She felt the searing pain in her chest again, and
doubled over, hugging herself tightly. She could hear
her own raspy breathing and admitted to herself for
the first time that she was ill. "I don't want to die,"
she said, the words freezing on her lips. "I won't die."

She scrambled through the brambles, each tree becoming a goal to reach and pass. She felt a surge of
hope, for she was certain that the trees were thinning
ahead of her. Yes, that was an opening. She was nearly
there, nearly free of the forest, nearly to Borhamwood.

Suddenly she went flying, stumbling on a large root
that stuck up through the moss on the forest floor.
She sprawled facedown on the frozen ground, stunned
by the force of her fall. She felt curiously warmed by
the thick moss.

She would remain here just a minute or two longer.
She sighed. She would rest just a little while longer,
then she would feel strong again. She would be so
strong she would run to Borhamwood.

4

"Bloody hell."

Phillip Edmund Mercerault, Viscount Derencourt, drew up his bay mare, Tasha, gazed about him at the forbidding wilderness, and continued his cursing. Damn Charles anyway. He liked Charles, truly he did, had known him for more years than either of them could remember, but this was too much. The directions he'd provided to reach his house, Moreland, had landed Phillip in the middle of a forest in the middle of a snowstorm that could very probably become a blizzard. Phillip would shoot him when he next saw Charles.

If he next saw him.

No, that was ridiculous. Tasha was strong and sound. He knew he was going east. He just had to get out of this damned forest soon. But he hadn't seen a sign for a village called Borhamwood, there hadn't even been a farmhouse at which he could stop and beg a cup of coffee to warm himself. Of course since this was a forest and not farmland, he supposed it made sense that no farmers were around. He cursed again. There hadn't even been a ditch where he could get Tasha out of the snow, if for just a minute or two.

He'd been a bloody fool to wave off his valet, Dambler, with his carriage and luggage. Dambler, despite all his lapses into martyrdom, had a nose for direction.

It was uncanny, this ability, but unfortunately, at this point in the afternoon, Dambler was probably roasting his toes in front of a nice kitchen fire at Moreland. And here his master was—cold and hungry with only two changes of clothes in the soft leather valise strapped to Tasha's saddle.

What had ever possessed him? Hunting and Christmas festivities at Moreland. He wondered if he'd find his way there by Boxing Day.

He patted Tasha's glossy neck and gently dug his heels into her sides. He swallowed snow even as he said, "Come on, Tasha, if we stay here much longer, that damned Charles will find us here thawing out in the spring."

Surely he was riding east. He tried concentrating on his nose, the way Dambler told him he drew the various latitudes and longitudes into his being—through his nose—but all he got out of it was a sneeze.

It was getting late. It would be dark soon. If he didn't find his way to somewhere, he would be in big trouble. Tasha suddenly snorted, jerking her head left. To his left was a cottage nestled in a small hollow, carved out, it seemed to him, from the midst of the forest itself. He wheeled Tasha about, the thought of hot coffee scalding his lips making him forget that he wanted to bash Charles the next time he had him in the ring at Gentleman Jackson's Boxing Salon.

No, it wasn't a simple cottage. It was a two-story red brick hunting box, its facade covered with ivy dusted white by the snow. He swung off Tasha's back in front of the columned entrance, stamped his cold feet, and thwacked the knocker loudly.

No answer and no wonder. It was indeed a hunting box. The owner, whoever he was, wouldn't return until spring. As he swung back into the saddle, he said, "Tasha, I promise you an extra bucket of oats if you get me to Moreland so that I may thrash Charles before dark."

Phillip groped with one gloved hand through the rich layer of his greatcoat to the watch in his waistcoat pocket. It was nearly four o'clock in the afternoon. He gazed apprehensively up at the snow, coming down more thickly now, and turned Tasha about again toward the narrow, rutted path. If he didn't find his way out of here, he would return to the hunting box. He'd give himself another half hour, no more.

Despite his fur-lined greatcoat, the swirling wind chilled him to his very bones. He shivered and lowered his head close to his mare's neck.

Snowflakes dusted the bridge of his nose when he chanced to look heavenward. He pulled his greatcoat more closely about his throat, pulled his scarf up nearly to his eyes, ducked his head closer to Tasha's neck, and urged her on. At a fork in the path, Phillip looked up again at the snow-filled sky. He had absolutely no notion of which direction to take. He drew a guinea from his waistcoat pocket, flipped it, and with a shrug turned Tasha to the path at his left. He wasn't about to forget the direction of the hunting box. If the impossible happened, then he would return there.

He grinned suddenly, imagining what his friends would be saying to him if they knew he was lost in the middle of a snowstorm in a forest in Yorkshire. He doubted he'd live it down for many a good year. He could just hear his long-time friend, Rohan Carrington, say in that amused drawl of his, "Well, Phillip, what is one to say? You can find your way all through Scotland, but when it comes to the backyard in Yorkshire, you lose yourself in a bloody blizzard."

And then there was Martine, his mistress. He could just see her lying there on her bed, wearing something frothy, something he could see through yet not really see through, something that would fill him with such lust that he wouldn't, frankly, care if she laughed her head off.

The snowfall became thicker, if that was possible. He couldn't see the path beyond three or four feet ahead. Tasha quickened her pace.

He kept his head pressed against Tasha's neck. She would stay on the path. There was nothing more he could do.

Except go back to that hunting box if they didn't clear the forest soon, very soon. Say in the next ten minutes, maybe even nine minutes. He had a marvelous sense of timing, even Martine told him that. Yes, he knew the exact moment when she wanted him to do this and then do that. He was smiling as he pulled out his watch. Yes, he'd give it ten more minutes, then it was back to the hunting box.

Martine, his languid, glorious mistress, swam again into his mind's eye. At least she was a warm thought. When he'd told her that he was traveling to the north for a round of Christmas parties and would be gone from London for some time, she'd roused herself, propping herself up on her elbows to gain his attention, and given a lazy laugh. "Ah, my beautiful man, you prefer the dead of winter to a live me. It's absurd." He grinned, knowing that he would most willingly part with the bulk of his worldly goods if he could at this moment be warm and naked in her large bed, his face buried in her glorious bosom, showing her yet again his wonderful timing.

The snow was driving down in earnest now, and he drew up Tasha once again in an effort to get his bearings. It was the absence of thick snow that caused him to look again upon a large splash of crimson. He hooded his eyes with his gloved hand.

What the devil was that mound of red? In another

few minutes it would be completely covered with snow.

He turned Tasha off the path. He drew her up and gazed down in some consternation at a deep red velvet cloak that covered an unconscious small female.

He jumped off Tasha's back and knelt down beside her. What the hell was wrong with her? Why was she here in the middle of the forest, in the middle of a blizzard? He gently turned her over and stared down at a young girl's face. She was as pale as the white snow around her and her lips were blue with cold. He could see the veins beneath her white flesh. Two narrow scratches slashed down her cheek, the blood congealed with a crust of snow. A thick hank of red hair fell over her forehead.

The viscount stripped off a leather glove and slipped his hand inside the cloak against her chest. She was alive, but her breathing was labored, and slow, too slow. He lightly slapped her face. There was no response. He slapped her harder and shook her by her shoulders, but he couldn't awaken her. He had seen many cases of severe exposure two winters ago, when he'd spent the winter in Poland, after the French retreat from Russia, and knew that the result was more often than not a slow numbing death. He quickly scooped her up in his arms, wrapping his greatcoat about her as best he could. She didn't weigh much, despite her soaked clothing.

He realized that he couldn't continue on, even if he were alone, for the snow was so thick now he could scarcely see Tasha who was standing but four feet from him. The hunting box was the only answer. Even if the caretaker of the place didn't return, it would at the very least allow them shelter.

He pressed her tightly against his chest in an effort

to warm her, and wheeled Tasha back toward the hunting box.

"Life becomes complicated," he said to his horse. Her ears twitched and she neighed.

Phillip dismounted in front of a small stable next to the hunting box and quickly led Tasha inside, carrying the girl in the crook of his right arm. He laid her gently down on a pile of hay, quickly removed Tasha's saddle and bridle, and covered her with a thick horse blanket. "I'll be back to feed you when I can, my girl." He patted her rump, picked up the unconscious female, and carried her to the hunting box.

The heavy oak front door was, not surprisingly, securely locked, just as he'd expected it would be. His boots crunched in the thick layers of icy snow as he walked quickly to the back of the house. He came upon another door, this one less sturdy. He took a step back, lifted his right leg, and sent his boot crashing into the door. It shuddered, but didn't give. He kicked again and this time it flew back on its hinges. Clutching the unconscious girl against his chest, he walked into a small kitchen.

He shoved the broken door closed and pulled a small table against it to keep out the freezing wind and blowing snow. The kitchen had a homey air, with many small personal items strewn about on the table and counters, a sure sign the place was not left abandoned during the winter months. A neat stack of logs climbed halfway up the wall next to the fireplace. Although he didn't take time to look into the pantry, he felt fairly certain that there would be sufficient food to keep them from starving.

He carried her quickly from the kitchen, down a narrow corridor that led to the center of the house. He gazed only cursorily into a small dining room and across the hall into a parlor. All the furnishings were covered in white holland covers.

Phillip felt the cold from her wet clothing and hurried up the staircase that wound up in circular fashion to the floor above, taking the steps two at a time.

He found a large bedchamber toward the end of the upstairs corridor, carried her to the wide bed in the center of the room, and whipped back the heavy counterpane. He held her against him, pulling off the cloak. Then came her gown, for it was soaked through as well. He laid her onto her back to unfasten the long row of tiny pearl buttons that went from the waist to the throat. His practiced eye noted the quality and style of the gown. She was no farmer's daughter, that was certain. He frowned at the sight of her boots. They were riding boots, not made for trekking about in a forest. Where had her horse been? Had she been thrown and her horse had run back to its stable? That seemed likely. But why had she even been riding on a day like this?

He quickly stripped off her petticoat and chemise, both beautifully hemmed and embroidered in soft white batiste, and pulled off her sturdy wool socks. He looked resolutely at her face, but soon realized there was no hope for it. He studied her carefully, feeling her arms and legs for broken bones, pressing his palm to the pulse in her neck, to her breast. Her heartbeat was still slow, but steady. There wasn't a mark on her. No broken anything. What had happened to her?

He also saw that she wasn't a girl, but a young woman. Long-legged, no, he wouldn't catalogue her female points. It wouldn't be well done of him. He quickly bundled her under the covers and drew the sheets to her chin. He gathered up her hair, thick, waving around his hand, and as red as a harlot's evening dress, and spread it onto the pillow away from her head. He stared down at her. She looked like an angel, a dead angel, her skin was so white, her body so absolutely still.

He sat down beside her, placing his palms first against her forehead, then against her cheeks. She was cold to the touch, yet he knew that when she was warm again, the fever would come and very probably snuff out her life. Just as it had killed Lucius, he thought angrily, his mind laying bare the raw memory. Lucius, his French half brother, who had willingly followed Napoleon into the savage wilds of Russia. Lucius had been a strong man, a rugged man, so unlike this slip of a girl. As he looked down at her, he saw for an instant Lucius's ravaged face, deeply etched from the weeks of hunger and the driving winter wind and snow. He'd made it to Poland where Phillip had found him.

His hands shaking, Phillip pressed the covers hard against her, molding them to her. He forced himself to shake off the painful memories that occasionally still haunted his dreams. He looked again, briefly, at the pale face and the mouth that was still blue-tinged with cold. She was so still. He quickly placed his palm over her chest to see if she still breathed. She did, just barely. He'd failed to save Lucius, but he was damned if he was going to let this young female die.

5

He stacked his arms with blankets from the linen closet and layered them over her, then took himself downstairs to the kitchen to fetch logs for a fire. The indolent, rather negligent air for which he was known among his acquaintances fell away from him as if it had never existed.

He laid a huge fire in the fireplace and fanned the embers until flames roared up the blackened chimney. He glanced once again at his patient, saw that there was no change in her, and went to the stables to see to Tasha and to retrieve his leather valise.

He shaded his eyes from the driving snow as he walked the short distance between the house and the stable. It was nearly a full-blown blizzard. It struck him forcibly that the servants who cared for the hunting box wouldn't be showing their faces until the blizzard blew itself out. Who knew how long that could be.

As he walked into the stable, he was greeted with a low whinny from Tasha. She was eating hay from an overflowing bin. At least he wouldn't have to worry about her starving. He patted Tasha's glossy neck, picked up his bag, and made his way quickly back to the house.

He felt cheered at the cozy warmth of the bedchamber. As he unpacked his two changes of clothing and laid them carefully over a chair, it occurred to him that he should put her in some sort of nightgown. He pulled the holland cover off a short, squat dresser and rifled through the drawers. They were filled with men's clothes, and all of them too small for him, he thought, as he lifted them out for inspection. Beneath some underthings, he found two old well-worn velvet dressing gowns.

He sat down beside her and again pressed his hands to her forehead and cheeks. Her skin was warm; her lips had lost that terrifying blue tinge. But she remained unconscious. He gently probed her head through the masses of auburn hair, but he could find no betraying lump. Gently, he eased the pile of blankets down below her breasts and pressed his cheek against her. Her breathing was labored and he heard a wet crackling sound. He tensed, remembering the same sound from Lucius's tortured lungs. She stirred, bringing her arms weakly over her breasts, and shivered violently. He quickly put her into one of the dressing gowns. He wrapped it twice around her and tied the belt. He put her into the other dressing gown as well. Why not? He sashed it at her waist, pulled the blankets back up to her chin again, and lightly slapped her cheeks. She'd been asleep long enough.

"Come on now, open your eyes for me. You can do it. Open your eyes."

She mumbled, and turned her face away from him. "Don't try to get away from me. I'm more tenacious than a tick. Wake up."

She moaned, deep in her throat.

"I wagered with my mare Tasha that you would have green eyes to go with that wicked red hair of yours. No, it's more a wicked auburn color, isn't it? No matter, it's still wicked. Come on, wake up, I want to collect my wager."

Her hand fluttered, then stilled.

"It's time to face the world, you know. And me. I'm not such a bad fellow. I'm a good friend. Come on, wake up." He remembered all too well the men whom the cold had kept from consciousness and drawn deeper away from life. He wouldn't stand for it. "Dammit, do as I tell you," he shouted at her. "Bloody hell, wake up!"

He clasped her shoulders in his hands and shook her. She whimpered softly, and tried to bring her hands up to strike him away. But she didn't have the strength to move the five thick blankets.

"Open your eyes and look at me or it will go very badly for you." He continued to shake her.

Sabrina heard his voice as if from a great distance and forced her eyes to open. She couldn't see clearly. She heard his voice again. He sounded angry with her. She blinked and her eyes cleared. A man was leaning over her. His hands were on her shoulders. She screamed, then whispered, "No, please no, Trevor, let me go. Let me go."

Phillip stared down into large violet eyes, slanted slightly and fringed with thick lashes, a darker red than her hair. He saw the fear—no, it was closer to sheer terror—and said very slowly, lowering his face close to hers, "I'm not Trevor and I won't hurt you. This fellow is nowhere around. It's just me and you. I won't hurt you. Do you understand me?"

She blinked rapidly several times. The man's voice was unknown to her. She strained to clear her mind and her vision. "You're not Trevor," she said slowly.

"No, I'm just me and not this Trevor. Don't be afraid of me. I'm here to help you."

"Did God send you?"

He had to think about that. "Well, perhaps He did. I was lost and just happened to see you lying in the forest."

"You don't look like a gift from God."

"My father told me that God's gifts came in many shapes, that they can even appear in the strangest disguises. Don't spurn me just because I don't look like a pious Methodist."

"Your hair is as black as a storm in the Irish Sea. I don't think Methodists have black hair. Come to think of it, I've never met any Methodists."

"Maybe so, but I wouldn't scoff at sin, if I were you. I'm a sinner and I'm the one who saved you."

He smiled down at her, knowing her wits were still scattered, but she was speaking and making some sense. He lightly touched his palm to her cheek. She was warm, but not too warm. She didn't flinch.

"If I were a man I'd want to look like you. Are you tall?"

"Nearly a giant."

"Most any man is a giant compared to me. I stopped growing. I was very down in the mouth about it, but Grandfather said it didn't matter one little bit. He said I was perfect."

"Perfection is usually tough to gain, but it's true, grandfathers are usually right."

"Maybe, but he loves me. That covers a whole lot of things. Could you help me, please? The covers, they're so heavy. I feel like they're pushing me into the floor." When he didn't move immediately, she began to push and struggle.

"No, hold still. I'll make it better."

"It's just that I can't breathe."

"I know, I'm hurrying." But he knew that even if he pulled the blankets from over her chest, she still probably wouldn't be able to breathe easily. He compromised.

"Is that better?"

She shook her head and continued to struggle, finally shoving down the other two blankets. Phillip caught up her hands in his own and held her tightly. "No, I've got to keep you warm. I'm sorry, but even without the blankets you won't be able to breathe all that easily. The trick is not to fight me or the pain. Take shallow breaths. Yes, that's right." He remembered his long-ago words to Lucius and spoke them aloud, over and over. "Slow, shallow breaths. I'm going to make it better, I promise."

"Yes, help me." Her eyes were closed, her fists heavy at her sides.

He took himself once again to the linen closet, grabbed several towels, and set them near the grate. Some minutes later, he lifted the top towel gingerly, for it was nearly too hot to touch, and carried it to the bed.

As he pulled back the covers and opened the two dressing gowns to bare her chest, he said, "This will hurt you for just a moment, but it will let you breathe more easily."

"Oh, God." She gasped as he laid the hot towel over her breasts and tried to strike it away.

He held her hands and drew the dressing gowns and blankets back over her. She made no sound, but tears were trickling down her cheeks.

He wiped the tears away with his finger. Then he caught up her hands in his again. "I'm sorry, but it must be done. Things will be better soon, you'll see. Now, why don't you tell me your name?"

"Name," she said, her voice faint and dulled with pain, "my name. You're trying to distract me. That's what you're doing, isn't it?"

"Certainly."

"All right then, my name is Bree."

"Brie is a French cheese that is particularly soft, even runny in the summer, and I've never cared for it. My mother adored it. I can't understand why the

French write music to it. You don't look at all French so why did your parents name you after a cheese?"

"No, no, Bree is my nickname. My real name is Sabrina."

He smiled down at her, lightly touching his fingertips to her nose. "It suits you. What's your last name?"

Her eyes were on his face, searching. He saw fear in those incredible violet eyes of hers, and doubt that he wasn't another man to hurt her.

"Stop it. I'm not Trevor."

"Perhaps. I pray you're not like him."

"I'm not. You can trust me on this." Her eyes were still wide on his face, but the fear was fading now, and the doubt as well. He grinned and patted her cheek. "My horse won the wager," he said, and sighed. "You don't have boring green eyes like I'd thought you'd have with all that red hair. No, yours are a very nice violet. Actually I've never seen violet eyes before."

"They're my grandmother's eyes. Her name was Camilla. My grandfather loved her very much. He never hurt her. You're the one with the green eyes and they're not at all boring. They look like wet moss."

"Wet moss and French cheese. We're some combination."

"The pain is less now. That's wonderful."

"Ready for another towel?"

"No, please, wait a moment. It doesn't hurt so badly now."

"My name is Phillip Mercerault."

"You don't live around here."

"No, I don't. Actually I was lost when I found you. Charles gave me damnable directions to his house, Moreland. That's where I was going."

She knew who Charles was, that was as clear on her face as if she'd said it aloud. For whatever reason, she wasn't going to tell him who she was. She was afraid to. Why?

Who cared for the moment? He loved a mystery, and he wagered she had as many secrets as a Renaissance nun.

"Have you ever heard of me?"

She shook her head.

"Well, no matter. I'm here now and I'm going to take care of you. Are you ready for another hot towel?"

She nodded, surprised that the pain in her chest had lessened, that the heat from the towel had seemed to seep deep within her.

She looked up at the face above her, a handsome young face with regular features. He couldn't be above twenty-six or twenty-seven. She found herself staring into his eyes, compelling eyes. Unfortunately he'd been on his way to Moreland. On the other hand, if he hadn't found her, she probably would have died there in Eppingham Forest.

"I'm going to get another hot towel now," he said, but didn't move as she pulled one of her hands free and raised it to his face. He didn't stir. He felt her fingertip lightly touch his jaw, his cheek, his nose. "No," she said, her voice slurred now, "you're not at all like Trevor, thank God." What little strength she had failed her and her hand fell weakly to her side.

"No, Sabrina, I'm not." He gathered her hands once again into his and looked down a moment at the tapering fingers. No calluses, not that he expected any. She was a young lady.

A shadow of pain crossed Sabrina's face and she turned her head away from him on the pillow, not wanting him to think her cowardly and weak. But she couldn't prevent the racking cough that made her body arch forward.

Phillip rose quickly and fetched another hot towel. She shuddered as he laid it over her breasts. He covered her again and rose to look for medicine, anything that would ease her pain. In a small room down the corridor, he found a cache of bandages, ointments, and laudanum, most things he would have expected to find in a hunting box. He measured a few drops of laudanum into a glass of water and walked back to Sabrina's bedchamber.

He slipped his arm beneath her head and brought her upright. "Here, Sabrina, this will help. Drink all of it. That's it."

Although she sipped slowly, she choked and began to cough. He pulled her up against him and began lightly hitting her back. "Shush, it's all right. The water just went down the wrong pipe. That's it, breathe in light shallow breaths. No, don't fight me."

He held her firmly until she regained her breath and again placed the glass to her lips. She managed to swallow the remainder of the laudanum between short, heaving breaths. Phillip gently eased her back down and she lay quietly, waiting for the pain to lessen.

Phillip stood over her, staring down, studying her. Oddly, he felt a strong tug of protectiveness toward her. She could be no more than eighteen years old, a young lady, and in all likelihood a virgin, for there was no wedding band on her left hand. He wondered who this bastard Trevor was, the man who had made her flee her home. He didn't have a doubt that this was what had happened.

He smoothed back a curling lock of auburn hair that had fallen over her brow. She seemed to have fallen asleep, her lashes dark against her white cheeks. She was really quite lovely, not that it made any difference to anything at all.

6

Phillip left the bedchamber door open so that he could hear her if she awakened, and walked downstairs to the kitchen. He remembered suddenly how he and his fellow officers had hunkered around campfires in the mountains in Spain, roasting birds and rabbits to survive. He had learned to make soup from the remains, had even watched his men bake flat bread in crude ovens they'd made from parts of guns and equipment. But damn, that was more than four years ago. Since that time, it had never occurred to him to wonder where his next meal would come from. He thought of the exquisite meals prepared by Cook at Dinwitty Manor, and nearly swooned. He made it a point to have very mundane fare in London to keep him skinny. He'd give Cook a raise when he returned to his country home.

He walked to a small, cold pantry just off the kitchen that he'd noticed earlier. He was pleased and relieved that the owner of this hunting box knew how to keep it stocked. A haunch of smoked ham, beautifully cured, hung from a hook in the ceiling; there was a bin of flour, sugar and salt, potatoes, onions, carrots, dried peas, and even a partially filled barrel of dried apples.

Phillip Edmund Mercerault, Viscount Derencourt, donned a large white apron and set himself to the task of making soup. He sliced vegetables, cut up a slab of ham into small pieces, and tossed the lot into a pot with the dried peas. He gazed about him for water, realized that it wouldn't magically appear, and took himself outside to fill a large pot with snow. The well was probably a foot under snow. Some minutes later, he stood next to a newly built-up fire in the grate, gazing down at his pot of soup. "Lord be praised. You're not such a useless fellow after all," he said aloud. He stripped off his apron, rinsed his hands, then strode back upstairs.

He walked quietly to the bedside and looked down at Sabrina. Her eyes were closed and her breathing so labored he didn't even have to bend over her to hear it. He gently touched his hand to her cheek and found her cool to the touch.

Sabrina felt fingers, featherlight, against her cheek and forced her eyes to open. She could make out a man's face above her and for an instant felt a stab of fear. Her memory righted itself and she whispered, "Phillip."

"Yes, Sabrina. Don't worry. I'm here." He kept his voice pitched low and calm. The last thing he wanted was to frighten her again.

For a moment she thought it strange that he should know her name. She remembered vague images of her flight from Monmouth Abbey, her mare going lame, and the bitter, unrelenting cold. And then that cold was inside her. "I'm so cold. Really, so cold, just like I was in the forest. But I'm not in the forest now. What's wrong?"

"No, nothing's wrong. You're safe with me, Sabrina. I want you to lie still. I'm going to make you warm."

Phillip retrieved another towel from the grate, this one so very hot that he had to toss it several times into the air so that she would be able to bear its heat. She hissed out her breath when he placed it over her.

"No, don't move. Don't fight it. Just let the warmth seep into you. It will if you let it. Just hold still, that's right."

"I don't like this, Phillip, I really don't. It hurts worse than the cold."

"It won't in just a moment, I promise."

She didn't move. It was very difficult, but she didn't even blink. She felt the scalding heat begin to seep into her. It was amazing. His fingers touched her hair and she heard him say, "Try not to move your head, your hair is still damp."

"It's better. I can't believe you were right. I feel warm to my bones."

He tucked the blankets close to her chin. "Good. Now you need to sleep. You'll get better faster the more you sleep. I remember my mother telling me that after I nearly drowned. It worked for me. It will work for you. I'll be right here if you need me." Her eyes were closed. She was already asleep.

Phillip walked to the long narrow windows and pulled back the draperies. He could see nothing save white snow swirling against the windowpanes. He couldn't help but smile. The fates and Charles's directions had certainly conspired to alter his life, at least for the present.

He was too old and too tired. Sometimes he just wanted to close his eyes and sleep, and never wake up. He hadn't deserved the long life he'd been granted, not after he'd let Camilla die. To lose her in childbirth, and all of it his own fault. He shouldn't have given in to her pleas for another chance to have a daughter. They'd been given only one son, and how she'd wanted a daughter. But he had given in to her and she'd died, the boy child with her. No, he wouldn't think about Camilla just now. He hunched forward in his chair and stared at his elder grand-daughter, Elizabeth. She was graceful, he'd give her that, and she would be pretty if it weren't for the discontent that dragged down the corners of her mouth, that leached out any sheen of contentment from her eyes.

Sabrina. She had come to tell him that Sabrina was dead? No, he wouldn't accept that, never.

She came to a halt in front of him, not too close, because she hated him. He knew it but it had taken him a very long time to figure out why. And then one day, he'd known. She hated his power, seeing herself as powerless. She hated his age, finding it repellent, frightening.

He could have told her it wasn't frightening at all. It was just a bloody bore. He'd told that to Sabrina and she'd lightly punched his arm, telling him not to be foolish, not to be bored because he had so many years in his dish because that was surely proof that God wanted him to remain here to watch over his lands and his people, to ensure their safety from the wicked that roamed the earth.

Wicked, he thought, and looked toward his nephew, Trevor. Aye, his nephew and heir, the future Earl of Monmouth, a pretty fellow who was always polite to him, any feelings he felt always held behind those veiled lying eyes of his.

He tried to keep the contempt from his voice as he forced himself back to Elizabeth. He forced himself to say the words aloud, but it was difficult, for to say them meant that they were true. He felt the gnawing of helplessness, felt nearly bowed to his knees with it. He swallowed, saying nothing for another moment, but Elizabeth held herself perfectly quiet, Trevor the

same. There was no news, he thought, and said, "It's
been two days now, two days without a word, without
a clue, without a sign of Sabrina. Have you brought
me no news at all then? You know very well, Elizabeth, that she wouldn't leave her home without some
powerful reason to motivate her." He pulled a crum-
pled piece of paper from his dressing-gown pocket and
waved it at Elizabeth, a granddaughter he'd tried to
love, tried to shield, but she'd not wanted that from
him. Fear clutched at him, making his belly twist and
knot. "As for the letter she left me—it tells me nothing. Damnation, what does this mean? She writes that
she can no longer remain here and must go to her
aunt Barresford in London?" He thought of Sabrina's
mare, her legs scratched from brambles, the left fore-
leg lame, returned yesterday to the Abbey, and felt
his blood run cold. His blood had been cold now for
two days. "No, don't you dare tell me again about her
depressed spirits, whatever that means. I want the
truth now, Elizabeth. I don't want any more of your
lies."

Elizabeth stood tall above the earl, almost wraithlike
in her slenderness, and nervously shifted her weight
to her other foot. What was she to say to this miserable old man who was the undisputed master, who
didn't even allow her to sit in his presence? How she
wanted him to suffer. He deserved to for the slights
he'd given her since the day Sabrina had been born.
But the tug of fear was still there. She felt what little
color she normally had fade until she knew her face
was as white as the wall behind her grandfather's
chair. She didn't move, something she'd managed to
master many years ago. She never fidgeted in front of
him, never showed him how much she despised him
for his disregard of her. She nearly smiled as she said,
"I have no lies to tell, Grandfather. It was as I first

told you. Sabrina was quiet, withdrawn from me. I know nothing more today, truly."

And Trevor, his too-pretty nephew with his grand manner, said, "Elizabeth doesn't wish to cause you more pain, sir." As he spoke he gently squeezed one of her pale slender hands. "Come, my dear, we must not further dissemble. You cannot protect your little sister forever."

Elizabeth's eyes widened at her husband's words. She felt the excitement coiled in him, the pleasure at delivering a death blow, but she was afraid, still afraid of this wretched old man who held the reins of power over her, and would hold them until he died. Sometimes she wondered if he'd come back even after he was dead, and he'd torment her and mock her and she'd whimper and want to give up. And he'd win, he'd always win.

It was her grandfather's words that decided her. Curse him to hell where he belonged. She shriveled as he said, his mouth twisted with dislike, "Well, girl, don't stand there like a stupid cow. Out with it. If you know something about Sabrina's leaving, I will hear it now, by God. And I'm tired of your supposed truths, Elizabeth, for they ring as hollow as a fool's wit."

Her head went back, she returned the pressure of her husband's hand. She even made herself shrug. "I'm sorry, my lord, but it is as Trevor said. I am loath to cause you pain. But since you insist upon hearing the truth, then I will give it to you." She felt power sing through her, making her strong, making her impervious, putting her in control, where she belonged. "If you must know, Sabrina was jealous of me. She wanted Trevor for herself."

She stopped abruptly at the growl that came from deep in her grandfather's throat.

"My love," Trevor said, "you must tell his lordship

the full of it. You can no longer protect your sister. As he says, she's been gone for two days. He is worried about her. Come, tell him the rest of the truth." Elizabeth felt his fingers tighten their grip on her hand, felt the bones push together. She hated pain, had always feared it, and he knew it, knew it well from their wedding night when she'd pleaded and pleaded but he hadn't listened, just smiled at her and gloried in the pain he'd caused her. But now she held silent. Slowly, very slowly, she pulled her hand away. He let her go.

She drew a deep breath. "I haven't wanted you to know this, my lord, but Sabrina tried to throw herself at Trevor. Yes, she tried to seduce him, so that in his honor, had he taken hers, he would have been compromised in your eyes. Mayhap even compelled to leave his home and me."

It was well said, she knew it. Her voice had rung out with sincerity, but the old man just stared at her, saying in that loud strident voice of his, "What utter nonsense, girl. Sabrina, seduce him? It is beyond ridiculous. She doesn't even like him. No, she didn't tell me that, but I knew. She tried to hide her dislike, but I knew. Why are you still lying to me?"

"I'm telling you the truth, Grandfather. Why would I lie to you? She's the one who ran away, not I. Indeed, I saw her, do you hear me? Yes, I saw her. She asked Trevor to accompany her to the portrait gallery, to see Grandmother Camilla's portrait. When they were alone, when she knew no servants were about, she tried to convince Trevor to make love to her."

Elizabeth faltered, but Trevor continued smoothly, his eyes sincere, his voice compelling. "I told her, my lord, that although I held her in great esteem, I would not betray Elizabeth. I told her she was now my sister, nothing more, nothing less. She was angry, sir, and in her anger she threatened to tell you that I had tried to make love to her. Elizabeth was there, sir, she saw everything. Neither of us would lie, sir. It is the truth, all of it."

Elizabeth said, "It was then that I told her that I had witnessed everything. She must have realized she was ruined."

Elizabeth watched the despicable old man look away from them. He stared down at his twisted fingers, then at the fire that roared in the fireplace, making the chamber so hot she had trouble breathing. The silence in the library was broken only by the occasional crackle of burning logs.

"So, you are asking me to believe that Sabrina fled her home with naught but a meaningless letter to me because of your noble rejection of her, Eversleigh?"

Trevor said calmly, regret brimming in his voice, "I would assume so, my lord. Perhaps she felt mortified at her behavior and dreaded the whole being told. My lord, she should have realized that as a gentleman I would not have let a word of what happened pass my lips. As for Elizabeth, I am quite certain that she has already forgiven her sister. Isn't that true, my love?"

His fingers tightened again on Elizabeth's hand and she said quickly, "Of course it is true. Trevor is right, Grandfather. Sabrina knows how much I love her. She knows that I've already forgiven her. After all, she is the spinster now, not I. That she wanted my place, my husband, well, that is something I have already set aside. My feelings of affection for her are deep."

"Deep, you say? Aye, I believe every word that falls from your lips, Elizabeth. I always have, for you have been a granddaughter to point to with pride, to hold up as a model to all girls."

She preened, and straightened her shoulders. The earl just looked at her, wondering how she could have believed his words when they'd dripped with sarcasm, but she obviously had. He turned in his chair to gaze through the long French windows at the end of the library at the storm, still full in its fury. And Sabrina had not reached Borhamwood to take the stage to London. None of the fifty men out searching for her had found a trace of her. He felt a spasm of grief grip him, such as he had not felt since Camilla had died. Sabrina was so very like Camilla, her eyes as deep a violet, her auburn hair glorious, thick, and curling. And she was good-hearted, open, and loyal, just as Camilla had been. He smiled for a moment, for she was vain about her hair, saying it was the same color as Queen Titania's, in *A Midsummer Night's Dream.* Perhaps it was. He remembered when she was eleven years old and she'd become deathly ill with a fever. They'd had to cut all her glorious hair off. He'd told her that she had to get well to grow it back. If she left him, why then, she would see him in heaven all bald. Surely that was worth getting well again. She'd improved almost immediately. Thank the gods for that small bit of vanity.

But not for an instant did he doubt Sabrina. Her sense of honor was as strong and unbending as was his own. He felt impotent rage sweep through him. Sabrina might be dead and he was forced to endure Elizabeth and Trevor's betrayal of her. What had really happened? Why had Sabrina run away? It was driving him mad for he could find no reason. But of course there was a possibility, a strong one, that Trevor had been the one to trap Sabrina in the portrait gallery, that he had tried to force himself on her. He looked at his heir from the corner of his eye. Yes, certainly it was possible, else how had they come up with that other tale? Aye, it was the boot on the other foot, that's what it was.

He felt tired to his soul. He would have given all his worldly goods to rise from his chair and pound Trevor into the floor. But there was no proof of anything.

What had happened? Whatever it was had terrified Sabrina so much that she hadn't come to him, and she'd come to him with all her problems since she'd been a little girl, even before her parents had died.

Without looking again at his granddaughter or his heir, the earl said coldly, "Send Jesperson to me. If there is any report on Sabrina, tell me immediately." He waved a hand in abrupt dismissal. He couldn't stand the sight of them, hovering near him, standing so close together they appeared as one.

"I will come to you the moment we hear anything, my lord," Trevor said. The earl watched him lead Elizabeth from the library. It looked as if Trevor was holding Elizabeth's hand tightly, so tightly that it was hurting her.

7

Once Trevor had pulled the library doors closed, he turned to his wife of less than three weeks. "Are you not all of twenty-three years of age, my dear?"

At her startled nod, he continued, his voice as soft as the rustling silk of her gown. "And Sabrina is but eighteen. Your failure amazes me. You had a full five years, my love, to win the old gentleman's regard before she entered the world. How miserably you failed."

Elizabeth looked at the beautifully carved mahogany of the balustrade on the stairs. She said, "She is gone now. Finally. Perhaps forever."

"Do you believe so? She is perhaps beyond earthly cares by this time, that is what you think?"

Elizabeth's lips tightened. "If she hadn't been such a whining little fool, running to me for protection, if only she'd simply held herself silent, why then, she wouldn't be where she is now. Can you believe she actually expected me to denounce you?"

"Come, Elizabeth, you have always hated Sabrina. If you were a different class of woman, why, you could tread the boards on Drury Lane. If I were a stranger overhearing you, I would think that your heart is near to breaking because she might be dead. Did she not prove what she was? She was nothing but a worthless little whore. Does that not please you?"

She looked up into that very pretty face of his, saw the faint sneer marring his mouth. "You and I both know that it isn't true, none of it. Tell me, Trevor, would you have kept after her until you'd finally managed to rape her? Really, what would you have done once you'd accomplished what you'd set out to?"

"Even though I have been your husband for but a very short time, my dear, know that I expect loyalty and obedience from you. I do not expect questions that hover on the disrespectful."

"Loyalty is what I've given you. Come, tell me the truth. Would you have continued to chase her after you'd managed to rape her?"

He laughed, actually laughed. "The truth is a strange thing, Elizabeth. You hate your sister yet you are choosing to believe what she told you. Why don't you believe me, Elizabeth? After all, I am your husband. I will father your children. Mine will be the last face you see when you lie dying."

For an instant she saw herself lying on her bed, quite dead, saw him staring down at her. He was smiling. "Stop it. Forget that I asked, forget everything."

"Very well, I shall. Now, I want loyalty even when we are alone. I don't want any more of these speculations, Elizabeth. I want compliance and obedience from you. I want you to bend utterly to me."

"I choose to give you my loyalty because it is in my interest to do so, Trevor. But as the future Countess of Monmouth, believe me, I shall not allow you to sully the Eversleigh name."

Trevor regarded his passionless bride and wondered if any man would be able to make her scream with lust, make her buck as her woman's pleasure overtook her. Probably not. He was an excellent lover, but she hated his touch, his using her. Since their wedding night, he'd treated her with unflagging gentleness, forcing himself to curb his demands. She didn't flinch anymore, didn't plead. That was a start. There would be a better time to show her that it was he who was her master, in all things. For the moment, it rather amused him to see her try to control him. She didn't even realize that it was the shadow of the old earl that held him in check, and not any warnings from her. After the old man died, he would do precisely as he pleased.

She would not allow him to sully the Eversleigh name? That alone would merit a punishment. He would gladly mete it out when the time came.

But for now, he gave Elizabeth his most engaging smile and said with a lover's gentle voice, "Alas, my dearest wife, men are sometimes weak. Wasn't your father like that as well? Didn't he seduce every woman who did not run from him? Ah, no need to answer. Perhaps you didn't even know. Perhaps it was a lie fashioned by my own father. Now, you need have no further worry—surely you know that I love and desire you above all women. Sabrina? She was nothing, merely a young girl who chanced to whet my appetites one long afternoon. Just consider what it has gained you. I believe you owe me a great debt of gratitude. She is gone."

Elizabeth let his words pass. Her father hadn't been a saint, for no man was a saint, but he hadn't been like Trevor. And she was married to him for as long as she lived. It made her cold to her bones. Well, she would mold him, change him, guide him into behavior that wouldn't shame her in the future. She stared down at the great emerald wedding ring on her third finger. It was something of which she should be proud, a symbol of what she had long thought she would never have in life. Yet, it still felt alien to her, as alien as it had almost two months ago when the earl had summarily called her to the library, placed the ring in her outstretched hand, and said without preamble, "You are to be married, Elizabeth. The Eversleigh emerald is yours. I trust you will like the fellow, for he will be the Earl of Monmouth after my death."

She'd stared at him, so startled she had to flounder for words. "My cousin, sir? Trevor?"

"Of course, my girl. I could have wished for another heir but God doesn't grant us that many choices. Of course it is Trevor. At least he isn't a stranger to you."

But Trevor Eversleigh was a stranger. Elizabeth had met him only twice in her life, when he'd visited from his home in Italy.

She was to marry him? She swallowed. "He is coming here, Grandfather?"

"Certainly, how else could you wed with him?" He expected no answer, and waved Elizabeth toward a chair opposite him. "Sit down, and I will tell you the whole of it."

The earl looked down at his hands a moment, then began. "As you know, Elizabeth, Trevor is the grandson of my younger brother. You will not remember Trevor's father, Vincent, for he besmirched the Eversleigh name and fled to the Continent with a divorced woman who was a harlot. I will not sully your ears with tales of his mother's despicable behavior in Italy. At least Vincent married her so that Trevor is legitimate. Suffice it to say that she contracted the pox some three months ago and died a wretched death. It was then that your cousin wrote me. I don't intend to hold the doings of Trevor's antecedents against him, for he is, after all, my heir and the future Earl of Monmouth. I grow old, Elizabeth. I want Trevor Eversleigh here, at Monmouth Abbey, so that he may learn what will be required of him as the future earl. You might as well know too that it is my right to bestow the Eversleigh wealth where I wish. I have told Trevor that the wealth would be his if he agreed to take you for his wife. His reply, of course, shows his good sense. He will, of a certainty, live here with you, at least until my death."

"I cannot remember that my cousin Trevor even liked me, Grandfather."

"It's been four years since you've seen each other. He is nearly twenty-eight, a man full grown, and you, I might add, are growing no younger with the passing summers. I will hear no romantic drivel from you, Elizabeth. He will treat you well enough, trust me for that."

"Yes, Grandfather," Elizabeth said, nodding obediently.

"He will be arriving next week. Your banns will be read then."

The earl turned away from her, as if she were no longer in the room. "You may go now, Elizabeth, to contemplate your good fortune. Send Sabrina to me."

She had felt like dancing from the library, but she'd forced herself to walk away serenely. She smiled widely. A servant saw that smile and stared at her. Whatever her uncertainties about her future husband, she forced them from her mind. She was to be married. And not just married to anyone, she would be the future Countess of Monmouth.

She'd given up hoping any suitable gentleman would want her, despite the handsome dowry. Her stay with her aunt, Lady Barresford, had netted only two offers for her hand, both from gentlemen with an obvious need for money. At long last she would be freed from snide comments about her inevitable spinsterhood, freed from unflattering comparisons between herself and Sabrina. And above all, she thought, her pale eyes shining, she would be the Countess of Monmouth. As soon as that old man died.

Elizabeth felt Trevor's fingers caressing her shoulders and flashed him a confident smile. She wondered, almost dispassionately, if her younger sister was dead.

"I fear for Sabrina's safety," she said aloud, trying to disregard his hand, which was caressing her upper arm, moving toward her breast. He released her abruptly.

"Yes, so do I." He turned away from her. "I would wish it could be different. It is really quite a pity, quite a pity."

Her chin went up just a bit as she said, "Perhaps she has found shelter. She is so pretty, so vivacious, anyone would help her, don't you think? I have seen gentlemen scramble over themselves to please her. She always just laughed and teased them."

"You want your dear little sister home in the bosom of her family? Yes, of course you would give all you have to have her with us again. Perhaps soon she will be home. I would enjoy that. I would try to please her perhaps even more than you would. Is it possible that is true, Elizabeth?"

She was trembling. He had won. Her voice was low, furious. "If she does return, if she dares to return here, I assure you, Trevor, that she will not long remain."

Phillip pulled off his cravat, tossed it on the settee, and sank down wearily into a chair beside Sabrina's bed. He looked down into the bowl of soup. It didn't look promising. He couldn't think of what he'd done wrong, but obviously he'd done something very wrong, so wrong that he wondered if he could even get the stuff down. Yes, he had to. He brought a spoon filled with a clump of stringy vegetables and too salty ham chunks. They didn't taste better with the brief bit of aging. He ate, didn't think about what he was eating, just ate until he had finished. He set the empty bowl down, leaned back, and closed his eyes. He wondered how long it would be before Charles became worried at his absence. Would he send men out to search for him? He smiled at his own silent idiot question. It was doubtful, yes, even more than quite doubtful. He imagined that a round of ribald jokes was very likely circulating among the gentlemen of his acquaintance at Moreland, each in turn, he thought, laying wagers on his imagined amorous encounter in the wilds of Yorkshire with some comely wench. What a pity he wasn't living up to their lecherous fantasies.

He gazed at Sabrina, who was sleeping fitfully, tossing from one side to the other. Her beautiful hair was tangled, but dry. He rose and leaned over her. He smoothed his fingers through the tangles, then braided her hair as best he could. It wasn't a sterling result, but it would have to do.

He found himself wondering about her family. She'd spoken in a soft cultured voice, with no Yorkshire accent. Although he realized he was rather an ass for doing it, he pictured a cold, domineering stepmother and a weak, absent father. How else, he wondered, shaking his head, could such a thing happen to a young, well-born girl?

"Well, my dear," he said to the silent Sabrina, "I'll even find out if you have a birthmark soon enough. I will burrow into that head of yours and discover every detail you have hidden from me." He laid the palm of his hand against her forehead, and cursed. Her skin was hot and dry to the touch. The fever he had so dreaded was upon her.

Suddenly she opened her eyes, unseeing eyes, and struggled frantically against the blankets. She looked blindly through him and shouted, "No, you cannot, Grandfather. No! My poor Diablo, no."

Phillip grabbed her shoulders and pressed her back. She struggled against him until she had no more strength. She looked up at him, her eyes still unseeing.

"Sabrina? Can you hear me? It's all right. You've got the fever, but you will be all right, I swear it to you."

She quieted, closing her eyes. He released her.

Suddenly she pulled her arms free of the blankets and struck him in the chest. "You bastard! Let me go, do you hear? Let me go!"

What was going on here? Was it Trevor she saw again? She began crying, choking on her own tears. He couldn't bear it. He pulled her up against his chest and began to rock her in his arms. "It will be all right, Sabrina. I wouldn't lie to you. Trust me. No one will ever hurt you again, I swear it. You must rest now to get well. Once you're well again you can hit me as many times as you wish."

She quieted at last. He thought she would sink back into sleep. But she reared back suddenly in his arms, trying to pull away from him. She stared straight at him and said, "It's so hot in here. Why is it so very hot? I don't like it at all. Have you no sense? Look, there's even a fire in the grate. Why?"

He remembered the awful fever that had eaten at Lucius, burning him from the inside out. "I'll make it cooler. Try not to think about the heat, all right?"

He gave her some water. She was trying to swallow it faster than she could breathe. She choked, coughing even as she tried to drink all the water at once. When at last she was done, the coughing stilled, she lay back and stared up at him. But it wasn't him she was seeing. "Please, Mary, I have tried not to think about the heat, but it does no good. Please open the window. I'm so hot, so very hot.''

She knew she was dying. She had wondered several times what it would be like. She just hadn't imagined that she'd be roasted alive from the inside out. It was strange, this heat that was cooking her slowly and thoroughly. Then she heard a man's voice, vague and far away from her, Phillip's voice. Who was Phillip? Somewhere deep inside her, she knew who Phillip was, but the knowledge of him escaped her. He said from above her, "Just lie still, Sabrina. The pain will stop in just a moment, and the heat.''

How could that be possible? She was dying from the fire burning her insides. Suddenly she felt a cold wet cloth against her face. She again heard a man's voice, clearer this time. "No, no, don't struggle. Just feel this. Don't you like it?''

She would give him a moment to make good on his words. She suddenly felt cool air on her chest closely followed by the cold wet cloth. She arched her back against it, wanting more, wanting it to cover all of her at once. She felt his hands about her waist, turning her over. She struggled until she felt the damp cloth moving up and down her back, and over her hips, cooling all of her.

Phillip bathed her with a cold wet towel several times an hour throughout the afternoon and into the evening. A weary smile lit his eyes when he touched his hands to her cheeks. For the time being, at least, he had broken the fever. He thought for a moment that he saw an answering smile before she closed her eyes in sleep.

Phillip shucked off his clothes, pulled off one of the blankets from Sabrina's bed, and stretched out in a large chair near the fireplace. He listened to the night wind howling outside, and the swirling gusts of snow slamming against the windowpanes. It was a comforting sound that relaxed him and soothed his mind. He wasn't concerned about hearing Sabrina if she awoke during the night, for he was a light sleeper, his years on the Peninsula having taught him that men who released themselves completely into sleep often never awoke in the morning. The French had deployed small bands of soldiers, disguised as peasants, to slip into English camps and dispatch as many of its members as possible. He would never forget the deep gurgling sound that had erupted from the throat of his sergeant, a campaign-hardened soldier from Devonshire. Phillip had caught his assassin and choked the life from the man with his bare hands, but of course, it had been too late for his sergeant. He felt again the wave of nausea and fury that had consumed him as he had stood helplessly watching his man die.

He shook his head. He was tired, tired to his very bones. But she was still alive. He leaned over to pinch out the flame from the one candle that sat at his elbow. He looked for a moment at his large hands, with their elegantly manicured nails. They were the hands of a gentleman, a man whose pleasures and pastimes gave no clue of any preoccupation with the memory of the bloody violence that had occurred on the Peninsula.

He pinched the candle wick, sighed deeply, and settled back into the chair. He thought it curious that this one sick girl had stirred the embers of his past, making him relive scenes he'd believed long buried within him, or forgotten.

8

Miss Teresa Elliott frowned down into her glass of champagne. She eyed her host, saw that he was no longer paying her sufficient attention, and said, "Really, Charles, you must have some idea where his lordship could be. I thought you said that you yourself gave Phillip directions to Moreland. He isn't here. I want him here. You will do something about this now."

"I did give him directions, yes. He should have come by now. I don't understand."

"It appears to me that your understanding isn't what is important here. Come, aren't you worried about Phillip? After all, this wretched snowstorm has turned the world white. Perhaps Phillip is hurt, lying helpless somewhere. I really expect you to do something of consequence right now, Charles."

Charles looked at Miss Elliott's very pretty face and thought for perhaps the dozenth time that wherever Phillip was, he was better off than being here. Perhaps even lying in the snow was better. Miss Elliott had charmed him in London. Here, at Moreland, she was driving him to Bedlam. He admitted he was impressed with her ability to hide this part of her character from prying eyes in town. Or perhaps she hadn't. After all, Phillip wasn't here and she wasn't as concerned about her manners. Damn Phillip.

"You act as if you don't care if poor Phillip is dying. And he could be, what with all that nonsensical snow. So irritating." She snapped down her glass of champagne onto a side table. The glass was one of his mother's favorite set. He hoped it hadn't cracked. "Didn't you say that Phillip's valet is here? What is the servant doing here doubtless all snug in front of a fire when his master is dying in the snow? Surely you have put questions to him, forced him to answer, have you not?"

Enough was enough. Charles had exquisite manners. He had three sisters. He knew how to employ manners, how to gently soothe maidenly sensibilities, but enough was enough. He said in the sweetest voice that any of his good friends would have recognized as dangerous, "I begin to believe, Teresa, that the champagne has taken its toll on your brain. Naturally I have spoken to Dambler. He is growing increasingly concerned. However, since he doesn't imbibe, he doesn't keep repeating himself. He has no notion of where Phillip is."

She was not a devotee of irony. She waved dismissal with a lovely hand that had never seen a day's labor in its life. "The man is obviously lying. He's lazy. He knows he doesn't have any duties to perform as long as his master isn't here. I don't for a moment believe that his lordship would send his valet ahead because he wanted to explore the countryside. And alone, of all things. It is absurd. What is there to explore? It is winter. It is not London or even Bath. There is nothing to be explored. You must deal with this, Charles. You must speak to him again, really question him closely this time, realizing what he is."

It was either leave the room or strangle her. Charles motioned to a footman to refill Miss Elliott's glass. That was it, he'd get her dead drunk. That should shut her up, maybe even send her to her bed with a head-ache. Dambler's story that the viscount wanted to roam Yorkshire didn't seem at all strange to him. He'd known Phillip since Eton. He'd always gone his own way. But in this instance, he thought it wildly unlikely that he was lying somewhere in the snow, lost and alone and freezing to death. Phillip wasn't the type of man to lose himself anywhere, unless, of course, he wished it. He felt Teresa's fingers tug at the sleeve of his exquisite coat that Gautier of Paris had fashioned exclusively for him.

"Unfortunately you are a man, Charles, and thus you don't wish to heed my warnings. I'm getting dire feelings about this. Very dire. Will you promise to send out a search party for Phillip in the morning?"

Charles gently disengaged his sleeve. Her sharp fingernails had left a pucker in the soft velvet. His valet would have a fit. He began smoothing it out as he said, "Teresa, as long as this blizzard continues, it simply isn't safe to send out anyone. They would themselves become lost within feet of the front gate. No, we must wait until the storm blows itself out, then if Phillip doesn't come, we will search." He looked at her lovely white throat. He pictured his fingers wrapped around that lovely white throat. He sighed, adopting a placating voice that worked each and every time with his mother. Whenever he used the voice, she called him her dear boy. "Come, there is nothing we can do now. Would you care for some cards? Perhaps some dancing?"

She drank down more of his late father's excellent champagne. A small smile played over his mouth. Actually, truth be told, he thought it more than likely that at this very moment, Phillip was probably quite at his ease in some inn or in a nearby residence, down-ing warm ale and seducing the prettiest girl about.

Since Phillip had returned from the Peninsula, suffering a wound in his shoulder from the battle of Ciudad Rodrigo, he had adopted the attitude that discomfort of any sort was to be avoided at all costs. He saw her thump down another empty glass. What was he to do? To say? He'd try it another way. "Don't forget, Teresa, that Phillip was a soldier. Even if he did find himself caught unawares in the blizzard, he would have the good sense not to continue on his way to Moreland. I'm certain he's well protected from the elements. Were it possible, I would imagine his very good manners would dictate that he send me a message. However, the blizzard is an effective dampener of manners." With a flash of inspiration, Charles realized what he had not said. "You know, wherever he is, I know that Phillip must be missing you terribly."

He was a genius. He had scored a perfect hit. She preened. Oh, Lord, he mustn't forget to beg the absent viscount's pardon tonight in his prayers.

"Do you really think, Charles, that Phillip is just at this very moment pining for me, that he is—"

Charles was saved by the appearance of Edgar Plummer, a marvelous guest in his newly revised opinion, and his sister, Margaret. Plummer was old as dirt but he was smart. He liked Charles and thus sought to save him. Mr. Plummer bowed over Teresa's hand. "Allow an old man to tell you how very lovely you look this evening, Miss Elliott. Won't you please play the pianoforte for us?"

She refused three times, the seemingly accepted number of refusals to denote modesty, then allowed Mr. Plummer to lead her to the pianoforte at the end of the long drawing room.

"Oh, goodness, Charlie, now we're in for it. She's going to play some more of her tedious French ballads. Just wait, I'll wager she'll dedicate them to poor Phillip."

Charles groaned. "Don't say that, Margaret, she just might hear you." He led his sister to a red brocade settee lovingly made for the family in the early part of the last century. "At last the lady is well occupied. Remind me to buy a Christmas present for Edgar. I will give him my favorite watch fob. Yes, that's it. Watch fobs are excellent gifts."

"Was she bothering you again about Phillip?"

"It's her Greek chorus. I think Miss Elliott has matrimony in mind for Phillip. I did have the good sense not to tell her that the viscount is likely relieving his tedium during the storm in the arms of some Yorkshire beauty."

Margaret, in all seriousness, said low, "But where, Charlie? At some inn? I thought Phillip was more discriminating in his taste. A taproom wench?"

Charles grinned. He'd rather expected to shock her, but it was not to be. She'd been married to Sir Hugh Drakemore for nearly a year now and his shy, frequently tongue-tied little sister was now worldly and assertive. He quite liked the change in her. As for her husband, Sir Hugh still seemed the same—serious, quiet, studied in his reflections. Ah, but there had to be more, a lot more, just look at the change wrought in Margaret. "No, you're right. That's a problem. Phillip is very selective. Perhaps he is visiting one of our neighbors and it is a daughter or wife he is currently enjoying."

"No, Charlie, Phillip wouldn't seduce a married woman."

"Now, how would you know that?"

"He told me."

"Margaret, surely you're jesting with me, surely—"

"No, really. I asked him, you see, once about two

years ago when I fancied myself in love with him. He was so nice. He knew exactly how I felt and he was very careful of my feelings. I had heard that he'd bedded Mrs. Stockton, the ambassador's wife, and he hadn't. As best he knew, he'd turned the lady down and out of spite she'd spread rumors that he'd seduced her. It angered him, Charlie. He said married ladies were no longer on the playing field."

Margaret, in love with Phillip? Charles had never guessed, never even speculated. "Come to think of it, I can't think of a single married lady that Phillip has bedded. You no longer, er, feel this way toward Phillip, do you, Margaret?"

"No, not after I met Hugh. One week with Hugh and every man I'd ever met faded out of my mind."

"Good."

"But you know, Charlie, I've often wondered why he has never married. I know for a fact how many lovely young ladies would gladly accept him."

"Now therein lies a tale. Have you ever met the Countess of Bufford?"

Margaret cocked her head to one side, making the brown ringlets over her left ears fall to her shoulder. "Of course. She's a leader among the ton. Mother dislikes her intensely, but she told me she is too powerful to cross, that I must always watch my back around her. I told Mother that she looks so lovely, so innocent, so guileless, but Mother just laughed and told me not to trust her. I know that Lord Bufford adores her. What does she have to do with Phillip?"

"When she came out six years ago, she quickly earned herself the title of the Ice Maiden. She was endowed with both splendid beauty and wealth, and her instant success followed naturally from both of these facts together. Phillip was a young captain in the hussars, in London that spring because his father, the late viscount, had just died. Phillip was young, inexperienced in the ways of women like Elaine, and raw with grief from the death of his father."

"Good God, you don't mean that Phillip fell in love with that awful woman?"

Charles shrugged his shoulders. "I'm not certain exactly what it was he felt for Elaine, but I do know that he wanted her. Is that love? I don't know, Margaret. Phillip was only twenty years old, a boy. And boys are prone to lust, no other way to put it. Ah, look, Edgar is pleading with Miss Elliott to continue her concert. Cross your fingers that he will succeed."

Miss Elliott broke out into another song, a doleful rendition of a French ballad of the last century. "At least she sings well," Charles said.

"Come, Charlie, tell me what happened."

9

Charles eyed his sister thoughtfully, wondering why he had brought up the matter now, after so many years. Of course he knew why. After their good friend Rohan Carrington, Baron Mountvale, had married, Phillip had fallen into a funk. He'd said once to Charles last fall, "Rohan is happy. Happy. Can you believe it? And Susannah is happy as well. Just maybe sometimes there is something that is honest and good between a man and a woman."

Charles said now, "Very well, Margaret, but you must promise to keep this knowledge tucked under your chestnut hair. Most people know a little of what occurred, but not everything. Rohan Carrington is the only other one to know the whole of it."

"I promise, Charlie."

Miss Elliott hit a high F. A champagne goblet trembled on a nearby table.

"Phillip asked Elaine to marry him and she agreed. The date was set for the following April, for no marriage could take place during Phillip's year of mourning for his father. It is too long ago for you to recall it, but during the fall of 1809 there were many violent skirmishes on the Peninsula. Phillip felt it his duty to rejoin his regiment, over Elaine's objections. I sometimes wonder," Charles added, "how we all could have been so wrong. A bloody pack of fools we were.

Phillip returned to London on leave in early February to resign his commission and set Dinwitty Manor in order for its new mistress. He had changed somewhat, I can remember thinking that, as if he had been catapulted too quickly into manhood. Remember, he was now only twenty-one years old."

"Yes, a veritable young lad for a gentleman and a spinster for a lady. Grossly unfair."

"That's as may be but not to the point."

"Do you know, Charles, I have sometimes thought that Phillip's eyes mirror his deepest thoughts. I've seen laughter in his eyes when there was none about his mouth, and sadness too. I've never known what to make of it."

Charles had no idea what she was talking about. Better yet, he didn't want to know. He said, "I'll never forget the night he came to my lodgings on Half Moon Street, vilely drunk, his face so white and set that I thought he'd been in a battle with the devil himself. I was scared to death." Charles spoke more slowly now as he remembered Phillip's young face, his mouth flattened in bitter humiliation, his eyes cold and dead, mirroring his disillusion. He could still hear his voice, cold as ice. "Elaine wants to wed now, Charlie, not in April as we had planned."

Charles had stared at his friend. What to say to that? Phillip was so young. None of his friends wanted him to wed. He said carefully, "Is it that she missed you more than you had believed? Surely this is a good sign."

Phillip's laugh was low and mean. "Miss me? God, that's a rare jest. Give me a glass of brandy, Charles, and be quick about it."

Silently, Charles moved to the sideboard, poured brandy from the crystal decanter, and handed it to his friend. Phillip tipped the brandy down his throat and, with a growl of fury, hurled the empty glass toward the grate, where it shattered.

Charles was now seriously frightened. "Dear God, Phillip, what happened? What's wrong with you?"

The viscount raised his eyes and said in a voice so flat and soft that Charles had to lean close to make out his words, "Elaine—my Ice Maiden—is pregnant, my friend. It took me quite a while to pry it out of her. Rest assured that I'm not the father."

Charles reeled back on his heels. "But who?"

"Exactly my question to dear Elaine, which, of course, she tearfully refused to answer. It wasn't very noble of me, but I waited patiently, then followed her. There is no doubt in my mind that the father of her child is her wastrel cousin, Roger." Phillip paused a moment, his eyes turning hard. "Of course he will never know the sex of his child, for I am going to kill him."

Charles sucked in his breath. Of a certainty he had seen Elaine much in her cousin's company, but he was, after all, part of her family. To the eyes of the polite world, there had been nothing questionable about her behavior.

"What do you intend to do about Elaine?"

"That panting little bitch?" He began to laugh, furiously wild laughter. "If she is an ice maiden, Charles, I ask you, what is every other lady? Well, my friend, I'll tell you what they are—sluts who have no honor, who will part their thighs to the closest male of their acquaintance. I thank God that I have seen the truth in time to escape. Never will I fall into such a trap again."

Charles shook the viscount's shoulders. "You're drunk as a loon, Phillip, and you don't know what you're saying. Come to bed. We'll decide what is to be done on the morrow, when you've a clear head and your wits about you."

"No, Charles. What must be done will be done now, tonight. I am off to kill that bastard, Roger. You will act as my second?"

"But the scandal, Phillip. Have you thought of what this would do to your mother? To Elaine's family? My God, man, you're the Viscount Derencourt."

Phillip regarded Charles for a brief moment, then said softly, "If I do not have my honor, Charles, I have nothing. Most likely, all of society will damn me to hell." He rose and shrugged into his greatcoat. "I'm not too drunk to get it done. Are you coming, Charles?"

Margaret was shaking. That such a thing could happen appalled her.

"There's more, isn't there, Charlie? You've trusted me thus far, please, you must tell me the rest of it."

"Needless to say, I accompanied Phillip to Roger Travers's lodging. Both he and his valet were gone. I remember that his housekeeper, a nervous little scarecrow of a woman, showed Phillip a note written by Roger saying that he'd left on an extended visit to the Continent. As you know, Margaret, there was no scandal. As for Elaine, obviously, she rid herself of the child. It is my opinion that she must have harmed herself irrevocably, for she has never borne Bufford an heir. Phillip left immediately for the Peninsula. It was Elaine who inserted a retraction of their engagement in the *Gazette*. The following June, she married Bufford. The rest, my dear Margaret, you know."

"That horrible bitch. Goodness, I should like to challenge her to a duel."

Charles took his sister's small hand into his. "What's really strange is that Elaine hates Phillip. She knows he has never said a word about what happened, but it seems that she can't remain civil around him. I know she tells tales about things he's supposedly done. Now, I know that you will guard this secret. Phillip would wring my neck if he knew I'd told you."

"It's because of Elaine that he's never married?"

Charles was silent for several moments, gazing toward Teresa, who had displayed herself charmingly at the pianoforte. "Perhaps such an experience would shape the lives of some men, embitter them, make them hate and distrust women, but not Phillip. He's much too perceptive a man to allow Elaine's despicable behavior to jade his view of the entire female sex. I at least hope to heaven that it's true."

"But why hasn't he married?"

"I'm not married either, Margaret, and Phillip and I are the same age, twenty-six. Goodness, woman, give us time. We've just begun to ripen, as Rohan Carrington says."

"What else does Rohan say?"

"Ladies ripen early. They must either wait for the boys to ripen or pluck the older ones."

"Yes, that makes sense," Margaret said, and punched her brother's arm. "But will either of you ever marry, Charlie?"

"I believe I shall be a bachelor, Margaret. As for Phillip, I can only say that he is a very careful man. Only time will tell."

"I'm so very happy. Marriage is amazing. I just never considered that there were so many things I was missing. There is so much more to life when there is another who cares about you and wants to make you happy. I just want you to know what it's like. Do reconsider, Charlie, do."

"I'll think about it. Promise me you won't tease Phillip. You won't make any veiled references to anything I've told you."

"I'm trustworthy, Charlie. I promise."

Charles's attention was drawn to the sound of Miss Elliott's raised voice. "No, I have no wish to play whist," he heard her say to the dowager Countess of Mowbray. "Viscount Derencourt is my partner and I shall wait for him before I play."

Charles said, "Actually, Lady Mowbray is very lucky. Teresa is a disaster at whist. I had the misfortune to partner her once. She trumped my ace of spades. I wanted to wring her neck. I remember that Phillip was watching. He just laughed."

"Another ice maiden, I think," Margaret said, patted her brother's arm, and took herself off to partner the countess in whist.

10

She whispered against the hollow of his throat, "Please, build up the fire, it is so very cold."

Phillip pulled Sabrina's body more tightly against him. He felt her low cracked breathing against his neck; he felt the pain each of those breaths cost her. Hair had worked its way loose from the braid he'd fashioned for her, tickling his nose, curling around his jaw. He smoothed her hair, moving his head slightly on the pillow. She followed, even closer now, trying to get inside him, he thought, to find his warmth and burrow into it. Her hands were clutching at his shirt, her legs pressing as hard as she could against his. He felt desire for her. It had happened before when he'd stripped off her clothes, when he'd bathed her. It didn't matter. He again ignored it. He was a man, not a randy boy. He treated it like any other discomfort that couldn't be changed, he controlled it, focusing on Lucius, remembering how he'd held his brother, just as he was holding Sabrina now, letting his heat flow into his body. But unlike Lucius, Sabrina was very small. He knew he must be nearly smothering her, covering nearly all of her, and what his body didn't touch, his large hands did. He rubbed his chin very lightly against the top of her head. He had no intention ever again of leaving London during future Christmas holidays. Then he realized if he hadn't been here, in this particular spot, she would have died. He didn't want her to die. He realized more than anything he wanted to see her smile, see life in those incredible violet eyes of hers, hear her speak, not necessarily telling him important things, just occasional thoughts she had. It didn't matter. He just wanted her well. He kissed her again. No, no more complaining. He'd never believed in an outside force that changed men's lives for no good reason, hurling them in an entirely new direction. No, he'd always reckoned that a man was master of his own destiny, until something he himself set into motion, be it wise or stupid, changed the course of his life. Well, maybe he'd been wrong. Fate had flung him into Sabrina's path and he'd accepted the responsibility of her. He wondered how much further his life would now change as a result.

He awoke the next morning sweating and stiff. He nearly groaned aloud at the cramp in his shoulder. Then he felt like giving a shout of sheer pleasure when he realized Sabrina was also sweating. Her fever had broken. "Sweat all you like, sweetheart," he said, kissing her temple. He gently eased himself away from her and out of the bed. She immediately rolled into a small ball, her sleep unbroken. He stood quietly, listening to her quiet, deep breathing.

"This time I've won," he said aloud to the silent room. He stood a moment longer, watching the rise and fall of her breasts, listening to her breathing. He felt happier at that moment than he had in many a long month. Actually he hadn't been this happy since Rohan and Susannah had visited Dinwitty Manor and they'd figured out the clues to the treasure. Yes, he was immensely pleased with himself.

The room was cold. He built up the fire, always one eye on her to see that she still breathed, to see that she still sweated.

While she slept, Viscount Derencourt heated water to wash his clothes in the kitchen. First though, he bathed himself, sighing at the feel of being clean again. He eyed the pile of dirty clothes, but knew there was no hope for it. Without a second thought, he dumped the clothes into the water and washed them as best he could. He grinned, picturing Dambler's face were he to see his master scrubbing his fine white lawn shirt in a rather dirty tub of water in front of a kitchen fire.

He hung his clothes to dry over the backs of chairs that sat around the big block wooden table in the kitchen. He dressed himself in his only remaining clean shirt and britches and went back upstairs to check on his patient.

She still slept, curled up on her side away from him. Her brow was cool, but her dressing gown was damp with sweat. Damnation, he hadn't thought to check. He stripped her, hoping she wouldn't awaken. Because he was a man, because he simply couldn't help himself, he looked at her, tried to touch her as little as possible because he wasn't completely lost to good sense, and gritted his teeth. But she was lovely, particularly since there was a flush on her cheeks.

The hair on her woman's mound was just a bit darker than the hair on her head. He wanted to touch her, touch her woman's flesh. He shouldn't be thinking such thoughts. Very well, he'd think about nonsexual parts of her. Her hands were very white, her fingers long. He imagined she played the pianoforte. There, that wasn't badly done of him. Not to mention her breasts that were actually very nice and—no, that wasn't well done of him either. He stared at her feet. Nice feet, arched, probably quite useful, as good feet went.

Then he laughed at himself, he couldn't help it. "Sorry, sweetheart," he said. "I'm trying to do the best I can. Please forgive me when I fall into these lapses.''

She moaned softly in her sleep, which was no answer, and made him think about sex.

Phillip straightened the man's white shirt over her, smoothing it down. It came halfway down her thighs, surely modest enough. He supposed he'd have to wash the two dressing gowns. No, he didn't think velvet could be washed. He looked down at her quiet face. He knew that face now; it was precious to him. It was odd, but it was true. He had no idea if she was a shrew, a devious liar, a saint. When they'd spoken, she'd seemed well enough, witty even, her voice soft and cultured, but he knew from long experience that she could just as easily be another virago like Elaine. *Elaine.* He hadn't thought about her in a very long time. In fact, the only time he ever thought about her was when he came face-to-face with her at a gathering in London. He rather hoped she was miserable, she deserved to be.

She still slept. Food, he thought, it was time to make something. He made bread. The two loaves of something that could pass for bread, maybe, he eased from the old iron oven. He swelled with pride. It didn't matter that they were flat and burned on the corners. It didn't matter that any sort of bread wasn't supposed to have corners. It was edible and he had made it. He was a fine human being. He could survive. No, it didn't matter a bit that the two loaves reminded him of the gray quarry stones his workers hauled from the sandstone pit near Dinwitty Manor to repair the ancient Elizabethan watchtower wall. They would use the same quarry stone when he finally managed to get started on his new crenellated tower that he'd spent most of the past summer designing. However, he still hadn't gotten it built, or even started it, probably because he'd been so shaken up by what had happened in Scotland with Rohan and Susannah Carrington. No, he wouldn't think about that bizarre experience. He allowed himself to remember all of it only late at night when he was alone, drinking brandy in his own library, staring into his own fire, seeing things no man should even imagine.

He broke off a burned corner. It didn't taste wonderful. On the other hand, he wasn't starving, and he knew from experience that starving indeed made a difference. His mouth was still spoiled from memories of food Cook made him at Dinwitty Manor. It didn't matter. It was nourishing and it could be eaten, if one was desperate enough, and surely both he and Sabrina were desperate enough.

She was still asleep. He wasn't worried, no, sleep was the best thing for her. He carefully wrapped his two loaves of bread in coarse cloths he found stacked on a shelf in the kitchen. Then he shrugged on his greatcoat and went to the stable to see to Tasha. The moment he stepped outside, the howling wind whipped against him, sending snow in his face. But the blizzard couldn't last for much longer, no storms in England ever did. He looked toward the path that wound its way to the front of the house, a white ribbon. No one would be coming for a while yet, not for at least several more days.

Tasha whinnied when he stepped into the stable. He rubbed her nose, laughed when she butted into his chest. "Yes, I know you're bloody bored, but there's no hope for it. Just a few more days, then you can gallop your way out of here." He looked down at the nearly empty bin of oats. "Actually, in another couple of days, you're going to be too fat to do anything except groan."

Phillip refilled the bin with hay, scooped up a bucketful of snow that would soon melt in the warmth of the stable into fresh water, sang Tasha a song, then walked slowly back to the house. The snow was nearly to the top of his boots. He shook his head and smiled. Damn, if Sabrina didn't wake up soon, whole-witted, he would soon be talking to the furniture. He just hoped if that happened, the furniture wouldn't talk back.

He'd nearly finished righting the havoc he'd created in the kitchen when he heard a soft thumping sound from overhead. He tore off the white apron in an instant and was up those stairs, two at a time, in three seconds flat, his heart pounding.

He pushed open the partially closed bedchamber door and stopped cold in his tracks. Sabrina stood next to the bed, clutching the bedpost for support. Her face was white, her breathing harsh, her braid flopped over her shoulder, oily and lank.

"What the devil are you doing out of bed?"

She stared at him, her face whiter than the man's shirt she was wearing.

"I can't get back into bed just yet."

"Why ever not?"

"I got up because I need to relieve myself. Do you know where the chamber pot is?"

"As a matter of fact I do. I wish you'd called me instead of trying to make the journey by yourself."

"But I don't even know who you are. Well I do, but I'd forgotten. You're a man. I don't want you to help me relieve myself. That wouldn't be right. It would be utterly mortifying."

"All right then. Let me help you over behind the screen. Call me when you're done so I can put you back to bed. I'll bet you have about as much strength as a flea."

"That's just about it," she said.

When she was back in bed again, the covers to her throat, he sat down beside her. Out of habit, he laid his palm on her forehead. "Not even a whisper of a fever. You're just fine now. Now, don't get me wrong. You're going to have to rest because you've been quite ill, but you will get well again."

"You know my name," she said, those strange colored eyes of hers on his face.

He wanted to tell her that he also knew about the small heart-shaped birthmark on her left buttock, but he didn't. He just smiled at her. "Yes, and I even know that your nickname is Bree. Do you remember that I'm Phillip? I don't have a nickname unless some enemy calls me a bastard."

"I remember now. Where are we?"

He smiled down at her and began to smooth loose tendrils of hair back behind her ear. "You have got your wits back again, thank the good Lord. Now, as to where we are, I haven't a clue. I'm a stranger to this particular part of Yorkshire. Do you remember what I told you? I found you lying in the forest in the snow. I'd passed this hunting box and brought you back here. We've been here two days now, wherever here is."

"What were you doing in the forest, my lord?"

"My lord? Now how would you know that I was a lord, a merchant, or otherwise?" Had he told her he was Viscount Derencourt? He couldn't remember.

Her eyes fell to his left hand, "You're wearing a signet ring. I'm not stupid or ignorant."

Phillip smiled as he looked down briefly at the heavy ruby signet ring passed from father to son in the Mercerault family for nearly three hundred years. Not all that long a stretch of time compared to some of the great families of England, but still three hundred years seemed a powerful long number of years

11

He wasn't mistaken. She did indeed hesitate before answering him. Was she still afraid of him?

Finally she said, "My name is Sabrina Eversleigh." She wasn't about to tell him that she was actually Lady Sabrina. That was none of his business. He could be anyone. He could even be a friend of Trevor's. Well, no, not that, but for the moment, she wasn't about to tell him anything.

The Eversleigh name was familiar to him. Where had he heard it before? Sabrina's eyes were tightly closed.

He touched his fingers to her cheeks. She was cool to the touch. "Sabrina, you can't go back to sleep just yet. I've made bread for you and some soup. You've got to eat something to gain your strength back. All right?"

"Yes," she said, not opening her eyes. "I'm hungry. Thank you."

He looked down at her awhile longer, then rose. He turned at the doorway and said over his shoulder, "Stay in bed. Just call out if you need me."

Five minutes later Phillip came back into the bed-chamber, a tray balanced on his arms. "Your servant, Sabrina. The best bread and soup available in these parts. Of course there are hay and oats in the stable, but I doubt Tasha would part with any of it." She cocked her head to one side. "My horse," he said. "Now, let me help you up on that pillow, my lady."

She opened her eyes at that. He wasn't mistaken. He saw panic. "I don't have a signet ring," she said, and he could hear the fear crawling in her voice. "I'm not a *my lady*. How could you ever think that I was?"

He wanted to tell her that he'd just been jesting with her, but no, not now. What was going on here? Who the devil was she?

"No, no signet ring," he said, looking down at her fingers. "It doesn't matter. Come now and eat." He clasped her under her arms and eased her to a sitting position, sat down beside her, and vigorously stirred the soup to cool it.

"Would you believe that this is a recipe from His Majesty's own kitchens? Brought to you here in Yorkshire by your humble servant? No, I didn't think you would believe that. Here, try some." He placed a spoonful of broth into her mouth.

To his relief and delight, she closed her eyes in bliss and looked ready to swoon. She downed nearly half the bowl before shaking her head and leaning back. "It's truly delicious, Phillip, but I can't swallow another drop. If you weren't a nobleman, why then, surely you could cook for the king, although since he's mad, perhaps he wouldn't appreciate your cooking."

"I'll let you try the bread before making a final decision on my cooking abilities." He brought out one of the loaves from the cloth. "I know it doesn't look aesthetically pleasing, but perhaps you'll be able to get it down."

He fed her a chunk of the still-warm bread.

She got it chewed and swallowed, he'd say that for her. Nor did she change expression. In fact, she smiled at him. "It's wonderful, my lord. You are indeed a find. Where did you learn how to cook?"

"If a viscount happens to spend some years on the Peninsula, I assure you that he learns quickly how to keep body and soul together, at least after a fashion. When you are better, I doubt you'll be so enthusiastic."

A shadow crossed her face. "My father was killed at the battle of Ciudad Rodrigo."

Eversleigh. Perhaps that was why her name was familiar to him. He tried to remember an officer of that name, but couldn't remember a face. "I'm sorry," he said. "Many good men were lost in that battle. I was wounded myself."

She opened her eyes wide.

"Yes, shot through the shoulder. I returned to England then. Sometimes when the weather suddenly changes, as it always is doing in England, my shoulder will ache. But I survived."

He saw it in her eyes. He saw how she wished her own father had suffered a simple wound and returned. But he hadn't. He was surprised when she said suddenly, "That loaf of bread looks like a turtle and I have just eaten off its head."

"That's a repellent thought."

Her smiled deepened, and dimples appeared on either side of her mouth. She looked really quite charming. He knew now that she was animated, full of life, full of energy. "I will be ready to eat its feet in just a few hours."

"Ah, so you are of a sadistic nature."

"What does that mean?"

He thought of that evil Frenchman, the Marquis de Sade. He just shook his head. "It just means that you think a bit differently. It's charming."

She withdrew. She didn't move an inch, but she withdrew from him. Why? He'd said nothing untoward. He said easily, "Actually, I was thinking that the loaf reminded me of the quarry stones mined near my home."

"Over the years Cook has occasionally taught me things. I do love your bread, my lord, but I would say that just a touch of yeast wouldn't come amiss."

"You're right. I'll see if I can find some." She smiled again, but weakly, and leaned her head back against the pillow. She stiffened when he laid the back of his hand against her cheek.

"No, no, don't pull away from me. I must check. There, you've no fever."

"How long have we been here?"

"By my best reckoning, about two and a half days. I don't think you could have been wandering around that forest for too long before I found you or you wouldn't have survived."

"It's Eppingham Forest."

"Ah, now I know you're an Eversleigh and this forbidding place is called Eppingham Forest. Would you like to tell me where you live?"

He saw a flash of something in her eyes. Was it temper? He hoped so. She said, "What is the day today?"

He had to think a moment about that. "It's Wednesday, I believe." It felt strange to be living outside of time.

Wednesday. She turned her head away from him, not wanting him to see her face. She had left Monmouth Abbey on Sunday. It seemed an eternity to her. She thought of the note she'd left her grandfather and blinked. She couldn't cry. It would do no good. It would only make Phillip more suspicious. But Grandfather knew by now that she hadn't reached Borhamwood. By now he might think her dead.

Something was seriously wrong. No more pushing her now. He rose. "We'll speak later of why you left your home, sweetheart. It's quite likely that your family is at this very moment searching for you. The blizzard will blow itself out very soon now." He closed his hand over hers. "No, don't worry just yet. All will be well, you'll see. Undoubtedly, my friends will be out soon searching for me as doubtless your family is searching for you."

She turned even whiter. He held his peace. She closed away thoughts of her grandfather, thoughts of Trevor. She felt weary, incredibly weary. She looked up at him for a long moment and said, "Your eyes. They're really quite beautiful. It seems so long ago, yet I remember now wanting to see you frown or smile so that I could read your eyes, so that I would know what kind of a man you were."

"My eyes wouldn't tell you whether or not I was a good man. Sleep now. When you next wake up, you'll be even stronger. I'll have some more bread and soup for you."

Phillip sat quietly beside her until he was certain that she slept. So I have beautiful eyes, have I, Sabrina? He realized that she hadn't said whether or not she'd found him a good man. He walked quietly to the window, staring out over the white landscape. The snow wasn't slapping so hard against the window. The winds had lessened. The blizzard was blowing itself out. Where had he heard the name Eversleigh before? Was it from Ciudad Rodrigo?

"Well, girl, don't stand there gawking. Get on with it. What news do you have for me?"

Elizabeth stood before the earl, her eyes downcast, her fingers nervously plucking at the folds of her gown. "I don't have any news. I'm sorry, Grandfather. All of our men have been searching since the blizzard lightened this morning, but as yet, there is no word."

"Trevor is searching with the men?"

"He began the search, Grandfather," she said, looking away from him, toward the open-draped windows.

"Just what does that mean?"

"Trevor is greatly affected by our severe weather. He was forced to return a short while ago. He is in his bedchamber, warming himself."

The earl slewed his head about and stared silently for several moments through the bowed library windows onto the frigid white landscape. "Sabrina isn't a fool," he said, more to himself than to Elizabeth.

She'd always been the fool, Elizabeth thought, bitterness twisting in her belly. "But I didn't run away," she said aloud, "disgracing myself and my family."

The earl's grizzled gray brows drew sharply together. He said in a voice colder than the frozen pond in the east gardens, "Sabrina isn't a slut, Elizabeth, even though it suits you to insist upon it. Your spite does you no credit. Sabrina throw herself at Trevor? Such a thing is nonsense, absurd." He saw Elizabeth pale, but doubted he could bully her into telling him the truth. He'd believed, foolishly perhaps, that Elizabeth's dislike of her sister would lessen once he'd secured her a husband, and not just any husband, but the future Earl of Monmouth. He had made certain that she would marry before Sabrina, even going so far as to deny a powerful nobleman Sabrina's hand until after Elizabeth was safely wedded. He shook his head, knowing that he wasn't being entirely honest with himself. No, the truth of the matter was that he'd wanted above all things to keep Sabrina with him for as long as possible. If only Clarendon had wanted Elizabeth instead of Sabrina. But of course, Richard Clarendon had been drawn to Sabrina the moment he'd seen her laughing with old Squire Frobisher as she'd helped him to his chair. He remembered seeing

the look on Richard's face and knowing, simply knowing, that Clarendon wanted her.

The earl looked back at Elizabeth's pale face.
"Well, don't you have anything to say to me?" It was
a meaningless question. He couldn't begin to imagine
what she would say, if she would say anything at all.

Elizabeth felt the old earl's eyes on her face. "Why
is it, sir, if Sabrina had decided to leave Monmouth
Abbey—for whatever reason—that she didn't come
and discuss her plans with you? You have said yourself that her letter told you nothing. Does that fact
not imply her guilt and shame in this entire matter?"

She'd shaken him. She wanted to smile. It took all
her resolve to keep still, to keep all her triumph, her
pleasure at her blow to herself. He appeared to shrink
visibly in his chair, and his fierce blue eyes dimmed.
Ah yes, she thought, your precious Sabrina, who's always shared her fancies and problems with you, her
doting grandfather—gone with only a meaningless letter to you.

The earl drew a deep breath. "I shall never believe
the story you and your husband have tried to foist on
me, Elizabeth. Leave me now."

Her shoulders squared, Elizabeth turned on her heel
and walked quickly from the library, without a backward glance. As she walked across the massive flagstone entrance hall, she wondered what would happen
to her and Trevor if Sabrina hadn't been consumed
by the blizzard.

"Lady Elizabeth."

She turned abruptly, her hand on the balustrade.
"Yes, Ribble?"

"Forgive me, my lady, but the Marquess of Arysdale has come to call on Lady Sabrina. He is in the
drawing room. I didn't think it my place to tell his
lordship that Lady Sabrina wasn't here."

Elizabeth felt a deep jolt of pleasure sweep through
her. She licked her dry lips. Good God, Richard
Clarendon was here. She saw that Ribble was watching her and nodded briskly. "I will see him, Ribble."
She felt both frightened and excited at the prospect
of seeing Richard, the man she'd fallen in love with
when she was sixteen and he, twenty-one. She had
given him every encouragement over the years, had
even blatantly talked of her dowry to him, one be-
fitting the heir to the Duke of Portsmouth. When his
young wife had died over two years ago, her hopes
had soared. She remembered the shock of betrayal
she'd felt when only six months ago she had overheard
him tell the earl that it was Sabrina he wanted. Her
humiliation was made all the worse by the fact that
neither of them seemed to care that she was within
earshot.

Every word spoken was still clear in her mind, the
pain of them still bowing her in on herself. The earl
had said in that deep smooth voice of his, his brows
beetled together, "My little Sabrina is like her grandmother. She won't tolerate a husband who isn't faithful to her. She knows of your reputation even though
she can't begin to understand it. No, I would never
give her over to a man who would betray her, and
that's how she would view a husband who bedded
other women. Make up your mind to mend your ways,
for I'll not push her into a marriage that would make
her unhappy."

"Sabrina is young, my lord," Richard Clarendon
had said in that honey-smooth deep voice of his.
"She's spirited, a beautiful unbroken filly. As my wife,
my lord, you can be assured that she will never desire
for anything more than I can give her. And that, sir,
includes other gentlemen."

"So, Richard, you believe your charm and prowess will satisfy my granddaughter, do you?"

"Lady Elizabeth."

She shook herself free of the memory and turned irritably to the butler. "Yes, Ribble?"

"If I may inquire, my lady. Is there any word of Lady Sabrina?"

Elizabeth knew that servants had their ways of discovering things. Surely this old fool of a butler knew that Sabrina had disgraced herself. Yet he had the temerity to approach her, the now undisputed mistress of Monmouth Abbey, to inquire after the little slut.

"I fear, Ribble," she said coldly, "that my sister could not have survived the blizzard. The men are still searching, as you know, but soon his lordship will realize the futility of it and call them back. Her body will undoubtedly be recovered when the snow melts."

She saw a spasm of grief pass over the old man's smooth forehead.

"It's naturally a tragedy," she continued more coldly still, moving away from him, "and a loss to all of us. But life continues. We continue. You may follow me to the drawing room now, Ribble. I don't wish to keep the marquess waiting."

12

The marquess was standing by the windows, staring out at the snow. Elizabeth felt her belly muscles clench at the sight of him. She'd never wanted another man, just Richard Clarendon. He was magnificent, all strength and muscle, beautifully made, his face hard and cold, drawing her easily to him, and any other woman he wanted. She swallowed and stretched out her hands. "Richard, why ever are you in Yorkshire, now of all times? Surely London is a more pleasant place than Yorkshire at this time of year."

The Marquess of Arysdale straightened from his negligent pose at the bowed windows. He strode across the room, his grace stunning her, making her hot and breathless. He raised her hand to his lips. "It's a pleasure to see you, Elizabeth. Marriage appears to agree with you. I only regret that I wasn't able to attend your wedding."

Elizabeth trembled when his mouth touched her wrist. She couldn't help it. She also knew that he was quite used to such a response. He was a rake, a womanizer, enjoying himself with any woman that pleased him at the moment. She had long known it, but she'd never cared. Now that she was married and knew well what men wanted of women's bodies, she wondered how different lovemaking would be if Richard were her husband. A stain of red deepened on her cheeks as she pictured Richard naked over her. He wouldn't be soft and smooth as Trevor was. He wouldn't be cruel.

"Where is Sabrina, Elizabeth?"

Sabrina, he wanted to see Sabrina. She felt the heat cool in her body. She lowered her eyes and said in a shaking voice, "Please sit down, Richard. The news I have for you isn't pleasant."

"Damn you, woman, what the devil do you mean by that?" She felt more than saw the instant difference in him. The lazy animal grace had disappeared. He was alert now, ready to kill, if need be.

"Please, Richard." She waved to a blue brocade settee.

"Enough of this. Where is Sabrina?" He took his seat unwillingly beside her. She felt the barely leashed energy in him. The violence so very close to the surface. It thrilled her and frightened her.

She wished she could tell him what Sabrina had done, tell him that the little princess was nothing more than a trollop, that she'd disgraced herself and run away from home, but she wasn't stupid. Richard was unpredictable. It was very possible that he'd go into a rage, perhaps even kill Trevor. If that happened, she wouldn't have anything. No, she had to be calm, to think clearly. "Sabrina has vanished," she said. She lowered her head and waited in silence.

"Sabrina's not a damned witch. I have never seen her with a broomstick. What the deuce do you mean, she's vanished?"

"It's just as I said, Richard. She fled the Abbey last Sunday, before the blizzard. She left Grandfather a vague letter telling him she intended to go to Aunt Barresford in London. But, of course, we have heard nothing. We fear that she could not have survived."

The marquess roared to his feet and stared down

hard at her, his dark eyes hard and dangerous. "Damnation, Elizabeth, what is this idiocy? Sabrina knew that I was coming to visit her. Indeed, there is no doubt in my mind that she knew the reason for my coming."

Elizabeth kept the smile hidden. He didn't realize that he'd just given her immense power, and all so very innocently. She raised her pale eyes to his harshly beautiful face. "Perhaps, Richard, you have just provided us with the reason for her running away."

If she'd been a man he would have struck her. She knew it and gloried in it. He had to rein himself in. "That's a damned lie, Elizabeth, and you know it." He turned on his heel and strode toward the door.

Elizabeth jumped to her feet, alarmed now. "Where are you going, Richard?"

He said over his shoulder, not even turning to face her, "I'm going to see the earl. It appears I won't get a sensible answer from you." He turned then, to look at her fully. "You know, Elizabeth, you haven't changed at all." Then he was gone and she was left standing there, alone, in the middle of the huge drawing room. She rubbed her arms. She was cold. What had he meant?

Sabrina was running down a long, narrow room. People were staring down at her, yet they made no move to help her. She whirled about in her flight at the sound of footsteps closing behind her. Trevor was coming toward her and she saw lust burning brightly in his eyes. She backed up. Something sharp dug into her back and she cried out as she turned. The people's eyes were watching her, uncaring and cold. He was nearly on her. He stretched out his hand. She screamed as a hand clutched her shoulder.

"Sabrina, wake up."

But her terror held her back in that room with all those faces staring at her. The hand shook her again, harder this time.

"Wake up, you're having a nightmare. Come, sweetheart, you can do it."

Her eyes flew open and she stared up at Phillip's face. She felt such tremendous relief that she didn't think. She reared up and threw her arms about his back. She said against his chest, "The faces. There were so many faces and none of them said anything, they just stared at me. They didn't care. None of them would help me."

Phillip held her tightly against him, smoothing tangled hair back from her forehead. "It's all right now, Sabrina. There's nothing to fear now. You're here and I'm here and I won't let that damned nightmare get close to you again. What faces did you see?"

She drew a deep, shuddering breath and leaned back in the circle of his arms to look up into his face. "Yes, the faces. They must have been the portraits in the gallery. So many of them, all long dead, they couldn't have helped me."

As calm as a vicar, he said, "So you fled to the portrait gallery to escape from Trevor?"

"Yes," she said, then gulped. She didn't say another word, just concentrated on getting a hold on herself.

"Who are you, Sabrina? And who is Trevor?"

She wanted to tell him everything, she truly wanted to, but she couldn't. So long as Trevor and Elizabeth stood together at Monmouth Abbey, she could never return, nor had she any wish to. She could well imagine Phillip's reaction were she to pour the whole sordid story into his ears. He would take her back and undoubtedly force a confrontation with Trevor. God only knew what her grandfather would do, what would happen to him. No, she couldn't allow it. She had made her plans and as soon as she gained her strength back, she would leave Yorkshire and go to her aunt Barresford. She never wanted to return to Monmouth Abbey for as long as Trevor and Elizabeth were there. And that would be always. She thought of her grandfather, of him not knowing if she was alive or dead, not understanding. She felt tears sting her eyes and shook her head. Crying wouldn't help and it would just make Phillip question her more. She forced herself to pull away from him.

"I told you that my name's Sabrina Eversleigh. Trevor is someone who is of no concern to you."

"That may be true, but I know he's a bastard and that he hurt you. I do wish you'd just tell me the truth, but if you still wish to keep it all inside you, well, then, I still have some time on my hands. A little mystery always amuses me. Yes, I have both patience and time on my side."

He eased her back onto her pillow. She immediately reared up again, balancing herself on her elbows. "My money. What did you do with my money?"

"I suppose you mean the three pounds and some odd shillings I found in your bodice?"

"You know very well that's what I mean. Where is it?"

He'd meant to embarrass her. Not well done of him, but he wasn't feeling all that much charity with her at the moment. He rose from her bed. "Obviously there isn't a gaming hall hereabouts where I could dissipate your fortune. Your three pounds are quite safe, I assure you. Since you are awake, I must insist that you eat some more of my soup. You don't wish to go home looking like an orphan from the workhouse."

She felt hated, useless tears burn her eyes. She said, as if by rote, "My home is in London. And it is to London that I must go when I'm well again."

"I suppose you'll tell me that you were out for a nice winter's stroll and got lost in your Eppingham Forest."

She shrugged. It infuriated him. "I was here visiting acquaintances of my family. I live with my aunt in London. Please, Phillip, you must help me return to her."

"Who are these acquaintances you were visiting?"

She just looked at him, that stubborn chin of hers up.

"What's your aunt's name?"

Her chin went higher, but he saw that it was costing her. She looked fixedly at a point just above his left shoulder. "She's married to a London merchant and lives in the city. Her name would mean nothing to you."

"Ah, I understand now. You are an orphan."

She was taken aback and he saw that she was. Actually she'd never thought of herself as an orphan, even though both of her parents were dead. She remembered her mother's face when she'd received word that her husband had been killed in the battle of Ciudad Rodrigo. Her mother had died shortly thereafter. Yes, she was an orphan. She nodded and was silent.

"God, but you're stubborn. How can you expect me to get you back to your aunt, if you will not tell me who she is?"

"I've told you that I was on my way to get the London stage that stops in Borhamwood. That was where I was going when my horse went lame. I didn't realize that it would snow; well, I did, but I thought it would hold off longer."

The viscount rose, giving her a look of acute dislike. "Enough, Sabrina. If you continue with these unbelievable tales when you're better, I just might be tempted to beat you."

"A man's threat," she said, eyeing him with contempt. "None of you think anything of threatening someone smaller than you are."

He just grinned at her. "Spare me your indignation. You know very well that you pulled those words out of a hat. Except, of course, for this Trevor fellow, who, when I discover his identity, I will kill with no hesitation at all. Now, calm yourself down, my lady. I'm going to fetch your soup now."

"Don't you dare call me that."

A very strong reaction, one that gave him the truth. And she knew she'd spilled it. Her face was frozen. He said easily, "Even though you're not wearing a signet ring, it doesn't matter. I'm not altogether ignorant of the ways of ladies of quality. And despite your spurts of impertinence, that's exactly what you are."

She shook her head back and forth on the pillow and fell into a spasm of coughing. Phillip leaned over and clasped her against him, gently rubbing her back until the hoarse coughs subsided.

"I feel so wretched."

He felt her warm breath against his shoulder. "I know." He pressed her gently back down and covered her. "No more inquisition for now."

Phillip paused at the doorway, then turned back to look at Sabrina. She was lying there stiff as a sapling, her hands fisted at her sides. What the devil would happen to her? And to him, if she didn't tell him the truth? Or if she did, for that matter?

13

"Your visit is poorly timed, Richard. It would have been better if you'd but come a week ago."

The marquess was pacing back and forth in front of his chair. The earl found the young man's energy exhausting.

The marquess whirled about then, saying, "I couldn't get anything from Elizabeth, my lord. Perhaps you will tell me where Sabrina has gone so that I may go fetch her."

"Stop staring down at me like Satan himself. Sit down, my boy. I have enough idiots in my own household without adding you to their numbers."

The marquess curbed his impatience and his rising temper and lowered his lean body into a leather chair facing the earl. He looked closely at the crippled old man and for the first time felt a stab of alarm. He'd aged years since the last time Richard had seen him. His eyes seemed sunken in his face and his shoulders drooped. Something had happened, something awful.

"Very well. I'm seated. Tell me what's happened to Sabrina."

"She's gone, Clarendon, with but a note to me. My men are scouring the area within a twelve-mile circle, but as yet there is no sign of her."

The marquess waved an elegant hand impatiently. "Yes, I know that. Elizabeth told me of the letter

Sabrina wrote to you. The letter said she'd gone to her aunt Barresford in London."

The earl's voice was flat, almost emotionless. "Yes, that damned letter. No one of Sabrina's description has left from the posting house in Borhamwood. She's well known in the village. No one has seen her."

"Then she's staying with friends near here."

"I'm sorry, Richard, but no."

The marquess bounded from his chair. He began his pacing again, back and forth in front of the earl. "Of course she's nearby. The people she's with are simply protecting her. From what? Well, I can easily imagine Elizabeth and Trevor dishing out more misery than she could endure. She left simply because she couldn't bear to stay."

"She would have come to me if that had been the case. She would have told me. She would have known that I'd deal with Trevor and Elizabeth. No, that isn't what happened."

"Damnation, this is bloody ridiculous!" The marquess leaned over the earl's chair and placed a hand on each arm. "Why, sir? Why did she leave?"

"What did Elizabeth tell you?"

"Elizabeth?" The marquess shrugged, then straightened, crossing his arms over his chest. "She told me some nonsense about Sabrina running away because I was coming to see her."

A travesty of a smile crossed the old earl's face, quickly to be gone. "It appears that Elizabeth is playing off all her stories. In a way, my boy, I wish I could believe that, but you must know the truth of it—to the best of my knowledge, Sabrina didn't remember that you were coming. You have been singularly unsuitorlike these past months, Clarendon, for a man who professes to care for my granddaughter."

Richard drew back, his dark eyes narrowing. "If you

will recall, my lord, I agreed to leave Sabrina be until she reached her eighteenth birthday. Her birthday was two weeks ago. It would appear that you have not much encouraged my suit with her."

To the marquess's appalled surprise, a long tear fell from the old earl's eye, falling crookedly down his wizened cheek. He pounded his fist against the arm of his chair. "Don't you understand what I've been telling you? She's gone. She's very likely dead by now. Her horse returned, lame, and we have had no sign of her. The blizzard blew hard for nearly three days— no one could have survived it. No one."

The marquess curbed a shaft of fear that tore through him, then he quashed it. "Sabrina is young, my lord, but she isn't a fool. She's safe, somewhere, she must be. Dammit, sir, do you have any idea why she left in the first place?"

The earl forced himself to think about his nephew and heir. Trevor Eversleigh would not make much of an earl, but at least he was an Eversleigh and the line would not die out. He knew that if he told Clarendon the story Elizabeth and Trevor had foisted upon him, the marquess would likely kill Trevor without a second thought.

"I'll not have you yelling at me, Richard. I'm sorry, but I simply don't know."

At the incredulous look on the marquess's face, the earl added, his voice hard and laced with pain, "The grief is more mine than yours, my boy. I have lost my granddaughter."

"I don't accept your answers, old man," the marquess said, his voice colder than the icicles hanging from the roof. "Sabrina isn't dead."

The earl turned his bony hand palm up in a helpless gesture.

The marquess strode quickly to the door. His hand

was on the doorknob when he turned back suddenly. "Where is your nephew, my lord? I would like to meet the fellow."

The earl couldn't manage to hide a frisson of distaste as he said, "Trevor is in his bedchamber, nursing a chill. He was leading the search when he was overcome by the cold."

The marquess didn't try to hide his contempt. "Are you certain this idiot is of your blood?"

It made the earl smile. "I'm certain. I suppose the explanation is logical enough. Trevor lived all of his life in Italy. Thus he isn't used to the harshness of our winters."

The marquess looked as if he would puke. "Will you send for the fellow, my lord, or shall I visit him in his sickroom?"

The earl saw there was no hope for it, and nodded slowly. "Fetch us both a glass of sherry, Richard. I will see if Trevor is well enough to see you." He raised his hand and tugged the gold tassel on the bell cord.

Trevor pulled open his dressing gown. The maid, Mary, lay on her back, her legs parted, her skirts and petticoats bunched up about her waist. She was still wearing her stout work boots and thick woolen stockings, fastened above her knees with black bands. "Please, sir, won't you come to me now?" She stretched out her arms to bring him down upon her.

Trevor slowly slid his fingers along the inside of her thighs. She moaned as he caressed her, and pushed her hips upward toward him.

"Such a slut you are, my girl," he said, his voice low and thick. He felt her tremble and quickly straddled her. She tried to clasp her arms about him to bring his mouth down to hers, but he struck them down. He pushed her skirts higher, until they were covering her face, then he dug his fingers into her flesh.

She cried out. He thrust deep and she moaned. Was it from pain or from pleasure? He didn't care. "Yes, Mary. You adore the pain, don't you? The pain and pleasure together move you, don't they?"

Trevor brought his hand up, riffled his way through all her petticoats and closed his fingers over her breast. He kneaded her as he spoke low to her, telling her how she pleased him, telling her she was a slut and he would give her what she craved. He smiled when he felt her stiffen beneath him. He leaned down and bit her, even as he went so deep it must hurt her. Even as she cried out in pain, she fell into spasms of pleasure. She loved it and hated herself for loving it. She knew with all the clarity of someone who rarely looked deeply into herself that he had recognized this weakness in her, this sinfulness, this perversion, yes, he'd recognized it and he'd come to her, calling to her as a master would to his dog. And she'd come.

Trevor tensed, then let his own release take him. He gave a shout of satisfaction. He called her a whore once again and she welcomed it for she knew it was only the truth. He lay beside her now, his face on the counterpane. Then suddenly he rolled off the bed and stood there, his dressing gown open, his fists clenched, cursing. Damn Sabrina. She was a slut like the rest of them, yet she'd denied him. Now she was dead and he would never have her. He gazed at Mary, who was lying on her side now, her clothes still frothed around her like icing on a cake. She was so easy, coming to him with scarce a backward glance or thought of her mistress, Elizabeth. She'd been easily had. She wasn't Sabrina. He wanted to hurt her because she was here and Sabrina wasn't, but he knew it wouldn't be wise. After the old man was dead, then he could do just as he pleased, but until that cherished day arrived, he would have to moderate his actions.

There was a knock on the bedchamber door. Mary's eyes flew open to look at him in consternation.

"Cover yourself, quickly." She jumped from the bed, frantically straightening her clothes. Trevor straightened the covers, and pulled his dressing gown closed. He motioned Mary behind the screen in the corner of the room.

"Who is it?" he called, his voice querulous, an invalid's voice.

"It's Jesperson, sir. His lordship wishes to speak with you in the library."

"A moment. I must dress. Are you certain this is important? What does his lordship want?"

"There is someone he wishes you to meet, sir."

"Very well. Send me my valet." He turned to Mary. "You might as well do something useful while you are here." He pointed to the chamber pot. "I will call you when I require you again."

She made a silent vow in that moment that she would never again come near him, but just as she thought it, she knew she probably would. She took the chamber pot and left the bedchamber. She knew he forgot about her the moment she was out of his sight. She also knew that when the old earl died, Monmouth Abbey would become a very different place. She thought of Lady Elizabeth. She hadn't much liking for that bitter young woman, but still, she knew Trevor would make her life a misery once he was the undisputed master here.

When she reached the door, she looked back at him over her shoulder. He had shucked off his dressing gown and stood naked by the fireplace. His body was not as beautifully formed as his face. He appeared soft and white, almost like a woman. But he wasn't anything like a woman. The pain he'd inflicted still remained, but it seemed only to heighten the memory of the ferocious pleasure he had given her as well. She passed his valet in the long corridor. The man knew she'd been with his master. He looked straight through her.

Trevor walked into the library some twenty-five minutes later.

It was about time, the earl thought, looking at him with as little dislike as possible showing on his face. "Ah, here you are, Trevor. This is the Marquess of Arysdale. Richard, my nephew, Trevor Eversleigh."

Trevor stretched out his beringed fingers and winced as the dark, powerfully built man mangled them in a strong handshake.

"My lord," he said in a soft, smooth voice, "it is an honor." He turned an emerald ring on his finger, away from the bitten skin that had been crushed by the marquess's large hand.

The marquess saw this gesture, took in Trevor's fobs, high shirt points, and lavender waistcoat, and instinctively drew back. God, he thought, disgusted, the man was a vain coxcomb. He hoped to heaven that he wasn't also a pederast. That would do no good at all for the Eversleigh line.

"Trevor, the marquess is here because of Sabrina. He is gravely concerned, just as we are, about her disappearance."

Trevor drew a lace handkerchief from his waistcoat pocket and daubed his forehead. "It is a tragedy, my lord. My poor Elizabeth is prostrate with grief. There has been no sign of Sabrina, nothing at all to help us find her."

The marquess wondered, dispassionately, if Elizabeth were still a virgin. He prayed not. He said pleasantly, although it was difficult faced with this vain idiot, "I'm to marry Sabrina, sir, and am looking for a logical explanation for her leaving."

A furious pulse beat in Trevor's neck. He wasn't, however, stupid. "I fear, my lord," he said, his voice high and lisping now, "that I can't be of assistance to you. Of course, my sister-in-law's precipitous departure has come as a great shock. No one has any idea why she left."

The marquess turned away, unable to hide his contempt, and quickly drew on his gloves. "I won't trouble you further," he said to the earl.

"What do you intend to do, Richard?"

"Scour the damned county for Sabrina, my lord. Good day, sir," he said to Trevor, and strode from the library.

Trevor looked after the marquess. "You didn't tell me that Sabrina was to wed that man."

"She hadn't as yet accepted him."

"I see," Trevor said. He began slowly and precisely to turn the gold fob on his waistcoat. "Such a brute of a fellow he is. Surely he is too large, too demanding, to wed a child like Sabrina."

"He is a man. Go back and nurse your chill, Trevor, I wish to think."

A slight sneer crossed Trevor's face. "I believe, my lord, that my chill has been sufficiently attended to. I shall speak with my poor Elizabeth now."

The earl's voice halted him at the door. "I would suggest, nephew, that your so-called reason for Sabrina's running away not reach the marquess's ears. He is not an understanding man and he would kill you with his bare hands. If you have ever exercised caution in your life, now is the time."

"I've been very cautious since I've come here to England." Trevor then shuddered delicately. "Did you say he would kill me with his bare hands? He does have very large hands, doesn't he?" He left the library, his footstep soft as his breath.

14

"No, tell me, Phillip, what happened next? Stop teasing me. Tell me."

"Very well. Without so much as flinching or batting an eyelid, Nell ordered him to drop his trousers. Then she marched him in front of her back to camp, naked as the day he was born, and said to the colonel, 'The lout tried to rape me, sir. I trust that you will see him hanged.' She handed the colonel the pistol and pulled the papers the fellow had stolen from her bodice. 'If attacking a defenseless woman isn't enough cause, sir,' she said, 'I trust these documents detailing the English strategy will settle the matter.' The colonel looked at Nell, then at the naked fellow, and dropped his monocle."

"Oh, goodness, that really didn't happen, did it?"

"Yes, indeed. After that, the colonel gave Nell the rank of corporal. To this day, she marches with the men and is always referred to as Corporal Nell."

Suddenly the laughter fell from her face, leaving it blank. Then fear took over. "He tried to rape her but she managed to save herself. She did it, Phillip. I wasn't strong enough. I tried, but I couldn't."

He started to take her in his arms, to comfort her, to tell her that he would never let anyone hurt her again. But he knew it wouldn't be the right thing to do. He didn't question why he was so certain, he just

accepted that he was. He looked down at his fingernails. "You know, Sabrina, you don't have to be at a
man's mercy."

She raised her face. "What do you mean?"

"I mean that I can teach you how to fight. If ever
again in the future a man tries to hurt you, you'll
know how to defend yourself. You'll know how to
hurt the man."

"That's truly possible? You're not just saying that
so that I won't weep about it anymore?"

"No. When you're well again, I'll give you your
first lesson."

Her eyes were shining. "I could kill him if he ever
tried to rape me again. I could kill him."

"Yes, but think if you didn't kill him, if, instead,
you caused him exquisite agony. Then every time he
looked at you he would be reminded of the god-awful
pain you inflicted on him. Wouldn't that be a far better punishment than just simple death?"

"Yes," she said slowly, her voice more intense than
any voice he'd ever heard. "Yes, I want to do it."
And then, she said to herself, "I'll go home."

"I heard from another military friend of mind that
Corporal Nell quit the army last year. She's now the
madam of a very fancy bordello in Brussels."

"How could she do that? She knew what men were
like, what they do to women if they're but given the
chance."

"I hear that she and all the other ladies are becoming quite rich off the men. Don't feel sorry for them,
Sabrina. Can you imagine any man ever trying to take
advantage of a girl who worked for Corporal Nell?"

"Well, maybe no, but I still don't like it. I don't
think I could ever do something like that."

"No," he said, and that was all he said.

He leaned forward then, smiling, and lightly patted

her cheek. Instead of drawing back, she said, "You've had so many adventures, seen so many exciting places. Of course you could have been killed, but still, you weren't, and now you have wonderful memories for the rest of your life."

"They're by no means all wonderful, Sabrina. Too many men, brave and loyal men like your father, died and are still dying. That's why all wars should be pronounced illegal by every government of the world. Can you begin to imagine a world that had no more fighting?"

She thought of all the books she'd read about the great military leaders in history. She said slowly, smiling just a bit now. "There wouldn't be as many books written if there weren't wars. Then there wouldn't be any more heroes."

"Oh yes, there would. A man doesn't have to kill people to be a hero." Again, he remembered Scotland; the experience, he knew, had changed the fundamental way he looked at life, and at death.

"Perhaps, but still, you're here and you're real and you've had some adventures that were wonderful. I've done nothing but ride, attend boring parties, learn how to manage serv—" Her voice disappeared. She looked down at her toes, wiggling beneath the covers.

He said smoothly, "How very enterprising of you, Sabrina, to be an accomplished horsewoman in London, particularly in Fleet Street."

She had no idea what Fleet Street was. "I would ride in Hyde Park. No one took anything amiss."

"There is excellent racing there, isn't that true? All along Rotten Row, so many people riding as fast as the wind."

"Oh yes, I loved it. That's how I became such a good horsewoman."

He just looked at her, shaking his head at himself,

not her. If a lady dared to race in Hyde Park, she'd be ostracized, but fast. He said then, smiling, "Do you know that Wellington is famed for his strategic retreats?"

"No, but what does that have to do with anything?"

"Nothing in particular." He rose. "It's just that right this moment, I'm retreating because I hope to return to win a final victory."

"It looks to me as if you can't get out of my room fast enough. Have I perhaps routed you?"

He stopped at the door. "I'm off to get you a bath-tub. I think you're strong enough to have a proper bath. What do you say?"

She picked up the thick braid that hung lifeless and dull over her shoulder.

"Yes, we'll wash your hair too. Now, what do you say?"

She looked ready to dance. "Oh yes, Phillip. I should like that very much. I'm beginning to feel crawly."

"Don't insult me. I've kept you quite clean."

She paled. She looked away, her lips clamped together.

He cursed under his breath, but she heard it and stared at him. "Forgive me, but if I hadn't taken care of you, then I fear you would be a lovely angel in heaven."

"I'm sorry, Phillip, truly I am. It's just that it's so very difficult. You've been very good to me and you don't even know me."

He'd know her better if she just told him who she really was. He nodded and left the bedchamber.

When he returned, two large buckets filled with hot water slung over his arms, Sabrina was sitting up in bed, staring at him as if he were bringing her Christmas presents. He laughed.

"No, don't leap out of bed just yet. I've got to fetch the tub."

Three minutes later, steam was rising out of the copper tub. "Do you have soap?"

"I wish you wouldn't doubt my scavenging skills." He lifted a bar of soap and smelled it. "It's jasmine. No, just stay there another moment. We need more water. You've lots of hair."

After he'd filled the tub, he turned and paused a moment, watching her unbraid her hair. "Who owns this hunting box?"

"Why, it's Ch—" She looked like she wanted to bite off her own tongue. She began pulling the tangles from her hair, not looking at him now. "Of course I don't know. I told you, Phillip. I live in London. I only visit Yorkshire rarely."

He slapped his palm to his forehead. "How could I be so stupid as to forget that?" He grinned, ignoring the killing look in those incredible eyes of hers, and pulled back the covers. "Come, Sabrina, your bath awaits."

She tucked the dressing gown tightly about her and swung her feet over the side of the bed. He held out his arms, but she ignored him. She stood up and almost immediately fell against him. "Oh, my, I can't believe I'm so weak. These were perfectly sturdy legs; just a week ago, they ran and jumped and danced in the drawing room. Why aren't they working as they should? It's very unsatisfactory." He just supported her, then kissed the top of her head.

She didn't notice. "If you would please just help me to the tub, Phillip, I'll be all right then. You can leave."

"Let's see just how much of your request I can give you." He picked her up in his arms and carried her to the bathtub. Very slowly, he eased her down at the side of the tub. She looked up at him then, her eyes clear, and said firmly, "Thank you. I'll be fine now. You can leave now, Phillip."

"I've no intention of nursing you back to health only to have you drown in a bathtub. Be quiet and hold still." He held her up with one arm and began to unknot the sash at her waist.

She was trying to keep her balance and slap his hands away at the same time. "Please, don't. I can see to myself, truly I can."

He knew she was embarrassed. Being unconscious while he cared for her was one thing, but being wide awake, knowing that he was looking at her, well, that was quite another. He sighed deeply. He set her firmly against the side of the tub. "Very well. I'll go see to our dinner. Call me if you get into trouble."

She grasped the edge of the tub, not even trying to move until he was gone. She heard his boots on the stairs. She got the sash unknotted. She shrugged out of the dressing gown. Then she looked at that tub. The rim seemed higher than it had just a moment before. She tried very hard. The third time she very nearly managed to pull herself over the edge of the tub. She gritted her teeth and concentrated all her energies on climbing over the side. It seemed higher than a mountain. Her fingers suddenly slipped on the edge of the tub, and she yelled as she fell backward onto the floor. She was stunned for a moment, then very cold, the wood hard and icy beneath her back. She had to get up, she had to. She could do it. She wasn't helpless. Very well, she'd lie here quietly, but just for another moment or two.

She heard him coming but she didn't have the strength to even pull the dressing gown over her. Then two strong arms clasped her about the waist and raised her to her feet.

She wished she were unconscious. She even closed her eyes tightly, praying for oblivion. Naturally oblivion wasn't anywhere near.

"It's all right, Sabrina," Phillip said, and lifted her into the tub.

The blessed hot water swirled up about her chin as he released her. She didn't look at him, she couldn't. She also knew she was being silly, but she couldn't help it. To the best of her memory, Phillip was the first person to ever see her without her clothes on, at least since she reached ten years and didn't need her nanny anymore.

He said easily as he rolled up his sleeves, "I'll wash your hair. Can you wash the rest of you?"

She had to think about that. "I'll try, but I still don't like this."

"Taking young virgins is not one of my pastimes of choice. Calm yourself and lie still. If you don't have the energy for the rest of you, I'll get to it." He didn't wait for her to perhaps curse him, which she didn't do well, not having had sufficient models in her young sheltered life. He washed her hair, complaining endlessly ". . . you've got too much hair. Look at all the bald men, you've got enough to cover every bald head in an entire village. There, about done. Now, I'm going to wash the rest of you, then we'll rinse everything at once."

She didn't try to fight him. No, she just tried to make herself into a small ball, but even that didn't work. When he soaped the sponge and washed her belly, she yelped. He ignored her, efficiently washing the rest of her even while she squirmed about. Actually, he was enjoying himself. Laughter was better than lust. She was an experience in contortions, not in seduction.

"Close your eyes, I'm going to wash your face."

Her mouth was opening to curse him, very probably, when the soapy sponge rubbed her face. She sputtered and cursed him then. He laughed at the indignant expression in her eyes, the only part of her face that wasn't white with suds.

"Hold your breath, under you go." He pushed her head into the bathwater. She came up, sputtering for breath.

"You did that on purpose. You're trying to make me mad so I won't be embarrassed. Well, it's working, but I want you to know that I realize that you're manipulating me and I don't know—"

He pushed her head under again.

"Now we've got your hair to deal with."

When all the soap was finally rinsed from her hair, he wound a towel about her head. He thought briefly about how he could save her further embarrassment, but saw that she was exhausted. If he hadn't come quickly to her, she would have slipped down into the water and drowned in the tub.

He picked her up and eased her down in front of the fire, holding her while he toweled her dry. She hung on to him, knowing she had no choice, not really caring now in any case. She just wanted to collapse onto the warm carpet and sleep until spring. But then something very strange happened. One moment she just wanted to sink into herself. The next moment she felt an awareness of him deep within her. She'd never felt anything like this in her entire eighteen years. She was naked and he wasn't, yet he wasn't doing anything hurtful to her. He was strong. His hands were large and steady as he moved the towel over her. He turned her slightly to dry the front of her. Oddly, she wasn't embarrassed. She stared up at him, into those beautiful eyes of his. It wasn't embarrassment that made her shudder when that towel traveled over her belly.

15

Phillip felt her shuddering, trying to pull away from him, and cursed to himself. He'd frightened her. "It's going to be all right. I'm nearly done drying you. Just hold still, Sabrina."

"I'm trying," she said, but then she looked up at him, met his eyes, and knew that if he didn't let her go very quickly she was going to embarrass him and kiss him until she was breathless. Oh, dear, surely she wasn't supposed to ever feel like that. It was because she was still ill, because she was still weak, because she trusted him, at least in this. In what?

Phillip felt a ton of lust bearing down on him. No, no, he wasn't about to take advantage of her. Here she was shuddering from fear, from cold, from—he didn't know what, and he wanted to mount her. He was a bastard. Without looking at her again, he bundled her up in the dressing gown and carried her to a chair next to the fire.

"It's time for your servant to carry out another duty. Behold your new maid." He turned away from her before she could reply and pulled the blankets and sheets from the bed.

Sabrina watched him work. He looked nice, despite his wrinkled shirt that was open a goodly way down his chest, a chest that had dark hair on it. She looked into the fireplace. This was better. He wasn't here to

make her think stupid things, to make her body feel
stupid things. Still, she wondered about those strange
feelings low in her belly when he'd touched her, stupid
feelings for all that, feelings a woman didn't need,
particularly this woman. She pictured Trevor in her
mind's eye. Now, the revulsion she'd felt for him, that
was what was appropriate to feel. That was safe because it was revolting. She'd just never imagined. Well,
now she knew. She shook her head, bemused, and
raised her head when he came back to brush her
wet hair.

Sabrina slept through the afternoon and awoke near
sunset. She lay quietly for some minutes, sniffing in
the faint lavender scent of the clean sheets and the
faint jasmine scent from her bath. She raised her hand
to her hair, carefully arranged about her head. It was
dry, all of it, and soft. No more oily braid. He'd com-
plained constantly for five minutes, the length of time
it took him to get all the tangles out of her wet hair. In
fact, she grinned, then laughed. That made her cough.

The cough brought her struggling up to her elbows
to catch her breath. She wasn't surprised at all to hear
Phillip's booted footsteps on the stairs.

"Drink this, Sabrina. It's got honey in it. I've kept
it warm for you, just in case. It will soothe your throat.
Slowly now. That's right."

It was strong hot tea. The honey in it made it slide
down her throat.

She lay back against the pillow and gave him a
brooding look. "I think that girl must have been
mad."

Phillip placed the teacup on the night table and sat
on the bed beside her. In an unconscious gesture, he
smoothed a lock of auburn hair from her forehead.

"What girl? Any girl I know?"

"The girl you were once engaged to, the girl you

mentioned when you were trying to pry me open yesterday, and her name slipped out of your mouth, and then I had you."

"Actually, she wasn't mad, but perhaps she is now. Who knows? One can only pray."

"What was she?"

"She wasn't honorable. Do you understand that?"

"All I know is that if I made a promise to someone, I would stick to it unless someone was torturing me too much for me to bear."

"Yes, that's exactly how I feel about honor."

"You don't still pine for her, do you, Phillip?"

"Pine? What a foolish word. No, I rarely even think about her now. It's just that she's in London so I still see her and remember. Perhaps the memories are good to have. They keep perspective. They discourage acting before thinking things through thoroughly. Just why do you think her mad?"

"It's obvious. With you about, Phillip, she would have been able to make so many economies. She would hardly have required more than one servant."

"I am rather a good servant, aren't I? Throughout my life I've done bits and pieces of things, but never so much in so little an amount of time. Actually, truth be told, I'm relieved that I was able to make food that we could digest. I have only one major failure."

"Oh no, surely not. Even the flat bread that you didn't mean to be flat was still all right. Come, what is this major failure? Come, tell me. I'm sure I can talk you out of it."

"You don't trust me. I've done everything I can think of, used every argument that came to mind, but it does no good. You don't trust me. I've told you stories that have spanned my twenty-six years, but the recounting left you unmoved. You still don't trust me. You haven't told me anything that would enable me to help you. Now, you are a good liar. With a few more years, you should be nearly as good as I am. But lies aren't what are needed here."

She'd made one stupid remark about that Elaine person and just look where it had gotten her. A sermon about trust. Well, curse it and curse him. She smoothed the green coverlet over her lap and stared at the bedposts.

She'd closed down again. Well, damn. He felt a surge of anger and savored it. "You must know," he said now, his voice turning hard, "that the servants who care for this house will be able to return any day now. The weather has warmed and the snow is melting. If I'm to help you return safely to your family— wherever they may live—you will have to make a clean breast of it. Was Diablo your horse, Sabrina? Did you grandfather shoot him?"

Her head snapped around so fast, he nearly laughed. But he didn't, just gave her that hard-eyed stare. "How do you know about Diablo? I was only ten years old. My sister took him without my knowing of it and crammed him over a fence." The memory swamped her. She felt her throat closing. It had been eight years ago.

"What happened?"

"He broke his leg on the landing. He had to be put down. How did you know about Diablo?"

"You were delirious in your fever. You cried out about him."

He read the fear on her face and he wanted to shake her. "Did I speak of anything else?"

"Trevor."

"Yes, Trevor," she repeated and turned away from him.

Phillip wanted to shake her but he couldn't. When she was well enough to shake but good, it would be too late. He rose and looked down at her. "If you don't tell me the truth, if you don't arm me with the facts I need to protect you, then you reduce me to nothing. Listen to me. No matter what happened, I can help you, if you'll but tell me the truth."

"What happened to me has nothing to do with you, Phillip. I'm nearly well. By tomorrow morning I should be completely fit. It you would take me to Borhamwood, to the posting house, you need never see me again."

"I can't do that, Sabrina, and you must know that I can't. You're a young lady. You're eighteen years old. I can't assist you to escape from your family and put you on a common stage to London. You cannot begin to imagine the sort of man you could meet on that stage. No, I would never do that. Forget it, and tell me the truth."

He would bend, but he wouldn't break. He'd drawn the line across the path. She didn't look at him, just shook her head. After he left her to go to the kitchen to make their dinner, she thought long and hard about her plan. It hadn't been fair to involve him even in that. No, she couldn't very well expect an honorable man to put her on a stage bound for London.

Phillip appeared thoughtful during the evening. He didn't say much, but she knew he was aware of her, aware of how many bites of his stew she'd eaten, how many mouthfuls of bread she'd chewed. She knew he was worried about her. For a moment she felt uncertain. Then she thought about the hideous chaos that would await her at Monmouth Abbey were she to allow him to take her back there. It was all she could do not to shudder.

"You told me you were visiting friends here in Yorkshire," she said, hating the interminable silence, for it wasn't a comfortable silence, a companionable silence.

"Yes, that's what I told you."

"Who is this friend?"

He was looking down at his filthy Hessians. He said without looking up, "Undoubtedly he's a friend of yours—Sir Charles Askbridge."

Charlie. She had to keep calm, act all sorts of ignorant and indifferent. She smiled. "Mayhap that name is a bit familiar to me."

He didn't pretend boredom now. "As you well know, Sabrina, Charles's Yorkshire home is called Moreland. Even though the directions he provided me led me into Eppingham Forest and thus to find you, I would wager that Moreland isn't too far distant from here."

Moreland was no more than seven miles distant. Charlie loved to hunt in the forest since he'd been a boy. And he knew Phillip. How very close Phillip had been to his destination. She shrugged and pretended to study her fingernails.

"I imagine that you quite like Charles. Everyone does. What do you think of his younger sister, Margaret? She's not much older than you are."

Margaret was twenty, just between Sabrina and Elizabeth. She shook her head and stared at him with a vacant expression. He was angry, but he held it in very well. She was impressed. "You were riding by yourself. Isn't that unusual for a viscount?"

"I left my incredible retinue of servants in Leeds. I struck out on my own, feeling brave and ready for adventure. Instead look what I got myself into. Would you like the rest of my traveling details? Of course you would. I imagine you are aware of the rounds of Christmas parties held outside of London at this time of year. Even though you look blank as a schoolboy's slate, I know that you do. Don't get me wrong. You're an excellent actress. It's just that I've come to know you very well. In any case, Charles invited me to Moreland and gave me directions that led me to this isolated place. I had sent my valet ahead. I had this romantic notion about becoming one with nature. What rot. So you see, Sabrina, it is probable that both Charles and your family are now out looking for us." He added, his voice so serious she again nearly spilled her innards, "It can't be longer than a day now, two at the most before they find us."

She knew that he was right, but held her tongue. At last she had an idea. She yawned and stretched. "Your delicious dinner has lulled my stomach and now my head. I think I'd like to sleep now." She yawned again and snuggled down under the covers.

"Thank the good Lord I was never burdened with a sister." He looked heavenward, then back down at her. His eyes were bleak. "There's a world waiting outside this room, Sabrina. I would that you think about that." He leaned over and patted her on the cheek. "Good night. Sleep well."

She wanted to thank him, but she couldn't, not now. "Good night, Phillip." She closed her eyes and turned her head away.

Phillip blew out the candle and walked from her room to a bedchamber down the hall. Since she no longer needed his constant attention during the night, he had begun the previous night to sleep in another room, in a lumpy bed that was marginally more comfortable than the cramped chair in Sabrina's room.

Sabrina lay quietly in the darkened room reviewing her plan. With the snow melting, her grandfather—no matter what he thought of her now—would have an army of men out searching for her. Even if her grandfather believed her dead, he would search. She couldn't begin to envision the bloody battleground at Monmouth Abbey if she were found and returned to him. He was too old and frail for that. She knew that there would be no way to keep the truth from him— Elizabeth's betrayal of her and Trevor's attempted rape—it would all come out. She wouldn't bring such bitter disillusion to her grandfather. She wouldn't destroy all his plans and hopes. She wondered if Trevor truly would try to kill him if she returned. She didn't know. She couldn't afford to find out.

She could never go home. No, she wouldn't cry. It wouldn't help, it would solve naught. She thought of her plan. It was simple and straightforward. So who cared if she was still a bit weak? Not all that weak, surely, not too weak to walk just a bit and ride just a bit. No, she could do that.

She slipped quietly from her bed, lit the candle on the night table, and padded on bare feet to the small desk near the fireplace. She found a pen and several scraps of paper and quickly wrote the lines she'd silently rehearsed for the past two hours. She felt sadness when she closed her note, ". . . please forgive me, Phillip, but I cannot stay here any longer. I thank you for saving my life. Now I must take care of myself." Her fingers paused, and then she quickly added, "I'll never forget you. Sabrina." She decided she'd write to her grandfather once she reached London.

She found her clothes and cloak, rumpled but dry, hanging in the armoire. She tugged off the man's dressing gown and pulled on her dress. She felt strong and certain of herself. This time she would succeed. She picked up the three pounds that Phillip had laid in a neat stack atop the table, and slipped them into the pocket of her cloak. She pulled the three blankets from the bed to wrap around herself once she was on her way.

Her boots didn't make any sound as she walked as quietly as she could down the front stairs, both hands on the railing. She still felt strong, still felt sure of herself and what she was going to do. By the time she reached the outside kitchen door, she was ready to run all the way to Borhamwood. It felt incredible to be well again, to be strong again, and competent.

The door latch clicked back with a loud grating sound that made her turn quickly and look back into the house. No, it hadn't been loud enough to awaken Phillip. She quickly stepped outside and pulled the door closed behind her.

She paused a moment in the cold moonless night and leaned for just a moment against an elm tree. The bark was rough beneath her cheek. The wood was sweet and cold. She thought of Phillip, of his gentleness and kindness to her. She'd known him for only a short time and yet he'd become a part of her life. Not just a part, he'd been in the center, taking such excellent care of her, always being there when she'd needed him. She shook her head. She couldn't think about him now. She pushed away from the elm tree and found to her astonishment that her vaunted strength wasn't quite as strong as she'd believed. It was absurd. Her strength would come back. She had to stop questioning herself. She had to stop whining. She forced her feet to move to the stable.

16

She unlatched the stable door and stepped into the dim interior. A beautiful mare craned her neck about and neighed softly.

"Hush, Tasha." She moved quickly to the bay mare's head, rubbing her ears, whispering nonsense in her ears. "That's right, just be quiet and get to know me. Aren't you ever a beauty. I can see why Phillip adores you, and he surely does."

When Tasha seemed calm and accepting of her, Sabrina started to reach for a saddle. Her arm was shaking. She cursed, not really toe-curling curses because she didn't know any, but they made her feel better. She simply didn't have the strength to haul a saddle onto Tasha's back. She slipped the bridle off a hook near Tasha's stall and tugged the mare's head down to slip it on.

An empty box was lying in the corner of the stable. It was heavier than it looked. Damnable sickness. She felt sweat on her forehead and under her arms by the time she'd hauled the wretched wooden box close enough to Tasha so she could climb up on it and pull herself onto Tasha's back.

Odd how Tasha's back looked higher than it had just a moment before. The mare's ears were twitching. "No, it's all right, Tasha. Please hold still. I don't weigh as much as Phillip. You'll see, it will be fun to carry me about. You'll barely know I'm even here."

It took her three attempts to get herself facedown over Tasha's broad back. She lay there, her feet dangling, rather like a heavy sack of grain, until her breathing slowed and calmed. Finally, she had enough strength to haul herself upright.

She leaned forward and grasped the reins in her hands. She'd made it. She click-clicked. Tasha didn't move. She dug her heels lightly into the mare's sides and flicked the reins again.

Tasha still didn't move.

What was she doing wrong? She'd ridden since she'd managed to stand up and grab a horse's stirrup. What was wrong here? She leaned over Tasha's neck and said directly into her ear, "Please, Tasha, we need to leave now. It's not far we're going, just to Borhamwood, but I do want us to get there. Please."

"I'm sorry, Sabrina. Tasha only lets me ride her. If you'd only bothered to ask me, I would have told you that and saved you countless wasted minutes."

She whipped about at the sound of Phillip's amused voice. He was leaning against the stable door, his arms folded across his chest. He didn't look particularly angry, but she knew he was. She wasn't certain how she knew, but she did. Well, if she'd been Phillip, she supposed she'd be pretty mad herself.

"I was so quiet. Couldn't you be a nightmare that I just conjured up to frighten myself? You really shouldn't be here, Phillip. You're not even wearing a coat. You could become ill. Why don't you go back to the house and I'll just be on my way?"

He didn't move, just smiled at her, the coldest smile she'd ever seen. "You of all people should realize what a light sleeper I am. You coughed and I was there beside you. You didn't breathe evenly and I was there beside you. It saved my life several occasions on the Peninsula. Now, perhaps, it has saved yours also."

"No, it hasn't. Listen to me, Phillip. I can't remain here. You said yourself that they were looking for us. I can't let them find me."

"Let who find you, Sabrina?"

She just waved her hand at him. "If Tasha won't let me ride her, then I'll just walk to Borhamwood. I'm a great walker. I've walked all my life. I can do it. You can't help me, Phillip, believe me on this. No one can do anything. I have to leave. It's the only chance I have. I won't tell you who I am. It would gain neither of us anything. I'm protecting you in this and protecting my family. Now, I do thank you for taking care of me but I have to leave. I must."

She slid off Tasha's back. When her feet touched the ground, she felt the damnable weakness hit her like a stone on the head. She held to Tasha's mane until she was stronger. She prayed that Phillip merely believed her to be saying good-bye to his horse. Finally she felt steady. She looked over at Phillip. He hadn't moved, was just looking at her, saying nothing. Perhaps he was seeing reason now. On the other hand, he was a man, and in her eighteen years' experience, it wasn't often that a male saw the same reason that a female saw. But Phillip was an exceptional man. Just perhaps he was ready to let her go.

Although the thought of trudging through Eppingham Forest in the middle of the night nearly made her hair stand on end, Sabrina was determined. She could do it. She stiffened her back, threw her head back, and marched up to him. "You see, I am just fine. Good-bye, Phillip."

The problem was that he didn't move from in front of the stable door. Then, suddenly, he straightened. She was staring up at a man who was much taller than she'd imagined. He was big. Strange how he hadn't seemed this big before. He was larger than Trevor, tougher, stronger. No, she wouldn't be frightened. This was Phillip. He would never hurt her, never.

"Please move," she said to the middle button of his wrinkled white shirt.

He straightened, taller now than just the moment before. "Come back to bed, Sabrina. I don't want you to make yourself ill again."

"No," she said, never looking away from that middle button. "Please move, Phillip." Then she did look up at him. "Listen to me, you don't know me. I'm nothing to you, not your sister, not your cousin, nothing. Believe me that you don't want to be involved with me. You wouldn't be at all happy were I to tell you all these things you wanted to know. Just let me go. You've done your good deed. But now it's over. Let me go. I'll never tell a soul I met you. You'll never have to see me again."

"That's the most pitiful logic I've ever heard. On the other hand, I haven't spent all this much time with a woman, so that must be it. Well, I have, but the time passed with other activities, not all this pleading and begging and ridiculous attempts at changing my mind, which I won't change. You think I'd let you go in the middle of the night into the forest? Do you think me a complete blockhead? Come, Sabrina, it's back to bed for you."

Still, he made no move to touch her. Her face was pale, her beautiful hair tangled now around her face. "Do you care so little for your life as to attempt a midnight walk with no protection? There are probably wolves out there. In fact, I know there are. I've heard them howling."

"There's a well-marked path. I will keep to it. I'll be warm enough with the three blankets." Her face was paler now than just a moment before. He had to bring this to an end.

"You're not going anywhere, Sabrina." He held out his hand. "Come here to me."

She was shaking her head. He knew she was very probably as cold as he was. And he was ready to let his teeth chatter. He hadn't even taken the time to throw on his coat. He wished he had it now so he could wrap her up in it.

"I've made up my mind, Phillip."

"Would you please remove Tasha's bridle?"

She wanted to drop in a heap right where she was and he wanted her to remove the damned mare's bridle? Without a word, she turned away and walked to Tasha. She unfastened the bridle and slipped it from Tasha's head. She tugged on the mare's mane and walked her back into the stall.

"You know," he said as he slowly approached her, "I should have hidden your clothes. It never occurred to me that you would even consider pulling such a stupid stunt as this."

She ignored him and pulled her cloak more closely about her face. "I'm leaving. Move aside, I won't tell you again." She felt his fingers tighten about her arms. Slowly, he pulled her closer until she was leaning against him. Even in the cold stable, he was warm. If she hadn't wanted to kill him she would have burrowed into that warmth, into him.

"You have no say whatsoever about my actions, and I won't be bullied. Let me go."

"I'm cold and I'm getting irritated, Sabrina. Either of these conditions should alarm you."

She lowered her head and bit into the back of his right hand.

He stiffened and released her. She got no farther than the stable door, tugging on the handle. His hand was above her head, pressing palm flat against the door. "You listen to me now, you little witch. Oh, what the devil, no more of this." He grabbed her about the waist, wrapped the three blankets about her, and tossed her over his shoulder. When she reared up, he slapped her bottom. "Hold still, damn you. I'm cold. I'm vastly annoyed with you. Just lie still." He slapped her bottom again.

She hit his back, but she knew she wasn't hurting him, just annoying him all the more. Then her strength was gone. She could do nothing more than just lie like a sack of flour, her face bumping up and down on his back. She felt tears sting her eyes.

Once in her bedchamber, Phillip eased her down to her feet and held her tightly against him for a moment.

"Please, Phillip," she whispered against his white shirt. "You don't understand. You must let me go. I'll hurt you if I remain with you."

"How the hell would you hurt me?"

She was silent as a stone.

"Hah, no answer for that."

She felt the warmth of his breath touching her forehead. "I won't allow you to kill yourself. You know your chances of making it safely to Borhamwood are slim at best. I can't take you to London, even if I just happened to know where you belong, even if you trusted me enough to tell me your aunt's name, which you've refused to do. No, such an act would be outrageous folly, and little better than kidnapping." He shook her slightly so that she looked up at him. "I won't be hurt. I'll stand by you, that is a promise." He had absolutely no idea what his promise might entail, but he didn't care. He meant his words. "Just tell me the truth. Who are you?"

Her lips were a thin closed line. He became suddenly brisk, aware that she was trembling. "Can you undress yourself?"

"Yes." She sounded utterly defeated. He hated it but had no idea what to do about it. He waited for her to straighten, to move away from him, but she didn't. She just leaned against him, her arms hanging limply at her sides.

"This is becoming a very long night. I'll help you. Don't move." She wanted to move, she really did, but she knew she just couldn't. If she tried, she'd fall on her face. That would be too much humiliation to bear. She felt him working at the buttons on the front of her gown.

Phillip pulled the gown over her head, scooped her up in his arms, and sat her down on the edge of the bed. He reached quickly for the dressing gown that she'd left on the floor in her hurry to escape. As he tossed her gown aside, he saw blood on it. He felt an instant panic.

"My God, what have you done to yourself?" He whipped about to look at her. She was staring down at herself, frozen.

"Lie down and let me look at you. However did you hurt your—"

"No!" Before his astonished eyes, she grabbed a blanket and clutched it to herself.

Appalled, he could only stare at her, holding the gown in his hands, looking from it to her. "But you're bleeding, you've hurt yourself, you've—" He understood then. He shut his mouth. She was still cowering away from him. Irritation washed over him. "For God's sake, don't be a ninny. I thank heaven that this is what's wrong. It's perfectly natural. It's next to nothing."

She quite simply wanted to die. She looked at him,

saw the relief on his man's face, and screamed, "Get out."

He stood there feeling helpless now, feeling out of his depth. She was embarrassed. He supposed he understood it. She was staring at him, the pulse pounding in her neck. Her bare neck. She must be freezing. He had to do something. "Put the dressing gown on. I'll go get you some cloths."

She looked like she wanted to both murder him and sink below the floor. Then she seemed to just give up, to collapse in on herself. He wanted to tell her not to be ridiculous, but she was only eighteen years old. Well, damn.

He returned to the bedchamber some minutes later and silently handed her strips of white cotton, carefully ripped strips he'd torn off a man's shirt. "Do you want some hot water so you can wash?"

She nodded mutely, her head still down. "Sabrina," he said, but then as she just shook her head, he shut his mouth.

"Thank you. Please go now."

Her voice sounded as flattened as she looked. After he'd placed a pitcher of warm water on the washstand and a bar of the jasmine soap beside it, he said, "Promise you'll call me if you have need of something more."

Again she nodded, and not knowing what else he could do to help her, he turned and left her room.

Sabrina didn't fall asleep for a long while. She'd just lain there all night feeling impotent and helpless. If Phillip had told her he felt the same way, she wouldn't have believed him. No, he had all the power. He'd certainly done what he'd pleased with her, even forcing her back here. What was worse was that she knew she wouldn't have managed to get through Eppingham Forest to Borhamwood. She probably would have died or been attacked by wolves. All she had left was a dreadful sense of the inevitable. She wrapped her arms about her stomach to ease her cramps and finally fell into an exhausted sleep.

Phillip took in her pale lifeless face the next morning, the dark smudges under her eyes. He set her breakfast tray on the table beside her and helped her to sit up. "I've brought you some good strong tea, toast and jam. It should make you feel more the thing."

She didn't look at him, just nodded.

"I have many chores to perform and will see you later."

He left her to herself for two hours. After he'd bathed and shaved, he returned to her bedchamber and lightly tapped on the door.

She looked bad, tired and ready to fold her tent and slink away. "You can't sleep?" Stupid question, but he had to say something. He walked over to her and sat on the side of the bed. He touched his hand to her cheek and said without thinking it through, "Perhaps a hot bath would make you feel better."

As soon as the words were out of his mouth he realized he was an idiot. "I'm sorry. I'm a man. I don't have a wife. This sort of thing simply hasn't come my way before. Listen, let me give you some laudanum. There's a bit left. You need to rest. All right?"

"Yes, all right," she said, and he wanted to take her in his arms at that moment and tell her—what?

Phillip shook the few remaining drops of laudanum into a glass of water and handed it to her. She downed the entire glass of water without taking a breath. She leaned back against her pillow, closed her eyes, and waited for oblivion.

Phillip moved quietly about the bedchamber,

straightening the disorder from the night before. He bent down and added several more logs to the sputtering fire, then turned slightly and looked toward the bed from the corner of his eye. To his dismay, Sabrina lay wide-eyed, staring blankly ahead of her.

He pulled the large chair closer to the fireplace and walked to her bed. "You're exhausted. You've got to rest. Trust me now." She didn't fight him when he lifted her into his arms, blankets and all, and carried her to the chair. He eased himself down, and drew her close against his chest. She gazed up at him for one long moment and closed her eyes. A small sigh escaped her and she turned her face inward against his shoulder.

Phillip laced his fingers under her back to hold her steady, leaning his head back against the chair top. It was some time before he felt her ease, before he heard her breathing even into sleep.

One moment Phillip was sleeping, the next he was alert, his eyes fastened to the half-open door. He heard soft boot steps on the stairs. He was on the point of dumping Sabrina onto the floor and flinging himself toward the door when a very familiar face appeared.

It was Charles Askbridge.

17

Charles opened his mouth and closed it. He quite simply couldn't believe his eyes. There was Phillip—long-lost Phillip—sitting in a large leather chair holding a sleeping female in his arms. At least he hoped she was sleeping and not unconscious or dead.

"Oh, my God," he managed to say at long last. He didn't move. He couldn't. All he could do was stare.

"Be quiet, Charles, I don't want you to awaken her. She had a hard night. Actually, I did as well."

Charles nodded. It was just as well since he couldn't think of anything to say in any case. He walked quietly toward Phillip and looked down into the half-hidden face of Sabrina Eversleigh. "My God," he said again, his voice barely above a whisper.

Sabrina stirred at the sound, but was too deep in sleep to awaken.

Phillip shook his head at Charles, then carefully rose. He carried Sabrina back to her bed and gently eased her down. He looked to the still openmouthed Charles and waved him from the room.

Phillip gazed down once more at her, lightly touched his palm to her forehead, and nodded to himself. She would be asleep for a good long time yet. He followed Charles from the room.

He was silent until they had reached the bottom of the stairs. "Well, Charlie," he said, shaking his friend's hand, "this is a surprise, I'll admit it. Do you often break into houses and creep up stairs?"

"You'd think I was a thief, wouldn't you? Actually, I'd think so myself. But you see, Phillip, this hunting box just happens to belong to me."

Phillip laughed, he couldn't help it. He felt unutterable relief, not to mention amusement at how the fates had worked this all out. "The devil you say. Well, Charlie, since the absentee landlord has decided to inspect his property, I don't think it would be all that wise to boot him out. Am I ever lucky. What if you'd shown up with half a dozen guests for hunting? No, I won't think about that. It's too painful.

"Now, come into your cozy front parlor and I shall serve you up a glass of your own sherry."

"Phillip, everyone has been frantic. What are you doing here? And not just you but Sabrina Eversleigh? Good God, man, the entire country is out scouring the forest for the both of you."

"So you know Sabrina, do you, Charles? Why of course you do. It only makes sense, particularly since she must live not far away from here, as do you as well." He handed Charles a full glass of sherry.

"I haven't tried it, but I know you have a fine cellar. Why would you stint here?"

"I wouldn't."

"Good. To your health, Charles." Phillip clinked his glass to his old friend's.

Charles downed the sherry in one long gulp, coughed, teared, then managed to get hold of himself.

"I do wish you would dispose of that gun, Charles. A lot of things have happened to me in the past week. I don't want to crown the week with a bullet in my gut." He poured Charles another glass of sherry.

Charles gulped it down, shook himself, and looked blankly down at the gun hanging out at an odd angle from his waistcoat pocket. He drew it out and laid it on top of a table. "You know, I did wonder if my intruder could be you, but to be honest, I didn't really believe it. I was starting to believe you dead, Phillip. It's good to see you well."

"Thank you. I must say that I'm also delighted to see you. Better me here than a criminal, I suppose. A criminal wouldn't have kept your house quite so clean and tidy as I have."

Charles shook his head and grinned. "Poor Stimson—he and his wife keep this place in good order for me during the winter months—he was white in the mouth with fear when he came to see me this morning at Moreland. You see I was the only one there, all the others out searching for you. I would have been gone in another ten minutes. In any case, Stimson saw smoke coming from the chimney and thought that rogues had taken over the house and that he should inform me immediately."

Charles dropped himself into a holland-covered chair. "How long have you had Sabrina here?"

"Five or six days now, I'm not really certain," Phillip said easily. "By the way, Charlie, just exactly who is she anyway?"

Charles raised incredulous eyes to the viscount's face. "What the devil kind of question is that? You don't know?"

"Come on, it can't be that bad. She isn't royalty, is she? As a matter of fact, she's refused to tell me who she is. You're my only hope."

Charles felt immense anger, the first time he'd ever felt such anger at Phillip in his life. "How could you? Where did you come across her? Don't you realize how very young she is? How innocent? Dear God, Phillip, I can't believe you would have seduced a young lady of quality. But you did, didn't you? You gave her that lazy smile of yours and she allowed herself to be seduced. Damn you, she's young and guileless, she didn't know any better. Oh, and then later she realized what she'd done. And that's why she must have refused to tell you who she was. She knew if she told you then even you wouldn't have brought her here."

"Charlie, who is she?"

"She's the Earl of Monmouth's granddaughter."

Phillip was stunned. Now he remembered where he'd heard her father's name. Yes, it was from the Peninsula, but it was from one of Wellington's men. Major Eversleigh had had to go home because his father, the Earl of Monmouth, had become very ill. And then he'd returned, only to die at Cuidad Rodrigo.

But he shouldn't be surprised. Damnation. He said, "Let me tell you something, Charles. I didn't seduce her. I was following your impossible directions to Moreland when I found her close to the edge of the forest, unconscious and suffering from severe exposure. Luckily for her, I remembered passing this place and brought her here, just as the blizzard gained its full strength. So she is the earl's granddaughter, you say? Why the devil didn't she want to tell me? Why was she so bloody frightened? What would it matter? It doesn't matter. Why? Ah, this teases my brain. You know what, Charles? I think I'll strangle her when she wakes up. Yes, now that she's finally well again, she deserves to be throttled."

Charles groaned and rose to fetch himself a third glass of sherry. He didn't like this and he knew he was going to like it less as time went on.

Phillip said from behind him, "Who is a man named Trevor?"

"Trevor? Oh, you mean Trevor Eversleigh, the Earl

of Monmouth's nephew and heir. He recently wed
Elizabeth—Sabrina's older sister—it wasn't above a
month ago. Quite a lot of flash and ceremony. Sabrina
seemed quite all right then. Why, Phillip? What is this
all about? What does Trevor have to do with Sabrina
being here with you? You said she was sick?"

"Yes, very ill. The fever came upon her. I feared
several times that I'd lose her, but she pulled through.
She's tough. She's just very weak now, but on the
mend. Have you known Sabrina long?"

"Little Bree? I've known her all her life. Monmouth
Abbey lies only about ten miles to the west of Moreland. She was really that ill? You're certain that she'll
be all right?"

"Yes. As I said, she's just very weak now. In a week
or so she should be quite fit again." Phillip turned
suddenly toward the door. "Follow me, if you please,
Charles, my bread should have sufficiently raised itself
by this time for baking. I finally found some yeast. It
certainly makes a difference."

"Your *what?*"

Phillip merely grinned and left the room, Charles
on his heels. When they reached the kitchen, a room
Charles had never been in in his entire life, he
watched Phillip walk to the big central block surface,
pick up an apron, and tie it around his waist.

Phillip looked up and grinned at him. "I'm lord and
master here," he said, waving his arm about the
kitchen. He tested the dough. "If my meager experience serves me, my yeast needs more time to work its
magic. Do sit down, Charles. I'm at present tied to
my kitchen."

For the first time, Charles took in the viscount's
appearance. His white shirt, though clean enough, was
wrinkled, as were his fawn-colored breeches. His Hes-

sians were a disaster. "Oh, God, wait until Dambler sees you. He's going to have apoplexy, Phillip."

"I'd prayed that Dambler was with you. I trust you've kept him from searching for me in the snow. He's a fine fellow but feels I'm still a lad to be shepherded and protected."

"He's very worried, as were all of us. He's out looking for you with the other men. Both you and Sabrina Eversleigh, I might add. I wish I had another sherry."

"Come, spit it out, Charlie."

"Teresa Elliott," Charles said, and that was enough, surely.

"What about her? She's at Moreland, right?"

"She's too much at Moreland. She's been driving everyone mad, utterly mad. She was trying to shove me out into the blizzard to search for you. It's a close call, Phillip, but now you don't have to worry about that harpy getting her quite pretty fingers into you."

"I would never have married Teresa Elliott. Not in a million years. Not until the earth crumbled to dust, not until my great-aunt Millie went to the hereafter, which likely won't be until the turn of the next century. No, not a worry there. Calm yourself, Charles."

"Well, even if she didn't bedazzle you with her beauty—which I can't deny is near to overpowering— it's now out of the question."

"Charles, what the devil are you talking about? If my faulty memory hasn't failed me, I recall having taken her for only one ride in the park. That certainly shouldn't give any lady hopes of marriage."

"Do you forget that you danced with her twice at Lady Branson's ball? Believe me, I didn't remember it, but she must have told me about it six times in the last three days. Evidently, Teresa places sufficiently high confidence in herself to think she would bring you about to bending your matrimonial knee. But as

I said, Phillip, she is no longer in the picture. You've jumped from the frying pan into the flames. Not that the flames aren't quite lovely."

"The three glasses of sherry you gulped down have addled your brain, Charlie. How about some coffee? That'll bring you back to reason. No, don't fall all over me with your thanks. I'm also the butler in this establishment. Coffee?"

"Sabrina Eversleigh is a charming girl," Charles said, ignoring Phillip's words. "She's eighteen now, I believe, quite old enough." He mentally ticked off the years in his mind. "Yes, eighteen. She's two years younger than my sister, Margaret."

"I've seen glimmers of charm in her, on rare occasion. However, usually she's been more stubborn, more closemouthed than my uncle Harvey's pet pig, Horace, a great animal, really, but once he'd made up his mind about something, that was it."

"Phillip, what's all this about a pet pig? Surely that isn't at all to the point. Now listen to me. I suppose it would be best if I seconded you to the altar. The old earl could obtain a special license and you could be wed by the end of the week. I'm certain the old earl would like to keep things as hushed up as possible." Charles looked up and beamed at Phillip. His relief was boundless. "You know, I think I'd like some coffee."

"Coffee," Phillip repeated as he stared at his friend. "A special license? Dear God, Charlie, you indeed did drink too much sherry. You believe I should marry Sabrina Eversleigh? That's more ridiculous than the ridiculous waistcoat you wore last month to White's, the one with the yellow tulips on it. I've known the young lady for less than a week."

"Don't you see? That's the point, Phillip. You've got a reputation that makes women want to creep into your bed and makes men envy you. You've kept a young unmarried girl with you for nearly a week. She's compromised, Phillip, all the way to her toes."

"She does have rather nice toes," Phillip said.

"I doubt that even Richard Clarendon would want her now."

"My brains have gone round the bend more than yours have, Charlie. That's another reason why her name was familiar to me. Richard told me one night while we were playing piquet that he was going to marry a young girl from Yorkshire. It's Sabrina. Now, listen to me. I'm not about to marry her. There's no reason to. Don't you understand? She nearly died. I kept her alive. I didn't have sex with her. I've cared for her the best I knew how, and that did not include having sex with her. I cooked all her meals and fed her, and dessert didn't include having sex with her. Now forget this nonsense about me marrying her. Richard wanted to marry her and now he can. I am and will remain the good Samaritan, nothing more."

"I doubt that. Once he realizes she's been with you, a gentleman with as great a reputation as his own, I doubt he will be inclined to wed her. Do you know he's been like a madman, nearly killed one of his horses in the snow, searching for Sabrina? He wants her powerfully bad. But now, when he finds out about you? I don't know, Phillip, but I strongly doubt it. I hope he doesn't want to kill you."

But Richard could not love Sabrina, Phillip thought, staring down at his bread dough. Why else would he have continued in his wicked ways, which he most certainly had? Why he'd even taken an opera girl under his protection but three weeks before. Maybe Charlie was wrong and it wasn't a love match. He racked his memory, trying to recall Richard's exact words about Sabrina. They were in White's, playing piquet, both men having left their mistresses but an hour before. Richard was slightly in his cups and the brandy had begun to curl pleasantly in Phillip's stomach as well when he'd said, "I've found me a wife." He didn't look at Phillip, but stared over at the flames in the fireplace. Phillip thought he was jesting. He laughed and refilled his glass.

"No, no, I'm serious about this, Phillip. She's a delightful girl, though I must wait some three more months for her. Old Eversleigh made me promise to let the girl reach her eighteenth birthday before taking her to wife."

Phillip had been surprised, no doubt about that. "But you've buried one wife, Richard, and you have your heir. You've told me more times than I can count that you would never again get yourself married, that one woman just couldn't keep you happy or content."

Richard grunted and downed another glass of brandy. "I want her," he said, his voice thick with lust and drink. "She's as vivid as life itself. Her hair is the color of those flames and long and thick. I want to bury my face in her hair, just breathe her in." He raised his eyes to Phillip's face then. "You know, she's the only comely female I know who hasn't used all her wiles to trap me. She is curiously unaware of passion, indeed, appears to be sublimely unaware of her effect on me. Yes," he said, looking away from the fire and back at the cards in his hand, "I want her."

Phillip became aware that Charles was speaking. "What did you say, Charlie?"

"I asked you what you intend to do."

"Didn't you hear me? I saved her bloody life, nothing more, nothing less. I'm going to return her to her family." No, it wasn't going to be quite that easy. There was Trevor to be dealt with. "You said that this Trevor is married to Sabrina's sister?"

"Yes. If you asked me, I'd say the whole thing was a bribe. Elizabeth isn't a very lovable woman. She makes me want to take to my heels."

"Does Sabrina have an aunt in London?"

"Certainly. Lady Barresford. You've been to several of her soirees, have you not?"

Sabrina's merchant aunt. He nodded absently. Obviously she'd intended to flee to her aunt for protection. At least Charles had added sufficient facts so Phillip would be able to force the whole truth from her. Then, he thought, he would decide exactly what was to be done.

"You still refuse to admit to having compromised her?"

"No, I haven't compromised her and I refuse to believe that saving that damned girl's life would cast me into the role of the major villain in this farce. Don't tell me you've ever wanted to ravage a girl who was so cold her teeth were chattering?"

"No, but I'm not a womanizer and you are. I have no idea what sorts of odd situations would make you mad with lust."

"Oh, just shut up."

"If it matters to you, of course I believe you. I've never known you to lie except when we were boys. But no one else will believe you. Sabrina will be ostracized the moment it's discovered that she was with you."

It was true and he didn't like it one little bit. He wasn't all that bad. He didn't hurt anyone, he merely did what he pleased. "My reputation is so very damning, Charles?"

"Damning? Well, I suppose you'd think that in this situation. Strange thing is, you know very well that you'd emerge unscathed from this, but Sabrina? Oh no. Odd the way society works, isn't it?"

Phillip felt a surge of anger. It was true that he'd felt lust for her. For God's sake, he wasn't dead. But he was an honorable man when all was said and done. He'd not taken advantage of her. Their intimacy had been forced upon her by her illness. He thought fleetingly of Martine, his mistress. By God, if only he'd stayed in London, passing long lazy hours in her bedchamber, none of this would have happened. Well, it had happened. Sabrina had happened.

There was no hope for it, if, that is, Charles was right. Phillip pounded his bread dough. Charles was right, no doubt about it, his reputation had come home to roost. "I don't suppose," he said, "there's any way of keeping the entire affair hushed up?"

"I don't see how, not with the entire county alerted to both your and Sabrina's disappearance. It must come out. Don't forget Richard Clarendon."

Phillip rose and began pounding mercilessly at the dough. He looked down at the white flour on his hands and smiled despite himself. He repeated to Charles the same words he had spoken to Sabrina. "I've done well by her, you know. I'll speak to Richard. Perhaps he'll believe me. Perhaps he'll still want to wed her. He is a marquess. That's certainly got more cachet than a measly miserable viscount."

"Yes, by all means speak to Richard. But I wouldn't count on him slapping you on the back, kissing both your cheeks with gratitude, and telling you he believes you saintly enough to be a vicar. No, Phillip. I'm sorry, but I think you must prepare yourself. In any case, it's time you wed. You need an heir. Even Rohan Carrington is married. It's your turn now."

Phillip cursed fluently.

Charles said, "It's the right thing to do, the honorable thing."

"Honor bedamned," he said, and sent his fist again into the dough.

"One can't bedamn honor."

Elaine bedamned my honor, Phillip thought with sudden bitter memory. His mind raced over the years, years he'd spent by himself, concerned with only his pleasures. He said slowly, "I suppose you're right. Someone must see to her. I have the distinct impression that left to her own devices, Sabrina Eversleigh would fall from one scrape into another. At least I can hold her on a tight rein."

To Phillip's surprise, Charles laughed.

Phillip raised an eyebrow. "I am eight years her senior. I will deal well with her."

"You've known her for less than a week, Phillip. And she's been ill. You'll have to ask Margaret about all the mischief Sabrina led her into over the years. Yes, I think you've spoken too soon. Sabrina is no malleable sheep, Phillip."

Phillip thought about her outrageous attempt to escape from him the night before. "She'll obey me. I haven't a doubt about that." He formed the dough into two loaves and slid them into the oven.

"You will join me for lunch, I trust, Charles. We must decide what is to be done. When Sabrina wakes up, I shall inform her."

18

Charles didn't remain to have luncheon with the viscount, the two men having decided that Sabrina's grandfather should be informed at once and the search halted. Phillip heard her awaken some two hours later. He prepared a tray and made his way upstairs to her bedchamber.

He didn't know if he felt more sorry for her or for himself. Both of them were caught in a trap of societal rules. He didn't see any escape. He'd done his best, gone out of his way, and it had gotten him a wife.

A wife.

He didn't want a wife. He was too young, too fond of doing exactly what he pleased whenever he wanted. Rohan Carrington had married, and he was so content it annoyed Phillip down to his toes. And made him just a bit envious, truth be told. But marrying a woman he'd selected was one thing; having a woman foisted on him was quite another matter. Still, there was no choice. He wasn't a villain; he wouldn't let a young lady be ruined when it was in his power to unruin her.

By the time he reached her bedchamber, he had pretty much accepted the consequences of his good deed. Sabrina Mercerault, Viscountess Derencourt. It had a certain ring to it. It wouldn't be all that difficult to be wed to her. Those violet eyes were unique and really quite lovely. As was the rest of her, which he'd seen at great length.

He found he was rather looking forward to her reaction when he told her that he knew who she was. She'd been a stubborn witch. He decided that he didn't dislike her stubbornness, certainly not a bad quality in a wife—if controlled. Yes, she would suit him as well as any other female. Better than Elaine would have suited him, that was certain, at least he prayed it was certain. Sabrina was lovely, she was bright. Few men knew their future brides as well. Yes, everything would be all right. She would become his wife as soon as it could be managed.

He stepped through the doorway of her bedchamber. She was looking away from him, toward the window. Bright afternoon sunlight poured through into the room, making her auburn hair a nimbus of fiery red around her head.

After they were married and she was safe, he would have to tell her that he had no intention of changing his life. Surely she would understand. Theirs wasn't a love match, but a marriage of convenience. No, he would continue as before and she would accept her role in his life and in society. She would do quite well.

She turned back from the window and closed her eyes. Her nose twitched. She said, "I know I smelled viscount's bread. I don't care if it's flat as my hand, I'll eat the whole thing."

Phillip smiled at her with new eyes, and set the tray down on the bed. "I brought an entire loaf."

There was soup, a bowl of honey, and his bread that she was eating as fast as she could get it in her mouth. Good, she was so thin. It worried him. When he took her to Dinwitty Manor, Cook would regard the new mistress with a zealot's eye and Sabrina would have to be careful, as he always was when staying in his country home, not to become fat as a stoat within a week. She was chewing vigorously when he said, "Eat all you want, you need it now, but be advised that I don't want a fat wife."

She stopped chewing. She stared at him, then shook her head and chewed faster. She swallowed, choked, and quickly drank down the glass of water on her tray.

She wiped her eyes and looked at him hard. She cocked her head to one side. "Excuse me, Phillip, I surely must have misunderstood you. What did you say? Perhaps you could say it again so that I could hear it aright this time?"

"As you will, Lady Sabrina."

"I told you I don't like that, Phillip."

"Very well. You may have your way for a while longer." He sat down beside her and took her hands in his. Her fingers were sticky with honey. "Sabrina, will you marry me? Will you be my wife? We've known each other for a full five days. I think we could do well together. What do you say?"

"Marry you," she repeated, never looking away from him.

"Yes. Just listen. We actually know quite a bit about each other. We've only disagreed when you've shut me out. That would have to end. You would have to trust me, to admit me into all your thoughts. Do you think you can do that?"

"You don't know what you're saying. Why are you doing this to yourself? Why do you want to marry me? I'm a stranger to you. You haven't any idea who I am or what I'm like or—"

"I know enough. Now, will you marry me?"

She gazed at him intently, trying to understand why he was doing this. It made no sense. She realized immediately, of course, that it would solve all her problems. She'd be free of Trevor. She'd be free of

Elizabeth. She could visit her grandfather without worrying about either of them hurting her. She wouldn't have to deal with Aunt Barresford whom Elizabeth had called an old dog. Why was he doing this? It made no sense at all. She said aloud, "No, Phillip, of course I won't marry you. Perhaps you'll be good enough to tell me why you asked me in the first place. Ah, I understand. Goodness, I guess my head is still fogged with sleep. I'm sorry it took me so long. You're obviously trying to protect me, but I assure you that isn't necessary."

"You need protection more than my lame cat, Dorkus."

"Why is she lame?"

"That's not to the point. Forget I said that. Dorkus went to cat afterlife five years ago. She managed to tip the years at twenty before she took her leave. Now, would you rather have Richard Clarendon, Sabrina? Is it because he's a marquess and is very probably richer than I am?"

"Richard," she said blankly. "Richard Clarendon? Of course I don't prefer him. I scarcely even know him. It's true that he visited us rather frequently during the summer." Her voice dropped off like a stone off a cliff. "Oh, dear, there's more to this, isn't there? How do you know about Richard?"

"Charles Askbridge has been here."

She nodded slowly and began tearing up the rest of the bread. He knew everything then.

"Yes, now everything is blindingly clear to me. It was Charlie who mentioned Clarendon and made me remember why it was that the name Eversleigh was so familiar to me. I thought it was a connection to your father, but it wasn't. Richard told me himself, some three months ago in London, that he wanted you, that he was waiting only until you reached your eighteenth birthday. I brought Richard's name into this to see if you had any tender feelings toward him. If you did, why then you would simply marry him, not me." He rose and sat down in the chair next to her bed, a chair he'd grown quite used to over the past five days. "Yes, I see that you understand everything now. Poor Charles, if only you had seen his face when he walked in here to see you sleeping in my arms and me staring at him ready to leap at him and tear out his throat."

"Why?"

"Why was he here? The caretaker for this house was scared that villains had taken over the house. Charles came to see what was going on. Although he wasn't overly surprised to see me, his shock at seeing you made him speechless for a good three minutes, a record for Charles. In short, Sabrina, Charles is off to tell your grandfather that you are all right and to fetch a carriage so that we can go back to Monmouth Abbey."

She turned whiter than the sheets. "Oh no. I can't go back there, Phillip, I can't. I won't. You can't force me back there."

"It's time you told me exactly what happened. It's time you told me all about Trevor and Elizabeth and why your grandfather couldn't protect you."

He already knew everything, but he wanted it out of her mouth. "There's no need for me to tell you anything."

"Trust is a very important thing, Sabrina. I demand your trust. Yes, I know that Trevor is your grandfather's nephew and heir and that he's married to your older sister Elizabeth. Now I want you to tell me the rest. I must know everything so that I can protect you."

"I really hoped Elizabeth would be happy."

He said nothing, merely nodded at her, his hands folded in his lap, and waited.

She looked at him straightly. "Trevor tried to rape me. But you know that."

"All right. The important thing is that he failed. Now tell me the rest of it."

"I thought when he first came to Monmouth Abbey that he was well enough, that he was charming, that he truly cared for Elizabeth. To be the future Countess of Monmouth was the most important thing in life to her. She floated about the Abbey, she was so pleased. But none of us saw beyond his handsome face and charming manners." She paused a moment. It was odd, but just thinking of him, saying the words to describe him, frightened her. She said, "It's odd. He's very handsome. He's slender, beautifully mannered, but he looked kind of soft, like a woman would look. The truth of the matter is that he's vicious and cruel. He seems to delight in inflicting pain. He trapped me in the picture gallery, away from the family and the servants. He would have succeeded in raping me had he not become overly excited, and thus for the time being, unable."

"You mean, he—"

"Yes, I suppose what you're thinking is what I mean. There was a big stain on his britches and he was all out of breath and seemed suddenly weak."

Thank the good Lord that the bastard hadn't been able to control himself. "Yes, I understand. Go on."

"I hurt him, but not badly. After he, well, lost himself, then I ran away."

"You mean you didn't take one of the portraits off the wall and hit him with it?"

"No. I wish I'd thought of it but I was just too afraid. I was a coward."

"No, you're not a coward. You were scared. It was

understandable." Rage was pouring through him but he knew it wouldn't help her at all to see it. It was very difficult to keep his voice calm. "What did you do then?"

"I went to Elizabeth and told her what Trevor had done. I could even prove it. He'd hit me again and again on the face. I looked frightful. There was no way she couldn't have believed me. But she refused to take my part. It was then that I realized that she's always disliked me."

Jealous, Phillip thought, the bitch was so jealous that she'd protect that bastard before she'd take care of her little sister. The rage nearly overflowed. He looked down. The last thing Sabrina needed was to see him red in the face with murder gleaming in his eyes.

"Elizabeth told me that if I went to Grandfather with my ridiculous story she would swear that it was I who tried to seduce her husband. She said it would be the two of them against me, and Trevor was Grandfather's heir.

"Then she reminded me that just such a disaster as this might topple Grandfather into his grave and if that happened, it would be my fault. I knew then that I couldn't stay at Monmouth Abbey. Trevor had told me he'd come to my bedchamber and that I'd better not lock my door against him. There was no one to stop him, least of all Elizabeth, his wife.

"I couldn't stay. I had to protect my grandfather and I had to protect myself." She raised bleak eyes to his face. "I should have returned to the Abbey after my horse went lame, but I couldn't, I just couldn't. It hadn't started snowing. I believed I could get to Borhamwood in time to catch the stage to London. I got lost and became ill in the cold. You found me."

Such a pitiful tale, she thought, staring down at her hands.

"When you return to the Abbey, you won't be alone. I'll be with you. You know, of course, that I want to kill Trevor."

"Yes. That's one reason I didn't want you to know anything. Phillip, try to understand. He's the future Earl of Monmouth. There is no other male to inherit the title. You can't kill him. Please promise me that you won't."

"I'm grinding my teeth over that one," he said, then stretched out his hand and took hers. "I promise, but it will be difficult. No, when we go back, I'll be with you. I won't let you out of my sight. If you will consent to be my wife, I'll have you out of that ménage within a week."

"Marry you? Oh no, I'd never do that, never. It wouldn't be fair, it wouldn't be honorable. I thank you for all you've done for me. Indeed, you saved my life. You guarded me and nursed me. I don't want to go back to Monmouth Abbey. I ask you for one more favor. Please escort me to Borhamwood so that I may take the stage to London, to my aunt Barresford. It is the only solution, the best solution. This is a favor I'm asking, since you owe me nothing."

19

Phillip drew back, releasing her hand. What was this? She didn't want to marry him? Was she so ignorant as to not understand that she could no longer be what she was, namely, an unmarried girl of good name? He realized that he would have to explain it to her. "Sabrina, listen to me. This is very serious. Although you're not aware of it, you have spent nearly a week with a man who's known for not being the most sober and serious of individuals. Actually, I've rather got a reputation for taking my pleasure with just about any female I please."

She was staring at him as if he'd grown another nose. "I'm sorry, but it's true. I suppose some people would call me a rake, perhaps even a womanizer. I'm really not all that bad, but it's my reputation, and that's what the world knows and accepts and believes. Even if you were to go to London, to your aunt Barresford, your reputation would be in shreds. No one would invite you to any parties. You would be a pariah.

"The best solution, the only solution, Sabrina, is that you marry me, and quickly." He waited to see that understanding of her predicament on her expressive face.

Instead, she gave him a tolerant smirk. "It's really very generous of you to offer to sacrifice yourself,

Phillip, but I won't allow it. Charles is trying to play God. I have no intention of having you saddle yourself with me—indeed, I would have no honor if I were to allow you to do so. Again, my lord, my answer is no."

"You're being foolish, Sabrina. I won't have it. You understand what's happened but you're just doing this to thwart me. Am I such a bad bargain? Do you think I would make such a wretched husband? Don't you like me at all?" She was just shaking her head at him. He added, his voice low and hard, "Even if you wanted Clarendon, let me tell you it's doubtful that he would still want you."

"Why?"

"You're damaged goods, Sabrina. It's that clear-cut. Accept it and marry me."

She reared up in the bed. She waved her fist at him. "You wretched men, you create and maintain two sides of the coin. The one side for you brave, honorable specimens, and the other for hapless women, whom you despise or protect depending on your whims of the moment. I tell you, I refuse to be bandied about among you. You may take yourself to the devil, my lord. Oh yes, and take Clarendon with you. To imagine that he wouldn't still want me just because I'd been with you for five days. *Damaged goods!* It makes me quite enraged, Phillip." She threw her pillow at him, then fell back, panting hard from the exertion.

Phillip thought inconsequentially that he shouldn't have let her eat so much bread. He wasn't particularly angry at her, for he saw some truth in what she said. He paused a moment, worried that she might make herself ill again, and said, "Please relax. I'm sorry. I shouldn't have thrown Clarendon at you, but I just want you to understand that everything is different now. Your life can never be again what it was. Trust me on this, Sabrina. Your best course, your only course, is to accept me as your husband."

She shook her head wearily. "Let's part friends, Phillip. I won't marry where there is no love. It's not you. It's not Richard. It's me and what I know I have to have to live my life with a modicum of contentment."

He was getting weary of his lack of success with logic, so why not try something utterly unexpected? He leaned forward, laying his hand on her arm. "Perhaps," he said, his voice thick and low, "I should take you now. It's certainly what everyone will believe, once it's known you've been with me. Believe me, Sabrina, I don't mind that you are, at the moment, at your most womanly."

She was speechless, for a good two seconds, then she pulled back her arm and sent her fist into his jaw. He jerked back and she caught his ear. She was strong and it hurt. She rolled away clumsily to the other side of the bed and sat up, wrapping the covers around her.

He cursed, then plowed his fingers through his hair. "I'm sorry. Damn, I was just trying to make a point. I was just trying to make you see the truth of the situation. I'm sorry," he said again. "I'm not a bad fellow, you know that. I'm not Trevor. That was all an act. Listen, Sabrina, we will manage to rub along quite well together. Can't you trust me in this?"

She said nothing. However, she did move back to the center of the bed. "I did something else," he said finally, since she was as silent as a clam, looking straight ahead, mutely suffering his presence. "Charles and I decided what had to be done. He is at this moment speaking to your grandfather, telling him that you're safe, telling him that your reputation will be safe, telling him that you and I will marry. When you next see your family, it will be as my betrothed."

"Phillip, I am not a fallen woman. I was simply very sick. Does that somehow make me immoral? I'm not sorry that you found me because you saved my life. Given that, do you ever believe I would make you pay for your kindness? Now, enough of all of this. Will you please take me to Borhamwood?"

He looked down at her, at a loss for words. He realized that he could not very well abduct her and force her to the altar. Well, he could, but it would require a lot of work, and frankly he was tired. Damnation, what the hell was he supposed to do?

He looked toward the window at the sound of horses and a carriage drawing up in front of the hunting box. Sabrina paled at the sound.

"Time's up, Sabrina." He turned, his brow raised.

She shook her head.

He turned and without a backward glance strode from the room.

He met Charles at the front door and saw that the carriage drawn up outside had no earl's crest on its door.

"It's my carriage," Charles said. "Come into the parlor, Phillip, we have a new and very different problem to deal with now."

Phillip shut his mouth on an oath and followed Charles into the parlor. "Well? Don't keep me waiting, Charles. Spit it out."

"The Earl of Monmouth has had a stroke. The physician will allow no one to see him. He assured me that he would tell the earl that Sabrina was safe and well, but he feared that the old man would not even understand."

"I see," Phillip said, and indeed he did see. "Trevor is now the master."

"Yes, both Trevor and Elizabeth. It would interest you to know that Elizabeth had already called in the men from their search for Sabrina. Actually, I think, from the looks they were giving each other, that the two of them had hoped she was dead. I really have difficulty believing this. Elizabeth was never a particularly likable girl, but now I find her cold and hard."

"Still, Charlie, why did you bring your carriage?"

"There's more, Phillip. When I told Elizabeth that Sabrina was safe, she inquired rather urgently, I thought, what Sabrina had told me about her running away. I told her that I didn't know the details, but that Sabrina had likely spoken to you. I saw her glance meaningfully at her husband. Then the both of them hastened to tell me that Sabrina had left the Abbey because she had tried to seduce Trevor and he had rebuffed her. They were surprised that she'd left, but thought it was because she was too ashamed to stay." Charles ran a distracted hand through his hair. "You know they'll be telling everyone in Yorkshire who will listen their version of this wretched affair. In any case, Elizabeth then told me in the coldest voice I've ever heard in my life that she would find it difficult to forgive her sister for what she had done. She did offer to take her back, but I realized I couldn't allow it."

"And what did Trevor say to this?"

"That was the final nail in the coffin as far as I was concerned. Trevor told me that he had forgiven Sabrina, that indeed he wanted Sabrina back, told me he would care for her himself, that he wanted her well again, that he'd missed her. He assured me that he loved his little sister and he would care for her always. My skin was crawling. I thought Elizabeth would leap on him."

"To hell with both of them. Surely no one would believe such drivel, particularly if they've known Sabrina all her life. Knowing her, no one could think she was anything other than painfully innocent and sweet as a—" He stopped. To Charles's astonishment, red stained his friend's cheeks, making his cheekbones more prominent. Phillip got hold of himself. "As I was saying, Sabrina finally told me, after much prodding, that Trevor tried to rape her and her dear sister took his side against her. And that, Charles, was why she ran away. I tell you, I've only known Sabrina for five days now, but I know that she wouldn't lie."

"And you're right about the folk hereabouts. Sabrina is known and well liked. No one would believe that she would try to seduce Elizabeth's husband. Not because they're all so generous, but because they know that Richard Clarendon wanted to marry her. They would think Trevor versus Richard, and come up with the proper answer."

"That's of little consolation," Phillip said. He raised his eyes to his friend's face. "Sabrina won't marry me. I'm not to be allowed to sacrifice myself, in her words. I tried everything. She wouldn't budge. Odd, you know, Charles, but I forgot my own ill treatment trying to get her to come around."

"No, I can't believe that. She won't have you? Impossible, Phillip. Wait a minute, there's Clarendon. She would rather have Richard?"

"No, she doesn't want Richard either. Indeed, she told me she barely knows him. He's nothing to her. Look, Charlie, I can't very well beat her. You want to take her to Moreland?"

"Yes. The only problem is that most of my guests are still there. Margaret will be delighted to see Sabrina, of course, and will most likely insist on taking over the care of her. Despite your efficiency, Phillip, once back in civilization, you must relinquish your patient."

"If we have her there, then it will buy us more time. It will be difficult to break all of this to her."

"There's no need."

Both men whipped about. Sabrina stood in the doorway, her hair streaming about her shoulders and down her back, holding the overlarge dressing gown tightly about her. There were circles beneath her eyes. She was too pale, too thin. She looked like she was teetering on the edge.

"Ah, Sabrina," Phillip began, and took a quick step toward her, his hands outstretched.

"It's nice to see you again, Charlie. I'm sorry that the circumstances are so horrid."

Charles was staring at her, he couldn't help it. She looked terrible. He felt a knot in his belly. "Sabrina, you're ill."

"Will Grandfather recover, Charlie?"

Charles knew he couldn't lie to her. "His physician doesn't know, Sabrina. I'm sorry."

"It's my fault," she said more to herself than to either of the two men. "If I hadn't run away, then he wouldn't have worried. He thought I was dead. I'm responsible for this, all of it."

Sabrina looked at Phillip, at his hands, which were still outstretched. She fell where she stood, the dressing gown flaring out about her like an unfurling green fan.

20

Phillip looked over the sloping west lawn of Moreland, watching the gray afternoon shadows lengthen into night. He turned at the sound of Richard Clarendon's angry voice.

"Damnation," Richard was saying to Charles, his dark eyes deepening as the frown of his forehead grew more pronounced. "Do you swear you've told me all of it? All right, I believe you. I'm going to put a bullet through that filthy bastard right now." One thing about Richard, Phillip thought, watching him draw on his gloves, when he made a decision, whether in anger or in infinite calm, he acted immediately.

"Richard," Phillip said, turning from the window, "stop this minute. I'm sorry, but unfortunately the old earl isn't in any shape to take Sabrina's side in this. He's too ill to refute what Elizabeth and Trevor have claimed happened. Very simply, it is their word against Sabrina's. And since she ran away, in the eyes of society such an action would point to her guilt rather than away from it."

"Don't be such a cold-blooded bastard, Phillip. You know as well as I do that Sabrina wouldn't have a clue about seducing any man, much less that little fop I met at Monmouth Abbey. Good God, he made my skin crawl with his softness and prettiness." He nearly shuddered with revulsion.

"Let me finish, Richard. The fact remains that Sabrina wasn't raped. Also, even though I promised Sabrina I wouldn't kill him, obviously that doesn't extend to you. But please consider this. There is simply no other male relative to inherit the title. It's Trevor or the earl's line is extinct. I believe you need to think very clearly about whether or not you want to dispatch the little fop to hell before he's had an heir off Elizabeth."

That made the marquess thoughtful. Slowly, he began to draw the exquisite black leather glove off his right hand. He said slowly, "You know, that's a powerful point, Phillip, and I think you've provided the answer. Once Elizabeth bears the heir, then I'll kill Trevor. Yes, that's a fine plan. I'd be a fool to tell him I'll kill him once his heir is born. He'd never bed Elizabeth if he knew the consequences of her bringing a child into the world. No, it will be our secret, just between the three of us."

"I agree," Phillip said. "But when the time comes, Richard, we will discuss it again. You will not simply act alone. Do you agree?"

"No," the marquess said.

"It might be ten years before there's an heir," Phillip said. "The world might be very different in ten years. Promise me, Richard."

"Damn you, Phillip. Very well. I promise."

"Yes, and another thing, Richard," Charles said, "you really don't want to have to escape to the Continent for killing the little rotter. Your father would likely offer himself in your place were you to do that."

"More likely your father would claim he'd killed Trevor," Phillip said. Both men knew that the Duke of Portsmouth regarded his son and heir as a god. Richard could do no wrong in his eyes. They both quite envied him his father.

"I'm blessed in my father," Richard said at last. "Oh,

all right. If we decide to kill the bastard after the heir is born, then it will have to be done in secret. I don't want to have to leave England, and I sure as hell don't want my father involved. And the both of you are right. He would involve himself. He would fling himself in front of a firing squad to save me." He sighed deeply, then slammed a fist against a table, making its legs tremble. "But not to do anything to him galls me."

"I know just what you mean," Charles said as he walked to the sideboard and poured three brandies.

"I've got it," Phillip said after he took a sip of the sinfully excellent brandy, doubtless smuggled from France. "I will go beat the little bounder to the ground. I won't kill him. I'll be very careful not to kill him in fact, but I'll hurt him. I think I'll break his nose. That will make women look at him and shudder."

"That's an excellent idea," Charles said, tipping his snifter to Phillip's. "I've heard that Trevor, married to Elizabeth only for a short time, is already bedding the comely maids at Monmouth Abbey. Yes, Phillip, break his nose, shove it off center, make him look like a gargoyle."

"No," Richard said, tossing his brandy down in one gulp. "I'm the one to marry her. I'm the one to avenge her even though it's Phillip's plan. Give me your plan, Phillip, and I'll smash that bastard's nose in within the hour."

"She won't marry you, Richard, so I'll keep my plan."

Charles stared at the two men, then he laughed. They both turned on him. "Actually, Sabrina doesn't want either of you. I've known her since she was born. Thus it is my responsibility to avenge her. I'll enjoy breaking his nose. How about his right arm as well?"

It was Phillip who began to chuckle. "We sound like a pair of boys, Richard. Cry peace. All right, Charles can break his nose."

"Oh, very well," the marquess said. "And his right arm as well, Charles. Don't muck it up."

"I won't."

"I don't know," Richard said slowly, frowning ferociously. "Perhaps I should go with you just to make certain you don't make any mistakes."

"Now if anyone should accompany me, it should be Phillip. After all, he's the one who saved Sabrina's life and nursed her back to health."

If Phillip had been closer, he would have been tempted to break Charlie's damned nose. Why the devil must he remind Richard about the role he had played in Sabrina's case? He waited for Richard to explode. He'd been only momentarily sidetracked. No longer. Richard regarded him as much a rake as himself, though it wasn't true.

But bless the fates, Richard had no chance to veer to this new fertile land. At that moment the library door was flung open and Teresa Elliott ran on graceful feet into the room, turned to Phillip, and threw her arms around him.

"Phillip! You're alive, you're well, you're here at last. You should have been here when I arrived, but you elected to be different and to ride your own path. It wasn't well done of you. Just look what happened. You found that wretched girl and had to hide yourself for five days. Five days, Phillip. It was unbearable without you here."

Phillip set her away from him. She didn't release her hold on his arms. He wanted to tell her that she'd reddened her lips too much.

Very carefully, he pulled away, catching her hands and holding her off a distance of a foot.

"Oh, dear, you must be exhausted. One can just imagine what you've had to do with that girl, being with her constantly. I don't suppose she was younger than fourteen, was she?"

He just shook his head. Teresa knew exactly how old Sabrina was, probably to the day and the hour, he'd bet on it.

But he asked anyway. "How is it that you know what I've been doing for the past five days?"

She pursed her lips into a pout she'd obviously been practicing in her mirror, and on other gentlemen as well. "It's obvious for all to see, my lord. Did you not arrive with her here? Did you not carry her upstairs and put her in her bed? Was not her head on your shoulder as if she'd become quite used to having her head resting in that exact place on your person?" She gave a laugh that was a bit on the shrill side. "You know what servants are, my lord. I've been hearing quite the oddest stories."

"You shouldn't listen to servants' gossip, Teresa. It isn't becoming." But he knew full well that the matter was no doubt being discussed with great relish among both gentry and servants. "Are you acquainted with Richard Clarendon, the Marquess of Arysdale? Richard, Miss Elliott."

She was forced to turn from Phillip. When she got a full view of Richard Clarendon, the turn was worth it. He was dark as the devil, he had the look of a man who always knew exactly what he was doing, and she knew right to her toes that he would take a woman and make her scream with pleasure. She knew this and she was still a virgin. Her hand trembled as he took it and lightly kissed her wrist. If she hadn't already promised Phillip her virginity, at least in her inner thoughts, Richard Clarendon would certainly be the next gentleman on her list. She'd heard about him, of course. She wondered if it was true that the number of married ladies he'd bedded exceeded three dozen.

"It's a wonderful pleasure, my lord," she said, watching his dark head bend over her wrist, seeing how finely he was put together. She'd never been this close to him before. It was a revelation. She smiled to herself, knowing that her beauty normally had such an effect on most gentlemen. The marquess would be no exception.

To her chagrin, the marquess said only, "My pleasure, Miss Elliott," and turned abruptly away.

Charles rolled his eyes. The last thing he wanted was a scene from this young lady who should have been drowned on her sixteenth birthday. He saw that her eyes were glittering dangerously. She wanted Richard to fall all over her. Damnation, what was he to do? He cleared his throat, shot a look fraught with pleading toward Phillip, which the viscount ignored, then said, "My dear Teresa, you've come upon us at a rather trying time. We were discussing business. It is something I swear to you would be more boring than death. May we be allowed to enjoy your company at dinner?"

"You know you're discussing what to do with that miserable girl, not business."

"We will see you later, Teresa," Phillip said in a firm tone his own father had often used with excellent effect on him when he'd been a boy.

Teresa was more than curious. Phillip was hers and she had to know what had gone on between him and the girl upstairs in a guest bedchamber. But even she had enough wit to realize that now wasn't the time. They were closing her out. It was aggravating. She frowned at the marquess, but he was staring into the fireplace. It was a nice fire, but it was she he should be looking at with such concentration. She would think about whether or not she would take him as a lover after she'd given Phillip his requisite heir. Why did he care about that girl upstairs?

She smiled. It was difficult, but she was accomplished, and she managed it. She waved an airy hand. "As you will, gentlemen. Do decide what to do with that stray girl upstairs. I would like to have a nice Christmas party, something Charles and Margaret promised me when I arrived, and we can't until she's gone."

"I repeat, Teresa," Phillip said, "you shouldn't listen to gossip." He was ready to leap upon her and strangle her with his bare hands. Sabrina, a stray girl? Damnation, he knew his face was red.

"As you will," she said in a submissive voice that her mother had forced her to learn, waved to the three of them again, indiscriminately, then walked gracefully from the room.

Charles watched her leave with distaste. "If you marry her I will never speak to you again, Phillip."

Phillip said to Charles, "I wouldn't ever speak to myself if I married her. Actually, I wouldn't marry her if I were randier than a dozen goats and she was the last female available."

"She's a bitch," Richard said, never one to mince words. "Now she's gone. Let's get back to the business at hand." But he continued to stare into the fireplace, his attention seemingly focused on the licking tongues of orange flame. He said, "I know your tastes don't run to innocent young virgins, Phillip. But Sabrina is so vibrant, so animated, so very different from any other lady of noble birth I've ever met, that you've ever met. She alternately charms me and ignores me. One minute she'll listen to me as if I were the smartest man alive, the next, she's laughing at me. I know she must have done the same to you. How could you resist her? You've seen her naked, Phillip. That I cannot tolerate. You've touched her and that I can tolerate even less."

"Stop gritting your teeth, Richard," Phillip said mildly.

"Damn you, she's never even let me kiss her." Actually he remembered that she'd laughed that innocent guileless laugh of hers when he'd made the attempt. He could still see those violet eyes of hers, looking at him, looking too far into him, and her good humor when she'd told him not to behave like Neddy Brickle, the blacksmith's son who'd grabbed her and pulled her behind a stable and tried to kiss her. "Damn you, she didn't even realize who I was."

"You mean," Charles said, "that she didn't realize what an honor it was to have you trying to kiss her?"

"Shut your mouth, Charlie. That isn't what I meant, exactly. But you, Phillip, she was with you for five nights as well as those days. Aren't her eyes incredible? Surely you noticed?"

"Yes, her eyes are unique."

"And that hair of hers, not red, but a very rich auburn color."

"Yes, she's got beautiful hair."

"Surely she intrigued you, didn't she?"

"No."

"You're lying, damn you. Did you lay a hand on her, Phillip?"

"Of course," Phillip said calmly. "Enough of this nonsense, Richard. She nearly died. I did everything in my power to keep her alive. Would you have preferred that I left her lying in the snow? She was nearly blue, you know."

"You know very well what I mean," Richard said, his hands fists at his sides. "I don't like this, Phillip. I just might have to kill you."

"Dear me, what a reward for a good Samaritan. Just stop it, Richard, and attend me. When Charles found us, he convinced me that I should offer for her, as five days spent alone with me, regardless of the circumstances, would ruin her reputation. She turned me down flat, Richard, as, I'm convinced, she will do to you, if you've still a mind to have her. However," he continued, looking straight into his friend's dark eyes, "I intend once she is better to push her again to accept me as her husband. She shouldn't be ruined and ostracized. She doesn't deserve it."

"If you haven't damaged her, then I'll take her to wife."

Phillip said only, "I didn't damage her." He thought that if the situation resolved itself and she became his wife, what had happened to her would not at all be such a bad thing. Although he didn't love her, he had come to like her and respect her. She seemed even-tempered, sweet. She was a mystery one minute, an open book the next. He would, he concluded, treat her much better than Richard would. To his mind, Clarendon merely wanted Sabrina to while away his boredom for a time. He could see the marquess setting her up as a new mother for his young son, while he resumed his own pleasures in London. Sabrina didn't deserve that.

Charles said, "Perhaps I should offer for her. I've known her forever. I'd keep her safe. What do you say?"

Both gentlemen turned frowns upon Charles, making him fling up his hands. "All right, forget it. But I'm here, should she need a sacrificial husband."

"Just shut your trap, Charles," the marquess said. "I'm going to see her now. Has that damned Dr. Simmons come down yet from her room?"

"I'll ask," Charles said and pulled the bell cord. He would be vastly relieved, he thought, if only Trevor got the broken nose out of this mess.

21

Sabrina didn't move even though her arm was getting numb. She didn't want Margaret to know she was awake yet. She felt the soft cotton of her own nightgown against her skin. It felt wonderful. How kind of Elizabeth to send her clothing to Moreland.

She felt consumed with misery at her own helplessness. She had to regain her strength soon so that she could go to her grandfather, assure herself that he would be all right, and convince him that it would be better for all of them if she went to London. It occurred to her that she would now have to apply to Trevor for her inheritance from her mother, the ten thousand pounds that was hers upon her eighteenth birthday. It belonged to her, and even Trevor couldn't prevent the solicitors from turning the funds over to her. How very disappointing for him that she hadn't died. A sob rose in her throat. She tried to keep it swallowed, but it was no good. The sob burst from her mouth like the sound of a dying chicken. That almost made her smile.

"Bree, my love, you're awake. How do you feel?"

Sabrina raised glazed eyes to Margaret's face as she poured Sabrina a cup of tea. Her childhood friend who'd married a man she loved; a childhood friend so happy it hurt to look at her. "I'm alive," Sabrina said.

"Really, I'm alive. No need for you to worry so, Margaret."

"Of course I'll worry. Do you have any pain, Bree? Shall I fetch Dr. Simmons for you? He's still downstairs, speaking to Phillip, I believe."

Sabrina felt Margaret's hand, soft, and featherlight on her forehead. She missed Phillip's hand, solid and strong. She grabbed Margaret's hand. "No, Margaret, I'm fine, really. I'm very grateful to you and Charlie for bringing me here to Moreland. I couldn't have gone back to the Abbey. Thank you. I'll be strong again, really soon now. You know me, I've always healed faster than I deserved. Soon, Margaret, soon I'll take my leave of you. Another day, perhaps two."

Sabrina wondered dispassionately what her aunt Barresford's reaction would be when she arrived on her doorstep. Would Elizabeth write to tell her that Sabrina was a slut, a trollop, a—? She didn't know any more words for loose immoral women. No, Elizabeth didn't want her to return to Monmouth Abbey. She'd keep her mouth shut.

From what she knew of Aunt Barresford, she didn't think the lady would turn her away, not with ten thousand pounds in her purse.

"You'll stop the nonsense, Sabrina. I won't hear another word out of you. You'll stay here until I tell you that you can leave. Listen to me, even at this moment, Charlie is getting rid of the Christmas guests. I won't have to leave you. My husband Hugh will be arriving from London in two days and we'll all celebrate Christmas together. It will be quite like old times.

Remember that one Christmas when you and I were angry at Charlie because he treated us like little girls, which we were, of course? Ah, but the revenge we exacted on him. He still shakes his head about that and shudders."

Sabrina managed a smile. "I'll never forget the look on his face when he came downstairs from his bath, and you and I were hiding inside the cupboard behind the stairs. He was green from head to foot. A lovely moss green. It was a magnificent revenge."

"Yes, and despite what you and I have done to him over the years, he is very fond of you. Ah, don't forget that Phillip is here, of course, and Richard Clarendon. He, Charles, and Phillip were closeted together in the library for the longest time. My maid told me that Teresa Elliott came out of there so angry she could barely speak. I'll bet she spewed her meanness on Phillip and he put her in her place."

"Richard Clarendon is here? At Moreland?"

"Yes. He was searching for you with all the other men. Even after your sister—no, never mind that. It's not important now."

"Tell me, Margaret."

"I don't want to. You're still ill. I don't want to make you mad."

"Tell me, Margaret."

"Very well, Sabrina, but I want it noted that I don't want to. Elizabeth and Trevor called off the search for you. Richard was so furious he went on a rampage."

Oddly enough, Sabrina felt nothing much at all with that news. She could understand how her presence would ruin the tales Trevor and Elizabeth had told.

"You say all the gentlemen were in the library?"

"Yes."

"They were undoubtedly discussing what was to be done with me. And now, Richard Clarendon must needs be part of it. Perhaps, Margaret, they're gambling, the loser will take me off everyone's hands. Sabrina Eversleigh, neatly wrapped up like a Christmas gift and dispensed with quickly, to the most unlucky of them."

"Don't be a fool, Sabrina. You know that's not true. Just stop it. You're feeling sorry for yourself and I must tell you that I don't like it. It doesn't suit you. It's really very unappealing."

"All right, I'm sorry. Tell me, is there any news of my grandfather?"

"No, as far as I know his condition remains the same." Margaret suddenly became brisk. "Now, Sabrina, it's time you had a cup of tea. It will make you feel better. Just remember, you're alive and soon will be well again. Your grandfather will recover, you'll see." Margaret wondered what was to become of her friend if she continued to refuse to marry Phillip. She realized that she was frankly amazed that any lady under the age of eighty would refuse Viscount Derencourt were he to offer for her. Sabrina wasn't a fool nor was she naive. She knew that she'd been compromised, through no fault of her own, but that never made any difference to anyone. If ever there was anything redeeming in any scandal, it was quickly brushed beneath the rug.

What would it be like to have Phillip taking care of you for five days? She wished, in a small hidden part of herself, that she knew the answer to that.

"Sabrina, don't you at least like Phillip?"

"Of course."

"But—"

There was a light knock on the bedchamber door. Sabrina clutched at Margaret's hand. Her teacup crashed to the floor. "Please, don't let anyone in, Margaret, please."

Margaret patted her hand. "What if it's Phillip?"

"No, particularly not Phillip. Please, Margaret."

"All right. Calm down. You're turning red in the face."

She walked slowly to the door, inched it open, and slipped out into the corridor.

The Marquess of Arysdale towered over her, Charles at his elbow.

"Richard wants to speak to Sabrina," Charles said. "Is she awake?"

She looked up into the marquess's darkly handsome face, dismissing the tug of attraction she felt. He was one of those rare men her mother had told her about, a man she could admire until her toes turned hot, but she wasn't to touch, ever. "I'm sorry, my lord, but she doesn't want to see anyone."

"She'll see me," Richard said and stepped forward. Margaret put her hand on his sleeve. "My lord, I beg you to listen to me. Sabrina is still not well. So much has happened to her, and in so little time."

"Come, Richard," Charles said quietly. "Margaret's right. You've got to give Sabrina some more time."

The marquess looked undecided, his eyes still upon the closed bedroom door. "I wouldn't make her worse."

"No, I agree," Charles said, "but Sabrina? Let her be for the moment, Richard."

Margaret thought she heard him curse softly under his breath. He turned back to her, bending his dark eyes upon her upturned face. "Please tell Sabrina that I will return to speak with her this evening. She will not deny me entrance then." Before Margaret could form a protest, the marquess had turned on his heel and was striding back down the corridor.

Charles looked after the marquess. He was worried, very worried. "Clarendon will see her, Margaret. He will have his way. Talk to Sabrina. At least now she'll have some hours to consider her decision. Now, my dear, Mother is in the midst of most charmingly ridding us of our guests. You must come downstairs and make your good-byes."

"Is Teresa Elliott gone yet?"

"Oh no. Phillip will probably have to lure her outside so that we may lock the door." He grinned down at his sister, chucked her under her chin, and said, "She'll leave. She's got enough wit to know that she can't stay."

Margaret nodded briskly. "The sooner the better for that lady. My maid told me that she was wheedling about the servants for any tidbit of gossip. Phillip's appearance with Sabrina turned her from a light breeze into a full-blown storm."

Charles shrugged. "There's really not a thing I can do about her except to see that her horses are healthy and ready to pull her carriage out of here."

Margaret nodded. "I'll speak to Sabrina. I don't understand, Phillip. Why doesn't she want either of them? What woman ever had such a choice?"

"Even I threw myself into the ring. It boggles the mind, doesn't it?"

So Sabrina had been right, Margaret thought. They hadn't drawn straws, but all three of them were ready to march to the altar with her.

"It was Phillip?" Sabrina asked when Margaret came back into the room.

Margaret shook her head. "No, it was the Marquess of Arysdale. He wants to speak to you, Sabrina. Charles helped me put him off, but only until this evening. You will have to talk with him or else he just might kick the door down."

Sabrina felt as if a small precious light had been extinguished. But what did it matter? "Very well. I'll preserve the door and speak to him." Where was Phillip? Why hadn't he come to her yet? Would he remain much longer at Moreland?

After Margaret left, Sabrina let her mind wander to the carriage trip from Charles's hunting box to Moreland. Phillip had cradled her in his arms; he'd said nothing much of anything, except to Charlie, and his face had been calm and blank. She'd been thankful for his silence, truly she had. But why hadn't he come to her? At least to say good-bye? She recognized her own perversity but she found no humor in it.

She stared grimly at the closed bedroom door. Had Richard Clarendon been chosen to be the sacrificial husband? Somehow, she could not imagine the marquess doing anything that was not precisely to his liking. Surely he still couldn't wish to marry her.

She sighed and closed her eyes. If Richard did indeed offer for her, she would just have to save him from himself.

Perhaps it was the flickering light of the candle touching her face that awakened her. Sabrina opened her eyes, followed the candlelight to its source, and saw Phillip seated on her bed, looking at her intently, his expression impassive.

She smiled. She was used to his being by her bed, in her bedchamber. There was no shock, just a pleasant recognition, a sense of safety because he was here and he wouldn't let anything bad happen.

He didn't smile back at her.

"What is the time?" she asked, trying to come up on her elbows.

He was up in an instant, his large hands on her shoulders, gently pressing her back down. "No, just stay put. I don't need you to be a hostess. It's just after midnight. I'd hoped the candlelight would awaken you sooner or later. I'm glad it was sooner or else I might have fallen asleep here."

"What are you doing here, Phillip? We're no longer

in Charles's hunting box. As you told me a number of times, you being alone with me is very improper." She laughed. "Not that it matters one whit. I could have a battalion of men parade through here and it wouldn't matter, would it?"

"So, at last you're being reasonable about all this."

"There is nothing reasonable about my reputation being ruined. It isn't fair or even close to the truth."

"So? What is your point?"

"There is no point," she said at last. "It's the way things are, the way things will remain."

"That's right, at least in the foreseeable future." He sat down beside her, laying his hand across her brow. "You're feeling better now?"

"Yes. What are you doing here, Phillip?"

"Richard told me—he was in the vilest of moods— that you wouldn't marry him. He wanted to beat me to a pulp, but decided that if you'd decided I was to be the lucky man, then I couldn't very well go to the altar with a blackened eye. I wanted to see if he was right, but I waited until everyone had gone to bed. I've only been here an hour or so. Watching you sleep. You look very peaceful when you're asleep, Sabrina. At one point you even smiled a bit. Do you remember what you were dreaming? No? Well, it doesn't matter."

"Richard was wrong. I told him I didn't intend to marry anyone." She closed her eyes a moment, picturing the marquess towering over her bed, his look so bewildered, so incredulous, that if she'd had it in her, she would have laughed. And when he spoke, he sounded as bewildered as he looked. "You refuse my offer, Sabrina?"

"Yes, Richard, but I do thank you for your kindness, for your concern."

"We're not talking about anything that is even close

to kindness or concern. Don't you muck around with those silly words with me. Dammit, I was to wed you in any case. It was all arranged. Your grandfather approved the match."

"My grandfather said nothing to me, my lord," she said, and the fire in her eye, the bit of ire, disconcerted Richard, but not for long.

"You knew I wanted you. Every female I've known has recognized when a man is interested in her in that particular way."

"Well, I didn't."

"So, I see the truth now. You spend five days with Phillip Mercerault and you are ready to whistle me down the wind."

If she'd had the strength, she would have leapt from the bed and pounded him into the carpet. The anger felt good. "My lord, you will listen to me. I'm not the sort of woman who teases a man, who leads him on, and then laughs at him. Now, you have made your gallant offer. I have said no. You are now freed of your obligation to me, if indeed there ever really was an obligation.

"My intention is to first of all visit my grandfather to assure myself that he is well cared for. Then I shall go to London, to my aunt Barresford. You know, of course, that there is no place for me now at Monmouth Abbey."

And Richard had raged and argued and insulted her, all without really realizing what he was doing.

Sabrina opened her eyes at the sound of Phillip's voice.

"Well, whatever you told Clarendon, it is still his opinion that I'm to be the lucky man. I came here to ensure that was indeed the case."

She shrugged. It annoyed him, but not all that much.

He wanted to see a reaction, even anger, anything but that flattened look of hers.

"He said you plan to go to your aunt Barresford. Just what makes you think, my dear, that your aunt would joyously welcome an unexpected visit from her niece?"

"I have ten thousand pounds."

Phillip cocked a brow. "An heiress, in short. As I live and breathe, an heiress. That's excellent. Now everyone will believe that I've married you for your fortune, and your no doubt sizable dowry. Actually I much prefer being thought a fortune hunter rather than a chivalrous fool."

"I won't wed for the wealth I would bring a gentleman."

He nodded agreeably. "That's no problem. We will put your fortune in your name or in trust for our children."

Sabrina stared at him, then opened and shut her mouth. He was building a wall of words, and she was throwing herself impotently against it. She thought she would prefer another interview with Richard Clarendon. At least with him, it had been she who had been the calm, rational one. "Phillip," she said, in an effort to focus his attention away from his logic, "it appears to me that you're taking your defeat at the wager as a good sportsman should. However, you may be sure that I shan't hold you to it. You may inform Charles and Richard that I can take care of myself without any of your powerful male assistance."

"What the devil did you just say?" Suddenly he was alert, and she saw it. "What defeat at what wager?" Even as he said the words, he remembered Charles's stupid jest about offering himself as the sacrificial husband. He looked away from her.

She meant her laugh to be filled with wonderful

scorn, but it came out bitter as old coffee. "You can't deny it, can you? You and Charles and the wretched marquess are all eyeing each other like crowing banty roosters, fighting to keep your ridiculous male honor as well as your freedom. Well, I'll tell you, Phillip, I won't have it. I'm not damaged goods and I refuse to shout to the world that I am by marrying any one of you. Now, I'm very tired and have found you a bore. Good night, Phillip. You always know your way about. Surely you can find your way out."

She turned onto her side, away from him.

Phillip was silent for some moments. She felt the bed give way as he rose.

He said slowly, and she heard the sadness in his voice, "The world is very seldom the way we wish it to be, Sabrina."

"Then the world must change, and I shall force it to."

"I see that you must learn for yourself. The world will not change its rules for you, Sabrina. I presume that I will see you in London."

"Yes," she said. "But first I am going to visit my grandfather. If he needs me, I shall, of course, do what I must."

He drew a deep breath. "You've refused to listen to me about anything else, Sabrina, but I ask you to listen to me now. Your grandfather is too ill even to recognize you. There is absolutely nothing you can do to help him."

She struggled up onto her elbows and turned toward him. "Don't you understand, Phillip? I must be certain that he is being properly taken care of. You don't know Trevor. He has no love for any of us, least of all Grandfather. And only he stands between Trevor and the earldom. All the Eversleigh wealth. I must go."

The viscount was silent, his gaze fastened on the dark shadows in the corner of the bedchamber. He looked down at her and said abruptly, "Will you trust me to see that the earl is properly cared for and that he is protected from your cousin?"

"But what can you do?"

"Answer me. Will you trust me to see that all is taken care of?"

"I suppose," she said slowly, too aware of her own helplessness, "that since I trusted you with my life, I can also trust you with his. Thank you, my lord, for all you have done for me."

"Could you not also trust me with your future?"

"No, my lord. I'm not the kind of person to use another person's honor against him."

She heard him sigh as he picked up the candle and turned to leave.

"Good-bye, Sabrina."

He didn't want her reply. No sooner had he spoken than he turned away from her. She saw a dim shaft of light from his candle in the hall before he closed the door behind him.

22

"Do allow me to congratulate you, Anissa. Your niece is such a charming girl, although I've heard some say that she is a bit arrogant, but arrogance is good, I always say, if, of course, it doesn't go too far. I've also heard it said that she is far too thin as well, what with those bony elbows, but one can certainly overlook that, given her delicious dowry. At least her bosom isn't quite as thin as her elbows, but one will hope that she gains just a bit of flesh while she is with you. Don't you agree?"

Anissa Barresford looked into Lucilla Morton's avid sharp eyes, wanting to smack her, but Lucilla had more money and thus more power, and, of course, they'd been best friends since their youth. Thus she smiled and simply nodded. Her turn would come. "Yes, if you'll recall, Lucilla, I told you that dear Sabrina—did you notice those incredible violet eyes of hers? No other girl has such unusual eyes." She was also cool and aloof and beautifully dressed.

"So thin she is," Lucilla said.

Anissa nodded. She could afford to be gracious. "Yes, skinny as a hen's leg—some sort of inflammation of the lung I was told—but she is on the mend now, at last. That pallor of hers is exactly the style at present, so fortunate, don't you agree?"

"Only if the pallor is from staying indoors, not from illness."

Anissa raised an eyebrow. Slowly, Lucilla nodded. At that moment her own daughter, Dorinda, now in her second season, was standing next to Sabrina, beneath a potted palm, and the comparison didn't make her happy.

"She's an improvement over Elizabeth."

Anissa laughed. "Any girl would be an improvement over Elizabeth."

"I trust Sabrina's character isn't quite so colorless as her sister's?"

"I trust not. She's been with me only a week now."

Actually, if she hadn't been talking to her best friend, she would have said that Sabrina was so very quiet, so docile, that she really had no idea at all if the girl was a saint or a shrew. Well, she had been very ill.

She said aloud now, "Madame Giselle performed a wonder with Sabrina's blue velvet gown. I'm very fond of the Russian style, though, naturally, I am just a bit too old to wear it comfortably."

Lucilla looked at her, said not a word. She admired the cut and was too old as well.

Lady Anissa smiled toward her niece who looked perhaps even colder than she had just a moment before, perhaps even more aloof as well. Unfortunately, she also looked as if she were ready to fall asleep as the young Earl of Grammercy led her in a cotillion. Perhaps she should tell Sabrina that just a hint of a smile, just a suspicion of wit, displayed very occasionally, might play to her advantage.

Lady Anissa said now, "I told her she must add pounds for the gown to be truly elegant. But do notice when she turns. She has a lovely back. Madame Giselle cut the gown lower to draw attention away from her lack of frontal endowments."

"Her hair is too long," Lucilla said finally.

"Bosh. Her hair is her secondary asset, after her eyes. Have you ever seen a more beautiful red?"

"It's not modern."

"The auburn is of course modern."

"No, the length. I vow that gentlemen aren't supposed to admire all that hair. Short is the style and everyone must applaud it, particularly gentlemen. If they don't, they have no taste."

"True," said Lady Anissa. She would have preferred to have Sabrina roundly clipped, but the girl had held firm. She'd never tell Sabrina that she was pleased she had that thick beautiful head of hair, but she was. It would be her own private secret.

Lady Lucilla had fired all her cannon. It was time to get down to business. "You say the girl is an heiress, Anissa?"

"Yes. Ten thousand pounds she's inherited from her mother. As to her dowry, I haven't inquired. Her grandfather is still very ill. Of course, it is bound to be generous."

Lady Lucilla looked fondly toward her younger son, Edward, who was currently wasting his time dancing with that plump girl of Blanche Halford's. When the dance was over, she would pull him aside and tell him how to gain his fortune and suffer no pain in the process.

Anissa Barresford was patting a crimped gray curl just in front of her ear when she stopped mid-pat and stared. "What is the meaning of this? Good heavens, I can't believe this."

Lady Lucilla followed Anissa's pointed finger to the drawing-room door. There stood Viscount Derencourt in the doorway, looking indolently about the crowded room. He was immaculate, elegant, and slothful-looking as a lizard.

Lucilla said, "What is Phillip Mercerault doing here? I specifically asked Jane if he would be here, thinking of my dear Dorinda, and she just shook her head sadly. She said he never comes to small dancing parties such as this. In addition, it's January. What is he even doing in town? To be sure, Jane did send him an invitation, but still it is an unexpected treat."

Lady Lucilla suddenly recalled her dearest daughter, whose future husband—if she had anything to say about it—was just standing there, all lazy and loose and lonely. She hurried to her daughter as Jane Balfour recalled her duties as hostess and nearly ran to the viscount, who smiled charmingly down at her.

Anissa Barresford thought Viscount Derencourt was about the most delicious man to come along in many a long year. Lucilla was mad if she believed Phillip Mercerault would ever give Dorinda a second glance. But Sabrina now, she was different. Why shouldn't he have Sabrina? Now that could prove interesting. She sank back deep in her chair and began plotting.

The cotillion drew to a close. She watched Sabrina curtsy to the young earl, dismiss him with a wave of her hand, and come back to her.

"You should have let him bring you back, Sabrina. It isn't done for a girl to just skip away from her escort like that."

"Yes, ma'am. I forgot." Sabrina sat down beside her. She was tired and hot and wanted to sleep for a year. She wondered how much longer it would be before her body didn't betray her, before she was completely well again.

"You do dance passably. That is something."

"Thank you, ma'am."

"You may call me Aunt. Also, I believe you should strive for just a bit of animation in your voice, not a great amount, naturally, but a bit. If I didn't see you talking, I would think you were dead. Yes, you must strive for a whisper of vigor. To be sure, gentlemen have no admiration for a girl who can be heard talking and laughing across a room, but still, they are put off by ladies who have nothing at all to say. Try to squeeze at least one compliment out to each gentleman you dance with. Sometimes it is difficult, since many gentlemen are so sadly deficient, but I have faith you will manage it."

"I will, Aunt. I'm sorry, but I'm so very tired."

Anissa looked at her closely. There were circles beneath those extraordinary eyes of hers. That wouldn't do at all. Nothing must detract from those eyes. "We will leave in a half an hour. Then you will sleep for as long as you like."

Sabrina wanted to tell her formidable aunt that she was more than just physically tired. She thought she could probably sleep for a week but her spirit would still be flattened. She forced a smile. Her aunt seemed pleased. "Yes," she said. "I just need to rest."

Anissa leaned close. "I would never wish you to be a flirt, child, but remember that this is your first appearance in London. Perhaps you could make just a small push—once you're not so tired—to be more charming." She paused a moment, remembering that she had spoken similar words to Sabrina's snippy sister, Elizabeth. Not, of course, that it had done any good at all. An entire season she had squired Elizabeth about, and all for naught. She sighed. "It was the longest season I've ever lived through," she said aloud. "Elizabeth simply didn't gain any ground, but that's neither here nor there now, thank the good

Lord. I had quite given up when I heard from your grandfather that she'd married your cousin. You know I imagine it was a bribe. Not that it matters now, of course. She is the future Countess of Monmouth. She is well set. Now we must see to you, Sabrina."

Anissa saw Jane Balfour leading Viscount Derencourt over to Dorinda Morton, Lucilla, like a dog, trailing after them. Her chin quivered. She would bide her time. She sent Sabrina after a cup of punch.

When Sabrina returned to her aunt, she heard Jane Balfour's voice from behind her. "Sabrina, allow me to introduce Viscount Derencourt. Phillip, you are acquainted with Lady Barresford naturally. This is her niece, Sabrina Eversleigh. Lady Sabrina."

She was relieved that she'd already handed her aunt her cup of punch. If she'd still held it, she would have dropped it, splashing it all over her beautiful velvet gown. She knew she'd see him in London, he'd told her that. But it was too soon. She hadn't had the time to gain distance from her feelings for him, or to school herself in how she must behave toward him. She slowly forced her eyes to his face.

He wasn't dressed at all like the man who'd taken care of her for five days. Of course, she wasn't dressed like that girl, either. She watched him bow over her aunt's hand, exquisitely polite. "Lady Barresford. A pleasure to see you again, Sabrina." The gentleness of his voice nearly undid her. She'd never heard that gentle voice during their time when she'd been so very ill. She nodded dumbly, unable to speak.

"What is this, my lord? Why, I had no idea you were acquainted with my niece." What was going on here? Sabrina had suddenly turned into a stick—thin, mute, and stiff.

"We met only briefly, my lady," Phillip said, forcing himself to look away from Sabrina to her aunt, an ambitious old biddy he'd always avoided in the past. "It was a Christmas party at Moreland."

"Ah, that is Charles Askbridge's country seat," Lady Barresford said. "And Charles's dear sister, Margaret, married Sir Hugh Drakemore. I was pleased to hear of it since Margaret has always been on the short side and her mother despaired of finding her an agreeable husband. How does she like marriage, my lord?"

Phillip thought of the glowing smile on Margaret's face when Hugh, a man Phillip had sworn would go to his grave a bachelor, had arrived at Moreland but one day before Christmas. He saw Hugh swing her up in his arms, laughing, kissing her. "I'd say she's tolerably happy with the institution, ma'am." The small orchestra at the far end of the drawing room struck up a lively country dance.

"Would you care to dance with me, Sabrina?"

"Yes, my lord." She didn't look at him, just placed her hand on his arm. "Is that all right, Aunt?"

"Yes, do enjoy yourself, child." As the viscount walked away with Sabrina at his side, Lady Barresford felt a stab of apprehension. The viscount, although a charming, handsome young man, and quite wealthy, was known as a slippery fish that no one had ever managed to net. Later, she must tell Sabrina that he'd never marry her. He was still too young to worry about begetting an heir, though it was well known that gentlemen could pass to the hereafter at any age. Only they never seemed to realize how very fragile they really were. A wife was the best thing to keep a man firmly planted above ground and not beneath it.

Yes, she would speak to Sabrina. There was no use in having her waste her time. Also, it was doubtful Sabrina had ever before met a man like Phillip Mercerault. Still, she did appear to know him well enough for him to address her by her first name. This was interesting.

Phillip was saying softly not an inch above Sabrina's ear, just before he bowed in the dance, "It's a pity you can't waltz yet."

"But I can waltz. Grandfather hired a dancing master for Elizabeth and me, just before her marriage." But she hadn't danced since she'd been here in London.

"That isn't what I meant," he said, looking down into her eyes. "You must have permission to waltz here in London."

"From whom?"

"From the patronesses at Almack's. Has your aunt gained admittance for you?"

"I don't know. She hasn't said." She couldn't look away from him. Here she was fully dressed, looked quite as well as she could look, and she was with Phillip. He turned to face her at the edge of the dance floor. She couldn't help herself. She swallowed, leaning toward him. He let her nearly touch his chest, then he pulled her back. "I cannot, Sabrina, as much as I want to, I cannot."

She stared up at him, not understanding. She felt an almost physical pain. It boggled her mind. She hadn't expected this. She didn't understand it. Where were these odd feelings coming from? "Why?"

They were close, much too close. She was wearing all those damned clothes. Not that she didn't look wonderful, because she did. The problem was he remembered her naked, every white inch of her. Then he heard her one spoken word. "A man doesn't just succumb to any lady, for fear she'll compromise him. But I don't mind telling you, it's a close thing. You'd best not tease me."

"I don't know anything about teasing."

He sighed. "No, of course you don't. Now, I asked you to dance because I want to speak to you."

The set formed and they were almost immediately separated. Sabrina set a smile on her mouth and let her feet move. She curtsied and walked down the line, giving her hand first to one gentleman, then to another. It wasn't particularly strenuous, yet she was out of breath at the end of the dance.

She felt his hand upon her arm. "I imagine you still tire easily."

"Yes, but it gets better every day."

"I don't want to return you just yet. As I said, I want to speak to you. Would you care for a glass of punch? It should help revive you."

She nodded. She laid her hand on his arm. They walked across the huge ballroom to the dining room where there were several long tables holding quantities of food, everything from oyster cakes to apple tortes.

"Are you hungry?"

She shook her head.

Phillip placed a filled glass in her hand and accepted a goblet of champagne from a footman. "To London and your evident success."

She sipped her punch. It was very sweet. She put it down. "Let's drink to a world that doesn't need to be changed. My success isn't just evident, it's a fact."

"No, Sabrina. It's just that the world doesn't as yet know."

"Do you intend to make an announcement?"

"It isn't necessary. Your world right now is made of glass. It will require but one thrown rock—but one vicious tongue—and it will shatter."

"But that makes no sense. I haven't done anything to anyone. I scarcely open my mouth. My aunt does all the talking. I just smile and nod and do what I'm told. No, Phillip, there'd be no reason for such viciousness as you describe."

He could only shake his head. "You're remarkably innocent, Sabrina. It will happen, you know. It's just a matter of time. Did you receive my letter?"

"Yes, just this morning." She gave him a brilliant smile. "Thank you, Phillip. I can never repay you."

"I trust you've stopped your worrying?"

"For the most part."

"You're lying, but that's all right. As I wrote in my letter, your grandfather is improving steadily. He's a tough old eagle. Your rapacious cousin, Trevor, will chomp at the bit for many years before taking his turn. Something I didn't write, just in case your aunt would read your mail, is that the earl is safe from Trevor, I promise you."

She frowned, her eyes upon his exquisitely tied cravat. "What did you do?"

"I went to Monmouth Abbey. I saw the rotter. I made things perfectly clear to him."

23

"You did what? What did you say, Phillip? You actually saw him? Did you shoot him? Please tell me it was just a little hole in his arm, nothing to kill him."

He laughed. "Actually, I believe in about six months I shall go back to Monmouth Abbey and beat him into the ground." He didn't add that Richard Clarendon would probably be with him, or get there before he did. The thought of it nearly made him rub his hands together. "Now listen to me, Sabrina. Yes, I went to Monmouth Abbey and cornered both Trevor and your blushing bride of a sister. They deserve each other, you know."

She looked up at him helplessly.

"But why?"

"They both have the moral fiber of ants."

"I don't really know about Aunt Barresford's moral fiber."

"No, not aunts. I was referring to the very small creature that always enjoys a picnic."

"Phillip, why did you go?"

"I went because I owed it to you."

"No, you didn't. You don't. I've told you. You owe me nothing. You saved my life, Phillip. Surely that's enough."

"All right. I went because I wanted to see this pretty little dandy who cooed all over Richard Clarendon. I wanted to see the bastard who tried to rape his sister-in-law, who should be under his protection."

"He is very pretty. You told him not to hurt my grandfather?"

"Yes. Whatever else Trevor Eversleigh may lack, he doesn't lack an instinct for self-preservation. I told both him and Elizabeth, quite succinctly, that I would put a bullet through the future earl's heart if the old earl died. There was a lot of outrage, sputtering about it being none of my business and the like, but eventually they believed me. But I admit, I did have to resort to a rather drastic demonstration. I had to knock Trevor to the floor and stomp on him a couple of times. Elizabeth stood by, shrieking. Actually, now that I think back on it, I think she might have been pleased that I hurt the little bastard. Who knows? It's strange. Trevor yelled for the butler—"

"Ribble."

"Yes, Ribble. He came to the doorway, stood there, saw what was happening, then just turned around and left."

"But, Phillip, you're talking about fighting a duel with Trevor if Grandfather dies. I can't approve of that. He could hurt you. Why would you risk your life for an old man you don't even know?"

"He's your grandfather, Sabrina."

"I've freed you of any obligations that Charles tried to foist on you. It puts me further in your debt. I can't bear it."

"It appears you will have to since it's done."

She'd told him the truth. She couldn't bear it. She fanned her hands in front of her. "I thank you, Phillip."

Phillip felt a surge of anger at the position she found herself in, through no fault of her own, through no fault of his either, but the defeat in her, the role of eternal supplicant, he hated it for her.

"I don't want any more thanks from you, Sabrina. They are growing quite boring. Yes, all these little mewlings don't fit you at all."

Ah, that did the trick. Color crept up from her breasts to her hairline. Ah, her breasts, he tore his gaze away and looked directly into her eyes.

"Little mewlings? You fool, that doesn't even mean anything. I have to thank you, there's no way around it. Why don't you do something more fitting your character, which Charlie told me was wild and reckless and selfish? Yes, I now about all these ladies you do things with that you really shouldn't do because they're married. Oh, enough of that. He also told me that you liked to build on your house, but that didn't really count, just the other, which should shame you to your toes."

"Selfish, am I? The other—wild and reckless—all right, I'll accept those. I'll even take your damned insults, but I draw the line at you calling me selfish. Don't you remember how I bathed you, Sabrina? How I toweled you dry? All of you? Every damned little inch of you? I proved to you that I wasn't selfish. I did everything for you."

"I was unconscious. Well, I was barely conscious. Only a complete villain would bathe me when I was barely conscious."

She was making no sense at all and he loved it. He wanted, quite simply, to see more. He fairly hummed with anticipation as he said, "You were nearly shrieking with pleasure when I suggested a bath. Unconscious? I don't think so, Sabrina."

"A gentleman wouldn't remember such fine details."

The color on her cheeks was blooming bright; her eyes were glittering with rage and life. Just a bit more, he thought, just enough so that she would growl at him. A growl would prove that she was regaining her fighting spirit.

"Now, now, Sabrina, a gentleman should remember fine details. That ability aids him in pleasing the lady even more the next time. Should I not speak of them? I will think about that later. Ah, but I do remember that you weren't at all unconscious that memorable day I bathed you. As for the earlier days, you weren't completely unconscious either. You were in a fevered, almost frenzied state." He looked at her left ear, framed by loose red curls. He said easily, knowing if there was a growl in her, it would explode upon him soon, "Don't you remember how I warmed you when you were so very cold?"

Hazy memory stirred and she felt her skin flush the color of her hair. He'd held her tightly against him, warming her with his own body. Now she remembered his hands moving up and down her back, cradling her against his chest. She remembered the dizzying warmth of him, how she'd tried to burrow into him.

"You're no gentleman." She backed away from him, splaying her hands in front of her to ward him off, to ward the memories off.

He'd gone too far, pushed her too hard. No growl this time. Well, hell.

He said now, his voice clipped and hard, "You're right. I apologize. Let me assure you that you were indeed unconscious. I did only what I had to do to save your life. Don't become hysterical on me. I promise I won't mention any of it again."

"I'm never hysterical."

He laughed, he couldn't help it. "No, and I beg you never to become so. I have the rankest fear of a female who shows the incipient signs. Come, let's go dance again. Or, if you're too angry with me, I'll simply return you to your aunt. The aunt married to a merchant, as I recall. No, forget I said that. You're breathing too hard. It bespeaks a nervous state. Calm down."

"Your wit would fell an oak," she said, whipped about, picked up her skirts, and walked stately as a queen down the corridor back to the drawing room, to the safety of her aunt.

"Now that insult really hurts," he called after her, laughing. "Perhaps it wasn't an insult?"

He said polite good nights to his hostess and took his leave. Some hours later, after having consumed a half bottle of brandy at White's, he went to Martine's rooms on Fitton Place.

It was some minutes before Annie, Martine's maid, butler, and chef, cracked the front door open a few inches at his insistent knocking, demanding irritably who was trying to raise the dead.

When she saw him, she drew back with a startled, "My lord, it's after two in the morning."

"A fine morning it is, my girl." He knew he'd had a skinful, and gave her a big grin. He tossed Annie his greatcoat and hat. "No need to announce me, I'll surprise your mistress."

He took the stairs two at a time, clutching at the banister several times to keep his balance, and burst unceremoniously into Martine's bedchamber.

A long candle suddenly spurted into wavering light.

There was Martine, propped up on her elbows, those beautiful lips of hers parted in a lazy smile.

"Good evening, madam," he said, and swept her a drunken bow.

She sat up and the covers, as if with a sigh, fell to her waist. She was naked. He stared at the expanse of white flesh and became instantly harder than a rock.

He groaned and jerked off his clothes, leaving them to lie where they fell.

"Quelle sottise," Martine said in a hard Manchester accent. "Come, my lord, I believe you need my assistance, and quickly." She pulled back the covers and drew him down into her arms. "You are drunk, Phillip? Too drunk to give us pleasure?"

"I'd have to be dead before that would happen. Trust me, Martine, I won't disappoint you. If I happen to skip some steps on the way, just remind me. I love to backtrack."

She just laughed and bit his shoulder. "I will, but I don't think you will miss any steps, they're too much a habit with you."

He grinned, and buried his face between her breasts. He knew she wanted him because she forgot to practice her French on him. At least some woman wanted him.

She stroked his dark hair, shiny and thick in the candlelight. She arched her back so he could kiss her breasts. "Ah, the pleasure of that."

"I could give every damned woman in London pleasure," he said between kisses, "including that stubborn little witch."

Now this was interesting, she thought, until pleasure poured through her and she pulled him to her mouth so she could kiss him until neither of them could breathe. After some minutes of absolute enjoyment, he suddenly reared back and stared down at her. She saw that his eyes weren't quite focused.

He fell onto his side, balancing himself on his elbow. His right hand, out of habit, stroked her, molding her flesh, making her sigh. "She's a fool, Martine. I compromised her but still she won't have me. Oh, I didn't ask her to marry me again this evening, I knew better than that. I already did enough of that. Why slap myself in the face again when I knew she'd refuse me yet again? No, I'm not that much of a fool.

"I don't know what to do about this. It gnaws at me. I hate this defeat in her. It doesn't suit her at all. But you know what? She had the gall to accuse me of losing some harebrained wager, in short, of having to be the sacrificial husband. Me, a sacrifice? I don't think so. It's a ludicrous thought."

Martine blinked her creamy brown eyes at this outpouring. His hand was no longer caressing her. He was clearly abstracted, far away from her, at least in spirit. Well, truth be told, this could prove just as interesting. "You compromised a lady, my lord?"

"Of course I didn't. Do you think so ill of me?"

Martine sifted her fingers through his tousled hair. "But didn't you just say that—"

"There was no compromising involved. She would have died if I hadn't taken care of her. She knows it, I know it. The whole damned bloody world should know it." He laid his hand on her stomach and began tapping his fingertips.

She smiled at him, encouraging him with her silence to talk. And he did. "Did you know that even Clarendon wanted her? Why the devil can't she see that social ruin is nipping close at her heels?"

"But if you didn't compromise her, then why would she be facing ruin?"

Phillip flipped over on his back. The weaving light from the single candle at the bedside was spiraling upward toward the shadowed ceiling. He could make out a patch of plaster that was cracked and in imminent danger of falling on the bed. "Call the damned carpenter, Martine. I don't want to have my head bashed in while we're in the midst of lovemaking."

She made a soothing, agreeable sound, then said, "I don't understand why this girl who hasn't been compromised refused Clarendon. A romantic figure, that one. I nearly swoon just speaking his name." She was laughing at him. He frowned as she added, "However, at the sound of your name, Phillip, I do a complete swoon. Why don't you want him to marry this girl?"

"He just wants her. He doesn't love her. He's a rake and he's not worthy of her."

"Do you love her?"

"Certainly not. I scarcely know her. You know I'm far too young to love anyone. Far far too young to wed."

"Aren't you also a rake?"

"No, not really. It's all a matter of degree. I'm a very low degree, as in I'm barely on the scale at all. Most of it is just gossip. I'm not as clean as Rohan Carrington is known to be now, but it's close. All right, not all that close, but I'm not a womanizer, not like Richard Clarendon."

"I've always enjoyed the degrees you've given to me, Phillip."

"Stop twisting my words, Martine. Clarendon would have really compromised her, taken gross advantage of her innocence, had it been he who had found her. She was very lucky in her rescuer. I'm honorable. I might have felt lust for her, but never would I have acted on it."

Martine pondered this for some minutes, then harked back to two words that quite struck her fancy. "Clarendon, he also wanted to be the sacrificial husband to this girl nobody compromised?"

"It wasn't ever a question of that. It was Charles Askbridge—the blockhead—who said that. Your romantic Clarendon would have shied away had he thought of himself as a sacrifice, no matter how much he shouted about his desire to marry her, if only I swore I hadn't damaged her. *Damaged*. Can you believe that? After hearing that she nearly died, he had the gall to ask me if I'd damaged her. Sometimes it's a sorry world, Martine. It's a world that ranks down there with slugs."

"Yes, that is true," Martine said as she ran the tips of her fingers over his chest, down to his belly. To be truthful, which she hoped she wouldn't have to be, she was getting bored with all this talk about a girl she didn't even know. She leaned up and kissed his throat. "How hard you are," she said, her fingers low on his belly now, touching him.

"You know I spar at Gentleman Jackson's Boxing Salon," he said absently, his attention returning to the cracked plaster overhead.

Martine chuckled and kissed him all over his chest. "No, Phillip, I don't think your Gentleman Jackson has anything to do with this particular hardness." She was holding him now and he sucked in his breath.

He pulled her on top of him. She said into his mouth, "I don't understand something here, Phillip. You've told me many times that you're too young to marry, that the last thing you want is a wife. But you act like a man with a very guilty conscience." Then she began to move over him. His mind very nearly blanked out.

She stopped for a moment, and he managed to say, "She spent nearly a week with me—alone. And that wretched pair, Elizabeth and Trevor, were spreading tales about her having tried to seduce her own brother-in-law. At least when I saw them, I made it clear—in no uncertain terms, mind you—that they were to keep their mouths closed. But no doubt the damage has already been done. It just hasn't reached London yet, but it will. Sabrina doesn't understand this, damn her for not trusting me, for not believing me."

Martine let him fill her completely. It was a wonderful feeling, particularly with Phillip. "This girl whom you did not seduce, would she like this?"

Phillip thought of Sabrina, small, slight, pressed hard against him during the worst of her fever. He could feel again her consummate embarrassment at his intimate care of her. Although his lust had very nearly overcome his wits, he managed to bring himself to heel. A gentleman didn't discuss a lady of quality in such a way, much less discuss the matter with his mistress. He knew, of course, that it wasn't Martine's fault this had happened. It was his.

"No more, Martine, no more. Just this. Yes, just this." He wrapped his fingers in her short fair curls and pulled her mouth down to his.

24

Dambler wasn't happy when he admitted his master at near dawn the following morning. He trailed after him up the wide staircase of Derencourt House. He knew very well what his master had been doing. He'd ceased being envious years ago. He was now happily sour about the entire business, a benefit of getting old. One of the very few. He sniffed. His master smelled of sex and brandy. More of the former than the latter.

"Don't you preach at me," Phillip said over his shoulder, thinking that at any minute Dambler would tread upon his heels.

Dambler didn't say a word. When he reached his bedchamber, Phillip tried his best to get off his rumpled clothing. His fingers didn't seem to want to work together.

"The nighttime, my lord, is for sleeping and not for carrying on," Dambler said as he helped his master undress.

"It's only for sleeping if you're old, Dambler, and you well know it. I remember my father telling me what a wild young man you were. You're just jealous now."

"I don't think so, my lord."

Phillip grunted. He couldn't imagine a man not being jealous. He slid in between the sheets. They were cold. He wanted to complain about it, but he was too sleepy.

"On the other hand, anything is possible," Dambler said. "I will think about this. I was just congratulating myself on enjoying one of the benefits of approaching my autumn years, that is, I don't have to bed a woman every night."

"Two women, if possible."

"As you say. I don't remember. Well, at best they're fleeting memories that sting only for a very brief instant."

"You sound like you're about to weep. Forget autumn years, Dambler. Go find yourself a laughing lady. But first, go to bed and don't wake me up unless the house is on fire or you feel a bout of apoplexy coming on. I didn't ask you to wait up for me, curse you."

"What would her ladyship say?" Dambler said as he blew out the candles.

"Since my mother passed to the hereafter some four years ago, I fear contact would prove difficult, even for you. Go to bed, Dambler. But you know, my mother was quite a bold wench in her heyday, all flash and good sport. Blood will tell, thank the good Lord."

He heard a low buzzing sound from Dambler and closed his eyes. He found himself wondering what his valet would say if he were to see Martine in all her natural glory. Apoplexy, he thought, very probably it would result in apoplexy.

Dambler said from the door of the bedchamber, "Do you have any activities planned for the evening, my lord?"

"I have just finished the evening, thank you. Go to bed."

"The next evening, my lord."

Phillip suddenly cursed. "Yes, I forgot. It's off to

that sacred boring Almack's, to play St. George again, not that it will do any good."

"A noble gentleman, St. George, my lord."

"If he was anything like me, then he was a bloody fool."

Miss Teresa Elliott, her arm placed gracefully upon her brother Wilfred's sleeve, glided toward the patronesses across the main hall at Almack's, where they were sitting on a dais, holding court.

"Old besoms," Wilfred said in his sister's ear as his myopic gaze took in the three ladies seated close together in their stiff-backed gilded chairs. "I'd rather face a hanging judge. If you hadn't worn Mama out with all those balls of yours and whatever else it is you do—"

"Be quiet, Wilfred. It won't hurt you to be away from your wretched books for one evening, and I must have an escort, you know that."

"Find yourself a husband, Teresa. Maybe you will snag some poor wretch who will be willing to let you diddle him about."

She gave him a loathsome, self-satisfied smile that made her brother want to smack her.

"For your information, I've decided upon one of the most eligible bachelors in London."

"And just who might the poor devil be?" Wilfred looked down at her classic profile and didn't appreciate it one bit.

"It's highly unlikely that he will attend this evening, for it's known he finds Almack's a bore. However, I expect he will come about, once we're married."

"Who is this weak-willed ass?"

She pinched his arm, no more, because the Duchess of Wigan was smiling toward her.

"You've smiled quite enough, Teresa. Now, who is this paragon you've set your sights on?"

"I doubt he would even give you a nod. He is too magnificent, too sporting—"

"Please stop. He's one of those useless men who do nothing except drink brandy, visit their mistresses, and race their horses."

"I'll have you know, you dunce, that it's Viscount Derencourt."

"Phillip Mercerault?"

"Yes," she said, ignoring the incredulity in his voice. "If you ever bothered to pull your nose from your infernal studies, you would know that I have ridden in the park with him and, indeed, was at Moreland with him before Christmas." That visit, however, hadn't lived up to her expectations. "If it hadn't been for that stupid girl who interfered, I know, I just know he would have—"

"I thought you said Phillip Mercerault never came to Almack's."

"He doesn't, more's the pity, for I look very fine tonight and—" She followed his pointed stare. She felt herself flush. "Good heavens, he must have found out that I would be here this evening. How clever and romantic of him to surprise me." She tugged at her brother's sleeve. "You'll be polite, Will, or I will make your tutor fall in love with me."

He wanted to say something to put her in her place, but he imagined that she could make his tutor, the hapless Mr. James, fall so deeply in love that he wouldn't be able to dig himself out. "I'll be all that's civil."

"Oh, dear, we've got to greet Lady Jersey and the Countess Lieven, and that cold Mrs. Drummond Burrell first."

"I'd rather go to Newgate."

Delicate color suffused Teresa's cheeks in her excitement as she greeted the patronesses. Wilfred, thank the Lord, was able to speak a civil sentence, which was all that was necessary from him.

"Pretty girl," Countess Lieven said behind her fan to Sally Jersey as Teresa and Wilfred drifted away. "She has nice manners. She dresses nicely too."

Sally Jersey gave her a superior smile, a malicious smile, truth be told. "Perhaps Miss Teresa Elliott's perfect manners will fall off a cliff when she meets the newest addition to the young misses making their coming-out this year. Indeed," she added thoughtfully, "it would appear that Sabrina Eversleigh has already made a notable conquest. Phillip Mercerault asked my permission to lead her in a waltz."

Mrs. Drummond Burrell, who had given no impression of even having attended to the ladies' conversation, turned her cold eyes to Lady Jersey and said, "It would appear to me that the viscount will shortly find himself caught between two ladies. The man has great charm. It will prove interesting to see how well he manages to extricate himself from this encounter."

Teresa dragged Wilfred toward the viscount, pausing to give only cursory greeting to a young gentleman who seemed more than willing to take Wilfred's place at her side.

She was within five feet of her goal when the viscount turned away to speak to a small, red-haired girl who was standing next to Lady Barresford. In the next moment he was leading her to the dance floor. Teresa stopped dead in her tracks. "How dare he do this to me? He must have seen me, I know that he did. Who is that miserable girl he's with? Oh, he will hear about this."

Wilfred, who'd expected to be bored silly, changed his mind in that instant. He looked at his sister's furious face, and drawled in a voice designed to make her explode into flame, "It looks to me like that little beauty has taken your viscount. Right from under your nose. Isn't she a lovely girl? Beautiful hair, titian, I'd call it. Looks innocent and sweet. Somehow I don't think that's your future husband, sister. I wonder if she'd dance with me. Do you think she might?"

"Shut up or I'll tell Mama. I know what it is. He's being polite, nothing more. Come, Will, I must pay my respects to Lady Barresford."

At that moment Lady Barresford lowered her turbaned head to hear something Lucilla Morton was saying. It would be unforgivable to break in. Teresa cursed under her breath.

She looked toward Phillip and the girl he was waltzing with, and saw him throw back his head and laugh at something the skinny twit said. Without warning, she grabbed Wilfred's arm.

"You're going to dance with me, Will. Don't complain and don't you dare step on my toes. These slippers are new and very white."

Phillip whirled Sabrina in a wide circle toward the periphery of the dance floor. She was breathless and laughing. "So what do you think of Almack's?" he asked, smiling down at her.

She smiled back. "This is wonderful. I love the waltz and you are so very good at it, better than the dancing master. He kept counting out loud and his hands were sweaty. Do you come here often, Phillip?"

"Rarely. Usually it's a bore."

"I hope you haven't put yourself out on my account."

"Oh no. Haven't you been told that I'm a thoroughly selfish creature? That I never put myself out on anyone's account? It's true, most of the time. I normally do exactly as I wish." Except where you are concerned, Sabrina, he finished silently to himself. She appeared to have forgotten their rather dazzling fight of the night before. He wondered if she was coming to her senses. No, little chance of that. There was no reason at all for her to change her view of society.

"You're breathing hard, Sabrina. Let's rest here a moment. I don't want you to overdo."

"I wouldn't want to bore you, my lord."

"I'll tell you if I feel a bout of boredom overcoming me."

Her violet eyes widened at his gentle thrust, which was, in truth, a mild jest. Let her growl, he thought, just once let her growl at him.

He smiled down at her and stoked the flames. "That's right, Sabrina. A little temper can't hurt. Richard spoke of your being as vivid as life itself. I wouldn't argue if you decided to impress me in the same way."

Before she could answer, the band began another waltz. He tightened his hand about her waist and whirled her about the perimeter of the dancing floor, in wide, dipping circles. She was panting breathlessly and laughing. The room was warm, the candlelight twinkled like a thousand prisms, and she could hear laughter all around her. She felt wonderful. Phillip drew her just a bit closer and slowed down.

"Please don't stop, Phillip. I love the way you whirl me around." He thought that if he released her, she'd hug herself in joy, that or simply keep waltzing by herself. He was charmed.

"You were wrong, you know. Just look around you. Everyone is happy and dancing and laughing. Almack's isn't a bore. And everyone is being so kind. My aunt even told me that the last person Mrs. Drummond Burrell smiled at was a hussar in uniform at the turn of the century. She smiled at me, Phillip. Well, nearly smiled. She showed her teeth, which, Aunt assured me, was well nigh a miracle."

He just shook his head and whirled her about again in the large circles she so much loved. When he slowed again, he said, "I must agree. This is a delightful evening. You dance rather well, I might add, for a merchant's relative."

"All the gentlemen I've danced with this evening have agreed with you." She looked up at him through her lashes. She was jesting with him. Perhaps even flirting, just a bit. He was enchanted.

"For a merchant's relative, you also dress well. I like your aunt's choice of the pale amber. The Italian crepe is exquisite."

"I selected it, not my aunt. How do you know this is Italian crepe? I didn't think any gentleman knew of such things."

"A man who is to enjoy a certain success with ladies must be a master of many things. If you like, I can take you to a small milliner's shop just off Bond Street. I can think of several charming bonnets that should set off your coloring to perfection."

She didn't know whether to be furious or to laugh, and he saw it clearly. He arched an eyebrow, saying, "Well, which will it be?"

"When I make up my mind I will tell you. But I do know that if I laugh, it will just encourage you."

"Probably so." He felt her fingertips tapping on his shoulder and thought, a slight smile on his lips, of his previous night with Martine. He whirled her about until she was panting. Just before the waltz ended, Phillip lowered his chin to the thick coronet of braids atop her head and said in a pensive voice, "I wish you would allow me to be the second St. George. You are a damsel in distress, Sabrina. It's true, you know, and nothing you want to believe will change it. Won't you reconsider?"

"I would never repay you by asking you to give up your life. Besides, just look around. Everyone likes me, Phillip. St. George really isn't necessary."

He just sighed. Then the orchestra struck up another waltz and he whirled her toward the middle of the dance floor.

"A third waltz. How very kind you are. I do so enjoy it."

If only you understood what a third waltz means, he thought, his laughing smile firmly in place.

25

He saw the avid curiosity in everyone's eyes. This was their third waltz. A second waltz was as good as an announcement in the *Gazette*. A third, and they were as good as married in the eyes of society. He'd been right that Sabrina, in her ignorance of London rules, was sublimely unaware that three waltzes as good as put a wedding ring on her finger. He refused to feel guilty about it. Let her aunt Barresford deal with it.

After some moments, he said, "I must leave London for several days, to go to my home near Oxford. I shall be back no later than Monday. Would you like to ride in the park with me when I return?"

"You mean they actually allow merchants' relatives in the park, my lord?"

She was trying not to laugh, and he was pleased. "Since," he said, bland as tepid tea, "you will be in my company, there's no need for you to worry. If anyone says anything about you not belonging, I will speak up and protect you."

She tilted her head back. "I swear that one day, Phillip Mercerault, I will have the last word."

"Since I am eight years your senior and come from clearly superior stock, I truly doubt it is possible, but we will see, won't we?"

"I doubt that," she said, but knew he'd outdone

her. She said, "I know where your home is. However, I know little else about it."

He laughed down at her, his white teeth flashing. So she wanted to know about his home, did she? Well, it would probably be her home, so he willingly said as he slowed their pace, "Have you ever traveled to Oxford, Sabrina?"

She shook her head. "I've heard that it's not as beautiful as the Cotswolds."

"Ah, a pox on you for that remark. It is glorious, actually. My family home is called Dinwitty Manor, a truly abysmal name but the heiress who saved my ancestors' hide demanded, I suppose, that the name be changed, and so it was. She renewed our wealth and fortunately since that time no viscount has been a wastrel. In fact, pleasantly enough, all have been fairly astute in matters of money. Dinwitty Manor has somewhat of a reputation of being rather oddly fashioned."

"Whatever does that mean?"

"Let's just say that all my ancestors had different architectural bents. There were many different styles. I am of a medieval bent, you could say. My father was of a Moorish bent. My grandfather was of a classical bent. It has made for a charming if unusual house."

"It sounds intriguing."

He cocked an eyebrow, lowered his voice, and said, "There is a very nice nursery."

He thought her eyes crossed.

"In addition to a nursery, there is also an exquisite library. The ballroom, my grandfather's addition, is at the back of the house and is fairly dripping with carved cherubs from the ceiling—really quite disconcerting, particularly when one is trying to mind one's steps."

The music came to a halt, and Phillip, curse his

scheming eyes, merely smiled at her and said, "Would you like to dance yet another dance?"

Her eyes were glowing. "Oh, drat. Look, Phillip, my aunt is waving to me. Goodness, she's frowning. Why would she be frowning? I've done absolutely nothing to displease anybody, since I've danced with you, and quite passably, at least according to you."

"I'll take you back to her. It's likely she wants you to meet other gentlemen." He wondered if Lady Barresford would shriek at Sabrina for dancing not two, but three dances with him.

"I suppose you're right. Will you waltz with me again after I've done my duty with the other gentlemen? I do so enjoy it."

"I'm sorry, not tonight. I have another engagement and must leave now."

He returned Sabrina to her aunt, noting well the speculative gleam in that lady's sharp eyes. "My lady. Sabrina, I'll return to London on Monday. We will go riding in the park then."

Sabrina nodded. She felt a stab of disappointment as she watched him make his way to the patronesses to bid them good night.

"It would appear," Mrs. Drummond Burrell said toward the viscount's retreating figure, "that his lordship managed to escape with his hide intact. A pity. I should have liked to see him tested."

"I must say that Miss Elliott doesn't look happy," Lady Jersey said. "Yes, a drama would have been enlivening tonight. A pity."

"At least the girl has the good sense not to dash after him," Countess Lieven said. Like the other two ladies, she'd hoped for just the opposite.

"Oh, dear," Lady Jersey said behind her fan. "Miss Elliott has decided to meet her rival. Oh, how I wish we were closer."

Teresa, a firm smile planted on her mouth, was saying, "Dear Lady Barresford. How delightful to see you again. My mama surely would have sent her best regards if she'd had the faintest notion that I would be speaking to you."

Sabrina turned about at Miss Elliott's words. What an incredibly lovely girl, she thought. She dismissed Phillip from her mind for the moment, promising herself that when she saw him on Monday, she'd flatten his ears. Her aunt had told her what he had done. Three waltzes. However had he managed to keep a straight face? He was trying to compromise her again. Why? She'd released him. He was free. Why didn't he bless her and run as fast as he could?

". . . And this is Wilfred, my brother, my lady."

Wilfred of the dreamy eyes, Sabrina thought. She watched him bow. It was odd how he was eyeing his sister who was now staring at her. There was no smile on her face.

Lady Barresford nodded pleasantly toward the uneasy Wilfred. "Sabrina, this is Teresa Elliott and her brother, Wilfred."

After polite greetings, Teresa said in a voice brimming with gaiety, "Do let me take Sabrina from you for a few minutes, my lady. I should like to get to know her better."

Wilfred opened his mouth to say something, but Teresa said quickly, "Why don't you dance with Miss Ainsley, Will. She's standing over there next to that woman who must weigh at least eighteen stone."

Sabrina smiled at the perfectly blank expression on Wilfred's face.

"But I don't—"

"Yes, you do," Teresa said firmly, and actually shoved him in Miss Ainsley's direction.

Teresa turned back to Sabrina. "Don't keep my

niece too long, Miss Elliott, for there are many other gentlemen she needs to meet."

"Certainly not," Teresa said and took Sabrina's arm. Her hold was strong.

"You're new to London," she said, sitting very close to the interloper on a small settee just behind a palm tree.

"Yes, I have been with my aunt but a week."

"I saw you dancing with Viscount Derencourt, Miss Barresford."

"My name is Eversleigh."

"Ah yes, Miss Eversleigh. Was dear Phillip giving you lessons?"

"Well, no, actually, I love to waltz and he is so very good at it."

"I don't suppose you realized that three waltzes will make everyone question your good sense? Your sense of propriety?"

Sabrina, who had been openly admiring this lovely girl, now wondered what was going on here. "No, I didn't realize it. Phillip was playing a jest on me."

"You call him Phillip? How long have you known the viscount, Miss Eversleigh?"

"Not very long. But he's a good friend."

"A good friend doesn't play fast and loose with a girl's reputation."

The good friend does if he wants the girl to marry him, Sabrina wanted to say, but didn't.

Teresa's eyes widened as memory suddenly fell into place. "Eversleigh, did you say?" Her heart began to pound. It couldn't be, no, she couldn't be that lucky. She cleared her throat. She had to tread carefully. "I don't suppose that you just arrived from Yorkshire, Miss Eversleigh?"

"Yes, my home is in Yorkshire, near Leeds." What was going on here? Why did this beautiful young lady care if she was from Yorkshire? Or from Africa, for that matter?

Miss Elliott's nostrils flared. She felt her heart begin to sing as she said, "Then you are, naturally, very well acquainted with Vicount Derencourt."

There was danger in the air and Sabrina smelled it. She realized that Miss Elliott was jealous because she wanted Phillip. That was why she wanted to know all about Sabrina. But then she saw that the young lady's eyes were slitted and mean, her lips tight. She wasn't stupid. The last place she wanted to be was here, with this beautiful young lady who looked ready to stick a knife in her ribs. She rose quickly. "I must return to my aunt, Miss Elliott. It was a pleasure to meet you and your brother. I was very ill and still tire quite quickly."

"You tire easily, Miss Eversleigh? I should imagine so, given how you spent that week you were supposedly ill. But you weren't at all ill, were you? No, you met the viscount at Charles's hunting box and you quite enjoyed yourself. I am only surprised that the viscount will still even speak to you. Surely he got his fill of you during that week."

She knew, Sabrina thought. She knew and she was going to use her knowledge to bury her. "Perhaps you'd best explain yourself, Miss Elliott. You're acting jealous and it ruins your looks, you know."

"Jealous, Miss Eversleigh? I assure you I am not. Come, you don't have to play innocent with me. I know who you are. I know all about you. Tell me, how many lies did you feed your aunt so that she would introduce you into society?"

"There is no reason for you to behave in such an ill-bred manner, Miss Elliott. There is no reason for you to attack me just because you want Phillip. You may have Phillip. As I said, he is a friend, nothing more. You are welcome to him. However, if he has a brain, he will see the spite in you and run in the other direction. You aren't at all nice, Miss Elliott."

Teresa jumped to her feet, shaking her fist in Sabrina's face. "You vulgar little slut. If Phillip is but a friend, then what would you term your cousin, Trevor Eversleigh?"

It didn't occur to Sabrina to wonder how Miss Elliott knew about Trevor. She knew and that was all that mattered. Phillip had been right. She'd been a fool. Her new life of one week was about to crumble into dust.

Teresa saw the color drain from Sabrina's face. She wanted to shout and dance. She had the little slut, she had her but good. "I was a guest at Moreland. Ah yes, I see that you won't even attempt to deny it. The gentlemen were in quite a fix, I assure you, trying to figure out what was to be done with you. Did you enjoy your five days with Phillip? I've heard that he is kindness itself to his discarded mistresses. And that, you little bitch, is why he bothered to dance with you."

Miss Elliott was just one person. She was jealous. That was why she wanted to kill Sabrina, to kick her dead body. Surely all of society wasn't like Teresa Elliott. She heard Miss Elliott continuing to speak, as if from a great distance. "Did you intend to continue your wanton behavior in London? Everyone at Moreland was appalled that a girl of good family would seduce her own cousin, and her sister's husband at that, then spend nearly a week with Phillip Mercerault."

Sabrina remembered her words to Phillip about making the world change. As she gazed into Miss Elliott's gloating face, she realized she'd been grossly wrong. Society would not change its rules for her; she was nothing better than an outcast. She threw back her head and said, "It's ridiculous that I should try to defend myself to the likes of you, Miss Elliott. You're a vicious, jealous girl. I pity you."

"I need no pity from a harlot."

Sabrina turned on her heel and made her way slowly back to her aunt. Perhaps she should have tried to reason with Miss Elliott, explained everything to her. But she knew it would have done no good. If she didn't have pride, she would have nothing. She wondered, almost dispassionately, what would happen to her now.

26

Sabrina stood quietly beside a window in the small drawing room of her suite at the Cavendish Hotel, looking over the tops of red and gray brick buildings toward Bond Street. Although the window was tightly closed against the winter wind, it made her feel less lonely if she fancied she could hear the people on the street below speaking to each other as they passed by her window, carrying on civil conversations about whatever it was people discussed when they were not alone. But their conversations would be civil. They would be friendly to one another.

She turned away from the window. She heard Hickles, her newly acquired maid, moving about in the next room. At least she was not completely alone, although it was difficult to count Hickles as anything remotely resembling a confidante. Sabrina grimaced as she pictured her maid, an obese older spinster who contrived to look somehow disapproving even when she smiled, a rare event during the past three days. But she couldn't afford to be choosy.

She chewed on her thumbnail. Things could be worse. At least she wasn't destitute. When she'd paid her visit to Hoare's Bank to secure her own inheritance, she knew it was on the tongue of every male employed there to tell her to hie herself to a drawing room and serve tea, as she was supposed to do. But she'd just kept her chin up and insisted, until, finally, she was allowed to see Mr. Boniface, the man responsible. At long last it had been done. Her funds were now in her name and there was nothing her aunt Barresford could do about it, and she knew the lady had tried, for Mr. Boniface had sent a clerk around to tell her of her aunt's machinations.

She sat wearily down in a stiff-backed brocade chair and stared blankly at the wall opposite her. A poorly painted picture of a milkmaid faced her. She smiled now, at herself, a tight little smile that meant nothing, remembering how she had still felt some hope after her disastrous confrontation with Teresa Elliott just five days before. Although her aunt had looked at her rather oddly when she'd pleaded a headache at Almack's, she'd taken her home without questioning her.

How glib she'd been, telling Phillip that she would change the world, insisting that no one would have any reason to hurt her. The very next day she'd learned what it was like to receive cold stares from ladies she'd never seen before in her life, to be ignored by supposed friends of her aunt's. One gentleman she'd met that disastrous evening at Almack's had actually leered at her and rubbed his hands together.

Sabrina's confrontation with her aunt came about that very afternoon. She'd intended to tell her aunt the whole of it, truly she had, but there was Lady Morton waiting for them upon their return, her face sharp with anticipation. Sabrina went to her room, reasoning that she was, after all, the granddaughter of an earl and not some poor relation. Perhaps Aunt Barresford would understand and be able to smooth the matter over with society. She had not long to wait for her aunt's summons to the library.

"Sit down, Sabrina."

Sabrina looked searchingly at her aunt. Her cheeks were a mottled red and her eyes were bright and hard. "Lady Morton has spoken to you?" She spoke very quietly, trying to keep her voice neutral. She glanced about the library, half expecting to see that lady still there, but they were quite alone. A library was a strange name for a room that held only Egyptian furnishings and heavy draperies.

"Can you doubt it?" Lady Barresford asked, her voice harder now, lower.

"Aunt, I can explain all of it. I should have told you last night, but I honestly didn't think anyone would care about what Teresa Elliott had said. I found out differently today. I would have told you, but Lady Morton was here and I gather she couldn't wait to fill your ears. I'm sorry, but please, let me explain."

"Yes, I'm positive you would have told me all of it, yes I certainly am. You would have smiled, I assume, while you confessed your trollop's behavior with Phillip Mercerault in Yorkshire. Lord, first Elizabeth and now you. At least your sister didn't come to my home with her reputation in shreds, hoping to pull the wool over my eyes."

"Aunt, I don't know what Lady Morton told you, but you must let me explain. You must believe that it is all lies, started by that wretched girl Teresa Elliott."

Lady Barresford stood directly in front of her, her hands fisted at her sides, her face very red. "I see. So you deny that you ran away from Monmouth Abbey?"

"No, of course not. I had to. Trevor tried to rape me. I couldn't stay because Elizabeth took his side. He would have come to my bedchamber if I hadn't run away. He would have succeeded."

"Trevor tried to rape you? That's your story. Not a very likely story that, my girl. He's been married to

Elizabeth for only a month. I suppose you'll tell me that you didn't spend five days—alone—with Phillip Mercerault."

"I was ill, very ill. He found me unconscious in the snow in Eppingham Forest. I was on my way to Borhamwood, to the stage. I wanted to come to you. He saved my life. There was nothing more than that, Aunt, you must believe me. I could have been his little sister for all he cared. He did nothing. Believe me, I was so ill I couldn't have done anything. It was Charles Askbridge who made Phillip believe he'd compromised me, but I would have none of it. I did nothing wrong."

Lady Barresford stared down at her in disbelief. "You're trying to tell me that the viscount agreed that he'd compromised you? You're claiming that he made you an offer? That is what you want me to believe now?"

Sabrina said quietly, "Yes, he made me an offer. I refused him. He didn't compromise me. He saved my life. Why should he have to marry me? He did nothing wrong. I did nothing wrong. We didn't even know each other."

"You miserable little liar," Lady Barresford fairly shrieked at her. She waved her fist in Sabrina's face. "No girl would be such a fool as to turn down Viscount Derencourt, much less one who has spent five days alone with him. What you really mean to tell me, isn't it, my girl, is that he offered to take you on as his mistress?"

"No, he couldn't do that. I'm an earl's granddaughter. I'm a lady. I don't understand you, Aunt."

"You seduced him and he offered to let you continue. There's nothing difficult to understand in that. He's a man, a very accomplished, a very handsome, sought-after man. You're a very stupid girl."

"Phillip could never act like that. Why do you insult him and then call him accomplished and handsome? He is those things and he is also very kind. He was very good to me."

Lady Barresford shook her head in disgust. "I'm not insulting him, but to call him kind merely shows what a provincial you are. He has a grand reputation with ladies. He can get any lady he wishes to toss up her skirts for him. He has no interest in marriage. All understand that. He is only twenty-six, after all. There is no way he would offer for you. You're lying and I won't have it." She hit her palm to her forehead. "But when all's said and done, you're still an earl's granddaughter. What in heaven's name am I to do with you now?"

Yet another person to decide what to do with Sabrina Eversleigh, she thought, and stared down at her toes.

"You will go home to Yorkshire," Lady Barresford said with sudden decision. "You will try to be conciliating with Elizabeth and Trevor, for there is your grandfather to think about. You don't want to make him more ill than he is now. Yes, you will be nice, you will be civil, you will apologize. I hope Trevor and Elizabeth will forgive you."

Sabrina raised her eyes to her aunt's face. "I can't go back to Monmouth Abbey, Aunt. Even though you don't wish to believe me, Trevor did try to rape me. I have no doubt that if I were to return unprotected, he would succeed unless I shot him, and I would have to. Then our line would die out since he's the only male heir. As to Elizabeth, I can no longer live in the same house with her. She has changed toward me."

"Do you blame her? You tried to seduce her husband of one month."

"I did not. Why won't you believe me?"

Lady Barresford looked like she wanted to shoot her. "Believe you? That is nonsense. You may well be stupid but I am not, Sabrina. Oh, good Lord, what do you intend to do? You must know that after all that has happened, you can't remain here."

Sabrina rose. "You're wrong, Aunt, about all of it. You won't even consider that I'm telling you the absolute truth. Why? You said I was stupid and it was nonsense, but it wasn't, it's not."

"Don't be ridiculous. Even blind old Mrs. Baggil could see the truth of this. You stayed with Phillip Mercerault for five days. Of course he bedded you."

"Very well. I'll be out of your house as soon as I can pack."

"And just where do you think you are going, miss?"

"I won't be on the streets, if that's what worries you. You forget that the money you have freely been lavishing on the both of us belongs to me. I bid you good-bye, Aunt."

"Miss Sabrina."

Sabrina drew her gaze from the wall to her maid's doughy, satisfied face. She just couldn't bear it another moment. Did every person, regardless of station, know of her disgrace and revel in it? She said, her chin up, "I am Lady Sabrina and that is what you will call me. Do you understand?"

Hickles obviously understood, but it was a trial for her. She was bored. Accepting the lady's position, she'd thought she would see a procession of gentlemen march through her rooms, but so far, nothing. Just the two of them, and the lady was silent and withdrawn. Finally, Hickles nodded. "Lady Sabrina, it's teatime. Would you like me to order it up?"

"Yes, thank you, Hickles." She saw the avid gleam in her maid's eyes, heard the ill-disguised impatience in her tone. How odd it is, she thought, staring after the woman, that even the servants knew of her disgrace. She certainly hadn't said anything. How had Hickles known? Of course, something else Hickles knew very well was that she was the only one to provide Sabrina—an eighteen-year-old-girl—with any respectability at all.

Sabrina watched the clock on the mantelpiece move its arms slowly into evening. She had no desire to leave the Cavendish Hotel for fear that she would meet someone she knew, or more accurately someone who knew her. She thought of the gentleman who had openly ogled her. She wished he were here so she could hit him.

When the clock finished chiming its four strokes, she realized with something of a start that it was Tuesday afternoon. She was to have ridden in the park with Phillip on Monday. She wondered if he'd been delayed at his home and was unaware of what had happened to her.

Phillip had known everything, had warned her again and again, and she'd laughed in his face. She looked at herself in the narrow mirror over the mantelpiece. Her face was a stranger's, set, thin, dark circles beneath her eyes.

"It's been proved," she said to that pathetic stranger in the mirror, "you're a fool. A very stupid fool. A fool who has no future. All you have is a string of days that will stretch out without end into months and then into years." She felt sudden fury at the injustice of it all and smashed her fisted hand into the mirror. The glass shattered and she looked at the blood that was beginning to trickle down her fingers.

Toward midnight, after hours of frustrated thinking, an idea came to her. The world hadn't changed, but she certainly had. She'd nurtured romantic ideas about a future that could no longer be hers, then she'd allowed herself to wallow in self-pity, to act the broken, helpless female.

Yes, finally an idea. She would have to have the resolve to get it done. But she could do it. She knew she could do it. She finally fell into a deep sleep.

Phillip didn't return to London on Monday. He returned from Dinwitty Manor on Saturday, earlier than expected. The fact of the matter was, he had missed her, curse those incredible violet eyes of hers. He couldn't stop thinking about her, wondering what she was doing, wondering if she was finally well and back to her former energy, which he imagined was formidable, hoping she was eating enough, wondering if she would like Cook's offerings here at Dinwitty Manor, and knew she'd swoon at the food here, everyone did.

He'd come back to disaster. He sat now in the library of his town house on Wednesday, staring thoughtfully into space, his fingers wrapped about a folded piece of stationery.

It had taken nearly more determination than he laid claim to not to go to Sabrina as soon as he'd known the full extent of her disgrace. He'd even had Dambler speak to other servants so that he would know everything. It was bad. But he'd stayed put. He guessed that if he'd gone to the Cavendish Hotel on Saturday or even Sunday or Monday, she would have been more furious than reasonable. He could easily imagine her anger, her bitterness, her sense of injustice at what had happened. He'd even wondered if she'd blamed him for being right. Of course she would. The messenger always got the knife in the innards.

He unfolded the note and read it swiftly through once again. At last. He doubted he could have stayed away from her much longer. She had a business matter to discuss with him, did she? At least she still had guts. She'd thought it all through and come up with a solution. He couldn't wait to hear what she had to say. It seemed to him now that he'd done the right thing by not going to her immediately, by offering his services yet again. No, now she was the one to offer. She'd finally come to her senses. He wondered as he allowed Dambler to assist him to dress exactly what she would say to him.

27

On Wednesday at half past four in the afternoon, Viscount Derencourt lightly knocked on the door of the suite of rooms at the Cavendish Hotel. Thank the good Lord she had money. He'd found that out quickly. If she hadn't secured her inheritance, he would have gone to her immediately.

A heavy woman of indeterminate age and frankly vulgar manner admitted him as if he were a prize goose for her dinner.

"I'm Viscount Derencourt. You may announce me to your mistress." He was haughty and cold, guessing that Sabrina had endured more than enough disapproval from this wretched person. There was an avidity in her that truly repelled him. He wondered how she behaved around Sabrina.

"After you've announced me, you may take yourself off." He saw the woman's slack-jawed disappointment before she turned and led him into a small drawing room.

"Lady Sabrina, Viscount Derencourt is here to see you."

Although Sabrina had dressed herself with care, Phillip was appalled at her appearance. Her face was pale and drawn and she looked at him as if she fully expected him to denounce her, just as everyone else had.

"My lord, I'm delighted you could come," she said with such fear he wanted to simply take her in his arms and tell her never to worry about another thing for as long as she lived. But he couldn't. She had a business proposition for him. He would play by the rules she'd set. He didn't move. He watched her turn to the officious maid. "Hickles, you may go now. Do dress warmly, for it is quite chilly outside."

Phillip shrugged out of his greatcoat and gloves. As Sabrina took them, he said, "What did you do to your hand? Hold still, let me see."

"It's nothing," she said and whipped her bandaged hand behind her. "Thank you for coming, my lord. Will you please be seated?"

"No, I first want to see what you did to your hand. Who bandaged it? A blind beggar?"

"No, I did. It was difficult to bandage it well with just one hand. I cut it on a mirror. It isn't important. It doesn't hurt at all."

But he just stood there, his hands out. Finally, with a snort, she brought up her hand. He unwrapped the bandage and laid the cut bare. "It's not too bad," he said finally, "but I want to pour some brandy on it, just to make sure it's really clean. Do you have anything of that sort here?"

She nodded and turned away to the sideboard. The brandy was probably very cheap, but as medicine it surely wouldn't matter.

"Come here," he said, and walked to the window. He opened it, then held her hand outside. He poured the brandy over her hand. She didn't even jerk or moan. Fortunately there was no one walking below at that particular moment.

"Now, let me bandage this right. Did that hurt?"

Her hand was burning like it was on fire, but she shook her head. He wrapped her own bandage very carefully around her hand, then knotted it. "There, how does that feel?"

"It's fine, thank you."

"Would you like to tell me how you did it?"

"No. I was simply clumsy. Really, it's not important. Please, my lord."

He nodded and sat down. He steepled his fingers and smiled at her.

"Would you care for tea?"

"No. I daresay that conversation is what I would like most of all right at this moment."

"Very well." She sat down opposite him. She was calm, seemingly in excellent control of herself. She was behaving quite well. If he showed her his concern, she would likely think that he was pitying her, and that, he knew, she would never accept.

She didn't say anything, just stared at him. To get her started, he said, "I received your note, Sabrina. You wrote that you have a business matter to discuss with me?"

"Yes, I do," she said finally, staring at a point just behind his left shoulder. "I suppose you know why I'm here."

"Oh, yes," he said easily. "I returned to London last Saturday. I must say that you're quite the talk. The stories have gotten so extraordinary that neither you nor I could be considered just ordinary human beings. My prowess alone must make every man in London gnash his teeth in envy."

She stared at him, in his face now. "You returned on Saturday? You knew what had happened and you did nothing? It's Wednesday. Wednesday!"

"Yes, that's true. Now, what is your business matter?"

She rose and drew herself up ramrod stiff. "You're right, my lord—"

"Phillip."

"Well, yes, you are Phillip. You were right about everything. I find that I'm disgraced, all because of one lady, Miss Teresa Elliott, who, I believe, wants you for herself. Even though I told her that she could have you, with my blessing, it didn't matter. As you said, my lord, it would take but one vicious tongue and the damage would be done. My aunt, unfortunately, was not at all inclined to take my part in the matter; indeed, she believed everything anyone told her. She wanted me to return to Monmouth Abbey. You know I couldn't do that, so I left her house."

"I won't waste your time reminding you that I told you this would happen."

"Thank you. I appreciate your restraint."

He just smiled at her. "Yes. And this famous business matter of yours?"

"I've thought about this a lot. I've never been without friends nor so much alone in my life, and I don't want to continue in this way. It's very difficult. It's perhaps even more than difficult. It's damning. I can't continue to do it."

He could well imagine. So even marriage to him was preferable, he thought, without too much pain to his own vanity. It had cost her a great deal to admit this, particularly to him.

"So you are lonely and alone. You don't like it. So what is it you want to do, Sabrina?"

"I want to make you an offer. I want you to marry me. It's an honorable offer, Phillip. If you agree, you can have my remaining nine thousand five hundred and fifty pounds and my dowry. I have no idea how large it is, but it is probably sizable. The reason the ten thousand pounds isn't intact is because my aunt Barresford dipped quite liberally into my funds, for both of us."

"You're doubtless an heiress, Sabrina. Probably as much of an heiress as the Dinwitty lady back in the last century. That in itself makes this a very tempting business offer. Now, let me understand you. If I marry you, you will turn all your fortune over to me?"

She hated the sound of it, hated giving away her independence. She'd only had it for five days. He sounded indifferent, as if they were counting sheep or turnips, as if it weren't about marriage and about her future and saving her. "Yes," she said, forcing herself to keep calm, matter-of-fact. "In addition to all my money, well, I have given this a lot of thought." She cleared her throat. It wouldn't be so difficult to say once it was out of her mouth. "I will also offer you your freedom. You're young for a man, which I don't understand since you're eight years older than I am, but you're considered younger than I for marriage purposes. In any case, you are not through spreading yourself throughout all the ladies of London. You may continue to spread yourself to the extent you wish to do so. My aunt told me that you'd never willingly wed as yet, because of all the still available ladies that you'd want to enjoy. Thus I knew I would have to make my offer worth your while."

"Ah, I understand now. You're offering me my freedom, without any interference from you."

"Yes."

Phillip laughed, he couldn't help himself. "I already have my freedom, Sabrina. Marriage doesn't curtail a man's freedom unless he's a fool. Isn't there something else besides all your funds to interest me?"

She looked away, unwilling to let him see how his careless words sliced into her. She said barely above a whisper, "You can also have me if that is of any interest to you. But I'm sure you already know that I'm young and ignorant and really not at all toothsome. I'm probably nothing close to the ladies you can choose from. But there it is. I have nothing else, other than my mare, who is at Monmouth Abbey, and she's lame."

"A mare is something, even a lame one."

She raised her head at that and he saw the beginnings of outrage. Excellent. "I am something as well."

"Yes, I suppose you are. Now, in addition to my freedom, which I already have, my part in all these machinations is to save you from disgrace. Give you the protection of my name."

"That's right." It sounded pathetic put that way. She was pathetic. There was no way around that. She waited to see what he'd say. She'd never hated anything quite so much in her life, except, of course, being at Trevor's mercy.

He rose and extended his hand. She gave him hers and he shook it. "I will accept your offer, Sabrina."

For a moment he thought she would faint with relief. Then color flooded her face, healthy color. He looked into that thin vivid face of hers, into those incredible eyes. "I seem to recall you saying that you wouldn't marry where there is no love."

She wanted to strike him, but she knew she couldn't. She was the supplicant. But she was furious and he knew she was furious and she was certain he mocked her. "You're not stupid," she said. "Everything has changed. My former life is gone. Actually, here I'm going to marry you and I don't even like you at this moment." And then the bitterness flowed out of her mouth. She simply couldn't help it. "I can't believe it! You're still wonderful, greeted warmly by both men and women, invited everywhere. You're not seen as morally bankrupt, but I am. It's not fair!"

"That's true. I've never understood it myself, but that's the way things work. I told you once that I knew this jungle very well and that you didn't. Play by the rules, Sabrina, and you'll survive this. You've already asked me to marry you. Marrying me was rule number one. You see, you're already learning."

He sat back down in his chair and stretched his long legs out in front of him. He leaned back, lacing his fingers behind his head.

"I will learn all your damnable rules. Now, would you care for more tea?"

Phillip sat forward suddenly and tapped his fingertips together. "Tell me, Sabrina, do you really offer yourself to me as well as your money and your horse?"

Her hand shook. He saw it and she cursed. He heard that and smiled. "If I must," she said at last. "But it's true, what I said. I'm not beautiful, I'm skinny, and I don't know anything. If you weren't disgusted with me, then you'd laugh."

"I see. Now, you offered me my freedom—"

"Yes."

"A freedom I already have. Now my question is do you intend to take a lover?"

She turned as white as the walls. "Oh no, that's repellent! After Trevor—oh no, never."

"But you've offered me your own precious self. Will you be able to survive it if I lay my hands on you?"

She looked at her feet. "I don't know. I also don't know what's involved in this mating business. From my experience with Trevor, I never want to have anything to do with any of it."

"What if I told you that it's not that bad at all? That, given the right man, you just may find you like lovemaking."

"No, at least I can't imagine enjoying it right now. I'll do my duty. I promised. Yes, I told you that you could have me if you wished. I will keep to my end of the bargain."

"That sounds just dandy," Phillip said, and pictured Sabrina lying still as a statue on the bed with him panting over her. It was an awful vision. Still, he knew what had happened to her. He'd been a bastard even to bring up the matter. She was terrified of men, and no wonder.

He rose and placed his hand on her shoulder. She stiffened. He wasn't surprised, but something inside him tightened, just a bit.

"Sabrina," he said, his voice gentle as a soft summer rain, "I'm sorry to frighten you. It wasn't well done of me. You're safe from me, I swear it to you. I will never force you to do anything that frightens or repels you. I'm happy to accept your offer. I will try to make you a good husband." He paused a moment and lightly flicked his finger over her cheek. "We will do well together, you'll see. Now, there is much to be done."

She looked up at him, her expression grave. "Is there a chance that my shame will bring you disgrace?"

"No. Most people will think that I've done the right thing. Trust me to see that no one will ever hurt you again. Will you?"

"My money is sufficient for you to make the sacrifice?"

"More than sufficient. However, if I ever find myself reduced to living in a ditch, why, I'll just strangle you and find myself another heiress."

He was kind. She was relieved. Indeed, she found the remnant of a smile. "I don't want you to live in a ditch. I will school myself to practice the most stringent economies."

He pulled her to her feet and lightly kissed her brow. "I'll teach you how to make viscount's bread."

"Our first economy," she said and let him draw her against his chest. For a moment she rested her cheek against his shoulder. She was no longer afraid. "I'll try to make you a good wife, Phillip, I swear it."

He gave a low, deep laugh, then hugged her tightly. "A good wife. Now that is an appalling thought."

28

Phillip stood by the mantelpiece in the library of his town house. He looked first at Charles Askbridge and then at Rohan Carrington.

"I believe that's the whole of it. Charlie, can you think of anything else to help Rohan get the full picture of this wretched debacle?"

"No, but I don't mind telling you I'm more relieved than I can say that Sabrina has finally come to her senses."

Rohan Carrington, Baron Mountvale, was shaking his head. "This makes my belly cramp, Phillip. Oh, I know it isn't all that unusual, but to actually hear firsthand how a supposedly honorable man tried to rape an innocent girl under his protection. I really would prefer to kill him. If I were the old earl, I wouldn't want that man's blood in my future generations."

Phillip nodded. "All of us would like to kill him, but it comes down to preserving the line. The rotter is the next earl, curse his miserable hide, bad blood and all."

Charles said, "At least Phillip has ensured that Trevor and Elizabeth will tell no more lies about Sabrina."

"I still would like to kill him. So would Susannah,"

Rohan added, picturing his wife of six months in his mind's eye and her rage upon hearing this.

Phillip said, "My God, the fellow will be my brother-in-law. How's that for a fist in the face?"

Rohan Carrington said, "What do you want us to do, Phillip?"

"I need you to be your most autocratic and persuasive, Rohan. Do you think we can pull it off?"

"Oh yes," Rohan said, sipping his brandy. "There's but one problem I see looming and that is the aunt, Lady Barresford. If she can be brought around to see reason, then I daresay we shouldn't have much difficulty with the rest of society. It's the relatives that always cause the most problems. It's a pity my mother isn't here. She could deal with Lady Barresford and still have enough energy to waltz the entire night."

"Ah no, Rohan, leave that lady to me." He actually rubbed his hands together. "Oh yes, I want the privilege of dealing with that one. Not only will she reinstate Sabrina in her good graces for all society to see, she will also hold the private ceremony at her home. The wedding festivities will, of course, be held here."

"How much time do we have?" Charles asked.

"I want the ring on her finger by Saturday afternoon. In short, gentlemen, we have four days." Actually, what Phillip wanted more than anything was to see Sabrina smile.

"This is close to a miracle you're asking for," Charles said.

"That's right," Phillip said and grinned at them. "Why do you think I got the two of you over here? Well, shall we take on the world?"

Rohan raised his glass. "To your imminent demise as a bachelor. It's not bad, Phillip, trust me. Susannah's my very best friend. Actually, truth be told, I really can't imagine how I got along without her."

"I'll remain a bachelor," Charles said. He drank down the rest of his brandy. "It's a challenge to while away the winter hours. Very well, Phillip. I'm off to White's to begin working my magic."

"And I," Rohan said, shaking Phillip's hand, "am off to see my dearest friend, Lady Sally Jersey."

"Thank you both," Phillip said. "Really, thank you."

After Rohan Carrington took his leave, Charles said, "What do you intend to do about Teresa Elliott? It is she, you know, who brought the whole thing about in the first place."

Phillip shrugged. "If it hadn't been Teresa, it would have been someone else."

"Teresa wanted you. What if she treats Sabrina badly?"

"Why, I'll ruin her."

Charles nodded. He believed him.

"Besides, Charles, after we get this damned wedding over with and Sabrina has a chance to settle down, Teresa Elliott will discover quickly that she's no match at all for Viscountess Derencourt."

The following morning, after fortifying himself with two strong cups of Spanish coffee and a haunch of rare sirloin, Phillip drove his curricle to the Barresford town house. Although the day was overcast, he was in good spirits; indeed, he was looking forward to his meeting with Lady Barresford. He jumped lightly from his curricle, tossed the reins to his tiger, Lanscombe, and walked up the wide front steps.

"I shall announce myself," he said to the butler. He heard the man groan as he made his way to the Barresford drawing room on the second floor. He wasn't at all surprised that the butler knew exactly who he was. He doubtless knew everything, like every servant in London.

"Good morning, ma'am," he said in an obnoxiously cheerful voice as he walked into the drawing room.

Lady Barresford was on her feet in a surprisingly short amount of time, given her bulk. "My lord. What are you doing here?"

He saw the pen and stationery spread on the small writing table. He wondered how many letters she'd already written, bemoaning her betrayal by her immoral niece. His smile never slipped.

"I hope you'll forgive me visiting at such an early hour, ma'am. However, you already seem to be quite busy writing letters. Now I can provide you with good news to write."

"You will leave, my lord. I have nothing at all to say to you." She took a step toward him and waved her fat hands toward the door. "I imagine you're here to plead for Sabrina, but it will do you no good. I will never speak to her again. Leave, if you please."

He eyed her with a joyful expression. "Surely, ma'am, you would like to visit for a little while with your future nephew-in-law?"

Lady Barresford slowly lowered her hand. She stared at him. "I don't believe you. You haven't offered for her, it's impossible. No gentleman would, at least not now, now that it's known what she is, and everyone has had the opportunity to chew it over for a week."

"Not so impossible. I've offered for Sabrina several times, ma'am. I suppose I must thank you. If you hadn't treated her so badly I doubt she would have ever accepted my offer."

"You wouldn't dare call my behavior into question, my lord."

"What I would say, ma'am, is that my future wife

doesn't appear to be blessed with relatives who care for her, protect her, and, naturally, take her side. However, I'm more concerned now with society's behavior. I think that we can, together, turn off most of the gossip. Within a month there will be a new and more diverting scandal that will make everyone forget everything."

Lady Barresford's mighty bosom was heaving. She was angry and she allowed her anger full rein. "That little creature is a disgrace to the Eversleighs and to the Barresfords. Lies she told me, all lies. Who could believe such absurd tales as she told?"

"Anyone who knows her even slightly would believe her. She doesn't lie. However, it's immaterial to me whether or not you believe her or me. What is important, however, is her acceptance by society, as my wife."

Lady Barresford said with a good deal of satisfaction, "No one with any decency will ever recognize her again. As for you, my lord, were I you, I should seriously wonder how many men she's been with before you marry her."

Phillip pictured her wrinkled throat between his hands. But telling her what he thought of her wasn't the best approach. He would save that for a special treat at a future date. But his voice was very hard as he said, "Listen to me, ma'am, I have had enough of your tiresome venom. You're speaking of your niece and my betrothed. You will now oblige me by sitting down and listening to what I have to say."

Lady Barresford didn't want to sit. She wanted to rant, to tell him how Sabrina had deceived her, but the viscount looked determined. It occurred to her then that perhaps it would be better if Sabrina could be rehabilitated. Surely it would reflect on her if Sabrina was tossed out of London. She sat down.

"Here is what's going to happen, ma'am. Sabrina and I will be married here in a small ceremony on Saturday. I will return her to you tomorrow and you will treat her with the respect she deserves."

"Let her back into my house? That's ridiculous. Why, look at all the little wretch has done to me! If my reputation weren't so excellent, her actions could have brought me low."

Phillip wanted to strangle her, but he smiled instead. "In short, ma'am, we could have a scandal that perhaps could touch you, bring you low, just as you said. Would it not be preferable to scotch all gossip now? Can you think of a better solution than to have Sabrina safely wed to me? I assure you that my friends are at this moment putting a stop to most of the gossip-mongering. You won't have to fear for your position in society, ma'am, if you give in now.

"However, let me add, that if forced, I would make a formidable enemy, as would my friends." He'd spoken so very quietly that it took her a moment to take in what he'd said.

She rose and took several stalking steps about the room. "You don't understand, young man. My friends are already well aware of my feelings. They sympathize with me. They have commingled their tears with mine. They would continue to sympathize. They would stick by me. They would continue to hold me in high esteem."

Both of them knew, naturally, that a true friend was as scarce as a sunny day in January and that the likelihood was that her dear friends were probably sniggering behind their hands, just out of her hearing. "Why don't you do this: inform your friends that new facts have come to light and your niece is quite innocent. Indeed, she has been much maligned, and you, because you are her aunt and a fair and just woman, wish to be the first to right all the wrongs done to her. This should start a fresh spate of tears among your friends, don't you think?"

"But a wedding on Saturday, it's impossible."

"It can be done. Do you agree?"

He thought he heard her curse under her breath. He merely waited. He looked down at his fingernails. Finally, she said, "Very well, I will do it, but it won't be easy. If she isn't accepted, you will have no one to blame but yourself."

"She will be accepted. I count on your striving your best to see that it happens. Now, would you like to have my secretary's services?"

She shook her head absently, and Phillip knew that she was already planning the necessary arrangements. He nodded. "I'll bring Sabrina to you tomorrow morning. Remember, if her two days with you aren't pleasant, you will answer to me. Ah, when circumstances dictate, ma'am, I can be a formidable enemy. Please don't forget that."

As he turned to take his leave, Lady Barresford said, "I hope you won't regret your chivalry, my lord."

He merely nodded. She stared at him a moment, then said, "What makes you so certain that the girl is telling the truth about Trevor?"

"I know Sabrina. I might also add that I've made the acquaintance of Trevor Eversleigh. I fear for the future of the Eversleigh name. He brings new meaning to the word *revolting*. Please don't forget that Sabrina is now in my care. I bid you good day, my lady."

29

"No one would ever believe you were a bride if it weren't for that expensive gown the viscount provided for you."

Sabrina turned away from the mirror. She looked worse than she had just the day before. "Phillip didn't buy the gown, Aunt, I did."

"It's all one and the same for you now," Lady Barresford said, fingering her own exquisitely fashioned silk gown. "The moment the vicar says you're his wife, you won't have a farthing. Since your dear grandfather is still too ill to be approached in the matter, I, of course, had my solicitors draw up a marriage contract. Your dowry is even larger than I had thought. As for you, all you have now is a husband, and one, I might add, who has many pleasant demands on his time."

Sabrina was thinking about the shakily written letter a footman had delivered the previous evening from her grandfather. He had assured her that he would be well enough to greet her and her new husband in but a short time. He had not mentioned any of the less pleasant circumstances surrounding her sudden marriage. She wondered how much of it he knew. Her pleasure at his letter had carried her through until now. She turned at her aunt's words. "When you speak of the viscount's pleasant demands, you're referring to his mistress?"

Lady Barresford snorted, not an edifying sound. "If indeed he has only one mistress, which is doubtful."

"It doesn't matter. I've given him his freedom to do whatever he pleases."

"He doesn't need your permission, my girl, to do anything he pleases. Let me tell you that Phillip Mercerault hasn't led anything like a celibate life. It will be interesting to see if he parades his mistresses in front of your nose."

Sabrina tugged at the itchy Brussels lace at her throat. "Phillip is very kind. He would never do such a thing."

"Ha. He's a man and men do whatever it pleases them to do. If he chooses to ignore you, then he will. If he chooses to humiliate you, then he will. However, in all truth, the viscount has a good reputation. He is known as an honorable man. We will see. I will say that I'm shocked that you managed to fool him. I had not taken him for such a blockhead."

Not for the first time in the last three days, Sabrina wished she could smack her aunt. Just one little smack, right in the middle of all those ridiculous crimped gray curls. "He isn't a blockhead," she said, swallowing her anger. Soon she would be out of her aunt's house. Soon she wouldn't have to see her at all. Well, perhaps once every six months. That would be more than enough. She straightened, then turned. "I believe it's time to go downstairs, ma'am."

"Yes, it's time. For God's sake, girl, pinch your cheeks. You look like I've abused you when it's been the other way around. The good Lord knows how much I've had to deal with, between you and your sister. But you, bringing scandal into my house and lying—" She broke off. Sabrina just might tell the viscount something less than truthful, and the truth was that she had treated Sabrina better than anyone could possibly expect, given what the girl had done to her. Lady Barresford turned on her heel and walked toward the door, not looking back.

Sabrina closed her thumb and forefinger about her cheek and pinched herself. Her maid, Hickles, emerged suddenly from the corner of the bedchamber where she'd conveniently withdrawn into the shadows. Sabrina jumped. She was certain Hickles had been eavesdropping. "Will you need anything else, my lady?" Hickles asked, her voice trembling with excitement.

"Yes," Sabrina said quietly, turning. "I never want to see your face again, Hickles. You truly are irritating." She swept up the train of her gown and walked from the room, without a backward glance at her maid.

"Sabrina was a lovely bride. Perhaps a trifle pale, but hardly a wooden doll." Margaret Drakemore turned away from Madeleine Bingly, her hands clenched at her sides.

Lady Bingly raised a painted eyebrow. "I do believe that you're taking loyalty a bit too far, Margaret. Do finish with that flounce, you stupid girl," she said to the maid who was kneeling before her mending a torn ruffle in her gown.

Lady Dorchester said from her seat before a mirror, "Now, Madeleine, surely it's time for some Christian charity." Particularly, she thought with a small grimace, since her spouse, Lord Dorchester, was a good friend of the groom's and Rohan Carrington's. She, for one, wouldn't gossip about the new viscountess, which was surely a pity—it would have meant many pleasurable hours.

Lady Bingly did a small pirouette. "There, no one could tell that Colonel Sandavar put his foot through the flounce, clumsy man." She waved away the maid and turned to Margaret. "I believe I hear a waltz strik-ing up. Shouldn't we go back into the ballroom before our husbands think we have run away from them? Ah, to run away after being wicked and still manage to finish off your adventure being married to Phillip Mer-cerault, that is more than luck. That would require cunning and planning. It quite makes me gnash my teeth with envy that she managed it."

Margaret, who wished suddenly that she and Lady Bingly were at the top of the stairs and she could shove her down, rose to her full height and said, "I have told you the facts of the entire matter, Made-leine. It is really quite mean-spirited of you to con-tinue these silly lies."

Lady Dorchester rose from her seat and gave a final pat to her dark hair. "Margaret is right, Madeleine. What's done is done. It's over." As she swept from the dressing room, she said over her bare shoulder, unable to help herself, "At least the viscount will not have a shrinking bride on his hands tonight. How per-fectly quaint that the wedding should follow the wed-ding night."

Her laughter rang out. Lady Bingly moved to follow her from the ladies withdrawing room. She called out, "Or was it a wedding week, my dear Lady Dorches-ter? With the viscount's winning manners, it must have been an exquisite experience for the, er, child."

"Bitches," Margaret said under her breath. She heard Madeleine call out, "I do wonder if the vis-countess is breeding. An excellent reason for placing a gold band so quickly on her finger."

Margaret heard the carrying words, as, she sus-pected, she was meant to. At least, she thought, her spirits rising a bit, most of the guests were behaving as they should, with no overt nastiness toward Sabrina. The small wedding, held in the drawing room of Lady

Barresford's town house, had gone off without a hitch, her brother, Charles, having acted in the stead of Sabrina's family. Rohan Carrington had been Phillip's best man. She wished that the wedding dinner and ball had been kept similarly small, but Phillip had insisted. "No, Sabrina will dance her wedding waltz with me before as many people as I can squeeze into the ballroom. This will be no fly-by-night wedding."

Naturally everyone had come.

Perhaps, Margaret thought, Phillip had been right. But it didn't help that Sabrina looked so white and drawn. Margaret dismissed the maids and walked slowly back down the oak staircase to the ballroom.

Sabrina shrank back into the shadows until Margaret disappeared from her view down the winding stairs. She hadn't been meant to hear the cutting words, but she had. What had she expected? Indeed, what could she expect? She drew a long sigh. At least it was nearly over. She forgot the thick braid that was coming loose and made her way quickly back downstairs.

"Hold still, Sabrina, and I'll fix your hair."

"Phillip," she said, praying he hadn't overheard the women. He stood two steps below her, a slight smile playing about his mouth. She realized with a start that she'd been so closed into herself for the entire day and evening that she had scarce even been aware of him. She looked at him now, devastatingly handsome in his severe black evening clothes. "You look beautiful," she said. "I hadn't really seen you today. I'm sorry. You've done so much for me and this is the first time I'm really seeing you. You have eyelashes thick as a girl's, only most girls I've seen don't have thick lashes either."

The smile became a wide grin. "Well, eyelashes is

a good place to start. You really think I'm beautiful? I'm just a man, Sabrina. Beautiful?"

"Now you're showing your conceit. You want me to reassure you all the while you're jesting with me. Very well, yes, it's true. You are beautiful. Does that please your vanity?"

"Yes. I trust that my thick eyelashes are all that a girl would want. Come here, Sabrina, before your hair falls into your face."

She obeyed, her steps slow and careful, for she feared tripping on the hem of her wedding gown. She felt his long fingers move deftly to draw the sagging braid back to where it belonged. She felt him slide in the pin to anchor it securely.

"There, now you're the perfect viscountess."

She stared up at him. "Goodness, you're right. That's what I am now. But I don't feel like a viscountess. All of this—" she waved her hand around her— "it all seems like a dream, like I'm not really me, that it's someone else who's done all this."

He hooked his thumb beneath her chin. "It's real, Sabrina. You're real, as am I. We're married now. It's done. What was the dream was all the nastiness before today. It's over and done with now."

She thought of the malicious words of the women just moments before, but she forced a smile. "Yes, it's almost all over now. Thank you, Phillip, for all you've done for me."

He hated her gratitude, and thus said without thinking, "It's your money that's paying for all of it. Thank yourself as much as me."

"Money," she said, anger deep in her voice now, "money is one thing, but what you, Phillip Mercerault, have done is quite another."

That was true, he thought, pleased. He found himself wondering what she was thinking, for her eyes were vague now, and she was looking away from him. She'd said so little during the day, just the vows required during the ceremony, nothing more. She looked too pale. but he would change that soon enough. "There's just one more waltz you must dance with me. Then, Sabrina, you may retire."

Lady Dorchester's words flashed through her mind. She shuddered, unable to prevent it. "No, I really don't want to retire. I want to remain down here, with you, with our guests." She saw that he was frowning at her and added in a strained voice, "No, I want to stay right here."

He saw her furtive glance back up the stairs. It occurred to him then that she was thinking about sex. Sex with him, her husband. The thought of it scared her to her very toes.

He wanted to tell her again that she had nothing to fear from him, that he wasn't about to force himself on her, but not now. Now wasn't the time for such a discussion. He held out his hand as the strains of a waltz floated to his ears. "My dance, Sabrina." He drew her hand through the crook of his arm.

"Keep your chin up. Try to smile. Don't forget, this is supposed to be the happiest day of your life." He gave her a huge smile. "It's my happiest day."

"You must be jesting with me," she said, but she did manage a small smile.

"Perhaps I am," he said, and led her into the waltz.

The colorfully attired group of ladies and gentlemen obligingly parted their ranks as Phillip whirled Sabrina around the dance floor.

She saw Lady Dorchester from the corner of her eye and missed a step. She felt Phillip's arm tighten about her waist.

He gave her another dazzling smile, even laughed

with those white teeth of his as he said, "Show the world how delirious you are to have me."

"It is possible that I am delirious."

"Not good enough. Think about my glorious eyelashes."

That brought a giggle. "Excellent," he said, dipped down his head, and lightly kissed her ear. "Just excellent."

30

As the waltz drew to a close, he said, "Are you convinced now that your grandfather is on the mend?"

A genuine smile lit up her face. "Oh yes, Phillip. But his handwriting isn't as firm as it used to be. That frightens me."

"His handwriting will recover fully, just as the rest of him will."

The music stopped and Phillip drew her into his arms and kissed her lightly on her mouth. "Well done. It's over." He kissed her hair amid applause and laughter from the ladies and gentlemen. He realized for the first time just how short she was. The top of her head barely came to his neck. Naturally he hadn't realized it before. Most of the time she'd been flat on her back in bed.

He also realized that she was now his—his responsibility and the future mother of his children. Now that was a thought to make a man pause.

He drew her forward to stand at his side to receive their guests' parting congratulations. A few were genuinely kind. More were cold, but polite. Some of the gentlemen gave her looks that if Phillip had seen, would have angered him. But for the most part, all had gone well.

One of the last guests to leave was Lady Barresford. She paused at Sabrina's side. "You've managed to carry this off quite well, niece. You are more than fortunate that the viscount is an honorable man."

"Yes, that is quite true. Thank you, Aunt." She kept her eyes fastened to a mirror just behind her aunt's right shoulder.

Lady Barresford nodded toward the viscount. "I bid you good evening, my lord. I leave you to your blushing bride."

Phillip took Sabrina's hand, raised it to his lips, and lightly kissed her knuckles. "Sabrina is too tired to blush, ma'am, though I'm certain that she would be inclined to do so at the tasteless comments she's been forced to endure this evening."

"That's as may be," Lady Barresford said, and drew herself up.

Sabrina saw with relief that Greybar was hovering beside Lady Barresford, her ermine wrap on his arm. "Thank you, Greybar. Her ladyship is on the point of leaving. Good night, Aunt."

Lady Barresford gave her a look that promised more spiteful words, then allowed Greybar to assist her into her wrap. "Well, niece, you've made your bed, and now you may lie in it."

It was a good shot, she knew it, but Sabrina just stared at her, her head cocked to one side. One thick braid looked in danger of falling. "Men adore innocence," Lady Barresford added, then turned on her heel, whipped the ermine wrap over her shoulder, and marched out the front door.

Phillip turned to Sabrina. "Ignore her. Ignore all of them. Are you ready to sleep now, Sabrina?"

She gazed up at him uncertainly.

He smiled down at her as he said, "You're not to worry about a thing. Trust me, Sabrina." He wasn't a randy boy with no control. The last thing he wanted to do was scare her witless. He'd said enough. He'd give her time to settle in, time to get to know him.

He supposed he needed time as well. He'd never had a wife before. He couldn't begin to imagine the adjustment that he would have to make in his very pleasant life. "Greybar told me that horrible maid, Hickles, is well and truly gone. He said Doris would suit you very well. I'll send her to you." He patted her hand and turned away.

"I've never seen an angel with beautiful red hair like yours, my lady," Doris said. "Even the pictures I've seen in books, all the angels are the loveliest little blond girls, with huge blue eyes. But I think a red-haired angel would be a nice change. She'd look just like you." If only you weren't so pale and lifeless, she thought as she twitched a beautifully embroidered batiste nightgown into place. She pictured his lordship in her mind and imagined herself swooning in his arms. Now there was a gentleman to please a lady. Such charm he had, such wicked eyes and manners, not that she'd ever had them turned on her. But she wasn't his wife. This little one who looked more frightened than a rabbit in the sight of a hunter's gun was the new viscountess. She didn't look like a loose girl who'd lost her virginity to the viscount and been lucky enough to have him marry her. She looked rather pathetic, except for all that lovely red hair and those strange eyes that probably would have gotten her burned at the stake in another time and place. No, she didn't look like the viscount could charm her out of her chemise.

Sabrina nodded abstractedly, and Doris smiled to herself. She couldn't imagine any lady not having a really fine time in bed with his lordship, even this pale little creature. She laid down the hairbrush and stepped back. "Can I be getting you anything else, my lady?"

"No, thank you, Doris."

Doris curtsied and quietly closed the door behind her.

Sabrina turned slowly from the mirror and let her eyes rove again over the large bedchamber. It was severe and masculine, not at all unlike its master, she thought. She looked at the huge bed, a carved oak affair set on a dais in the middle of the bedchamber, with no hangings to soften its stark presence. She picked up a branch of candles, carried it to the bed, and set it on the bedside table. Phillip had told her that carpenters would be at her disposal to redo the adjoining bedchamber that had been his mother's. He'd been sorry but there hadn't been time to make it right in time for her. So she had to sleep in this bed tonight.

With him. She'd never slept with a man before. Well, she had, when she'd been fevered and he'd held her, but that wasn't real, that wasn't something that she'd actually chosen to be a party to, something she'd experienced as she was sure she would experience this.

She was married. She'd even offered herself to him as part of the bargain. She didn't remember that he'd been very enthusiastic.

Sabrina slipped in between the sheets and drew the covers up to her chin. She stared up at the dark oak beams that crisscrossed the length of the ceiling. She strained to hear Phillip's footsteps. She felt the night-gown slide over her skin as she drew her knees up to her chest.

Phillip would be kind. There was no reason for him

not to be kind. He wouldn't maul her. Not like Trevor had. He'd told her to trust him, and she would.

The room was so silent. She couldn't bear it. She began humming, hummed and hummed until her throat hurt.

He didn't come.

At least she knew her husband a lot better than every other girl knew her bridegroom. He'd given her a bath. He'd told her many of his adventures. He'd cooked for her. She'd tried to escape him that one miserable night but his damned horse wouldn't budge. And the other, her woman's monthly flow. He even knew about things like that. He'd even helped her. She squeezed her eyes closed.

Yes, she knew Phillip. Or, more's the truth, he knew her, inside and out.

The clock on the mantel stroked one long single stroke. Perhaps he wasn't coming to her. But where would he sleep? She was in his bed. If he hadn't wanted her here, then he should have said something. Was he perhaps sleeping in a guest chamber down the corridor? She got out of the huge bed.

It wasn't fair that Phillip not sleep in his own bed. It was his home, his bed. She lit a candle and managed to get on her dressing gown. Barefoot, she opened the bedchamber door. She didn't hear anything. Slowly she walked down the vast corridor, opening each door along the way.

Empty. They were all empty. Where was he?

She walked downstairs, carefully cupping the slender candle flame. She finally saw a light coming from beneath a door toward the back of the house. She had no idea what room it was.

She raised her hand to knock, then pressed her ear to the door. She heard nothing at all. She very slowly turned the doorknob. The door opened silently. It was a man's study of some sort, filled with leather and wainscoting, like her upstairs bedchamber. There was a large winged chair that faced the fireplace. A sluggish fire was burning. She walked silently toward that chair.

Suddenly he rose and faced her. He was still dressed in his evening wear, except he'd pulled his cravat loose and his hair was disheveled. He just stared at her. He was holding a snifter of brandy in his right hand.

"Sabrina?" He took a step toward her, then stopped. "Did something happen? Is something wrong? Did you have a nightmare?"

"Oh no. I'm sorry to disturb you, Phillip, but you didn't come to bed. It isn't fair, so I came to find you and tell you to come."

He shook his head at her, as if he were uncertain what she'd said. He said finally, "Surely this is a very strange offer from a girl who would probably prefer to see any man locked up in chains so he couldn't touch her. Let me get this straight. You want me to come to my bedchamber?"

"Yes, it's only right. You shouldn't be down here. This is your home."

"Well, I suppose it's now your home as well. Let me get this straight again. You want me to come to my bedchamber? With you there as well?"

"Of course. Why else would I come to find you? If you would prefer that I not be there with you, then you must simply say so. It won't hurt my feelings. Surely we know each other well enough not to see hurt where none is intended." It was strange, but in that instant, he would have sworn that he heard hurt in her voice as she said, "You weren't impressed with me offering myself. Therefore you needn't worry because I do understand. It's a very large bed. I'm certain that there's more than enough space for both of us. We won't have to disturb each other."

He cleared his throat. He plowed his fingers through his hair, making it stand on end. "This is excessively strange, Sabrina. I had meant to speak to you about sex, no, that's too stark a word. No, I had meant to speak to you about intimacy between a husband and wife, but I decided to do it tomorrow. You're very tired. You don't need to have any of this tonight. You should be asleep. You shouldn't be wandering about at one o'clock in the morning, wearing that embroidered thing that makes you look really quite lovely." He stopped. "Well?"

She looked down at her toes. She was glad she was standing on a thick rug. The wooden floor would be cold. She cleared her throat. "Well what? Listen, Phillip, what do you want from me?"

"I want you to go to sleep and then tomorrow when there aren't any bruises under your eyes and you aren't as white as newly laundered sheets, I want to very gently speak to you about how a man and his wife do things at night, in bed, in the dark. But you're here and it's very late, and you don't look all that pale anymore." He stopped, then cursed.

"That was very good. I'd never heard any curse involving a horse's bodily parts before."

"Forget that, I didn't mean anything by it. It's just that you've taken me by surprise."

"I'm just here to see if you want to come to bed, Phillip," she said patiently. "It's very late, just like you said. You should be in bed. You probably have many things planned on the morrow. You need your rest. You've done so much this week. You've done so much for me."

"All right," he said and walked to her. She took a step back. He held out his hand but she didn't give him hers. She gave him the candle.

He smiled down at her then, a gentle smile, the sort of smile a parent would bestow on a child.

"You're very brave, Sabrina." He gave her back the candle. He patted her cheek. "Go to bed. Tomorrow, one of us can move into another bedchamber."

"You'll also talk to me about those other things as well?"

He nodded at her again before she left. Phillip waited in the drawing room until he heard the door of the study open and close. He pictured her walking back up the stairs, that lovely white gown billowing ever so slightly around her bare ankles. Even if he hadn't had woman for a year, even if he was chewing on his knuckles, even if lust was threatening to drive him over the edge, he wouldn't have touched that innocent fairy creature. And she'd sought him out, offering herself to him. He felt a surge of lust and with it a bolt of anger at himself. He wouldn't defile her, scare her, as he knew any sort of lovemaking would.

No, he'd protect her from himself. He would leave. Greybar was standing right outside the drawing-room door beaming. "It was a splendid occasion, my lord."

Phillip nodded, his thoughts still on Sabrina, on protecting her. "Yes, thank everyone for me, Greybar."

"Allow me and the entire staff to wish you and the viscountess happiness." Greybar hoped his master would understand his subtlety, but he wasn't too hopeful. His lordship had the look of a man on a mission after drinking a good deal of brandy. Why was he leaving? On his wedding night? He'd watched from the shadows as the new viscountess had trailed back up the stairs, alone. Then the truth struck him right between the eyes. His lordship was being noble. Even the lowest scullery maid was well aware of the facts surrounding the viscount's hurried wedding. "Poor little mite," Mrs. Hawley, the housekeeper, had said earlier that day, shaking her soft gray curls, of which she was inordinately proud, "after the wedding we'll keep her safe and sound with us."

Greybar was very proud of his master at that moment. He'd risen above himself. He was showing immense gallantry. He wasn't giving in to a man's baser instincts. No, as a gentleman with money, he would take those instincts elsewhere, where they belonged, and not upstairs where that poor scared little girl was now lying in her virginal nightgown, quite alone and doubtless better off that way. Not that a newly married man should visit his mistress, but perhaps in this case, it was more well done of him than not. The master was young and lusty. Because he didn't want to scare his little wife out of her wits, he was taking himself off to relieve himself elsewhere.

He helped his master into his greatcoat and handed him his hat and gloves. Phillip said, "I know you're aware that the new mistress has come through a rather trying time. But it's over now. She's young, Greybar, and untried in London ways. I've decided against taking her to Dinwitty Manor, at least for the time being. She must learn her way here, in London, and I trust that you will assist her. A dinner party, say next week, will be just the thing to start her off."

"Oh yes, my lord, that sounds like an excellent start. We've a week to get color back into her cheeks, perhaps to add a bit of flesh on her little bones. Oh yes, that would be perfect."

Two hours and five minutes later, after shouting his second release to Martine's newly replastered bedchamber ceiling, Phillip rolled off her and onto his back. He crossed his arms behind his head. He thought of Sabrina benignly now, without any nagging lust getting in the way, thought of her lying in his big bed, soft and asleep and him not attacking her.

"You know, Martine," he said now, feeling quite pleased with himself and her, "all my friends pulled the wedding off quite nicely. And you have helped me return my thoughts to more practical matters and away from matters of the flesh. Now I can assist Sabrina to recover her spirit without wanting to kiss her and caress her and just bloody look at her until she's so terrified that she'd just swoon right away onto the floor. No, with your help, I can regard her as a pupil who's bright and willing to learn. But it will be up to her to make her own mark in society. She'll be quite acceptable once she puts a bit more meat on her bones, that's what Greybar said, and he's right. But what's important is that I give her time to get over Trevor, that mangy bastard. Yes, once that happens, then I can introduce her to what goes on between a husband and a wife.

"Exactly how I'm going to proceed I haven't figured out yet, but I thank you for granting me respite. You know how Greybar loves to entertain. Why I already told him that we'll have a dinner party next week and then—"

There was a soft snore beside him. Martine was fast asleep. Phillip grinned as he dressed himself and took himself back home.

He fell asleep in a too-short bed in a guest bedchamber just as the dawn was turning the sky a pale pink outside the window. He thought of Sabrina, again

31

Early the next morning, the viscount, wearing a pleased, sated smile, turned to his wife at the breakfast table. "Some bacon, Sabrina? It will help put some meat on you, that's what Cook said. Did you sleep well?"

"I don't care for bacon, but I did sleep well, once I managed to get to sleep. That bed is very big and I'm not used to your house. It was very quiet and then there'd be a creak and a little shudder. I dreamed about ghosts and things of that sort."

"I'm sorry, but soon you'll be used to everything." She merely nodded and chewed on a slice of toast. She was dressed charmingly, in a high-necked pale pink muslin gown. The pink did wonderful things to her auburn hair and to that white skin of hers, not to mention how it seemed to deepen the violet eyes. He started to compliment her, then decided that it might frighten her, that she might think that he was flattering her so he could hoist her skirts up. So he said nothing, merely kept smiling, determinedly.

"You won't have to get used to my bed. Perhaps, if you wish, you can select another bedchamber until we have the viscountess's bedchamber redone. All right?"

"Did you sleep in one of the other bedchambers last night, Phillip?"

"Yes. The bed was a bit on the short side. But it wasn't bad."

She toyed with a crust of toast. He handed her a pot of jam. She said suddenly, "Doris told me I looked like a redheaded angel."

That brought his head up. He'd been carving himself a slice of rare beef when she'd said that, and he very nearly cut his finger. "A redheaded angel, huh? I'll ask Rohan what he thinks."

"He's very nice."

"Yes. We've known each other since we were boys. He and Susannah are very close."

"I know. He really missed her. All he could do was talk about her, about Marianne, his daughter, Toby, his brother-in-law, and Jamie, who seems to be a stable lad and sings limericks to his horses."

"Yes, he's still besotted with his wife. She's pregnant and that's why she didn't come. He said every time someone said something funny within her hearing, she vomited. He said it's difficult to be melancholy all the time around her but that's what everyone has to do."

"Yes, I know. Will I ever meet her?"

"Certainly. Indeed, we can visit them at Mountvale Manor and go to a cat race."

"I've heard that cat races are very popular in the south of England. Grandfather told me all about them. I think he's always wanted to attend one."

"Perhaps all of us can. The most famous is the McCaulty Racetrack near Eastbourne. They've met for years every Saturday from April to October." He paused a moment, playing with his fork. "I always wanted a racing cat, but the Harker brothers—they're the big trainers down there—they didn't think I had enough commitment. Oh, well, we'll see how you like the competition. They won't begin until the fourth of

April. As for right now, I just thought we would remain in London for a while."

She kept chewing on that piece of toast. She heard the rustling of the newspaper and said to the painting of very large painted fruits on the opposite wall, "I don't really feel married at all. I don't feel at all different than I did last night, except that Aunt Barresford isn't here, and that, I can tell you, is very nice."

She was still afraid her world was caved in, he thought. She needed assurance from him and he freely gave it. "Just look at the Mercerault emerald on your finger, Sabrina. That ring has adorned many a Mercerault lady's finger. I hope you like it since you will wear it until you decide to give it to our son's bride someday. You're good and married. There's nothing for you to fear now, I swear it to you. Folk will come about, they always do. There'll be a new scandal that will titillate them and they'll forget all about you. By the time you have our first child, they will remember only that you're an earl's granddaughter and that you married a very handsome man who dotes on you. What do you think?"

She supposed that he could be said to dote, at least in the way he treated her, as if she were a shepherdess figurine atop the mantel. No one had ever treated her like that before. It was very depressing. She looked at him as he forked down a thick bite of sirloin. She smiled. "I think you've very nice, Phillip. But perhaps there is more than just simple doting?"

"Yes, there is. Now is as good a time to tell you as any. You met Peter Straddling, my solicitor. He will be drawing up the necessary papers so that your funds will return to your name."

He gave her a fat smile. He knew he was a prince among men. She was just staring at him as if she couldn't believe she'd heard him aright. Her mouth was actually open. He continued, his voice soft and rich and utterly serious, "I don't want you to feel that I ever married you for the wealth you bring me. I am keeping your dowry, that's as it should be, but your inheritance of ten thousand pounds will be yours again to do with as you please. Also, you'll have a quarterly allowance."

She was still as a stone and wore a particularly vacant look on her face.

"What don't you understand?"

"I just don't understand you, my lord."

"The bloody ten thousand pounds is yours again, that's all. What's to understand? What's right is right. There's nothing more to it than that."

Sabrina carefully lowered her fork to her plate. "But there was no reason for you to do that. Why did you do it?"

"I told you. I don't need your money. I don't want anyone saying that's why I married you. For heaven's sake, Sabrina, you might at least thank me. You're quite independent now."

She felt the anger bubbling up in her, but it was a helpless anger, an impotent anger, one that was going to choke her if she didn't do something, say something, ah, but to say anything would make her look like an ungrateful idiot. Still, she just couldn't help herself. She slowly rose from her chair, splaying her hands on the table. "Is it, my lord, that you believe that since I'm only a simple female, such concepts involving bargains and honor are beyond my ability to comprehend? It isn't *my* money, Phillip. We made a bargain, a business agreement, don't you remember? The moment you accepted my offer, it was your money."

"Our bargain," he said mildly, "was at your insistence." He shrugged. "Listen, Sabrina, that offer of yours allowed you to save face and the both of us to do what had to be done, namely marry before you were buried under the fast-accumulating piles of nastiness."

She leaned toward him now. He saw the furious pulse in her neck. She was clearly enraged. But what had he done? "You make me ill. You are so smug, so certain you are the titan of generosity." She was shaking now. "How dare you treat me like some brainless little female whose only motive was to lure your high and mighty lordship into marriage? Save face, ha! What I offered you in return for your precious Mercerault name was all that I could, my lord. It isn't a piddling amount of money. It's a great deal. It was an honorable offer and I had thought that your acceptance was to be taken in the same light."

He said slowly, not understanding her fury but certainly feeling it, "Why are you twisting what happened? I have never even hinted that anything you've done was to lure me into marrying you. I saved your hide, and that's the long and short of it.

"I saved you, Sabrina. It's the truth. Get used to it. Also, get used to having your money back. What the devil is wrong with you? Didn't you hear what I just said? Good Lord, I must be losing what little bit of brain I still possess."

"Your brain is your own problem, my lord. You refuse to see the point. Why do you want to destroy my honor and treat me like some idiot? Surely you can understand that."

He rose slowly now, their faces not a foot apart. "Very well, madam, it will be as you wish. I shall keep your bloody money, all ten thousand pounds of it. Maybe I'll even gamble it away, though I've never enjoyed gambling that much. Further, madam, if you wish it, we can hold a reckoning at the end of each quarter. I will expect you not to exceed your allowance. Is that what you want, Sabrina, to dance to my tune?"

She was shaking. It wasn't his tune she was dancing to, it was society's tune. But he represented society. He represented all the ridiculous strictures that had brought her low. She said, "Anything, Phillip, anything is preferable to being in your debt. Even the humiliation of a quarterly accounting. As for your noble male honor, I hope that you choke on it."

"I wanted you to get your spirit back after you were safely wedded to me, madam. However, if that means that you're going to be an irrational, stubborn mule, a girl who is so trapped in her petty little concerns that—"

"I'd rather be a mule than a stubborn blind ass."

"I am your husband. You won't interrupt me again, Sabrina."

"I'll do precisely as I wish. I have, after all, paid you quite dearly for that right."

"You have a lot to learn, Viscountess," he said easily, for he was in control again. "As for rights, you have none. You will do what I tell you. An earl's granddaughter you may be, but more to the point is that you are now my wife. Why don't you go to your bedchamber and think about your nonsensical charges and insults? When you're ready to apologize to me, tell Greybar, and he will inform me."

A jar of jam flew past his head.

He could only stare at her. Her breasts were heaving she was breathing so hard. If he shook her, which is what she deserved, he would probably hurt her. "Go to your room, Sabrina."

"I don't think so," she said finally. "No, I believe I'll send a message to Charles Askbridge. Perhaps he would like to take me for a ride in the park. He, at least, isn't an officious tyrant."

"Don't push me, Sabrina, else I shall remove you to Dinwitty Manor where you could cool your ridiculous temper in peaceful solitude."

"You'd like that, wouldn't you? Then you could spend all your nights with your mistress." She paused a moment at the shocked expression on his face. There were two spots of color on his cheekbones. He looked chagrined. He looked embarrassed and guilty. She wasn't mistaken about that. She blinked as understanding flooded into her brain. She said slowly, "That's what you did last night, isn't it? You left just after you dismissed me. I thought I heard the front door open and close just before I was back in your bedchamber.

"You went to your mistress on our wedding night, didn't you? You couldn't be bothered to bed your wife, even spend one night with her, even stay in a bedchamber close to hers, no, you bedded your damned mistress."

He was silent as a stone.

She flung back her head, looking through him. "It amazes me that you could bed your mistress all the while telling me and anyone else who will listen about how chivalrous you are, how noble."

"I haven't done that."

"Ha! If not out loud, you've preened and strutted about, all confident and smug in your damnable generosity. Should I throw myself at your feet, Phillip, for saving me? Should I then kiss your boots? Should I perhaps send a little token of appreciation to your mistress for keeping you away from me on the most special night of a woman's life?"

He stared at this wife of his, hearing her rage, her disbelief. He said slowly, getting to what was the most important thing she'd said, "Is it really the most special night in a woman's life?"

"Only if the woman knows nothing of what men are really like."

"Enough baiting me. Answer me. Did you want me to stay with you last night?"

There came a discreet knock at the dining-room door. "Oh, hell," Phillip said. He pointed his finger at her. "You will answer that question, Sabrina. Oh yes, you most certainly will, as soon as I get rid of this wretched person who is knocking and probably won't leave until I answer. And you won't write to Charles. Damn you, obey me."

He straightened. "Come," he called out.

"Your carriage is ready, my lord," Greybar announced, his eyes fastened on his master's snowy cravat. He wasn't deaf. His relief at seeing the carriage had been boundless. His relief that they were only shouting and not throwing dishes was even more boundless.

"I have no further wish for the carriage, Greybar. Her ladyship will be remaining here. You may tell Lanscombe to bring around my curricle."

Greybar looked ready to argue. He popped his knuckles, something Phillip had never seen him do in his life. He cleared his throat. It nearly sent Phillip over the edge. "The curricle, Greybar. Now. No arguments. Get to it."

"Yes, my lord."

When Greybar had closed the dining-room door behind him, Phillip turned again to his wife. "Answer my question, Sabrina. Did you want me to stay with you last night?"

She'd had two minutes to ready herself. She examined her fingernail. "I said it was the most special night in a woman's life unless she knew what men were really like." She raised her violet eyes, startlingly dark in her anger. "I have had experience with men, my lord. Trevor taught me a lot. You have taught me even more. Do you think I would want you to maul me as men do women? Do you think I'm completely and utterly stupid?"

It wasn't what she would have said before Greybar's unfortunate timing, he was sure of that, but for now, she'd dug in her heels. Given the short amount of time she'd had to prepare, she'd done a good job at slamming him into the floor. "Very well. Since it's obvious you have no wish for my company, I shall take myself off. It is one of your duties to plan the menus with Mrs. Hawley. You will tell her that I shall be eating at my club this evening and won't be here for dinner. Good day, Sabrina. I hope you won't choke on your misplaced resentment."

Sabrina didn't leap on him, though she did have two ready fists. "You never told me if I should buy a small token of my appreciation for your mistress."

"You will forget that my mistress exists," he said, and left the dining room before he put her over his knee and pounded her bottom. But he paused, saying over his shoulder, "You will not throw her up to me again. I forbid it."

He left before she could hurl another pot of jam at him. He'd seen another pot on the table, not far from her right hand.

32

He was pulsing with furious energy, wanting to pound someone, but seeing no likely candidate. Then he smiled. He would be at Gentleman Jackson's Boxing Saloon in twenty minutes. He spent the next two hours exhausting himself, hurting four men, and sweating until he was blinded with it.

"I would have thought, Derencourt, that you had found more pleasant ways to relieve yourself of such excesses of energy."

Phillip lowered the towel he was using to mop his face. The Earl of March, not long married himself, was regarding him with a good deal of amusement.

"Good afternoon, St. Clair. I wish you had come earlier, you could have come into the ring with me."

"And let you pound me into the dirt? I don't think so. Allow both Kate and me to wish you happy on your marriage. We only just returned last evening from St. Clair, else I would have been there to waltz with your lovely bride."

"My damned lovely bride is at this moment amusing herself with Charles Askbridge. I told her she wasn't to see him but I know, I just know, St. Clair, that she disobeyed me the moment I stepped into my curricle, maybe the instant I had stepped out of the front door, maybe while I was still putting my gloves on. She informs me that Charles isn't a tyrant."

"And you, I take it, are?"

"Yes, the silly twit, and after all I've done for her."

The earl looked with some interest at this outburst from a normally self-possessed and rational man. "I suppose it's a stupid question, Phillip, but what have you done for her?"

"Why, I—well, you know, I did save her life."

"Yes, that was well done of you."

Phillip stared down at his hands. Damnation, Julien was right. Sabrina had been right. He'd held himself up as a veritable god among men, noble, generous, selfless. He wanted to punch himself. Instead, he just stared at his friend of some fifteen years.

The earl said easily, "It would appear to me that you managed to marry a lovely girl of good breeding and excellent dowry, a lovely girl, who, in the normal course of events, you would have met here in London. Would you have fallen in love with her? Wanted to marry her? Who knows? From what I've heard, she's a beauty. Any number of gentlemen would have pursued her. Would you have been the one to win her? Who can say?"

"Damn you, Julien, I hate it when you're right, not that you're necessarily right in this particular instance, but still, it's an annoying habit you have."

He flung down the towel. "I'll thank you to keep your valued opinions to yourself. The fact is that she is my wife and it doesn't matter who would have proposed to her if not for this wretched misadventure. She's mine now and she'll do as I tell her and that's an end to it."

"Charles Askbridge, confirmed bachelor that he is, would likely agree with you. I, on the other hand, will offer you but one more opinion. Don't try to break her to bridle, Phillip. With that, my friend, I bid you good day. I have a wife who adores the ices at Gunthers. It pleases me to please her. In fact, it makes my innards melt."

Phillip watched his friend leave the room. He slowly flexed his tired muscles. He hated being wrong. He hated being wrong even more when it was pointed out to him.

Sabrina handed her sable-lined cloak to an unhappy Greybar and stood quietly as a footman divested Charles of his greatcoat and gloves.

When they were in the drawing room, waiting for tea, Charles said, "What's wrong with Greybar? I thought he would cry. That, or hit me."

"He is his master's servant. His master didn't want me to even see you, thus he didn't either. One thing's for certain, this bunch is loyal to Phillip, all the way to their bone marrow."

Charles walked to the fireplace to warm his hands over the bright blaze. After some moments, he turned to watch Sabrina fidget about the room, unable, it seemed to him, to contain her restless energy. Although he'd thought it odd for her to ask him to escort her to the park, he'd agreed, even managing throughout the afternoon to keep his questions to himself. Sabrina had chattered away so persistently throughout their ride, about the most trivial of topics, boring him until he thought he'd begin snoring on his chest, that Charles was now thrilled that she was at last still. But the fact was he'd known Sabrina all of her life. It hurt him that she was hurt and trying to hide it.

He said, "Where is Phillip? I expected to see him upon our return."

She turned to face him. Her face was flushed from the cold wind, her hair in some disarray around her thin face. She shrugged, a nice gesture of indifference that didn't fool him a bit. "I have no idea, Charlie."

"Do you expect him soon?"

"This is his house. I assume he'll come back when it pleases him to do so."

Anger, not defeat, he thought, and said, "Listen to me, Sabrina Eversleigh, for the past two hours I've been battered by silly chatter that has numbed me to my toes. Now I ask you a simple question as to the whereabouts of your husband, and you turn into a snarling dog. You've only been married for two days. What the hell is going on here?"

"I might have known you'd side with him."

"Side with Phillip? Dammit, I don't even know where he is. Come on, Sabrina," he said, softening his voice at the misery he saw in those incredible eyes of hers, "tell me what's wrong. You've known me forever. You know you can trust me. Talk to me."

Greybar entered bearing the heavy silver tea tray. While Sabrina was fussing with the cups, Charles was left to warm his hands and wonder just what the devil was going on here.

When Greybar bowed himself out of the drawing room, looking as disapproving as a nun in a room of harlots, Charles said, "Now, tell me what happened to make Phillip escape from his own house."

He jumped when Sabrina yelled, "You see, Charlie, you are siding with him. Why do you automatically blame me? Can't you even consider for a single minute that his absence might not be my fault?"

"No, I won't consider it. I've known you all your life. I'm used to you and the way you think and the mischief you led poor Margaret into for years and years. But poor Phillip, he—"

"Poor Phillip, you say? He's not poor, damn him. He has my dowry, which is magnificent, and he also has my ten-thousand-pound inheritance. Poor Phillip, ha!"

"That's not what I meant and you know it."

"Very well, your poor Phillip informed me at the breakfast table that he was returning my inheritance to me, so that I would be financially independent."

"Hang the bastard, I say."

"Are you telling me, Charlie, that Phillip didn't tell you about our business agreement?"

"A business agreement with you? That makes no sense at all. First of all, gentlemen don't indulge in business, much less indulge in business with ladies."

She looked down at her hands and began to pull relentlessly at her thumbnail. "After that horrible night at Almack's, Phillip stayed away from me. It was I who approached him about marriage. It was an honorable bargain we struck, Charlie. He gave me the impression that he needed my money, that we had come to an agreement that benefited us both."

"By all that's holy, surely Phillip wouldn't say anything of the kind. Ever since the Dinwitty heiress back in the early part of the last century, the Merceraults have never needed funds. They've only increased their wealth the past two generations. Phillip needs your money about as much as he needs a case of the hives."

"I suppose I realized that after this morning at the breakfast table." She sighed deeply. "I'm an heiress, Charlie."

"I know that. Naturally you would be. Now, tell me the truth. Well, now you know that Phillip never wanted nor needed your precious money. Lord, he would have followed the same course even if you hadn't a sou. It sounds to me as if you forced him to subterfuge so that he could do the right thing by you."

"I guess I did know it," she said in a low voice that made him lean toward her to hear her. "It was all a sham, a lie."

"I wish you would remember how you turned him down several times. He was responsible for you, even though it was you who plunged him into this entire mess. Well, you certainly didn't mean to, it wasn't at all your fault, but if you hadn't been there, it wouldn't have happened."

"He'd still be free if not for me. Oh, don't you understand, Charlie? I didn't want him to marry me for those dreadful reasons. I didn't want a sacrificial husband. I wanted to bring him something, anything besides my sullied reputation."

"If you would just stop worrying about your own honor and think about his for a moment—"

Sabrina felt tears swim in her eyes. She hated them but she couldn't keep them back. She gulped, raising her eyes. "He doesn't love me, Charlie. He would never even have known me, much less married me, if it hadn't been for what happened."

"Of course he doesn't love you. How could he? The two of you hardly know each other. As for the other, naturally he would have met you, here in London, when you'd come this spring for the season. He probably would have taken one look at you and thrown himself at your feet." He sat down beside her and patted her shoulder. She turned and buried her face in his neck. "He didn't spend last night—our wedding night—with me. He went to his mistress."

Charles felt deep waters close over his head. No, surely Phillip wouldn't have done that. Surely. It wasn't as if Sabrina were as ugly as a doorknob. She was lovely. In the next instant, he realized his friend's motive. He patted her back. She wasn't crying, just leaning into him, all boneless, like a child. "Listen, Sabrina. He didn't want to rush you. He wanted to give you time to get over what Trevor tried to do to you. He didn't want you to be frightened of him. Also you were very ill. You're still so pale it scares me. No, he was being careful of you and your feelings. Don't hate him for trying to do the right thing by you."

Her bones returned in a flash, her whole body stiffening. Her eyes were narrowed and mean. "Ah, I see it all now. He's so wonderful that he went off and bedded his mistress. It would seem to me, Charlie, that if Phillip were truly the saintly man you've been painting, he wouldn't go sleep with his mistress. He'd have stayed here in his own house, in his own bed. I could have slept next to him. He wouldn't have to touch me, not that saintly man. Or, idea of ideas, he could have slept by himself, the entire night, not just the hours before dawn, which is when he probably returned home. He's a pig, Charlie."

"No, he's not a pig, trust me on this, Sabrina. The problem is that Phillip is a man who's used to women, he's used to having—" He pulled back, aware of what almost spurted out of his mouth. "I didn't mean that. Just forget it."

"Yes, I see," she said slowly, and he thought that she was now in control of herself. It was an unspeakable relief. A crying woman annihilated him. She said slowly, pulling herself together, "That would make sense. Of course Phillip would want to bed a woman at night. It's the way he is. He didn't bed me because he was afraid he'd scare me. Ah yes, now I understand." She jumped to her feet and began pacing to and fro in front of him. "Then I suppose it's up to me to show him that I'm quite well again and I won't run shrieking out of the bedchamber if he kisses me."

"There's, er, more to what happens between men and women than just kissing."

"I know." Then she whirled about to face him and she was grinning.

Charles just looked at the bright girl in front of him. It was difficult not to burst into laughter. It was a concept that boggled the brain—Phillip Mercerault was going to be seduced by an eighteen-year-old girl who just also happened to be his wife. He hoped she would succeed. He would also say thirteen prayers that she didn't remember Trevor and get frightened.

"But you know, Charlie, I don't know what to do about his mistress. I gave him his freedom, you see."

"You won't do anything, Sabrina," Charles said in his firmest voice. "You will let well enough alone. Your courtship with Phillip, it hasn't exactly been conventional. Take everything slowly. That's my advice. Just don't yell at him. He isn't used to it. He's quite used to having women coo at him and kiss him and tell him he's wonderful."

"Yes, but he has to pay them to do that. He doesn't have to pay me. I'm his wife." She paused, then added, "Well, he will give me a quarterly allowance."

"It's true that he pays them, in some cases." He started to say more but decided against it. Charles smiled at her and squeezed her hand. "Yes, let things progress slowly. Just wait, Sabrina. You know that Phillip probably doesn't know what to do any more than you do. Just give him time. He is quite new to marriage."

"I know, and I suppose I'm an old hand at it. Goodness, Charlie, I'm only eighteen years old."

"That's true, but ladies seem to know things before gentlemen do, particularly things that involve feelings and such. Yes, Sabrina, keep that tongue of yours leashed. Give him a chance."

"I'll wager you've never heard Phillip unleash his tongue."

"Well, I have, but that's different. Men are sup-

33

For a moment Martine just stared at her lover. He was the last person she'd expected at her door. "Phillip, what the devil are you doing here? It's early evening. It's the second evening of your marriage. Surely this isn't how things are done. You were here last night, after all. Don't you like this wife of yours who, I understand, is quite young and lovely and rich as anything? What's wrong?"

Martine always prided herself on acting the languid beauty. She was serene, she was smoothly flowing in her speech and in the way she made love. But now, she couldn't help herself, she stared nearly open-mouthed at him.

"Good evening, Martine," Phillip said, tossing his greatcoat onto the back of a chair. "Yes, I'm here. Yes, it's the second night of my marriage. So? Am I suddenly not welcome?" He strolled over to his staring mistress and kissed her.

"You are always welcome, you know that." He straightened. She searched his face, drawn as she suspected most women were to his beautiful eyes and that passionate mouth of his.

"You are newly married."

"I, more than you, know that. Why are you chiding me? Oh yes, I know that tone of voice. I just heard it this morning, along with anger and resentment and illogic. So, don't you do it. Just leave me be and be yourself."

"This girl you didn't compromise, she's angry with you? That doesn't make much sense, Phillip. Surely she would be grateful to you, worship at your feet for the nobility of your character."

He had the grace to wince. "Whatever else she may be, at least she's now safe."

Phillip turned to the sideboard and poured himself a glass of port. Martine watched him silently as he quickly downed the port and filled his glass again.

"Did the carpenter come and fix the damned ceiling?"

"Yesterday. Didn't you notice last night?"

He nodded. Yes, he remembered now.

"He was a saucy man, that one. He grinned at me and said that his lordship didn't have to worry anymore about having his brains splattered on my pillows."

"Now that's an unappetizing vision."

He set down his glass and gave her a bow, waving his hand toward the door. "Will you join me upstairs, Martine? My need for you is great."

She didn't think that was the case at all, but she gave him a sweet smile and her hand.

As she was removing her gown upstairs in her elegant, very feminine bedchamber, she turned to the viscount, who was standing next to the fireplace staring at nothing in particular. "Phillip."

He grunted, not looking up from the flames.

"The little one, she is alone?"

Phillip's head came up at those words. "Why the devil do you call her that?"

Martine drew off the straps of her chemise and allowed the soft material to float to her waist. Oddly, his eyes didn't waver from her face. Now this was strange. "I called her that because I saw her."

"Where would you see my wife?"

"In the park today. She was riding in Charles Askbridge's phaeton."

She saw his lovely eyes darken, a fascinating sight. She wasn't at all fooled by his indifferent shrug. She wriggled lazily out of the rest of her clothes, stood naked before him for a moment, then walked slowly to the bed.

He didn't move. "How did she look?"

"She looked as if she was trying to forget something unpleasant, perhaps. I heard her laugh, and she was smiling, but none of it was real, do you understand what I mean?"

"I'll thank you not to pry, Martine."

She displayed herself on the bed. He still didn't move. "I'm not prying, Phillip. It was you, after all, who did the asking."

"I told her not to have anything to do with Charles. She wanted to send him a message, on the second day of her marriage to me, she wanted to be with another man. But since you saw her, then she disobeyed me. Not that I'm surprised, of course." He began to pull off his clothes. Suddenly he stopped.

"The little one, she has very unusual eyes. A soft violet. Unique. Just imagine what your children will look like. They will be magnificent."

He didn't move. The firelight played behind him, framing him. He was utterly silent.

"Ah, yes, her eyes are very vivid."

Suddenly he began again to pull off his clothes. "Dammit, I'll always have my freedom. I'll not be tied to her, not to anybody, it's nonsense. I'm too young. I don't want my hatches battened down. I know she wanted me to come to her last night, she as good as admitted it, but I also know that the moment I touched her, she'd be terrified to her toes. No, I won't do it. But I'll do exactly what I wish. Yes, I'll always have my freedom. I don't care if I have to keep proving it to everyone—both to her and to me. It just doesn't matter."

He was nearly naked. She just smiled at him, not really understanding him. He'd changed, she knew that, and he'd changed so very quickly, and he was fighting it with all his might. Men, in her experience, had a lot of might.

Then he was naked and he was on top of her, kissing her, caressing her fiercely.

Then he stopped. He looked up at the headboard. Then he rolled off her and out of the bed. He didn't say a word, just walked back to the fireplace and began dressing himself again. He said as he was pulling up his britches, "You know that Rohan Carrington had the reputation of an utter womanizer."

"Yes, it came as a shock when he turned up with a wife and a daughter four years old. He is faithful, it's said. Completely faithful. It's said too that he loves his wife and he's besotted with his little daughter."

"Yes, he is, but he was different from me, Martine. He never worried about freedom, losing it or gaining it. We're very different men."

He raised his head and looked over at her. She was lying on her side in the most seductive pose a woman would manage, but he really didn't notice. He said, "Yes, I'm very different from Rohan. It seems I must cause hurt where there was none before."

He finished dressing. He walked to the bed and kissed her lightly, passionlessly, on the mouth.

"I'll see you again, my lord?" She lightly caressed her palm against his cheek.

"Of course," he said.

"Ah yes. It's all a matter of your freedom, isn't it?"

He stared at her hard for a long moment. "Perhaps," he said finally, then he left her, not looking back.

She stared for a very long time into the fireplace.

The small ormolu clock on the mantel chimed out midnight. Sabrina lay wide awake in the darkness, waiting to hear Phillip's footsteps on the stairs. She wasn't at all certain how one went about seducing one's husband, but she was confident that if she managed to kiss him, he would kiss her back. Surely that was enough to get a man started down the road of lust.

She stiffened suddenly at the sound of footsteps outside the bedchamber door. She heard him pause and then his footsteps sounded down the corridor until they were lost to her hearing. Very well, he'd given her enough time to recover from her fear of men. She forced herself to lie quietly for some minutes longer to give him time to remove his clothing and settle into his bed.

She rose finally and walked to her dressing table to light a candle. She looked at herself in the mirror. It wasn't a frightening sight. Her eyes looked larger than usual and very bright. As for her clothing, she was wearing the embroidered nightgown. Her hair was shining clean, free down her back, and dark as burgundy in the candlelight. She slipped out into the corridor and walked to his temporary bedchamber.

She inched the door open and paused, blinking at the sound of his loud snoring. But she hadn't taken all that much time. Goodness, he was fast asleep. It was time to wake him up in a very unexpected way. She grinned in the darkness and walked on bare feet to the bed. He was lying on his back, still dressed in his evening clothes. His arms were at his sides. It wasn't the scene she'd imagined, she thought, as she bent over to touch him.

She stiffened suddenly and whipped her hand back. She smelled brandy. She wondered how much he'd drunk. Probably a lot. Maybe he had passed out and really hadn't just fallen asleep. She sniffed again. She smelled the rose scent this time and she strongly doubted that he'd splashed himself with it to smell more manly. No, it was his mistress's perfume. He'd been with her again this evening.

To spare his virgin bride.

Enough was enough. It didn't matter if he was drunk enough to float away. She was still going to seduce him.

Very slowly, she slipped the soft nightgown from her shoulders. It fell in a gentle pool at her feet. Now that she was naked, she realized that he wasn't. What to do?

She wouldn't worry about it. She eased down beside him. She lightly stroked her fingers over his face—the length of his nose, his jaw, the outline of his mouth. How she loved his mouth. She leaned over and kissed him.

He stopped snoring. His eyes opened and he stared up at her. "Martine?"

"No, Phillip. It's your wife. It's Sabrina."

"No, that's not possible. Sabrina is terrified of men. She wouldn't be here, kissing me." His eyes fell to her breasts, pressed against him. "She wouldn't be here naked unless she was too sick to care, like before. I remember that I tried not to look at her breasts, but they were so white and soft. It was difficult, but most of the time I didn't look."

His voice was slurred and soft. She lightly shook his shoulder. "Please look at me now. I'm naked so I can seduce you." She kissed him again.

"No, it's you, Martine. You're playing a game with me. Very well, let's play."

His hands came down on her bare back. "You've lost flesh, Martine, but by God you're soft, I love the feel of you. Kiss me some more."

Phillip realized it was his wife the very instant he eased into her. From one moment to the next, he became instantly and completely full-witted, the brandy gone from his brain. She was very small and he had to push hard. Then he butted against her maidenhead. He raised his head and saw that her eyes were tightly closed. He tried, but he couldn't pull out of her, he just couldn't.

"Sabrina?"

She opened her eyes. "Phillip, I'm sorry, but it hurts. It hurts a whole lot."

"I know, I know. Hold still and I'll try to hold still as well. Maybe the pain will lessen, I don't know. I've never taken a virgin before. Do you know how you feel to me? Do you have any idea at all what it's like to be inside you?"

She wanted to laugh but he was pressing harder against her now and the burning increased. "I'm inside me all the time."

"I want to be also," he said, kissed her hard, then shoved through her maidenhead.

She screamed, unable to keep her mouth shut.

So did he, after but a few moments of pounding into her, his head thrown back, his back arched, so wild were the roaring feelings deep inside him and he was deep inside her, so surely she must feel all that he was feeling too.

She was crying, tears seeping from beneath her closed eyelids.

He began kissing her again when he could move, when he could function, barely.

"You weren't afraid of me?"

"No. Well, just a bit, but only when you were looking at me. It wasn't the same way you looked at me when I was ill."

"I hope not. You're beautiful, Sabrina. I'm sorry I hurt you. It won't hurt next time. Thank you for coming to me."

"You're welcome, Phillip."

He rolled off her, brought her against his side, pressed her cheek down against his chest and in three minutes, he was lightly snoring.

Sabrina lay there, her palm on his chest, over his heart, and she said, "I love you, Phillip. I realized I loved you when I was lying in bed at Moreland and woke up to find you there with me, just watching me in that soft candlelight. I loved you then."

"If you loved me then why didn't you accept my proposal?"

She went stiff as a board, then tried to rear up, but his arm held her against him. "Don't fight me. Why didn't you accept my proposal then? All this would have been avoided, well, probably not, but Teresa would have had to take both of us on, not just you."

"You're asleep. I heard you snoring."

"I'm a light sleeper. The snoring is the way I relax myself."

"You're lying." She sighed. He said nothing, not that she expected him to. Then, suddenly, he turned to face her. He began kissing her, his hands on every patch of her, kneading her flesh, caressing her, saying sex words into her mouth, words she didn't understand. When he raised her in his hands and brought her to his mouth, she pulled on his hair and said, "Phillip, isn't this a very strange thing for you to do to me? It's very embarrassing."

"Shut up. Try to enjoy this, Sabrina. I'd like for you to have pleasure this time."

But she was locked into such embarrassment all she could do was bite her mouth and keep her eyes tightly closed. Finally, she heard him sigh. He opened her legs and slowly, gently, came into her. She was sore, but it didn't hurt too badly. He was moving inside her now and she knew that this was why she'd been ostracized. Everyone had believed that this is what they'd done at Charles's hunting box. Why would any woman believe that? She lay there, feeling him deep inside her body. She loved him but this was only something she'd do if he wanted it. She sighed. It seemed to be very important to him.

She hurt deep inside. He kept moving, kissing her mouth, her breasts, fondling every part of her he could reach. She was skinny. Why would he want to do that?

When he moaned his release, she braced herself for the torrent of stiffening muscles, the tightening of his body against hers, the wet of him inside her. Finally it was over.

"I will sleep now, Sabrina. I'm sorry."

"Sorry about what?"

He laughed. "I swear to you that I'll teach you soon enough. You're just not ready yet to be a woman, but you will."

His light snoring was real this time. Slowly she pulled away from him and rose. She washed herself in the basin of water on the bedside table. In the dim light of the single candle, she saw that there was blood and his seed on the cloth.

This was what everyone had believed she'd done. It was amazing. She rinsed out the cloth as best she could, then climbed back into bed beside her husband. She leaned up and blew out the candle.

She fell asleep with the pounding of his heart beneath her hand and the sound of his snoring in her ear.

Dawn light softened the blackness when she felt him again inside her, moving slowly, deeply. She hurt, but he was her husband. She loved him and if he wanted to do this a dozen times to her, then she'd not argue. Well, maybe she'd say something about it on the eighth time, but not yet. He was only to three. She could still bear it. She kissed him back, taking his moans into her mouth, and stroking her hands over his back. It wasn't long before she felt the stiffening in him, heard the sharp intake of breath, then his yell of release.

Yet again he was instantly asleep. Yet again she was washing herself in the basin, wondering what woman would ever agree to do this unless she was married and had to. Or unless she loved a man and wanted desperately to please him.

Sabrina supposed she fell into both categories.

At least now he was hers. She would let him do this whenever he wished to. He wouldn't have the time or the energy to go back to Martine. She fell asleep wondering if men wanted to do this during the day. If so, she would have to be close to him so he could use her whenever he wanted to. She thought of him touching her down there, kissing her down there. She shuddered with embarrassment. What if he wanted to do that during the day, when he could see her?

34

"My secretary, Paul Blackador, has many times told me that the devil was in the details. What do you think, Sabrina?"

"I don't know what that means." It was a bright winter morning, sun flooding into the breakfast room. He was smiling and eating and talking nonsense. Sabrina was tired and very sore, but she loved him, curse him for not asking her how she felt. He'd been the one to hurt her yet now all he could talk about was the devil and his damned details.

Couldn't he at least tell her that he was just a bit fond of her?

"It means that if a man isn't careful, it's the little things, the details, that will rise up and bite him. Do him in."

"I still don't know in what direction your mind is going."

"It's really very simple. I don't want you to love me, Sabrina." He was chewing a piece of bacon as he said that. She wasn't worth enough for him to even stop eating for a moment.

"I really can't help it."

"You said last night you realized it at Moreland when you woke up and I was sitting there watching you. I'm sorry for it. Don't get me wrong. I'm fond of you, very fond, but things won't change." He thought of his hands on her soft flesh. She'd felt to him like no other woman had in his life. And being inside her, the smallness of her, the tightening of her muscles, no, he wouldn't think about that. It was just sex. He looked at her. He realized he wanted to touch all of her, all at the same time, right now. He closed his eyes a moment.

"What things?"

He merely shrugged. "I enjoyed last night. Thank you for coming to me. I hope you're not too sore this morning?" He remembered how difficult it was to come into her. She'd been so small, her flesh so resistant to him, all his fault, of course. He should have taken more time, been more patient. Damn the surfeit of brandy and his own lust.

"Yes, I am. I had no idea that men did those sorts of things so much."

His eyes nearly crossed. Actually, he wanted to toss his breakfast plate to the floor, pull her up against him, and lay her onto her back on the table. He wanted to push her this morning, push her to pleasure, teach her. He wanted to hear her yell, and not in pain.

But he wasn't about to accept this girl's love offering. "Men like to do all sorts of things. Women do too."

She said absolutely nothing.

"You'll believe me soon enough. Now, get rid of this little girl's infatuation. That's all it is, you know. I'm your hero and thus you feel that you must love me. It's the stuff of novels, Sabrina, not real life." He tossed down his napkin and rose.

He stopped beside her chair, leaned down, and lightly kissed her mouth. "You're lovely, Sabrina. I very much enjoyed you last night; well, at least a bit since I'm a man and can enjoy a woman even if she's as still as a fallen tree. That will change, I promise you. Yes, you and I will do very well together, each in our own way." Then he was gone from the breakfast room, whistling.

She threw her plate at the closed door.

Phillip heard that plate. He paused a moment, then shook his head. No, let her hurl plates if it helped her realize what was real and what wasn't. He would bring her to pleasure and that would improve her opinion of him. A woman always liked a man who brought her to pleasure, always was more ready to excuse him, always was more ready to forgive him. He began whistling again, out the door and onto Tasha's back for a gallop on Heathrow common.

"Is her ladyship about, Greybar?"

It was late afternoon. Phillip had enjoyed a full day and was ready to see the slip of a girl who was his wife, the slip of a girl he'd teach pleasure to this very evening. Then he frowned. Perhaps that would be spoiling her. Perhaps he should be gone this evening. He didn't want her to think he was some sort of panting dog to sit at her feet.

"I believe her ladyship is with Mr. Blackador, my lord, planning the menu for the dinner party."

"Well hell, I'd forgotten all about that."

"It would be wise for you to refresh your brain, my lord. It's three evenings from now. If you don't mind my saying so, her ladyship is one who knows just how things should be done. Mr. Blackador has already sent out the invitations. Don't you recall? You scrutinized the list yourself yesterday."

"Oh yes, I did. This party will be just the thing to make her ladyship shine." He rubbed his hands together. "Ah, yes, Greybar, trust me to ensure that she's smiling, quite a lot."

Greybar looked as if he'd swallow his teeth. He

knew, of course, that the bride was no longer a virgin, the maid having informed Mrs. Hawley of the blood in the basin, and Mrs. Hawley having duly informed him, over tea in her rooms, as was proper. His lordship was being fatuous. Greybar, not for the first time in the past week, wanted to hit his master. Instead, he stared fixedly at the wainscoting.

"I've decided I want her in the bedchamber adjoining mine. It will be much easier that way. Do have the carpenter and all those folk to help select furnishings and wallpaper come and talk to me. Or rather, perhaps it would be better for them to see her ladyship. Yes, there's no reason why she couldn't see to this. She's young but I don't think she's particularly incompetent."

"My lord, she's your wife."

"She certainly is now," Phillip said, and went off to find his wife.

He found both Sabrina and Paul Blackador in the library, Paul sitting near her, a tablet on his lap and a pen in his hand.

"Hello, Paul, Sabrina," he said easily as he strolled into the room. "I see the two of you are planning our orgy. Is everything all right?" Even as he spoke, Phillip saw that even though Sabrina was wearing a very pretty pale yellow gown that did incredibly wonderful things to that glorious auburn hair of hers, her face was pale and there were dark smudges under her violet eyes. Damn, he shouldn't have indulged himself with her so much the previous night. Three times was excessive, particularly for a new wife and a virgin. But he'd wanted her, very much and she'd given herself to him. She'd told him she loved him, had loved him since that long-ago evening at Moreland. It was nonsense.

Her voice sounded equal parts anger and defeat,

surely an odd combination. "Good afternoon, my lord. It's such a pleasure to see you again. One would hardly imagine that this is your home, given the small number of hours you spend here, but whose business is that?"

"Certainly not yours, madam," he said, then softened it because Paul was there, and he looked so nervous he just might faint. "I see you're working on our party."

"Yes, we're planning the menu. Paul has excellent advice."

Paul Blackador had seldom ever given Phillip advice. He usually just nodded and kept his head down. Was she making fun of his secretary? Phillip looked at Paul, whose pleasant, sensitive face was undergoing a series of contortions. "Shall we discuss this over tea, Sabrina?"

"I'm not thirsty, my lord. There is a lot still to be done. Paul and I are quite busy, as you can surely see."

"Then you will eat some of Cook's lemon cakes. Come, Sabrina. I won't ask you again."

She wanted to tell him to hie himself to the devil along with all the details, but she saw that Paul was in agony. "Very well, my lord. Paul, can you carry on without me?"

"Certainly. I have many other matters to attend to, my lady." He looked first at his master, then at his mistress, who had two spots of color high on her cheekbones. Then he dropped his tablet. Phillip arched an eyebrow. He could have sworn he heard his very mild-tempered secretary curse. He had to grin, but he did manage to keep his mouth shut.

When she was pouring him tea, strong and dark, as he liked it, he said, "I hope you're still not angry with me about my misplaced gallantry regarding your inheritance."

"No," she said as she handed him the teacup. "I've decided I want it all. I want to be financially independent. I don't want to be pulled about on your string. Thank you for offering it back to me. I accept. If you would like to reconsider giving me back my dowry, why I'll take that too, gladly."

"No, not the dowry. You may have the other. That's fine. It's what I wanted." He frowned at her. He didn't like the way she'd changed her mind. The manner of it wasn't particularly as he would envision it should be, and it was obvious to even a blockhead that she was goading him, her sarcasm slamming him right between the eyes. Of course she didn't need to be financially independent. It was the grand gesture, merely an affirmation of his beneficence. She was his wife. Did she believe he'd throw her in a ditch and let her starve?

"Is there anything else I've done to offend you? After all, in the short time I've known you, you've pointed out a large number of flaws in my character. Do you wish to continue pointing now?"

"No, I have no more for the moment. I trust you enjoyed yourself all day today wherever you went, whatever you did, and with whomever you did it."

"Yes, thank you." He sipped his tea. It was China black tea, his favorite. "Now, tell me about the arrangements for your first dinner party."

"*My* dinner party? Aren't you going to attend? Oh, I see, you have more important activities planned for that evening. Perhaps you're escorting Martine to Vauxhall?"

"Eat a lemon cake."

"I'm not hungry."

"You're supposed to be flourishing now that you're safe with me."

"Flourishing?"

"Yes, in the manner of a beautiful tight flower bud gradually opening to the brilliant sunlight."

"That's ridiculous. You're ridiculous."

"Well, yes, but at least you're smiling a bit now. Now, tell me what you've planned so I can either approve or disapprove of your schemes. No, don't throw anything at me. Yes, just sit there and eat something. If you must, throw the cup at me, at least it's nearly empty."

She set the cup in its saucer. She folded her hands in her lap and looked down at the yellow toes of her slippers. "I never threw anything in my life before I met you."

"Perhaps you've just never suffered from excess bile before."

"I will try to control my bile."

"Good. Now tell me what you've planned." Phillip handed her a cake and gave himself one. She began nibbling on it. He was pleased. It was a start. "What delights have you in store for me?"

She thought of the kind of delights that he obviously preferred and grew so angry she bit her cheek.

She had a sudden memory of him bending over her, his face calm, as he touched his palm to her forehead. "Thank you for saving my life."

"Where the devil did that come from?" He didn't like that. He preferred a plate tossed at his head. Well, not really, but he didn't want her to go on believing she loved him. He'd be delighted to settle for something in the middle.

"I don't know. It was just a fleeting memory. You were there a lot in my mind, perhaps when I wasn't even fully conscious."

"I'd never bathed a woman before or washed her hair. I would like to do that again."

"To me or to your mistress?" The instant the words had spurted from her mouth, she was horrified. She'd meant to keep it to herself, at least most of it, most of the time. The words hung between them.

However, Phillip didn't say anything. He took another sip of his tea and appeared to study the Aubusson carpet beneath his boots.

Finally, he said mildly, "The schemes, Sabrina? For the dinner party?"

She told him what she was planning. When she paused, he said, "Impressive, Sabrina. Perhaps it's not at all a bad thing to have one's wife bred in the wilds of Yorkshire. Allow me to select the wines, and I vow we will have to drag our guests from the dinner table."

Sabrina turned pink with his praise. It was infuriating, but she couldn't help it. She was too easily pleased, she thought, but couldn't help herself. She didn't mind at all that he was changing her wines. She was smiling slightly as she said, "I had Paul commission the Huxley group for the dancing. I do so love to waltz, and Greybar told me that they have quite a fine way with the music. A lot of enthusiasm and energy. Greybar said they were even more lively than the group that played for our wedding."

Phillip cocked an eyebrow. "Dancing? I'd thought this would only be a dinner party."

"I know that it would cost quite dearly, but since I'm now financially independent, I shall pay for the orchestra myself."

She was so defensive with him. He didn't even raise an eyebrow again, just said easily, "That's fine. Do so, with my compliments at your show of independence. You pay for the entertainment and I'm the one who benefits. I enjoy waltzing with you."

"And I with you," she said, although she didn't want to. But when she wasn't infuriated with him, she remembered that she did love him, despite his belief that she was a little girl and this was naught but infatuation. The fool.

"If you ever find yourself short in the pocket or purse and in need of a loan, please feel free to approach me. I'm a generous man. I'd be more generous if I didn't feel you would dislike it so much."

"Let us talk of something other than money, Phillip."

"Yes, I suppose so. It's depressing, talking about money, that is."

She rose. "Will you be dining here tonight?"

She looked lovely and scared and defensive. He rose slowly to face her. He lightly touched his fingertips to her jaw. Freedom, he thought. He couldn't forget his freedom. Nor could he ever afford to let her forget it. He wanted to take her right this instant, on the beautiful Aubusson at their feet.

No, he wouldn't ever allow himself to be a pet dog at her feet. "Yes, I'll certainly dine here, but then I'm off. I have an engagement this evening and won't be home until very late. Then if you like, I'll come to you, Sabrina, or if you please, you can come to me, and we can try again to make you scream with pleasure."

She pulled her arm back, but he caught her fist at least six inches from his jaw. "I thought you loved me," he said.

She stared into his hazel eyes. "Yes, but I still want to kill you."

He laughed, released her, and stepped back. At least his wife was no longer a virgin. She still wasn't a satisfied woman, but he had time. They had the rest of their lives. He didn't like the sound of that in his mind, but somehow he liked the feel of it in his gut.

Freedom, it was all a matter of freedom. He took another step away from her, then said, "What gown do you intend to wear?"

What was in his mind? "Rose satin," she said. "It hasn't yet arrived from the dressmaker."

"It should go well with your hair."

"I hope so. Charlie thought that it would."

"I don't give a good damn about Charles's opinion about anything regarding my wife."

That made her smile, and he saw it. "I'm not jealous of that blockhead, Sabrina."

"Certainly not, my lord. That would be a very petty thing and if there's anything at all I understand about you, it's that you're never petty."

She didn't know exactly what he was, but she imagined, being a wife for life, that she would discover everything about him in the years to come. Years during which he would have mistresses. And spend time with them. She supposed, fool that she was, that she'd really expected him to stay with her after last night. She'd given him everything she had.

It still wasn't enough. She met with Mrs. Hawley and discussed new sheets.

The arrival of her rose satin gown the next day from the dressmaker's didn't make her smile.

35

Sabrina stared at herself in the mirror. The rose satin gown with its layers of Valenciennes lace edging the bodice and sleeves made her look more like a medieval lady than a modern one. But it was unusual and lovely. She didn't look too bad either, praise be to God.

He hadn't come to her. She'd wanted to go to him, but she hadn't. She was afraid she'd smell his mistress's perfume on him again.

He could have at least come to her once, just once, but he hadn't.

She was reaching for a single strand of pearls when there was a knock on the door. She was in one of the smaller bedchambers. She assumed he was back in his own.

"Come," she called out. She nodded absently to Doris and began to finger the clasp on the necklace.

"Oh, it's you, my lord. Do come in. Her ladyship is lovely, isn't she? I was worried about the shade of the gown, you know, but it's very elegant."

Sabrina was grinning at her maid's enthusiasm when she turned around and nearly froze her tongue in her mouth. Phillip stood in the doorway, dressed in severe black, his cravat and shirt as white as new snow. It would be cold to the touch, surely. She'd never seen a more beautiful man in all her life, not that her life

was all that long, but still, there could be no man on
the earth to compare to him. Well, at least in London.
She wanted to just spit it out and kiss him and run
her hands over him, but she stood still, waiting.

He was just standing there, after he'd dismissed
Doris, studying her, like a man deciding whether or
not he'd buy a hunter.

Then he smiled and stepped to her. "Just one more
small item, Sabrina, and all the gentlemen will fall
inert at your feet."

He was the only man she wanted inert at her feet
and she didn't want him inert at all. "Good evening,
Phillip. What are you talking about? What item?"

Phillip opened a narrow jewelry box. Nestled on a
bed of black velvet was a delicate diamond necklace.

It was the most beautiful thing she'd ever seen. She
just stared at it.

"I saw your gown earlier. I think the diamonds will
be more striking than the pearls. What do you think?"

She picked up the necklace, watching the diamonds
spill over her palm. "It's incredible. Oh, Phillip, thank
you." She threw her arms around his neck.

He didn't move, his arms remaining at his sides. But
he did kiss her temple. "Let me fasten the necklace."

She felt the coldness of the diamonds flat against
her throat, then the warmth of his fingers touching the
back of her neck. He said, "I wanted something new
for you. All the other Mercerault pieces are heavy and
old, too big for you. There, do you like it?"

But she didn't look at the necklace first. She looked
in the mirror at him, standing behind her. "Beautiful,"
she said. "Simply beautiful."

He looked suddenly embarrassed.

"The necklace, Sabrina."

"I don't look like myself. It glitters so much it will
blind our guests."

"Good. That will keep all the men from staring at you."

Staring at her? Now that was a jest that didn't deserve to be repeated.

He was looking about her bedchamber. "Mrs. Hawley told me you moved in here yesterday. Will it be all right until we can have the viscountess's bedchamber redone for you?"

"It's fine."

Phillip ran his hand over the top of a French chair covered in a pale blue velvet that she'd found in another room and moved in here. It was a lovely chair, one that surely wouldn't hold his weight.

"I didn't buy that chair."

"No, I know that you didn't."

"But if I had bought the chair, then I would have paid for it myself."

"That's kind of you. Now, shall we go downstairs?"

As they walked down the wide staircase, she remembered the gown and gulped. "I must tell you the truth, Phillip. The gown was very expensive. I forgot about it, really. Would you like me to pay for it?"

"No. Consider the necklace and the gown wedding presents from your doting husband."

He gazed thoughtfully at her a moment. "There's one guest you're not expecting. I hope you'll enjoy seeing him."

She had no idea what man he could possible have invited for her. And he wouldn't even give her a hint.

The twenty guests who sat down at the long dining table amid laughter and rustling gowns included not one unknown face. She looked down at the head of the table when there was a shout of laughter. Everyone around Phillip was laughing at something he'd said. She gave over her attention to the Countess of

March, a beautiful young lady who was ready to amuse and be amused.

As the meal progressed to the baked pheasant, Sabrina glanced down to where her aunt Barresford was seated and was relieved to see a smile on her relative's face. No one had refused her invitation, and Sabrina wondered with some cynicism if the guests had come merely to see if she would embarrass herself.

She was forced to marvel at her husband's adept handling of their guests. Both gentlemen and ladies alike appeared to bask in his attention, tossed with cavalier charm first to one, then to another. To her prejudiced eye, there was but one other gentleman to rival him. The Earl of March, seated near the middle of the long table, next to Aunt Barresford, appeared to be in his element, just as was the viscount. As for the Countess of March, that young lady had been very kind to her. "My dear," she whispered low just as they were leaving the dining room, "we must discuss how best to strip this masculine stronghold of its bachelor trappings. At last Phillip has seen the light. It's a good thing. I've always liked him, but now that he has you, I daresay he'll improve nearly to the sainthood of my husband. Yes, you must visit me in Grosvenor Square and we will settle upon a strategy."

By ten o'clock the ballroom was filled with more guests than had their wedding reception just a week ago, Sabrina thought. Only a week.

"Your husband has done quite well by you, Sabrina," her aunt Barresford remarked, surveying the beautifully dressed men and women. "I imagine that Teresa Elliott must be having a fit not to have been invited, not that she should have expected to be, given what she did to you."

Aunt Barresford appeared to have changed her stripes. Sabrina just smiled. "Phillip said if he ever saw her again he would wring her neck, but I told him that if we didn't invite her, I would have just one more enemy to deal with. He agreed, but he didn't want to. I'm sorry she's evidently decided not to come."

A half hour later Teresa Elliott arrived on the arm of her brother, Wilfred. He didn't look at all happy. Resigned, yes, that was how poor Wilfred looked. As for Teresa, she looked beautiful, but there was a dangerous glitter in her eyes. Sabrina prayed she'd keep a hold on herself.

Wilfred was saying to his sister, his voice low and controlled, "You've ranted and acted like a fishwife for the entire past week. If you have a brain in your head, if you have an ounce of sense, you'll make a push to be pleasant."

"Just look at her, Wilfred, lording it all over everybody, just like she belonged."

"She does belong. If you value your social position, you'd best wipe that nasty look off your face. You don't want everyone to know you've had a telling blow, do you?"

Teresa was forced to hold her peace as she and Wilfred came to the viscount and viscountess in the receiving line.

"How delightful that you could come," Sabrina said, nodding pleasantly to both Miss Elliott and her brother.

Teresa inclined her head, her eyes on the viscount's profile.

"Phillip," Sabrina said, tugging slightly on his sleeve. "Miss Elliott and her brother, Wilfred."

Phillip turned from a brief conversation with Lord William Ramsey. His hazel eyes instantly lost their compelling warmth.

"I was just telling Wilfred, my lord, that you were

so naughty to wed Miss Eversleigh so very quickly. None of us scarce had time to get to know her."

Phillip gave Sabrina a lazy smile, then said easily, "I would rather say, Teresa, that if I hadn't finally managed to convince her to wed me so quickly, I might have lost the most beautiful lady in London to another gentleman. We Merceraults have always been noted for our brains, you know. Wilfred, I trust your studies are continuing?"

"Oh yes, my lord."

Phillip watched the brother and sister go into the ballroom. "This could afford me some amusement. If she tries anything unpleasant with you, Sabrina, you have my permission to hurl a plate or a glass at her. Then, if she doesn't subside, you can kick her."

"Thank you. Perhaps I'll even stick close to her in hopes that she will insult me. May I really kick her?"

"Yes, but try not to let too many of our guests see you."

Another couple claimed her attention and it was some ten more minutes before Phillip turned again to Sabrina. "Waltz with me, Sabrina. I think we have finally greeted every guest."

"And not one of them your 'surprise,' Phillip."

"I assume that he decided he didn't wish to come," he said as he took her arm.

Within minutes, Sabrina was laughing, her eyes alight with pleasure. "You see, Phillip, not everyone is unkind in London."

"You're jesting with me. Even you can't be that thick."

"Very well, but I can so easily forget when we're waltzing. Oh, I very much like the Earl and Countess of March. They're charming."

Phillip remembered the earl's words to him several days before at Gentleman Jackson's. He said more to himself than to her, "Julien certainly follows his own advice. Never have I seen a young lady less broken to bridle."

"Breaking to bridle? What's this about?"

A space cleared on the dance floor and Phillip suddenly whirled her around in smooth, wide circles. When he drew her back into a more sedate pace, she was panting and laughing at the same time. "Oh, that was wonderful."

He dropped a kiss on the fat braid on top of her head. A rose ribbon was threaded through the braids. It was an excellent style on her. She moved closer to him. He frowned. He hadn't meant to do that, he hadn't.

"I believe," he said as the music came to an end, "that our surprise guest has arrived. If I'm not mistaken, he wishes to dance with you."

Sabrina turned to face Richard Clarendon. She cocked her head to one side. There'd been just a hint of chill in Phillip's voice. How odd.

"Richard," she said, and swept him a curtsy.

Richard Clarendon gazed down at the slender, vibrant girl before him and for a moment forgot all his gallant banter, compliments so much a part of him that he could speak them while continuing his own thoughts. "You're well, Sabrina?"

"Yes, Richard, I'm very well."

"I'm delighted you could come, Richard," Phillip said. "My wife dearly loves to waltz. Perhaps you would like to indulge her?"

She forgot their last meeting at Moreland when she'd been flat on her back, sicker than she'd care to admit, and he'd tried to bend her to his will. She looked up at him, seeing an extraordinarily handsome man who looked altogether dark and dangerous. "Perhaps Richard doesn't want to dance, Phillip."

Richard Clarendon merely nodded to Phillip and took Sabrina's arm. She smiled up at him, craning her neck, for he was some inches taller even than Phillip. He whirled her away into the throng.

"Good God, Phillip, what the devil are you doing? Have you lost your good sense?"

Phillip turned to see Charles Askbridge standing at his elbow.

Phillip looked down a moment at his well-manicured fingernails. He said mildly, "Clarendon just arrived in town. He's a friend, Charles. Would you that I barred him from my home?"

"He still wants her. Just look at the way he's staring at her. You're placing Sabrina in a rather awkward position. I wouldn't do it."

Phillip just shrugged. "Excuse me, Charles, I believe I'll dance with Teresa. I can't wait to see what she has to say. I'll either start laughing at the absurdity of it all or strangle her on the dance floor. Which do you think is preferable?"

36

Sabrina turned, smiling, and said to Richard Clarendon, "Your mother and son are well?"

"Yes." He sounded angry.

"Have I offended you in some way, Richard?"

His dark eyes flashed a moment. "Of course not. It is I who have offended myself."

"I don't understand."

"Many times I don't understand myself." The girl in his arms was now the Viscountess Derencourt and there was nothing on earth that could change that fact. "I read of your marriage."

"It's been nearly a week now. It seems much longer, truth be told."

He wondered, looking down at her, what would have happened if he hadn't gone to one of his northern estates after her refusal of him at Moreland. If he'd been in London at the time of her ruin, would he, like Phillip, have tried yet again to convince her to marry him? He didn't fault Phillip for his course of action; he only wished that it had been he who had been her rescuer. He saw that she was looking at him, a clear question in those incredible eyes of hers, and quickly changed the topic.

"I visited Monmouth Abbey again before coming to London. Your grandfather does much better. That weasel cousin of yours assured me a dozen times if he assured me once that the earl would recover. Trevor really is a paltry fellow, Sabrina, but I swear to you that I didn't knock his teeth down his throat. I did, however, grab the weasel by his cravat and lift him a good six inches off the floor and shake him until his head snapped."

She grinned up at him. "That was well done of you. Actually, I'd like to do that, too. I had another letter from Grandfather just yesterday. He sounds better. Thank you for going there, Richard. It's very kind of you. Did you visit with him?"

"Yes, briefly. His color is better. He's very pleased that you're safe."

He saw that she didn't want to ask, and said quickly, "Yes, I also saw Elizabeth. She appears to enjoy being mistress of the manor. But you know as well as I do that it has to be one of her only pleasures. It's becoming common knowledge that Trevor indulges himself with the Monmouth servants. And Elizabeth knows it. Every day he is less discreet. I heard that he was even bedding her maid, Mary."

"But does Trevor at least treat her well in public?"

"Yes, he's not altogether stupid. I'm glad you're out of that household."

"Poor Elizabeth," she said. "She doesn't deserve to be tied to a man like him, no woman does. I told her the truth but she wouldn't listen to me."

"I don't remember Elizabeth ever listening to anybody. You're still too thin, Sabrina."

"Give me time, Richard," she said easily. "Phillip tells me that if we go to Dinwitty Manor, the cook there will make me fat as a flawn within a week."

"He's right. It's a dangerous place to go." She felt his hand tighten about her waist and blinked at him. His dark eyes glittered.

Richard wished now that he hadn't come. There was

still a tug of attraction for her. It was still too strong for his own peace of mind. Although he enjoyed married ladies, the thought of flirting with Sabrina, of trying to seduce her, was distasteful to him and that smacked of a morality he didn't want to see in himself. "Your ball is a success."

"Yes. Phillip has done well by me, don't you think?"

"You don't sound very pleased. What's wrong? Aren't you happy?" His grip tightened about her fingers.

"Of course I'm happy. It's also a good thing that I'm no longer that silly young girl from Yorkshire."

The waltz drew to a close. Richard drew her hand through his arm, his fingers warm and caressing over hers. "Come, Sabrina, let us try some of your punch. I heard from one very happy lady that there's superb champagne in it. Phillip's cellars have an excellent reputation."

She nodded, looking for her husband from the corner of her eye. She finally saw him in laughing conversation with a striking girl whose name she couldn't remember.

Suddenly there was a rending sound. Sabrina stopped dead in her tracks. "Oh, drat, just look what I've done. My beautiful gown, I've caught the hem and ripped it. Do forgive me, Richard. I must go fix it."

"Allow me to fix it for you, Sabrina. I'm really quite accomplished at such tasks, you know."

She couldn't imagine how that could be so.

"Come, trust me."

Sabrina shook her head, laughing. "You and Phillip are like two peas from the same pod. The both of you must always have the last word. Very well, there's a small room just down the corridor that should provide you, me, and my flounce sufficient privacy."

Phillip watched Sabrina and Richard Clarendon leave the ballroom. What was going on?

He excused himself from Miss Patterson, and made good his escape from the ballroom. He saw Sabrina laugh up at Richard and walk away with him down the corridor toward the back of the house. Although he hated what he was doing, he still walked after them. He saw Sabrina open the door to the small room she'd just begun using for her own private parlor and close it after her.

His fists clenched at his sides and he felt cold fury wash over him. He admitted to himself that his invitation of a man who'd been a good friend for many years had been in the nature of a test. He simply had to know if Sabrina cared anything about the marquess. He wasn't proud of himself. But there it was. He'd said nothing, done nothing. He'd simply let them do what they wanted to do. He'd simply watched them go into that room. He'd simply watched the damned door close.

Her behavior was inexcusable. He was angrier than he'd been in a very long time. He turned on his heel and strode back to the ballroom.

In the small ladies' room, Sabrina was laughing as she said, "Some assistant you are, Richard, just look at what you're doing." He was actually on his knees in front of her sticking pins in strategic places in the ripped hem.

Their heads were nearly touching.

He looked up. He couldn't seem to stop staring at her mouth. "Consider me both your inspiration and your servant."

"No, that pin is all crooked. Here." She was laughing when she took the pin from him. She jabbed her finger.

"Oh, goodness, look what I've done." She put the injured finger in her mouth.

"Now I can truly be of assistance, Sabrina." Richard knelt up in front of her, taking the finger and inspecting it. A small drop of blood welled up. Without thought, he licked it away, then gently kissed the finger.

Sabrina sat very quietly, gazing down at his bent head. "Richard." She stopped. She didn't know what to say. She looked down at the handsome man who was kneeling in front of her. She felt embarrassed and strangely ashamed.

He groaned, dropped her hand as if it were something to bite him, and rose quickly. He ran his hand distractedly through his hair.

"I'm sorry, Sabrina. I didn't mean to do that."

Sabrina rose and placed her hand on his sleeve. "Please, it's all right, Richard. It's forgotten. You're an excellent friend and—"

"Dammit, I never wanted to be your bloody friend. You know I would have married you, despite what happened between you and Phillip."

She raised her head and looked him straight in his dark eyes. "I'm no longer a virgin, as of four nights ago. I now know what men do to women. Phillip did it to me three times. So, what I find absolutely astounding is that anyone with any sort of brain at all would think that a woman would willingly let a man do those things to her. It's ridiculous. If you honestly believe that while I was very ill I let Phillip somehow seduce me, then you're an idiot, Richard, very simply, an idiot."

He was treading on very swampy ground, but Richard Clarendon was a man used to speaking his mind. Her words didn't make sense. "You mean to tell me that Phillip didn't please you? Sabrina, Phillip is an experienced man. He isn't a clod. This is impossible. He made love to you three times and you had no pleasure with him?" He realized then what he was saying. Her face was perfectly white. She looked both pale and ill and ready to kill. "I'm sorry, forgive me. That wasn't something I should have said. I could have thought it but not said it."

He ran his hand through his hair again. "You're in love with him and yet he hasn't pleased you. That's astonishing, truly it is, if you but realized it." Suddenly the impropriety of the situation struck him forcibly. In her innocence, she'd thought nothing of accompanying him to this room, alone. All she needed at this point was more vicious gossiping. And just look what had happened. No fault of hers. All his. He smiled at her very gently, slowly lifted her hand, and lightly kissed her fingers. "I'm a fool. Everything will right itself, Sabrina, you will see. Now, I must take my leave. You must return to the ballroom and your guests before you're missed. Good-bye."

He turned on his heel and left the room, leaving her to stare after him.

At two o'clock in the morning Sabrina was so weary that she could barely restrain her yawns as Doris brushed out her hair. Her bedchamber door opened suddenly and Phillip's reflection appeared in her mirror.

He dismissed her maid. He didn't say a word until Doris was out of the room. Then he kicked the door closed with the heel of his boot.

She smiled at him in the mirror. "You've sent away the final guests?" Sabrina turned in her chair and looked at him with some surprise. He wasn't smiling back at her. He didn't look at all tired. He looked angry.

"Yes, they're all gone. The champagne punch is gone as well. Greybar is so tired I thought he'd collapse in the entry hall." He sprawled into a chair opposite her and began to tap his fingertips together.

"We only waltzed two times, Phillip. I'd hoped for more, perhaps six times would have been sufficient for me. Indeed, you were slathering your charm on so wondrously that I didn't think the ladies would ever let you out of their sight."

He waved away her words. He said slowly, his voice low and careful, "You, at least, had the good sense to return to the ballroom before the gossips took notice."

It took her a moment to realize what he was saying. She just shook her head at him. "I tore the flounce on my gown and had to pin it up. If you'd only asked me to dance when I got back to the ballroom, I would have told you that."

"Did you come up with that or did Richard?"

She became very still.

"I don't blame you for keeping quiet. I wouldn't tell me either. Unfortunately for you, Sabrina, I saw you go to that very private little room of yours with Richard Clarendon."

"What are you saying, my lord?"

"How formal you've become, but perhaps the situation warrants it. What I'm saying, Sabrina, is that I gave you the opportunity to prove your indifference to Clarendon but you did just the opposite. You waltzed with him, then immediately left with him."

She slowly rose from the stool, her face flooding with angry color. "You're saying that Richard was here so you could conduct some sort of test?"

"Yes. You didn't pass."

"I don't believe this, Phillip, I truly don't. You have the gall to tell me that you didn't ever believe me when I told you I had no interest in Richard? You have the further gall to tell me that's the only reason he was here? To tempt your wife?"

"No, of course not." He rose, staring at her, his hands at his sides. "I can well control my own wife without recourse to subterfuge."

"If this wasn't subterfuge, then what was it?"

"It was nothing more than an opportunity for you to prove yourself to me. As I said, you failed. Now I must question your feelings toward Clarendon."

"If I had a knife, I'd stab you in your faithless hypocritical heart! You bastard, I'm not the faithless one here, it's you. You throw Richard up at me with no evidence of anything at all, yet you even call me by your own damned mistress's name. It's Martine, damn you!"

She picked up a scent bottle and hurled it at him. Then she wanted to kill him because he laughed and ducked it, then laughed harder. Then he stopped laughing. He said, "I am a man. You are my wife. You will obey me and you will not even consider being unfaithful."

She was shuddering with rage. No, she didn't want to throw anything else at him. It was childish. She had to use her wits, but it was difficult, for he made her so angry her brain dissolved into red mist. She drew several deep breaths. "I want you to leave, Phillip. I can't deal with any more of this now."

He walked to her and took her arms in his hands. He shook her slightly until she looked up at him. "You will deal with anything I tell you to. You are my wife, this is my house."

"You are my husband."

"Certainly. You will always have the protection of my name. I simply shan't allow you to tarnish it. Listen carefully to me, Sabrina. I will not tolerate Richard Clarendon as your lover, or any other man for that matter."

"I told Richard that I was no longer a virgin. Naturally he believed that you'd taken my virginity when I was vilely ill at the hunting box. I set him straight. I told him that you'd taken me three times and that I found it ridiculous for anyone to believe that a woman could ever be willingly seduced. It is humiliating and wretched what men do to women, what you did to me. I don't want a lover, Phillip. It's laughable even to think about it."

He looked utterly appalled. "You told Richard that I didn't give you pleasure?"

She could only stare up at him. She would never understand a man's mind. Her chin went up as high as she could get it. "I told him you were a clod."

"No," he said slowly, studying her pale face, "no, you love me. You would never tell another man something that would lessen my worth."

"None of this makes any sense. I either love you, in which case, how could I ever think to take a lover?"

"I don't know if you really love me. I think it's just infatuation, which might lead you astray, as in leading you directly to Richard. He has a way with women, I know that, only I do wish that you hadn't told him I'd been a clod. I wasn't, really, it's just that because of what Trevor did to you, you're still frozen and—" His eyes were on her face now. He didn't say anything more, just stared down at her. He lightly touched his fingertips to her cheek.

"So soft," he said, then leaned down to kiss her. She leapt back.

"How can you want to do that to me when you think I'm a horrible woman?"

"No, it's just possible that perhaps you could be led down a path that would end in a place that wouldn't be good for you, a place I wouldn't like you to be."

She said flatly, "You sound like a jealous husband, Phillip. Where there is no love—and surely you have none for me—then the ground must be too arid to cultivate such a feeling."

"I will never be jealous of a woman, particularly if the woman is my damned wife. I won't be cuckolded, Sabrina. You had your flirtation with Clarendon this evening, but there it will end. I would that you contrive to show some gratitude after all I have done for you."

She'd sworn never to throw anything again, but she just had no control over the hand that reached down and grabbed her hairbrush. She watched that hand rise, then hurl the hairbrush at him. It hit him on the jaw, a clean hit, that caused him pain. The hairbrush bounced off and hit the carpet at his feet. He didn't say anything, just rubbed his jaw.

"You're a fool, Phillip. Get out of my room."

"Not just yet, madam." He was on her in the next instant. He threw her over his shoulder and walked to her bed. He pulled her over his legs and struck her with the flat of his hand. She tried to rear up, but he just smacked her again.

She cursed him but he just laughed. He gave her one extra smack, then pulled her to her feet to stand beside him.

"In the future when you throw things at me, this will be your punishment. Next time, I'll pull up that gown and petticoat of yours and you'll feel my hand. This was nothing, so don't you ever throw it up to me. Good night, Sabrina."

He left her room without a backward glance. She yelled after him, "To think I actually believed living with you here was preferable to that miserable hotel. What a fool I was."

The door slammed open and he stuck his head in. "Don't push me, Sabrina."

"Push you? I've done nothing to you if you but had the brain to realize it."

She was standing there, panting, and he heard the dreadful pain in her voice. He couldn't stand it. He stepped into her bedchamber. "Sabrina," he said, his hand stretched out toward her.

She gave a small cry and ran to the other side of the bed. It gave her courage and both of them knew it. "You've said, my lord, that this is your house. Tell me, how much would you say that this bedchamber is worth? I would gladly pay you for it. Perhaps then you would stop reminding me how I must be grateful to you."

"You may have this room. Good night again, Sabrina."

"So you don't want to hear about how I made Richard follow me to that private room, how I locked the door against the curious, and how, despite his noble protests, I seduced the Marquess of Arysdale? It's in my blood, don't you think? After all, I did spend five days and nights with you. Yes, I'm a trollop, no doubt about that. I want to bed every man I meet after the enjoyment it brought me to be bedded by you. All that pleasure has driven my slut's soul to seek more and more. Richard is so very dark and brooding, I'll wager any number of ladies are after him. It makes my palms itch to touch him, just thinking about him."

Phillip kept his mouth shut. He heard the hysterical pitch in her voice. He merely nodded to her and shut the door behind him. She stood there, staring at that door, biting her lip, her eyes bright with tears she prayed wouldn't fall. She wouldn't cry for him.

No, she would never cry again.

37

He said to her over luncheon three days later, "Listen to me, Sabrina. We live in the same house. But when I see you, you simply look through me. You're agreeable, I won't deny that, but you're just not here. You avoid me. It's enough. There's no reason for this false submissiveness of yours. It's driving me mad. I want you to change."

She'd set down her fork and looked at him with great seriousness as he spoke, all her attention seemingly focused on him. But he knew it wasn't true. It was in that instant that he decided to take her to Dinwitty Manor. Out of London, away from all the cursed memories. Things would be different at Dinwitty. Cook could stuff food into her face, food that was ambrosia. She could help him design his tower. He hadn't looked at his drawings since last summer. But he was getting the itch again. He was ready now to begin again. He loved to build. He wondered if Sabrina would enjoy all the planning, watching the builders curse and sweat and fashion what he'd drawn. He'd write to Rohan and Susannah and invite them to come visit. Yes, that's what he'd do.

"How would you like me to change, Phillip? Whatever you wish, I will certainly do my best to comply."

At that moment he believed he'd give just about anything to have her hurl a plate at his head. But she didn't. She was sitting silently, her hands now folded in her lap. All that immense vitality of hers was extinguished. He hated it. Hell, he would lock her into the tower once it was built, if she was still acting this way.

"I want you to stand up. I want you to walk to me. I want you to kiss me."

Without hesitation, she rose and walked to him. She stood beside his chair, then leaned down and touched her mouth to his. A fleeting light touch, nothing at all behind it, no feeling, no anger, just nothing.

Then she simply walked away, toward the window. She pulled back the draperies and looked out at the gray, overcast winter day.

"Would you like to go to Almack's this evening? You love to waltz. Would that please you?"

"If it would please you, then naturally it would be my pleasure as well."

She didn't even turn to face him as she spoke. It enraged him. "I'm asking what you'd prefer, Sabrina."

She turned and lowered her head. The toes of her slippers were more important, more interesting, than he was. She said, "I thought you found Almack's boring. It also looks as if it might snow today. The clouds are low and very dark."

"Who cares if it bloody well snows? I like to waltz with you."

"I see," she said. She drew her shawl more closely around her shoulders, nodding to him, and said, "I will naturally do your bidding."

"Don't leave. Sit down."

Without a word, she sat down.

"I've asked you for your wishes in this matter. It's not a question of your doing my bidding."

"But my desire must perforce be to do your bidding, my lord."

"Very well. My bidding is for you to cease acting

like a spiritless old horse." He thought he saw a spark of anger in her eyes and found that he wanted nothing more than to fan that spark into a flame that would burn him but good. He wanted blood in her eyes. He wanted to see her fists. But she remained infuriatingly silent.

He continued, doggedly, "Perhaps Richard Clarendon will be there. I realize that he's just a friend, to both of us. Perhaps you would like to see him." It was as close as he'd ever get to an apology. He didn't believe that men were fashioned for abject apologies. It didn't matter how wrong they were. But it was an offer of one. Surely she saw that.

"In that case, my lord," she said, raising her head to face him, "yes, I should very much like to go."

"What the devil did you say?"

"I said I'd really like to go. And as you said, it matters not if it snows."

He wasn't at all certain now that she'd understood his apology. Did she want to go just because Clarendon would be there? He didn't know. He eyed her with growing frustration.

"I don't like this marriage business," he said finally, rose from the table, flung down his napkin, and strode from the dining room.

"I know you don't," she called after him. "As a matter of fact, I don't much like it either." Yes, she thought, staring again toward the window, this marriage business is the very devil.

Sabrina walked slowly to the windows and pressed her cheek to the chill glass. She supposed she'd wanted to goad him, and she had succeeded, not that it had solved anything.

She wandered into the library. For want of anything better to do, she pulled out a novel from one of the lower shelves and curled up in a curtained window seat.

She opened the small vellum tome of Voltaire and forced herself to concentrate on the French that was surely brimming with wit. Her attention soon wandered to the light flakes of snow that pattered gently against the windowpane, dissolved into small drops of water, and streaked in slender rivulets down the glass. She traced the brief existence of each splashing snowflake with the tip of her finger.

She must have dozed, for her head snapped up at the sound of voices in the library.

"I merely wanted to ask you, my lord," she heard Paul Blackador say to Phillip, "for it indeed is a strange bill to receive from a tradesman."

She was alert in an instant. Phillip's voice held her utterly still.

"Ah yes, the carpenter. Martine told me he was a saucy one. For your information, Paul, I had thought I'd be smashed during the night by a piece of falling plaster in the bedroom. Do pay the man."

Sabrina's fingers tightened about the thin book until she could picture the male grins on their faces. She'd never felt such fury in her entire life. Well, maybe she had, but all her grand fury had happened only since she'd met Phillip.

"There's another bill, my lord, for a gown from Madame Giselle. The total, I think, is a trifle excessive."

Sabrina heard the brief rustling of paper as, she supposed, the bill changed hands.

"It is a bit much," Phillip said, without much interest. "As I'm off to see the lady, I'll ask her about it. Anything else pressing, Paul?"

There was nothing more except a speech about the Corn Laws that Paul wanted him to present to the

House of Lords. After a bit of discussion, Phillip left, Paul after him.

The library door closed upon the rest of Paul's words. Sabrina bounded from her hiding place and shook her fist at the closed door. She had married the greatest hypocrite imaginable. She was to remain chaste—he was even jealous of Richard Clarendon—while he continued doing what he'd always done.

Phillip had told her to cease being a spiritless old horse. Very well, she would certainly grant him his wish. She felt life and rage sing in her blood.

She found Martine Nicholsby's direction on the carpenter's bill. She memorized the address on Fitton Place, then tossed the paper back on its neat stack.

Ten minutes later, a warm cloak around her and gloves on her hands, she met Greybar in the entrance hall. He was staring at her, as if she'd suddenly become someone else. Well, she had.

"His lordship has left, Greybar?" At his nod, she said then, "Call me a hackney. I wish to leave right now, no longer than a minute from now."

For a minute it looked like he would question her. She gave him the most arrogant look she'd ever seen her grandfather make. It worked.

Thirty minutes later Sabrina found herself staring at a two-story brick town house, sandwiched between other houses in a very quiet, unpretentious street, not a mile from Phillip's house. She pulled her ermine-lined cloak more closely about her and stepped quickly from the hackney. From the corner of her eye, Sabrina saw Lanscombe, Phillip's tiger, climb into the box and prepare to drive the curricle around the corner. How like Phillip, she thought, to ensure that his horses received the proper exercise while he made love to his mistress inside. She wondered how long poor Lanscombe was to tool the curricle about before fetching his master. Sabrina saw Lanscombe's jaw drop open when he spotted her. He gazed at her dumbly, shaking his head.

Sabrina turned her back on him, walked up the front steps, raised her gloved hand, and pounded upon the door.

After some moments the door slid cautiously open and a frowning maid's face appeared.

"What do you want?"

"I want my husband," Sabrina said coldly, and shoved the door open, knocking the maid aside. She was standing in a square entranceway. On one side she could see into a small drawing room. Straight ahead of her was a slightly winding staircase that led to the upper floor. She heard a light, tinkling laugh from above, and without further thought, she grasped her skirts and rushed to the stairs.

"Oh, Gawd, wait, miss, wait! You can't go up there."

"You just watch me," Sabrina said over her shoulder, and began running up the stairs. She followed the sound of a woman's lovely husky voice from inside a room. The door stood some inches open. She stood for an instant, indecisive. At the sound of Phillip's low laugh, she pushed the door open and rushed inside. She drew up short, panting.

She stood inside a large bedchamber, dominated by a huge bed. Upon the bed a woman lay upon her back, clothed in nothing but alabaster skin. In an instant, Sabrina took in every detail of her exquisite body. She looked like a painting, damn her.

But it was Phillip who quickly captured her attention. He was standing next to the bed, his cravat hanging loose, his coat flung over a chair. At least he wasn't naked, but it didn't matter. He would have been as naked as his mistress in another three minutes.

The brief frozen tableau suddenly turned into furious life.

Phillip, who had been laughing at Martine's verbal baiting of him, turned to see his wife burst into the bedchamber.

He stared at her openmouthed, incredulous, disbelieving. Then he yelled, "What the devil are you doing here?"

38

"My goodness," Martine said, rising on her elbow as she slowly pulled her peignoir over her lovely self. "I hadn't expected this."

Sabrina looked again at his now nearly naked mistress, and yelled back at him, "I wish the plaster had fallen on your head while you were making love to her, you bastard! How dare you even be here? It makes me want to slay you, Phillip. Damn you, you're my husband!"

"What are you yammering about plaster? Oh! So you were eavesdropping, were you? Not a very lady-like thing to do, Sabrina." He stopped. He'd never felt such a fool in his life. Dammit, this couldn't be happening, not to him. It was more worthy of a farce in Drury Lane. He took several furious steps toward her.

"Ladylike! You rotter, you're mine, yet you won't even give me a chance."

"It's true that you're my wife, and as such, why the devil aren't you at home, where you belong?"

"It's *your* home, you faithless bastard, not mine. I don't belong there, I merely reside there. She could reside there as well. It wouldn't matter to you."

"Dammit, Sabrina, that makes no sense at all. I won't tolerate any more of this. Go home now. I'll deal with you later."

"Later? You mean after you've bedded her? Then perhaps you'll have time to spend with me? How kind you are. My heart nearly expires with the joy of it."

"What I do with her is none of your business. You're the one who offered me my freedom, freedom I told you I already had and always would have."

"You dared to accuse me of flirting with Richard Clarendon and all the while you have a mistress. A mistress!" Sabrina waved toward Martine who was sitting on the side of the bed. "How dare you do this to me? Do I mean so little to you that you don't hesitate to humiliate me? Does our marriage mean so little to you?"

"Enough of this idiocy. Listen. Our marriage, madam, was meant to provide you a home and the protection of my name. You wanted that, don't you remember? You offered me marriage, don't you remember? You offered me my freedom."

She actually shook her fist at him, yelling, "That was then. This is now. I love you. You're my husband. I won't allow you any more freedom unless the freedom is with me!" She looked over at Martine to see the woman smiling at her, nodding. It made no sense. It didn't stop her. "I know that she is beautiful and much more nicely put together than I am, but she didn't get ruined, I did. You didn't have to marry her, you had to marry me. So it's done. Accept it, damn you."

"Accept it like I did when I saw you take Richard Clarendon into that very private little room of yours?"

"Will you forever play that same tired song? It's absurd, and you know it." Then her eyes narrowed, her hands were on her hips. "Well, perhaps you weren't wrong. Perhaps Richard is so pleasing to me that I just might go see him right now while you remain here to enjoy yourself."

"You won't take Richard Clarendon as your lover. You won't take any man as a lover."

She stared at him, unable to believe his perversity.

He smote his forehead with his palm. "Ah, you're driving me to the brink of madness. Go home, Sabrina. I won't take any more of this. Get out of here. By God, you're ranting like the lowest trollop in Soho."

"You bastard," she screamed at him. "I catch you with your mistress and you have the gall to call me a trollop?" She ran at him, pounding on his chest with her fists with all her strength.

Martine came to her feet, then just shook her head and sat back down again.

Phillip clamped his arms about his wife and dragged her to the small dressing room adjoining the bedchamber. He kicked the door closed with his booted foot. "Stop it, Sabrina, stop it." He was shaking her until her neck snapped back.

She became rigid in his arms and he released her. She took a stumbling step backward. She opened her mouth, but he interrupted her.

"Your behavior is inexcusable. You won't question what I do. Now you will take yourself quietly away from here, else I will seriously consider sending you to Dinwitty Manor to learn your place."

"My place? I don't have a place, Phillip. Now that I've seen how you've humiliated me, stripped me of even any pretense of worth—" She broke off. "You don't even understand, do you?"

"I understand enough to want to thrash you," he said low and grabbed her shoulders.

Sabrina drove her knee with all her strength into his groin. He dropped his hands and stared at her in amazement. "I'm a big man. You could have kicked me anywhere but there." Then he doubled over in pain.

Sabrina ran from the small dressing room. She wouldn't think about him holding himself, on his knees. She pulled the door open and, without another look at his mistress, fled from the bedchamber.

For several minutes Phillip thought death would be preferable to the exquisite bowing pain that had brought him to his knees. As the bouts of nausea slowly lessened, thank God, it was Sabrina's death he thought about. He pulled himself shakily to his feet and walked slowly back into the bedchamber. Without a word, he pulled on his coat.

"You look whiter than a trout's belly. What happened?"

"She kicked me in the groin," he said as he grabbed his greatcoat.

"That is an extreme thing to do, but she was very angry, the little one."

"She'll regret it soon enough," he said as he jerked on his gloves.

"You will beat her? Surely not, Phillip. She's half your size. That would hardly be fair. Besides, you're a gentleman. A gentleman wouldn't beat his wife."

He was already to her bedchamber door.

"But she's in love with you," Martine shouted. "She told you that."

"Ha! It's a girl's infatuation, nothing more. Surely she lost that after I took her three times in one night and never once gave her pleasure. Yes, she's over that. She's just saying it by rote. It means nothing at all. Now I'm going to murder her."

He turned at the door. "I will always have my freedom. I will always do just as I please. I'll be back later, Martine."

Martine sat back down on the bed and leaned back

against the pillows, listening to his galloping footsteps on the stairs.

Lanscombe said not a word as his master jumped into the curricle and grabbed the reins. The furious working of the viscount's jaw didn't bode well for the viscountess. Like a frightened little animal, she'd flown down the steps, running full speed toward a hackney.

Ten minutes later the viscount pulled his stallions to a steaming halt.

"Stable them," he said over his shoulder to Lanscombe as he took the front steps of the Derencourt town house two at a time.

"Where is the viscountess?" Phillip said the moment he saw Greybar.

"She returned just a short time ago, my lord. I believe she went up to her room."

Phillip stopped in front of Sabrina's bedchamber door. He turned the handle. The door was locked. The pulse pounded in his neck.

"Open the door, Sabrina."

Her voice came back to him, loud and quite clear. "Go away, Phillip. Go back to Martine. I don't want to see you. Go away."

"I'll go back to Martine whenever it pleases me to do so," he shouted, took a step back, raised his booted leg, and crashed it against the door. He heard splintering wood. He aimed one more kick nearer to the lock and the door flew open, straining at its hinges.

Sabrina stood with her back against the windows. She stared at him, standing there in her doorway, breathing hard. "Go away, Phillip. Go away."

He walked toward her, slowly, his eyes never leaving her face. He was very, very angry.

Sabrina pulled her hand up from the folds of her skirt. She was clutching a riding crop tightly in her fingers. "Stay away from me, Phillip, or I'll hurt you, I swear it."

"The only thing I'll stay away from is your damned knee."

"I mean it. Go away." She raised the riding crop and shook it at him.

"Try your best, you little witch." He was on her. She swung it wildly at him, but he took a quick sideways step, and she merely flicked his sleeve. He lunged forward and gripped her arm just above the elbow. As he forced her arm down she tried again to kick him. He turned to his side, letting her strike his thigh.

He gripped her arm more tightly. She felt the numbness, felt the riding crop slip from her fingers. He pulled her close. "I can't believe you struck me," he said.

"In your groin or now?"

He looked down at the riding crop. She'd hit him. He looked at her now, saw her face washed of color, saw the bruises beneath her expressive eyes, saw the fear in them. Lightly, he caressed his fingers over her cheek. He said quietly, "What have we come to, Sabrina?"

She shook her head, saying nothing.

"I never meant to hurt you when I took you as my wife. I always meant to honor you, to protect you, yet we've come to this. It's damnable. What will we do now?"

"I don't know," she said, "but I can't bear it, Phillip, I really can't."

"You unmanned me."

"I was very angry. I'm sorry, but I'd do it again. You were with her."

"I was there for a reason, Sabrina."

"Yes, I imagine that you were."

He sighed and let her go. He leaned down and picked up the riding crop. "You knew I'd come back here. You were going to protect yourself with this?"

"I had nothing else. It seems like another lifetime, but I still remember. When we were at the hunting box, when you were taking care of me, you told me you'd show me how to fight. You didn't. You forgot."

"Yes, I suppose I did. If I'd taught you, I wonder what damage you would have inflicted on me at Martine's."

"Go away, Phillip. I've really said everything I wanted to. Please just leave me alone."

"Yes," he said finally, "I suppose there really isn't anything more to say at the moment." He left her then, walking away from her, lightly hitting the riding crop against his leg.

She turned to stare blindly into the glowing embers in the fireplace. He was right. There wasn't anything more to say.

Downstairs, Greybar said to Dambler just after the viscount had slammed his way out the front door, "I don't know what's going on, but it's bad."

"I know," Dambler said. "I've never seen his lordship like this."

"We've both never seen him married." Greybar shuddered. "What will happen now?"

39

Sabrina slowly laid down the pen. She looked away from the letter she'd spent the past hour writing. She looked out her bedchamber windows. Heavy-bellied clouds, laden with snow, hung low in the early morning sky. She glanced at the clock on the mantelpiece, quickly added several more lines to her letter, and turned away to finish packing her portmanteau.

She fastened the straps, dragged the portmanteau to the door, then saw her letter on the writing desk, and returned to read it one last time.

"Dear Phillip," she read. "I've returned to Monmouth Abbey. I'm truly sorry if my abrupt departure causes you embarrassment. I'm also sorry for many other things, Phillip, least among them my outrageous behavior of yesterday. You were perfectly right. I had no right to act the wounded wife and kick you in the groin for having a mistress, although I didn't care at the time, I was so angry.

"You will perhaps believe me the perfect hypocrite now, but I find that I simply cannot continue as we have. You've said that your freedom is important to you, you've said it many times, I just never listened. Now I hear you. It's just that now I realize that I simply can't be but one of the women to share your life. I want more than that. I'm worth more than that, at least I think I am, hope I am. Perhaps I'm wrong.

"It's time for me to return where I belong. I no longer have any real fear of Trevor, for as you have said, he values his own survival above all things.

"I know you're a proud man, Phillip, and that's as it should be. I ask that in your pride you will not feel yourself honorbound to come after me. I've thought hard about this. It's the only thing to do. It's what I want. Good-bye. I'm truly sorry for all the misery I brought into your life. You didn't deserve it."

Sabrina glanced one last time about her bedchamber, pulled her cloak closely about her, and made her way downstairs.

She stopped right in front of Greybar and said in her coldest voice, "Is my hired carriage here?"

Greybar was wringing his hands. "Wouldn't you prefer to wait for his lordship to return? He should be back shortly. It shouldn't be long now. Surely he wouldn't want you to travel in a hired carriage. A viscountess shouldn't ever travel in a hired carriage with hired horses. It isn't safe. Please, my lady, just wait a moment longer, perhaps just ten minutes. All right?"

"Good-bye, Greybar. You've been kind to me. But I must go now. Surely you understand that."

She carried her own portmanteau out the front door, leaving Greybar to stare after her, still wringing his hands.

She walked quickly from the house into the cold morning. She stepped into the carriage and waved her gloved hand to the butler, who stood shivering and uncertain on the front steps, still wringing his hands.

The horses started forward and she was tossed back onto the squabs. She drew a carriage blanket over her legs and sat there, staring out at nothing at all.

The weary horses pulled to a steaming halt in front of Monmouth Abbey early four evenings later. Sabrina looked at the great weathered stone building, half castle, half manor house, its jagged surfaces worn smooth through the centuries. Smoke billowed from the massive fireplaces that towered twenty feet above the slate roof. Sharp points of candlelight dotted the latticed windows.

It was very cold but at least it wasn't snowing. It was quite dark, a quarter moon lighting the sky.

She paused a moment before the great oak doors, her stomach knotting at the thought of facing down Trevor. But she could do it. She would face him down. She would, quite simply, kill him if he ever tried to touch her again. She pounded hard on the huge brass griffin knocker.

Ribble opened the massive doors. He just stared at her, then shouted, "Lady Sabrina! Oh, my dear child, you're home. Do come in. Oh, gracious, it's wonderful to see you again."

He hugged her against him and she nearly burst into tears. "It's so good to see you again, Ribble. You're looking well. Is Grandfather all right? It's been almost a week since I've heard anything. Please tell me he's all right."

"Yes, he improves every day, I promise you." Ribble set her away from him. She looked disheveled, thin, pale. He wanted to wrap her in three blankets, set her in front of a fireplace, and feed her. Instead, because he knew her, he said, "No, it's all right. Everything will be fine. You're home and we'll all take care of you. Now, where is his lordship? Is he behind you?"

"He isn't with me," Sabrina said simply, and walked into the large flagstone entrance hall.

"Sabrina!"

She looked up to see Elizabeth clutching the railing at the bottom of the staircase.

"Hello, Elizabeth. Just a moment, please." She turned back to Ribble. "Please see to my coachman and have my portmanteau brought in. Thank you."

She was aware of Ribble giving instructions to two footmen who were gawking at the returned prodigal. What had everyone been told? What did they believe?

She walked to where her sister still stood, staring at her as if she were a ghost, that or something depraved that had wandered by accident into her view. "You're looking very well, Elizabeth. I hope you are feeling just the thing."

"Why wouldn't I be? I didn't run away and get caught in a snowstorm and nearly die."

To think she'd nearly held out her arms to her sister. "No, I expect you're just fine. Your gown is very stylish." Actually, the gown was lovely, but it seemed that Elizabeth had lost flesh. The gown hung off her thin shoulders. But her glorious fair hair was full and thick in braids around her face, wisps dangling down her neck. Sabrina tried to smile. She knew she had to be conciliating.

Elizabeth took the last step and stood not a foot from her sister. "What are you doing here? I don't recall asking you to come back. I know that Grandfather hasn't. Well, maybe the old fool has written to ask you to come. I don't know since he won't allow either Trevor or me to read his letters."

"No, Grandfather didn't ask me to come. I came on my own. I would like to stay with you for a while."

Elizabeth said coldly, "Now that you're here, standing right in front of me, I suppose I can't send you away, at least tonight. Where is your husband?"

"He's still in London. I wanted to see Grandfather, Elizabeth. I've felt so helpless not being here with him."

"Doubtless he will want to see you. You nearly

caused his death, Sabrina. I hope this time you'll behave as you should, as a lady should."

"Ah, conduct myself as a lady should. Now what does that mean? I wonder. Does it mean that a lady would simply lie helplessly in her bed to wait for her brother-in-law to come and rape her? Is that what you mean? You say nothing. Listen to me. Please don't distort the truth now, at least not to yourself."

To her surprise, Elizabeth stared her down. Sabrina blinked, looked away. Elizabeth grabbed her sleeve and brought her close. "You little slut, don't you try to preach at me." Then she released Sabrina and laughed. "If you were guilty of nothing, sister, how is it that you are so very brave now? With your husband still in London, you have no protection from Trevor—if it is protection you need."

"It's very simple, Elizabeth. Both you and Trevor know that Phillip would kill him without hesitation if he so much as laid a hand on me, or even thought about it."

"Since it never happened, neither of us need to worry, do we?"

"Good God, what have we here? If it isn't my little sister. What an unexpected surprise."

Sabrina saw Elizabeth go rigid at her husband's voice. She turned to watch him come down the stairs, his walk lazy, the expression on his too-pretty face filled with rich humor. He never looked away from her face.

"Yes, it is I, Trevor. I have come back to see Grandfather."

He stopped at the bottom of the stairs, making no move toward her. "And where is your marvelously fierce husband?"

Elizabeth said, "The viscount is still in London. He

will arrive shortly. As she said, she's here to visit Grandfather."

"How delighted the old gentleman will be. His precious little Sabrina, returned to the fold. You will find him sadly changed, little sister, but quite alive."

"Yes. Both Phillip and Richard Clarendon assured me that Grandfather would continue to improve in his health, that you would see to it, Trevor."

"How could one not see to that dear old man? Is he not my great-uncle? I have all the loyalty and tender feelings of a grandson. Yes, the old man will live until the next century."

Sabrina merely nodded and said to Elizabeth, "If you wouldn't mind, Elizabeth, I would like to visit Grandfather now. I shall be quite content with a tray, if it wouldn't be too much trouble for Cook."

"Perhaps there is something remaining."

"But, my dear Elizabeth," Trevor said, "have you forgotten? Why, we haven't dined yet. Surely there will be a veritable feast of food, some of which we can share with your dear little sister. Perhaps I can even bring a tray to her myself. Perhaps she'd like me to remain with her and chat while she eats."

Sabrina didn't feel the numbing fear she'd felt before. It was odd, but she was strong now, and it wasn't simply because she knew Trevor was afraid of Phillip. No, she knew that she'd kill the bastard if he came near her. Why not tell him so? Then she saw her sister's face. No, if he dared to come near her, then she'd tell him.

She said, "Since I'll be with Grandfather, Trevor, he will doubtless entertain me." She nodded to both of them, then walked up the stairs, her back straight.

Trevor called up after her, "Do ask the old gentleman if he would like to see either Elizabeth or me. It's been a while since he's enjoyed our company."

"I can believe that," Sabrina said over her shoulder. Neither of them said anything as she kept walking.

Trevor walked to his wife. He smiled down at her, raised his fingers, and lightly stroked them over her cheek. Then he drew her hand through his arm. "Of course, your sister is pleased to see me again, don't you think? It will give us an excellent opportunity to become better friends, don't you agree, Elizabeth?"

Elizabeth stared at the toes of her slippers that were peeping out from beneath the hem of her gown. She nodded numbly.

"I believe I asked you a question, Elizabeth."

Sabrina had turned at the sound of Trevor's voice, all low and oily. She felt the blood pound at her temples as she watched Trevor slide his fingers to the soft skin on the inside of Elizabeth's arm and pinch her. She couldn't help herself. She raced down the stairs, yelling, "Don't you touch her, you filthy bastard! Don't you dare hurt her."

Elizabeth said calmly, "Be quiet, Sabrina. Go on your way. Visit with Grandfather. Leave us alone." Then she smiled up at her husband. "As you say, Trevor, that's perfectly true."

"Perhaps," Trevor said, "just perhaps, Sabrina, after Elizabeth has retired, you and I can have tea. Would you like that?"

"I'd like for you to change into a human being, but that is unlikely to happen, isn't it?" She turned on her heel and walked back up the stairs.

"Until tomorrow then, little sister," Trevor called after her; something in his voice would have scared her to her toes, regardless of Phillip's threat to Trevor, if she hadn't stolen Phillip's derringer and had it in her reticule at this very moment.

40

Jesperson, the earl's valet, opened the door to the vast bedchamber and sitting room. "Oh, my, it's you, Lady Sabrina. Welcome home. Ah, this is a wonderful surprise for all of us." Jesperson, normally quite solemn in the presence of any member of the family, was actually smiling at her, lightly touching his fingers to her shoulder. "Let me tell his lordship that you're here. Oh, he'll be so pleased. You can dine with him."

She took his large hand between hers. "Thank you, Jesperson, for taking care of him, for protecting him."

A flash of deep emotion crossed his face, then he was calm again. "This way, my lady."

Childhood memories stirred as Sabrina followed Jesperson through the sitting room to the long, rectangular bedchamber beyond. The small treasures she'd collected in her younger days and presented proudly to her grandfather were still displayed atop a huge mahogany desk: colored rocks from the streambed, polished by the rushing water to a smooth surface; a string of amber beads left her by her mother; a tattered kite whose long cloth tail lay wrapped limply about it.

Her grandfather's bedchamber hadn't changed since before she was born. It was dominated by dark blue damask hangings. Thick Turkey carpets covered the planked floor, swallowing the sound of her heeled slippers. The earl sat in his chair before the roaring fire-place, wrapped in his favorite velvet burgundy dressing gown, his twisted fingers clutching the arms.

"Grandfather," she said very quietly so as not to startle him. When he turned and saw her, she saw the love for her in his dark eyes. She shouted and ran to him, hurling herself at his feet, her arms going around him.

She felt his gnarled fingers stroke her hair, and she pressed closer and laid her head upon his legs.

He was long silent, and Sabrina felt sudden fear that he had believed Trevor and Elizabeth's stories about her. In her letters to him, she hadn't written of what had happened, fearing to hurl him into a confrontation. She raised her head slowly and gazed into his fierce blue eyes.

"You are so very much like her," the old earl said, the tips of his fingers gently tracing her jaw, her nose, her eyebrows. "It's such a pity that you never knew your grandmother. Camilla had such grace, such good-ness, just as you do. And those eyes, they are her eyes as well, Sabrina." He gave her a grave smile, his twisted fingers cupping her face. "You're a beautiful, vibrant woman, Sabrina. I am very pleased to see you, relieved, truth be told. Is your husband here? I must look him over, you know, make certain that he is in-deed the sort of man to deserve you."

Jesperson said from beside the earl's chair, "Dinner is here, my lord. My lady, would you please sit in this chair? Then you may continue conversing while you eat."

But Sabrina didn't want the formal chair. She eased down on her grandfather's footstool, where she'd spent so many happy hours. Of course then he hadn't been ill. No, he'd be working at his desk, dealing with

family matters, with estate matters, vigorous and bois-
terous and laughing.

"You're looking well, Grandfather," she said,
watching him eat a small bite of roasted chicken in
Cook's famous cream sauce, quite in the French way,
Cook would say with a superior smile.

"I'm but an old eagle chained to his nest, Sabrina.
Even my spirit grows weary."

She laughed and said, "You're an old poet who
loves the simile and I refuse to allow you sole claim
to tired spirits."

"What does a girl like you know about weary spirits
and such?" Then he frowned. "You've seen your
sister?"

"Yes." She tried to keep all feeling from her voice,
but the earl had known her since she was born. He
wasn't having it.

"She's become even more a whining termagant now
that she's married to that scoundrel. Bedamned, if
only I'd seen through him. I could have protected all
of us."

"Please eat, Grandfather."

He forked down a bite of potatoes. "She's not
happy, but then, how could she be?" The old earl
looked away from her, toward the fireplace, where
comfortable flames flared and danced. "Elizabeth
won't ever be happy, Sabrina. I should have realized
that long ago, but I didn't. I thought all she needed
was a husband. I looked upon Trevor and believed
him a gift from a beneficent God. More fool I. But
you see, even if she were married to a kind man, she
would still be miserable because she dislikes herself.

"I did give her what she wanted. She is now mistress
of Monmouth Abbey. Someday she will be the Countess of Monmouth. She has always wanted to be the
great lady, lording it over those about her, but it has

brought her nothing. No, less than nothing. Now her misery is based on the behavior of someone outside herself. It is a pity, Sabrina, but there is nothing anyone can do about it."

Sabrina laid aside her tray. She slipped back to the floor, nestling her cheek against the earl's dressing gown. She felt the skin of his leg stretch against the bone.

"She never comes to me anymore," the earl said, his fingers patting her hair. "It's probably because she feels guilty. No, don't look so surprised, Sabrina. Now you've insulted me. How could you ever imagine that I'd believe the filth she and Trevor told me.

"In all truth, I'd like to kill him, but then my family would be done. But perhaps it would be best if the line died with me. It makes me shudder to think of the sort of children Trevor and Elizabeth will have." He paused a moment, still running his fingers through her hair. His breathing sounded calm, normal. It relieved her enormously.

"I remember when I brought that honey-voiced pretty boy here to Monmouth Abbey. I believed he was a fop, but harmless for all that. He's not, Sabrina. I know that it's your husband's hand and Richard Clarendon's that keep him from murdering me. Still, it grates that I could have been so wrong with respect to his character."

Was he seriously considering killing Trevor? She didn't know. She'd never thought of her grandfather in a way that would allow him to do such a thing. She leaned back, looking up at him. "Thank you for believing me."

"Your husband told Jesperson what had happened. Jesperson told me. I'm in your husband's debt for all my days, Sabrina."

She paused just a moment, just a veritable instant.

"Phillip is very kind. He is honest and honorable. Oh, enough of this. We are together again and I want us to talk and laugh the way we used to until you groaned with weariness and finally sent me to my bed."

"You came home because you have no place else to go."

She couldn't look away from those eyes of his that seemed to see everything both outside and inside her all her life. She ran her tongue over her bottom lip. How could he know that she'd left her husband? She tried to smile, but it wasn't much of a success. "Could you read Grandmother Camilla's thoughts?"

"No, love, but I read what you didn't write to me in your letters. I know you very well, Sabrina. There was little joy in the words you wrote, then there was none at all. If I hadn't been tied here, I would have been in London immediately. Probably I would have challenged that viscount of yours to a duel."

"No, I doubt you would have done that."

"Well, possibly you're right. Richard Clarendon told me all about him."

"Richard? He praised Phillip?"

"Richard also is an honorable man. He told me the truth. By the time he'd finished, I felt as if I knew your husband. I can't tell you how relieved I was, Sabrina, that you didn't fall into the hands of another rotter, like Trevor."

"Oh no, Phillip isn't a rotter by any stretch of the imagination. So now you know what sort of man he is." She paused a moment, looking at the dancing flames in the fireplace. She said slowly, "It's just that London, all that fine society, it's very different, Grandfather. I didn't do well there. Actually, I did until it came out that I'd spent the five days with Phillip and

everyone called me a trollop. No, it's the rules there.
I don't understand them. I couldn't live with them."

"What rules?"

"Phillip wanted his freedom. He has a mistress. Her
name is Martine. He makes no secret of it. I just
couldn't accept it."

"I see."

"Only if Phillip hadn't *damaged* me. Can you believe that word, Grandfather? *Damaged*. As if I were
something that could be torn apart, like a bundle. It's
difficult to accept that people think like that, but they
do. Not just men, but women as well."

She stared down at the faded pattern in the carpet.
"Phillip is generous, Grandfather, and as I said, he's
kind and honorable."

The earl nodded for her to continue.

"We fought. I never thought anyone could rival
your temper, but Phillip does."

"You fought about his mistress?"

"Among other things. It wasn't well done of me.
You see, when I made him an offer to marry me, I
told him he could have his freedom."

The old earl would have choked if he'd been drinking anything. "You told this young man that he could
continue bedding women who weren't his wife?"

"Yes. He rudely told me that he already had his
freedom, that he'd do just as he pleased. And he did."

"And that's why you left him?"

She was so transparent, she thought, looking down
at her short, blunt fingernails. "Actually, I love him.
He doesn't love me. He is responsible for me. He
protects me, but he doesn't love me. Oh, Grandfather,
I did the most terrible thing to him, and yet, I know
that I would do it again. That's why I had to leave. I
knew I could never accept the other women."

"What did you do? Something outrageous and worthy of an Eversleigh?"

She smiled, but it quickly turned into a moan. She buried her face in his dressing gown. "I went to his mistress's rooms and found them together. No, he wasn't actually in bed with her nor was he naked. She was, or very nearly. I went mad. I kicked him in the groin, Grandfather, then I ran back home. He found me there. He didn't retaliate, didn't hurt me at all, regardless of what I'd done to him. But I knew at that moment that it was all over."

"Oh, my God," the old earl said. "You kicked him? There?"

"Yes, I brought him low. I didn't realize that it would be so awful for a man to be kicked there."

"There is no worse a place to be kicked."

"After he left me at home, I knew I couldn't remain. Everything was in a shambles. There was no hope, else I would have stayed. So I left the next morning. I hired a carriage and came here."

The earl looked thoughtfully into her violet eyes, Camilla's eyes. He thought it likely upon brief reflection that his ferociously loyal and loving wife would have done the same to him had he been inclined to take a mistress, which had never even occurred to him to do.

The earl leaned forward in his chair and took one of her hands into his. "You love him, with all your heart? You would give your life for him? You would do your best to protect him, no matter the cost?"

"Yes."

He laughed. "Is he a blockhead then? Hasn't he the brains to see clearly and deeply into things? Into people? Surely a wifely kick in the groin should have convinced him of your feelings." He wished that he'd actually met the viscount. He stroked her rich auburn hair, now tumbled down her back. "Well, I suppose we'll just have to wait and see what happens." He looked into the orange flames in the fireplace and saw another face, so like Sabrina's, from a past that had long since turned to ashes and memories. "I've told you this before. You are Camilla's granddaughter. Believe me, Sabrina, no man who knew her would have ever willingly let her go. Once I saw her, once I *really* saw her, I never did."

41

Ribble pulled open the front doors and stared at the gentleman in front of him. He grinned. He laughed. He held out his hand, surely not what a butler should do, but he didn't think, just did it.

Phillip didn't hesitate. He shook the man's hand. "It's good to see you again, Ribble."

"Thank you, my lord. Oh, dear, this is passing strange and yet wonderful, don't misunderstand me. Her ladyship will be so very happy to see you. She didn't tell us precisely when to expect you. But you have come so quickly. Do come in, my lord. Yes, let me take your greatcoat and your gloves. Yes, this is a happy day."

"You're right. Her ladyship will doubtless be very surprised to see me." Phillip looked around the huge entrance hall. He saw a door open, heard the rustling of silk. There was Elizabeth. She didn't say a word until she stood a foot from him.

"So, you've come."

He gave her a mocking bow and smiled at her, showing his teeth. "Of course. I trust you've taken good care of my wife." Now he would find out what Sabrina had told her damned sister. He waited, all calm and composed, an eyebrow arched.

"She only arrived yesterday evening, my lord. She went immediately up to her grandfather. I've scarce had time to even see her. I doubt she even left his room last night."

"Well, that wouldn't be surprising, now would it, Elizabeth?"

"I don't know what you're talking about, my lord."

"Don't you now? A very beautiful young girl just might fear becoming a victim to roaming villains in the halls. She could be afraid that one of those villains might try to break into her bedchamber."

"That's ridiculous. There are no roaming villains here. But were I to guess, I would have to say that your metaphor was rude."

"It wasn't a metaphor."

She froze. He waved his hand. "All right, no more, Elizabeth. The earl continues to improve?"

Elizabeth got hold of herself. She even managed to shrug. "Naturally. Everyone lives and breathes to see that he continues to do so. He will outlive all of us. I will be the Countess of Monmouth, yet sometimes I wonder if I will enjoy it if I only gain it when I'm an old woman." She shrugged again. "Undoubtedly the arrival of his precious Sabrina has made him feel even better."

"I've found that Sabrina's presence enlivens the spirits of most around her. Where is she, Elizabeth?"

"With the earl, I would imagine. As I told you, she hasn't left his rooms, as far as I know."

"I should be delighted to escort his lordship to the earl, my lady," Ribble said.

Elizabeth merely waved them away.

"Perhaps I shall see you later," Phillip said as he turned to follow Ribble up the great staircase. "Oh, I should also enjoy seeing your sterling husband again. Does he flourish?"

"He will always flourish."

Was that a note of bitterness he heard? "That's a pity," he said. "But you know, I'm not surprised."

Phillip dismissed the butler with a pleasant smile and knocked on the earl's door.

"My lord!"

"Good day to you, Jesperson. How goes the earl?"

"Ah, the laughter I've heard since Lady Sabrina returned. He is smiling again and he has so much more strength. Don't get me wrong. He will be very happy to see you as well, I'm sure of it."

Phillip wasn't quite as sure as Jesperson was, but he only nodded. He wondered what Sabrina had told her grandfather.

As they walked through the sitting room to the bedchamber beyond, Phillip asked quietly, "You've had no interference in your care of the earl?"

"None whatsoever, my lord, not since you and the marquess came to see Master Trevor."

"So the little worm has kept his distance?"

"A very goodly distance," Jesperson said, and grinned widely. "I hear him carp and whine outside the door, but he never tries to push his way in."

"Is my wife with the earl now?"

"No, my lord. He sent her away about an hour ago. Wanted her to get some color in her cheeks, he said. She's always loved the outdoors."

"She's riding?" Phillip asked. "It's very cold outside, Jesperson."

Jesperson shook his head. "No, my lord. She said something about visiting Miss Pixel's new kittens in the stables."

"You mean the damned cat isn't even married?"

Jesperson laughed. He opened the adjoining door to the earl's bedchamber and motioned the viscount into the room. Phillip drew to a halt and looked at the old man who sat hunched forward in a chair by the fireplace, a tartan blanket wrapped about his legs. The earl turned his head slowly and the viscount found himself staring into a pair of lively blue eyes, sunk beneath a craggy brow. He looked like a tough old bird. Phillip smiled at him.

"You, I presume, are Sabrina's husband?" the earl said in a rich deep voice, a strong voice, not that of an invalid.

Phillip walked forward and took the earl's twisted fingers in his hand. "Yes, sir, I'm Sabrina's husband. Phillip Mercerault."

"Sit down, my lord."

Phillip did as he was bid, and sat on a faded brocade chair opposite the earl.

"Forgive my travel dirt, sir. I didn't wish to take the time to change."

The earl waved an indifferent hand. "Richard Clarendon told me good things about you, my lord. He said you were a man of honor, no matter that you'd poached upon his preserves."

"Richard and I have known each other since we were boys at Eton. I'm pleased he didn't paint me as another devil to you."

"Oh no. The dear lad wanted desperately to kill Trevor, to strangle the cur, he told me. He said you'd told him he could kill Trevor only after you were done with him."

Phillip laughed. "That's close enough. Is Sabrina all right, sir?"

"Well, now, my lord, she will be vastly surprised to see you though I must admit I'm not."

"Yes, she will be surprised. She has yet to recover her confidence from the drubbing she took in London. Also, she doesn't seem to understand what effect she has on people, particularly the effect she has on me. I'm here to fetch her home."

The viscount was handsome, the earl would give him that. He was well spoken, well made. There was no cruelty in his face, no signs of discontent, or displeasure at what he was. He was a man's man, but with the charm to seduce the skirts easily off any woman he set his sights on. Perhaps he'd been like Phillip Mercerault when he'd been young. He honestly couldn't remember the man he was before Camilla had come into his life.

A man's hands told him a lot as well. They were strong hands, well formed. Capable hands. The earl approved of what he saw. He said slowly, his eyes going back to the viscount's face, "You've set yourself a goodly problem, lad. Sabrina just might not choose to go back with you. This is her home, you know, and I won't force her to return with you if she doesn't wish to."

Phillip, tired to his bones, so worried he was nearly cross-eyed, sat forward in his chair, his hands clasped between his knees, and said, "Forgive me, my lord, for being blunt, but Sabrina is my wife, and will do as I bid her. She isn't yet in the habit of obeying me, but perhaps that will change once she understands what I'm about. Yes, I'm here to get her. That's an end to it."

The earl's blue eyes twinkled. "It surprises me, lad, that my granddaughter hasn't taken a whip to you, called you a tyrant, and tried to shoot you."

Phillip smiled, a pained smile. "Actually, she kicked me in the groin. It wasn't pleasant. I thought I was going to die and for a few minutes there I would have welcomed it. I don't know how I can smile about it now. I suppose it's because I'm here and have nearly got her again and I know that she didn't render me impotent."

The earl couldn't help himself. He laughed out loud.

He squared his shoulders at the quick burst of pain, a bit difficult, but he managed it. He said quickly, seeing the look of concern on the viscount's face, "Keep your seat, my lord. Age and infirmity are a damned bore, but it's what awaits all of us. What is of the most importance now is my granddaughter. She spoke of you as being kind, my lord, kind and noble."

"She has alternately yelled at me that I'm a conceited ass, then tried to strangle me with what she perceives as my blasted nobility. It will stop."

"You didn't wed Sabrina out of duty then? Nobility, if you will?"

Phillip was silent for a moment. He said, finally, "There are rules, sir, codes of behavior that must govern society, else we might well find ourselves back in trees and caves, wearing animal skins. I suppose that in the beginning my offer of marriage to Sabrina was motivated by a sense of duty. She refused me upon several occasions. As you are undoubtedly aware, it was her imminent ruin in London society that finally forced her to wed me. It was she who offered for me then. I didn't regret wedding her. I doubt I ever will, even if she strikes me in my manhood again. Well, perhaps I'll entertain visions of strangling her if she does it again. A man can take just so much, you understand."

"I well understand you. Now, you say you don't regret marrying her. Still, it was a marriage forced upon both of you, by the rules of society. I wonder how such a marriage can flourish if there is nothing else to support it."

"Sabrina loves me. She told me she did."

"Did you believe her?" The old earl looked down at his twisted fingers, blast the pain of them. "Or did you just think that she was a little girl playing a woman and it was all just infatuation?"

"Yes, that's exactly what I thought because, you see, I didn't want her to love me. It scared me to my toes, this love of hers that offered me everything. I told her it was just infatuation. I was a fool. I freely admit it. I plan to tell her that, as soon as I get my hands on her."

"She's very proud. She's also very stubborn, just like her grandmother. That woman would get something mired in her mind and it would take the earth tilting to change her opinion. I wish you luck."

"These two qualities make us well suited, I think."

"Possibly. But it will lead you both to ferocious ragtag fights. Doubt it not, my lord."

"Just so long as she doesn't try to destroy my manhood, she can screech at me as much as she wishes. Actually, she excels at hurling things such as jam pots, plates, and such, at my head." Phillip rose then. "Sabrina did me a great disservice by leaving London before I could speak with her again." He frowned. "Actually, that's not exactly true. I left her. I was sunk in a sinkhole and couldn't get my brains together. It's also true that we haven't dealt well together since our marriage. However, it is my intention to assure that she will never again have the opportunity to misinterpret my feelings. Now, if you will tell me where I may find her."

"And if she refuses to speak with you?"

A singularly gentle smile touched the viscount's hazel eyes. "Then I'll kiss her until she's silly. If I have to I'll even tie her down, then kiss her some more."

"It's likely you'll find her either in the orchard or in the stables, playing with Miss Pixel's new kittens."

"I wonder if there's a possible racing kitten among them?"

"Ah yes, even I've heard of the Mountvale racing cat trainers in southern England. It's a wonderful sport

though it has yet to catch on up here in the north.
But everyone has heard of the McCaultry Racecourse
near Eastbourne. Do you have a racing cat?"

"No, not yet. If she's with the kittens, I'll look them
over for possible racing potential. Who says I have to
be sanctioned by the trainers? Given time perhaps I
could even figure out some of their strategies."

Phillip took the earl's hands once again into his and
pressed them slightly. "I thank you, sir. Sabrina is
mine now. I haven't done well by her since our marriage. However, I will take very good care of her from
now on. And I will tie her down if I have to. She will
listen to me."

"Perhaps she will," the old earl said and waved the
viscount off. "Good luck. You will need it."

"I bid you good-bye, sir, for both your granddaughter and myself. We shall come—together—in a couple
of weeks to see you again." He grinned. "No, I won't
kill Trevor, if he doesn't push me, that is. It's just that
even thinking about the rotter pushes me."

Phillip met Ribble downstairs. "You have her ladyship's portmanteau all packed?" He had no intention
of spending this night beneath the same roof with her
brother-in-law.

"Yes, my lord."

But she wasn't in the orchard. Nor was she in the
stables, playing with Miss Pixel's kittens. He didn't
take the time to see if there could possibly be a potential racing cat among the litter.

She was gone, damn her beautiful eyes. Phillip
yelled to the rafters.

It was the head stable lad, Elbert, who came running. He said, "Lady Sabrina ain't here, m'lord. She
told me to give ye a message."

The man stopped, shuffled his feet, and looked like
he wanted to sink into the hay. Phillip was on the

edge of strangling him. "What, damn you? Connect your brain and your mouth.'

"She said, m'lord, to tell ye that she's left the Abbey and that she won't be back until ye take yer leave. She said she didn't want to see ye, that ye had to leave her be."

"Did she tell you where she was going?" Phillip asked, his voice furiously calm. The man shook his head. "Did she take a horse?"

"The brown mare."

"What sort of brown mare?"

"Jest yer average sort, m'lord. Nothing here, nothing there, jest a brown mare. I don't know no more, m'lord. None of us know no more."

He knew then that he was in the middle of a conspiracy. He wanted to knock their heads together, but time was of the essence. He had to find her. He honestly doubted she'd told them where she'd gone because she knew he'd probably intimidate them. Well, if he believed they knew anything, he'd threaten to gullet them. "Well, hell," he said, turned on his heel, and left the stable.

42

Dinwitty Manor

"Hello, my dear, You must be Phillip's new wife, Sabrina. That's a lovely name and you have very seductive eyes. The color, it's violet? Yes, how unique, not a boring blue like mine. I will teach you to use those eyes to good effect. You're very young. You have a long time to learn, but you will have to apply yourself. I'm Charlotte Carrington, of course. Rohan's mother."

"You can really teach me how to use my eyes to make men wild?"

"That is the point, my dear. One begins, naturally, with one's husband."

"That could pose a problem, Charlotte."

Sabrina took a step back and the most beautiful woman she'd ever seen in her life floated into the house like a fairy princess wearing golden slippers. Cotter, the Mercerault butler, was staring as well. She saw from the corner of her eyes that three footmen were all stacked upon each other to see her. She was a goddess, her beautiful thick blond hair piled artfully on her perfect head, her eyes a brilliant blue, not boring as she claimed, but mesmerizing. Just the purity of her features was enough to make any breathing person come to a full stop and stare at her.

Sabrina stuck out her hand. "How do you do, Charlotte? I'm sorry that the viscount isn't here. Actually I don't know where he is. Why are you here? May I assist you with something? Perhaps if you have time, you could give me a lesson in using one's eyes?"

"Hmmm. I adore those Moorish arches, I always have. I believe a seventeenth-century Mercerault had them built."

"Oh yes, Dinwitty Manor is one of the strangest houses I've ever seen. Phillip told me I might just take one look and double over laughing, but I didn't. Perhaps it was because I was a mite unhappy, but I don't think so. The house and grounds are charming. They feel right. I'm sorry, please come into the drawing room. I'm just standing here staring at you, forgetting my manners, because you're so incredibly beautiful. It's hard to believe that you're Rohan's mother."

"I know, but it's true. I understand that my sweet son was Phillip's best man at your wedding in London?"

"Yes, he was. Unfortunately, his wife couldn't come. Why didn't you come, ma'am?"

"I was in Paris, my dear. I just arrived at Mountvale Hall two days ago. Augustus and I have just returned from Moscow, a fascinating place. Fortunately everyone speaks French. Isn't that odd? There are more people living in that country than you can begin to imagine and yet all the aristocrats and all the royals, of course, speak French."

"Ho, Mother, are you rolling over poor Sabrina?"

It was Rohan Carrington, smiling brilliantly, coming to stand behind the vision, who surely couldn't be his mother.

"She is truly your mother, Rohan? I know it must be true in theory, but seeing her, it surely isn't possible."

"Yes. Amazing, isn't it? Toby, he's my brother-in-law, he swore he believed her to be my younger sister. Now, here's my own glorious wife, Susannah. Susannah, my love, this is Phillip's new wife, Sabrina."

Sabrina, who'd been utterly blinded by Charlotte, had to shake her head. She shook hands with a very pretty young woman who appeared to be just a bit older than herself. She invited everyone into the drawing room.

"Have you gained flesh yet, Sabrina?" Susannah asked, grinning like an unrepentant sinner as she stripped off her gloves.

"So, you've been here before then. Oh, goodness, it's so difficult, isn't it? Cook took one look at me and vowed I couldn't leave until she had me bursting out of my gowns." Suddenly, embarrassed, she stopped talking. Cotter, fond of his new mistress not really because she was sweet and lost and rather pathetic, but fond of her because she would doubtless settle the master, if they would only speak to each other again, was absolutely delighted to see Baron Mountvale and his reinforcements. Things would happen now. He began to rub his hands together.

He stepped forward and assisted their guests with their cloaks, handing them off to two silent footmen who couldn't take their eyes off Charlotte Carrington. He then said in a very gentle voice, "My lady, would you like Cook to send tea to the drawing room?"

"Oh yes, thank you, Cotter." She led them into the drawing room. They all sat. Suddenly Sabrina dropped her head. Her shoulders slumped. Then she blurted out to Rohan, "I'm sorry, my lord. Phillip isn't here. Actually, I don't know where he is. I don't know why I'm here, really, but it seemed the only place to come. You see, I ran away from Monmouth Abbey when he arrived there. I've been here three days now, but Phillip hasn't come. Everything is a mess and I don't know what to do."

"I thrive on messes," Rohan said, and kissed her fingers. "Listen, undoubtedly Phillip knows what he's doing. He usually does." He turned to his wife. "My dear, how is your belly at this particular moment in time?"

Susannah appeared to consult her innards. "Fine, really. It's so amazing," she said to Sabrina. "Rohan had to stop the carriage just an hour ago. I was so ill. That was why I couldn't come to your wedding. Do forgive me."

Charlotte, dowager Lady Mountvale, smiled at Sabrina and said, "I believe I must inspect the Tudor wing. It's been a good half-dozen years since I've seen it. Phillip, the dear boy, told me he was going to make some changes."

"Well, ma'am," Sabrina said, "I believe Phillip is more interested in the medieval period."

"Ah, yes, his crenelated tower," Rohan said. "He said it bored him and so he stopped with his plans late last summer, after we all got back from Scotland."

Charlotte waved at them. "Cotter, bring two of those lovely footmen and take me to the Tudors. The four of us can rattle through those magnificent corridors and avoid Cook's apple tarts." She turned to Sabrina. "You and I will become friends. Ah, those eyes of yours. It will be a pleasure to take you in hand."

"She's so beautiful," Sabrina said, staring after her. "It must be difficult to be her daughter-in-law."

"Yes, it is, particularly when it's just the two of us and we're walking together and all the gentlemen stop in their tracks and swoon," Susannah said. "You know, Charlotte's never said anything about taking me under her wing. That's hardly fair."

"Well, this man only swoons when he sees you.

Don't be jealous of my mother. It's disheartening. She doesn't tutor you because she knows it wouldn't please me if you began to attract the gentlemen like leeches."

Susannah laughed and poked his arm.

"I'm sorry that Phillip isn't here, Rohan."

"Ah well, I suspect that it shouldn't be too long before he discovers your whereabouts."

"He might discover where I am, but that doesn't mean he'll come here. Trust me."

Rohan and Susannah Carrington just smiled. As one, they turned toward the open doorway. There, with no warning at all, stood Phillip. He nodded to them, then said easily, "That's bloody nonsense and you know it, Sabrina. If you hadn't run away from Monmouth Abbey like a racing cat, then you would have seen me raving around and tearing out my hair because you weren't there."

"Phillip!" She jumped to her feet, a hand outstretched toward him. Then she didn't move. She just stood there, so thin and pale that it smote him.

"Actually, let me tell you the truth now. I enlisted Rohan and Susannah and Charlotte. They're my protectors, my witnesses, my frontal force. They were to get themselves through the door, perhaps soften you up a bit, then I could make my grand entrance. What do you think? Was this a good strategy?"

She stared at each of them in turn as if she'd lost her wits.

"Promising," Phillip said, nodding. "Yes, they came just ahead of me. That was the plan. I was afraid that you'd run away again if it was just me. You do understand, don't you, that you can't leave our guests in the lurch? It wouldn't be the done thing. And they are our guests and they deserve a hostess."

She was still just standing there, her hands bunching

and unbunching the soft muslin of her gown. "Won't you at least say hello to me, Sabrina?"

"Hello, my lord. I've been here three days. All your people have been very kind to me. When I arrived and told them who I was, they immediately accepted me. I was worried because I had to walk from the village. I was cold and dirty, but still they took me in without hesitation and Cook's tried to fatten me up. I was very grateful, but it's been so cold and there's been no sun and all one can do is just wander through the Moorish arches, walk beneath the Ionic columns, and dream about medieval towers that could possibly be built beside the suite of Italian music rooms at the corner of the east wing."

"Was that an attempt at humor?"

"Yes, it was. I'm very sorry I ran, Phillip, but I didn't know what else to do. Don't worry that I didn't have enough money, I did. I would have hired a carriage to bring me here, but there wasn't time. I thought you'd track me down, so I took the stage."

A spasm crossed his face. "Yes, I know you took a stage, but by the time I found out, it was too late. You'd nearly arrived here."

"I left you wanting to strangle me."

"What makes you think I still don't?"

"I don't blame you. I'd probably still want to strangle me if I were you." She turned to Rohan and Susannah, who were sitting very quietly side by side on a lovely pale blue settee, holding hands. "Don't you see? I kicked him in the groin because I found him with his mistress—"

"Yes, that's true, but I wasn't doing anything with her. I was, in fact, on the point of telling her that I'd decided to become like Rohan. I was going to design medieval towers, Rohan was going to design his gardens, and the two of us would forever tread the straight and narrow. I was also going to promise you that I wouldn't gain flesh from Cook's incredible cooking."

"But I hurt you dreadfully, Phillip." She turned wild eyes to Rohan. "After I kicked him, he fell to his knees and moaned. I thought he was dying." Then to her husband, she said, "When you came back to the house, I thought you would strangle me then, or beat me, but you didn't."

"What I did was worse. I left you. I'm sorry for that, Sabrina, but I honestly didn't know what was going on in my brain, if anything. My wits were roiling about like bat's wings and lizard's toes in a witch's cauldron."

"Cook is now serving, so all conversation must come to a halt," Cotter said, motioning in two footmen, different ones from those who'd taken everyone's cloaks and gloves, and gone off with Charlotte Carrington. They carried in trays piled high with food.

"I thought you went with my mother, Cotter," Rohan said.

"Her ladyship is currently in the protective company of three stable lads, two footmen, two maids, the tweenie, and the pug, Orion. I deemed it proper to see if everything was going as planned here."

"Planned?" Sabrina said.

Smells began to waft outward. Susannah groaned. "You're thin, Sabrina. You can afford to stuff yourself, but I suggest you don't do it for longer than a week. You might get in the habit, then I firmly believe you'd be lost. You'd become the fattest lady in all of England. Is that a bilberry tart I see, Phillip? Oh, goodness, just smell it. Hand it to me, please."

"Yes, Susannah," he said even while he took a big bite of gooseberry tansy. He closed his eyes as he chewed, groaned, then said, "Do you swear you won't run away from me again, Sabrina? That you'll stay with me and together we'll figure out what we want to do?"

"But you don't love me. What is that, Cotter?"

"It's a damson tart. Cook is rather consumed by all things fruit this week."

Susannah, her mouth full, actually stopped chewing. This was getting very personal. She looked at her husband, but he just nodded, making no move. He said out of the corner of his mouth, "Just be a piece of furniture, Susannah. That's all that's necessary right now. Phillip will tell us if he needs more or wants us to leave. Sabrina is talking. We're succeeding."

Phillip said, "Why don't you think I love you? Don't you think you're worthy of being loved?"

"But your freedom, Phillip. I tried, really, I tried, but you want to have mistresses and I just can't do it."

"Then why did you come here, to Dinwitty Manor? You don't think I could bring mistresses here if I wished to?"

She took the blow, then straightened, those thin shoulders back. "No, if you ever take another mistress, I'll do you in."

Phillip, relieved to his toes at that show of possessiveness, said to Susannah and Rohan, "See, I wasn't wrong. She hasn't forgotten that she adores me. She worships me. She's very protective of me. Do you think she'd really do me in if I dared bed another woman? Yes, she would, I can see the blood in her eyes. She wants me all to herself. So many ladies want me, but she won't allow it. She's a greedy wench."

Sabrina threw a quince comfit at him.

Susannah gasped, not because she was horrified that it would strike Phillip, but because she'd wanted that comfit for herself. Only the Dinwitty cook still made the old-fashioned treat. Phillip, now used to her bombardments, handily caught the comfit and immediately gave it to Susannah. "No, just one. Remember, Rohan, my vow to never let Cook make me fat? Just two goodies a day, never more. Now, Sabrina, do you love me? Are you willing to say it in front of these two fine upstanding witnesses?"

43

Sabrina knew she should be embarrassed to the toes of her slippers that two people were watching this very strange confrontation between them, but oddly, she wasn't. But she didn't know what was in Phillip's head. She'd never known. She looked at him helplessly, her hands splayed in front of her. "You know that I love you. I'll promise that to anyone who wants to listen to me. But I'm not the one who wants mistresses, Phillip."

"A lover for you, Sabrina? No, never. Forget it. Not in this lifetime."

"But you know that was always only in your own mind. I told you that lovemaking was utterly miserable, that no woman could possible enjoy herself doing that. It was unpleasant, it was—" She stopped. Phillip was flushed, two spots of color high on his cheekbones.

Rohan choked on his apple Charlotte. Susannah thumped him on his back. He sucked in enough breath to blurt out, "Phillip, I don't believe this. You? You left your wife unsatisfied? You were so rotten that she doesn't want anything more to do with you? Good God, you never told me this! This may be insurmountable. I don't know if I should encourage her to take you back if you can't do things right. It's a repellent thought. It's unacceptable."

"Now, just calm yourself and think back for a moment. I believed the same thing she did, Rohan," Susannah said with alarming candor. "It was Charlotte—no, not the apple Charlotte—who kept talking about her precious Rohan, how he could make a toad sing with pleasure if he but put his mind to it, his mind and all the skills his dear papa saw to it he learned from his own mistresses beginning when Rohan was only fourteen years old."

"That's quite enough, Susannah. The fact is that you were quickly disabused of your silly beliefs. All I needed was a very short time in our bed to change your mind, don't you remember? Not more than two minutes or so, very little so."

Sabrina said, "And then it was all right? You truly enjoyed this, Susannah?"

"Yes, I truly did. I truly do."

"But Phillip did this to me three times, all in one night, one after the other. It wasn't very nice at all, but because I loved him, I endured. What else can a woman do when she loves a man but endure?"

"Exactly right," Phillip said.

"Phillip, what the hell happened?"

He looked at his boyhood friend and said simply, "I was a blockhead. She wouldn't accept my expertise, but I should have known that it would take more than simple expertise. But I won't ever be a blockhead again." He was no longer flushed. He took two steps toward his wife. "No, don't retreat from me, Sabrina. Do you swear before these witnesses that you love me?"

"I swear."

"Good. Now I swear that I love you as well. Actually I probably love you more. My love for you has been simmering, like a damned stew, for a very long time. It's grown stronger and stronger, it just took me longer to realize what it was and to admit it. It's still boiling over a steady flame. I daresay that flame won't ever go out."

"That makes no sense at all. You'll just keep boiling? You won't boil away?"

"Never. I also swear to you that tonight, just after we can politely leave our guests, you and I are going to enjoy ourselves, immensely. Will you trust me on this?"

She didn't say a word, just stared at him.

"Trust him," Susannah said. "Yes, you should trust him. A man and a woman together, it can be glorious, Sabrina. Life is so very uncertain, so unwieldy sometimes, that coming together with a man you truly love can make sense of everything, make everything very clear to you. It can make problems disappear. It can make annoyances, burdens, much lighter."

Rohan said, "If you agree to trust him, Sabrina, to give him another chance, then I'll give him the gift Susannah and I brought him from Mountvale Hall. Your trust would turn the tide, I should say. I would believe him worthy of the gift then. It would prove that commitment wasn't abhorrent to him. It would prove that he's become a steady man."

"Do you know," Sabrina said slowly, looking at each of them in turn, "this is quite the oddest thing that has ever happened to me. Phillip, you invited them here because you were afraid I wouldn't listen to you?"

"I felt I needed character witnesses."

"Will you tell him you trust him, Sabrina?" Susannah said, sitting forward.

Sabrina said slowly, "I believe that now I'm going to go find Charlotte beneath the Moorish arches. I want her to give me some lessons in how to make the best use of my eyes."

Phillip groaned. "I will be undone by your mother, Rohan."

"Think of my mother as another character witness, Phillip," Rohan said, grabbed a delicate mulberry cream cake in the shape of a cat, gave his wife a beatific smile, and rolled his eyes.

His mouth was on her belly, nibbling as he would on one of Cook's lemon spice cakes, then smoothing where he'd nipped with his tongue. It tickled and she giggled. Much of her nervousness fell away when he looked up at her, and smiled widely. "That's a wonderful sound. It warms me to my, er, never mind what. Just relax, Sabrina. Remember now, you trust me."

"Yes," she said when his mouth was on hers. Since he'd kissed her until she was nearly out of her mind, it didn't take long for her to scream, arch off the bed, and fling her hair into her eyes. "Phillip!"

He pushed her and pushed her, then drew back, calming her, slowing down his rhythm, until she was drawing heaving breaths, and again, he smiled. Her pleasure was beautiful to him. It warmed him to his toes. "Now," he said and came over her, and very gently, very slowly, he came into her. She raised her hips, her hands stroking down his back. "Oh yes, I like that," she said and bit his shoulder. "I'm glad Charlotte told me to trust you. Oh, goodness, Phillip, this is very strange. It feels like nothing any person could possibly imagine. Can we do it again after we finish it this time?"

He groaned, threw back his head, and let himself take his release. It was rending and powerful and he was nearly dead with the pleasure of it.

"Yes," he said five minutes later when he was finally able to speak again. "Yes, in a few more minutes, we'll do it again."

Between kisses, she said, "The candlelight is too dim for me to practice my eye lessons on you."

"Trust me again, Sabrina. You don't need any lessons."

Her hand stroked down his back, over his flanks. "All right," he said, and brought her over on top of him. He grinned up at her. "What do you say, wife? Do you want to be the one in control?"

"I don't understand."

When she did, she very much enjoyed herself. As did Phillip. When she was sprawled atop him, her face against his neck, breathing hard, she said, "Did I ride you well?"

"Oh yes, you did. I also like the way you bite me. It's almost like my sweet old mare, she bites my shoulder, then smiles at me."

"That's ridiculous, a mare smile?"

"Yes, I found her moldering in a stable in Scotland last summer when Rohan and Susannah and I were there. She nipped me and smiled at me. I sent for her, as I promised her I would do. She's been with me since last October. She neighs whenever I come near."

"I met her. She didn't seem to like me at all. She didn't try to bite me."

"I will try to talk her into accepting you."

"Phillip, I'm glad I trusted you. That is really very nice, all those things you do."

"Would you like to learn things to do to me?"

She came up on her elbows, her hair tumbling down on either side of her face, forming a curtain around their faces. Her eyes were sparkling. "Yes, oh, please. What?"

"Tomorrow. Tonight, now that I've pleasured you twice, I feel free to tell you that if you ever run away from me again, I'll strangle you and throw your body into the River Ledlow. It's an ugly muddy excuse for a river, but you'll deserve it. Do you swear you'll not run out on me again?"

"I swear. Shall I also swear not to throw things at you?"

He thought about that for a moment. "No, I'm learning how to move quickly. It'll keep me on my toes, else I'll get a plate or a lemon tart in my face." He became suddenly serious again. He eased her onto her back, and came up on his elbow to look down at her. "You're beautiful, Sabrina. You must accustom yourself to hearing that from me. But you want to know something else? You're the woman God fashioned just for me. You're precious. You mean more to me than the crenelated tower you and I will build together. I love you and I will love you until I cock up my toes. Will you accept my word? Will you accept me?"

She raised her hand to lightly stroke her fingers over his cheek. "I will thank God each night for bringing Trevor into the world."

"Trevor? What's this about?"

"If it weren't for Trevor, I wouldn't have met you. Well, if I had eventually met you in London, I doubt you would have given me a second glance."

Phillip didn't agree with her at all, but he smiled down at her, kissed her yet again, and said, "We will drink to Trevor on the morrow then. Can I pound the bastard into the ground again?"

"Perhaps, in the future. But we'll do it together."

Together, he thought. He'd never been part of a together before. It felt quite nice. He fell asleep with Sabrina pressed against him, the memory of her featherlight kisses on his chest deep in his dreams.

He jerked bolt upright in bed. He was wide awake. It was the middle of the night.

"Phillip? What's the matter? Are you all right? Do you want me to trust you some more? I'd like that."

"Yes, I would too, but now I want my gift that Rohan promised me. Do you know what it is? I forgot all about it. He said he'd give it to me if I pleased you."

"I'll tell him you pleased me. You'll get your gift."

"I want a silly grin on your face when you tell him," he said, getting out of bed. "The sillier the grin the more likely it is he'll believe you."

"It's the middle of the night."

"Yes, so it is, but Rohan deserves to be awakened. He should have given me my gift on speculation. He should have given me my gift because he knew I wouldn't let you down again."

The floor was icy beneath his bare feet. He grabbed his dressing gown and pulled it on. He fastened the belt tightly. "I want my gift now. What room are he and Susannah in?"

"The Blue Damson Room. Phillip, wait for me!"

Three minutes later, after a sharp knock on the door of the Blue Damson Room, Rohan awoke to see a candle shining toward him and Susannah. Something was wrong. Oh, God, what had happened? Wait, it was Phillip. What was going on? Sabrina was standing right behind him.

"Phillip, what's going on? What are you and Sabrina doing in our bedchamber in the middle of the night? Susannah, no, love, it's all right. It's just Phillip and Sabrina. Doubtless they'll tell us why they're here at this particular moment in time."

"I want my gift, Rohan. You said you brought me a gift."

"Oh, that," Rohan said and yawned. He straightened in the bed and scratched his belly. "Susannah,

Phillip wakes us up in the middle of the night to get his gift. Should we give it to him?"

Susannah looked at him, then at Sabrina. "He pleased you?"

"Oh yes, please give him his gift now."

"If I haven't squashed her," Rohan said. "Where is she?"

"It's true," Phillip nearly shouted, running to the bed. "You brought me a racing kitten! I've wanted a racing cat since I was a little boy, but the Harker brothers never deemed me worthy of one. They always said I wasn't responsible enough, that a true racer always needed commitment, just what they always said about you, Rohan, and they finally gave you Gilly's son. Now I've got my own racing kitten to train and to teach." He quickly set the candle down on the night stand, turned and hauled Sabrina up against him. He picked her up and whirled her around. "A racing kitten, Sabrina. Finally!"

"Let me find her, Phillip. Ah, here she is." Susannah pulled a boneless kitten, still asleep, from beneath the covers. "She's just nine weeks old. The Harker brothers say she's ready to begin training. They've sent instructions. I wrote them down for you. You're to swear to keep them confidential. You know how the Harker brothers are. Now, here she is."

Phillip reverently took the tiny kitten from Susannah's hands. It was black and white, soft as Sabrina's skin just behind her knees. It opened its eyes and looked up at him, gold eyes unblinking. Phillip gently rubbed his finger beneath the kitten's chin. "She's wonderful. What shall we name her, Sabrina?"

Sabrina took the kitten and cuddled her against her breast. "Nothing sentimental. A racing cat doesn't want to sound sentimental, no one would take her seriously. Let's give her a grand name, one that calls forth great feats. Let's name her Olympia."

"Oh yes," Phillip said, taking the kitten back. He kissed the small face, smoothed back the whiskers. "Olympia. That has a ring to it, doesn't it? I'm already thinking of great feats. When we visit your grandfather in a couple of weeks, we'll take Olympia with us. Your grandfather has an interest in racing cats. He knew all about the Mountvale trainers, about the cat races at the McCaultry Racetrack."

Phillip, his wife, and his new racing kitten left the Blue Damson Room, Phillip whistling softly to the kitten.

Sabrina turned in the doorway. Both Rohan and Susannah were smiling toward her. "Thank you both. You've made him very happy."

"It's not even close, Sabrina," Rohan said. "You're at his center now. No, not even close."

"Do you think, then, that he might carry me around and whistle to me?"

Sabrina left them laughing. Life was wonderful. Just wonderful.

Phillip said as he and Sabrina settled back into their bed, "I have both a wife and a racing kitten to train to become one of the top racing cats in all of England. I doubt building a dozen crenelated towers can get better than this."

Sabrina rubbed her palm over his belly. "I wonder," she said between nipping bits, "which you prefer, me or Olympia?"

"There's no contest. Er, how fast do you think you can run, Sabrina?"

She fell asleep with laughter still in her heart, her head on Phillip's shoulder, her nose nearly touching Olympia's small outstretched paw, the kitten sprawled on his chest.

Epilogue

The crowd was shrieking. There were six racers, but only Gilly from Mountvale Mews and Olympia from Dinwitty stables were now in contention. Gilly was running his paws off to reach Jamie, who stood at the finish line, singing Gilly's favorite limerick. Just behind Gilly, on the inside, ran Olympia, her long legs eating up the ground, her eyes focused on the Dinwitty strategy, namely, Cook from Dinwitty Manor, who was just standing at the finish line, beside the singing Jamie, her arms crossed over her massive bosom, calling out in a piercing voice that nearly drowned out Jamie, "Here, my sweetie. Here, my little kitty. Here's your favorite—steak and smoked oyster pie. Just think of all those kidneys, diced up real nice and small, and the steak, in long thin strips, just as you like it, and the smoked oysters, that will have your tongue singing. Come to Cook, Olympia. That's my darling, come to Cook."

Then Cook pulled a packet out of her bosom, unwrapped it, and held up a long strip of steak. The odor wafted down the track. Olympia jumped a foot in the air, kicked dirt in Gilly's face, and within seconds was across the finish line, the clear winner, bounding toward Cook and that strip of steak.

Phillip Mercerault was holding his small son, Alexander, in his arms when Olympia came flying over the finish line, tail fluffed, fluting a high meow of victory. Alexander screamed with laughter when Olympia jumped into Cook's arms and ripped the strip of steak from her hand.

There was wild applause intermingled with grumbling for those who had bet on one of the other racers. As for the champion, Gilly, he left the track, his head held high, allowing Jamie to carry him to where Susannah and Rohan stood.

Susannah Carrington was yelling congratulations to Olympia, even as she leaned down and picked up Gilly, holding him close and kissing his dusty neck. Then she let her daughter, Violette, give him a consoling pat. Marianne, now nearly seven, was saying to Rohan, "I could smell that steak. Are you certain that's fair, Papa? I started drooling when I smelled that wonderful smell."

"A new racing technique, pumpkin," Rohan said, and kissed his daughter. "The Harker brothers will just invent something else for us, something more powerful that will have your aunt Sabrina and uncle Phillip gnashing their teeth when next we win. You'll see."

Later that evening, back at Mountvale, Julien and Katherine St. Clair, the Earl and Countess of March, joined the Carringtons and the Meceraults at the dining table. They'd just produced a son, Damien, the previous year, who was now sleeping in the nursery with all the other offspring. They spoke of marriage contracts among the children, but then Phillip, sighing, said, "All of you know as well as I do that the chance of any of our children doing anything that we wish them to do will be equal to the number of races Gilly will win with Olympia in the race."

Rohan threw a muffin at his friend. "We will see. I have infinite faith in the Harker brothers. Now, back to our children. There aren't yet enough to have a really good mix. We must get to it, Susannah," he said to his wife, "and provide more choices for all the offspring."

"We must help in this also," Phillip said, patting his wife's shoulder, a lovely shoulder that was very white and not as thin as it was when they'd first married.

"Perhaps," Sabrina said, "just perhaps we shall."

"And you, my lord?" the Countess of March said to her husband. "Will we also do our share?"

"I believe we will, Kate. Yes, I do believe we will."

Talk turned to Richard Clarendon, the Marquess of Arysdale, whose beloved father had recently died, making Richard the Duke of Portsmouth. "I wonder," Phillip said over a glass of tart white wine, "if Richard will ever find a woman who will make him realize what he's all about."

"Yes, a woman who will claim him right and tight," said Sabrina. "Just as I did you, Phillip."

"Who knows?" said Rohan Carrington, and raised his glass to all his friends.

Susannah said, "To well-fought cat races and good friends."

"Amen to that," Phillip said. He sipped his wine, then leaned over to lightly kiss his wife on her mouth.

September 10, 1974–May 2, 1997
Gilly, my old warrior, died quickly and easily
on Friday, May 2nd.
He leaves many people who loved him dearly.